2/1

A
Monster's
Notes

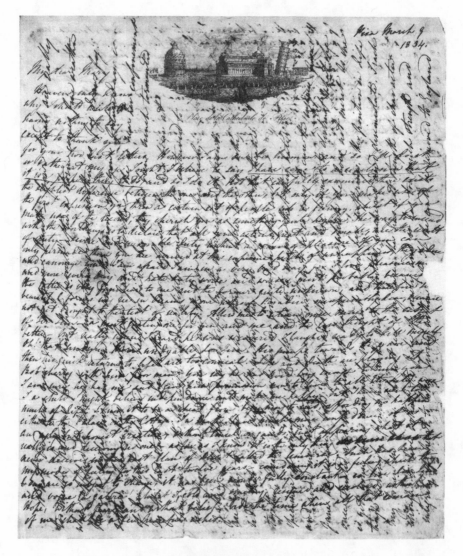

"Crosswriting" in an 1834 letter from Claire Clairemont to Mary Shelley.
Courtesy of Lord Abinger and the Bodleian Library, Oxford.

A
Monster's
Notes

LAURIE SHECK

ALFRED A. KNOPF
NEW YORK
2009

THIS IS A BORZOI BOOK
PUBLISHED BY ALFRED A. KNOPF

Library of Congress Cataloguing-in-Publication Data
Sheck, Laurie.
A monster's notes / by Laurie Sheck.—1st ed.
p. cm.
"This is a Borzoi book."
Includes bibliographical references.
ISBN 978-0-307-27105-1
I. Frankenstein (Fictitious character)—Fiction. 2. Self-realization—Fiction. I. Title.
PS3569.H3917M66 2009
813'.54—dc22
2008055081

Manufactured in the United States of America
First Edition

For my friends

{ CONTENTS }

❧ Preface ❧

I long for some circumstance that may assure me that I am not utterly
disjointed from my species
   these hauntings of the mind   *and very tenderly to prove*
        My dearest Hogg my baby is dead—Will you come you are
so calm a creature & Shelley is afraid
into the regions of frost   *crushed by fortune—I am nothing—*
       It became necessary that I should conceal myself
  But I am not confined to my own identity   *I am still here still*
thinking still existing
I shrank from the monster—he held out his hand but I couldn't touch it
Yours tenderly   *Your Exiled,*   *I am &c &c*   *Addio Cara Mia*
I am, Sir

             Your obedient Srv'
             Mary Shelley

London, Milan, Naples, Pisa, Marlow, Geneva, Leghorn, Florence, Genoa, Rome, Cadenabbia, Paris . . . The handwriting in gray or chestnut ink, in the early years sometimes accompanied by her husband's; sometimes the letters are turned sidewise, the text continuing over the first in the practice of cross-writing used to save paper in the nineteenth century. Of her *Frankenstein* copybooks, the first, "Notebook A," as it's now known, survives as seventy-seven leaves of laid paper with a light blue tint and five sewing holes along the side. The paper was probably purchased in Geneva. The second, Notebook "B," consists of seventy-five surviving pages on thicker, British, cream-colored paper. The bindings and covers of both notebooks have long since disappeared. On the first notebook's pages she penciled in a left-hand margin, and there Percy Shelley left his comments and marks. Picture two hands moving side by side, she writing "creature," he (in some impulse of tenderness, kindness?) crossing it out, replacing it with "being."

  I open one of her letters and a clear envelope containing a lock of auburn hair falls out. A lock she'd sent to her friend Hogg. Often the paper is thin and worn, and many of the letters are held within larger envelopes stamped with an auction-house purchase number and date of sale. This strange condition of ownership, what would her monster have thought of it? And she, who was often short of money.

By the time she died of a brain tumor at age fifty-four, twenty-nine years after her husband's drowning, and thirty-four years after the writing of *Frankenstein*, erratic undiagnosed symptoms had mostly kept her from writing for over a decade. Her monster long behind her by then, and all but one of her children long dead.

So much of a life is invisible, inscrutable: layers of thoughts, feelings, outward events entwined with secrecies, ambiguities, ambivalences, obscurities, darknesses strongly present even to the one who's lived it—maybe especially to the one who's lived it. Why should it be otherwise? I didn't seek to find her, wandered instead within and among her fragments of language—notebooks, drafts, journals, fictions, letters, essays, and found there whole worlds like spinning planets, lived in their cold light and burning light, wondering where I was, where they might take me. Curious, I heard a monster's voice and followed—

NYC, May 31, 2008

A
Monster's
Notes

A Letter

June 30, 2007

Dear Mr. Emilson,

This is to inform you that the final closing on your building
on East Street was successfully completed at 10:15 this morning.
I have deposited the check as you instructed. The new owners will
begin renovations tomorrow. In our previous communications,
I asserted that the structure, now in great disrepair, was completely
abandoned. However, yesterday afternoon as I made my last
walk-through, I found on the second floor a short note, a
manuscript wrapped in a rubber band, and an old computer. As
these technically belong to you, please let me know if you would
like them forwarded to your London address. I have not unbound
the manuscript, but reproduce for you here the short note left
on top:

> So much blurs . . . I write then forget what I write . . . walk these
> streets, a stranger to myself and others . . . Then sometimes it all sud-
> denly flares back—my breath catches, my brain aches. How long have
> I wandered, talking in my thoughts to the one who made me from
> dead, discarded things, then left me? Why did he need to see me as
> frightful, misbegotten? I know he'll never hear, never answer.
>
> Walking, I remember the other ones as well, those three I watched
> though none of them could see me. Isn't seeing a wounding and caress-
> ing both? All of them gone now, though once I held them with my
> secret eyes and in my own way loved them. Mary, Claire, Cler-
> val . . . All those hours they visited me in air, came to me as voices
> made of flesh, ripe with shades of meaning, though in the end all that's
> left of them is absence.
>
> Why did she need to portray me as she did? For so long I tried not
> to think of our days in the graveyard, the clicking of pebbles in her
> hands as she sat near the bushes, listening while I read. Even now the
> details grow faint . . . I try to forget . . . banish it all from my
> mind . . . though part of me wants only to remember. She was a child
> of eight sitting by her mother's grave. I sat behind the bushes with my

books. *Once we briefly spoke. Mostly I read to her, that's all. And her stepsister Claire, how strange that she came to me years later, long after I'd been wandering, heading north, far off in the Arctic by then. Why did she need to come to me, or was it I who needed her? And Clerval, that gentle man who everyone thought dead—in fact he traveled east as he'd wanted. Even now I sometimes picture his hand moving in patient transcription as day after day he translated the* Dream of the Red Chamber *in his house at the foot of Xiangshan Hill, and wrote letters to his friend in Aosta.*

Isn't any voice largely mute and partial, even those that speak openly and plainly (though of course I mostly hide). Why do I leave this? These words absorbed into the garbage dumps, the flames—

{ NOTES }

Notes on the Earth Seen from Space

Over and over the word *fragile.*

"It looked so fragile, so delicate, that if you touched it with a finger it would crumble and fall apart." This from James Irwin, crew member of *Apollo 15.*

Astronaut Loren Acton spoke of seeing it "contained in the thin, moving, incredibly fragile shell of the biosphere."

To Aleksei Leonov, the first man to walk in space, the Earth looked "touchingly alone."

And when Vitali Sevastyanov was asked by ground control what he saw, he replied, "Half a world to the left, half a world to the right, I can see it all. The Earth is so small."

Neil Armstrong said, "I put up my thumb and shut one eye, and my thumb blotted out the planet Earth. I didn't feel like a giant. I felt very, very small."

And Ulf Merbold: "For the first time in my life I saw the horizon line as curved, accentuated by a thin seam of dark blue light. I was terrified by its fragile appearance."

(Is this what frightened you, is this what you sought to combat and to flee? This fragility, this somehow-knowledge even then before anyone had ever left the Earth or seen it from a distance, of how small it is and delicate, as we are too, how finite, how beside-the-point, how fleeting.)

(Might this partly account for my monstrous proportions, as if you were building a shield, a fortress of flesh, as if the vertiginous wings of blood in us could somehow be made to tremble less. But I'm a blunt and narrow piece of materiality. Imprinting and imprinted.

As were you. Footprints, strands of broken hair dropped here and there. }

On March 18, 1965, Alexei Leonov exited the main capsule of *Voskohod 2* by pushing himself headfirst out of the opening. A sixteen-foot lifeline held him to the ship. If it broke he would drift off forever. Although the spacecraft traveled at great speed, there was no air rushing past to let him feel it. He spun slowly for ten minutes. But when the copilot Belyayev told him to come back he didn't want to return.

(He didn't want to return. And yet it seems a lonely thing—that feeling of nothing pushing back. }

Several months later, Edward White walked in space for twenty minutes, though the term is deceptive as the motion is of free fall or floating. Seen from 120 miles away, Earth was nearly featureless. When he returned to the spaceship he had lost five kilograms of body mass, and two kilograms of perspiration had collected in his boots.

But he, too, didn't want to return to the capsule.

When told to come back to the spacecraft he said, "This is the saddest moment of my life."

His copilot pulled him back in.

(And you will work in sorrow the fields . . . As if your laboratory were a field, a wound always to be worked, a rivenness of mind needing to be healed. But when he floated there, in that region without weight or mass or shadow, all fields fell away, all shattering turned soft and pliant, there was no need anymore either to build or to destroy— }

(But how my mind builds and destroys you over and over. }

On January 27, 1967, two years after his space walk, Edward White died in a fire on Launch Complex 34 at the Cape Canaveral Air Station. He had entered *Apollo 1* for a simulated countdown along with Command Pilot Gus Grissom and Pilot Roger Chaffee when the fire broke out.

Years later White's wife took her own life.

{ How strange to see the Earth from the sky and then come back . . . to float in space like that, barely tethered, Earth a modest uncrowned thing. "So peaceful and so fragile," one said of it. The size of a marble or a pearl "hanging delicately," said another. And another: "But I did not see the Great Wall." }

Still, there are many practicalities to be addressed (as you would have known even from your rudimentary laboratory). "It's a very sobering feeling to be up in space and realize one's safety factor's been determined by the lowest bidder on a government contract," the astronaut Alan Shepard pointed out.

And Neil Armstrong spoke of a feeling that was "complex, unforgiving."

Lyndon Johnson said, "It's too bad, but the way the American people are, now that they have all this capability, instead of taking advantage of it, they'll probably just piss it away."

{ But what would it mean to *take advantage*? }

{ And what of how small, and of how fragile . . . }

{ Over and over the word *fragile* describing this world that has taught me such resistance, the hard of it and brutal, and yet, still– }

Numerous inventions made for space have been adapted by private industry, resulting in studless snow tires, scratchproof eyeglasses (White needed to shield his eyes from the extreme glare of sunlight), the five-year flashlight and cordless power tools.

The U.S. Space Walk of Fame Foundation was formed in the 1990s as a "major component of a redevelopment master plan designed for Titusville's urban waterfront." There you can "visit the gift shop at the museum and treat yourself, a friend or a relative to a truly unique space-related gift."

{ When Leonov and White floated in space they didn't want to come back. They couldn't have known this beforehand. What is a footstep then, after that, and the feeling of Earth–so fragile, so small–beneath a shoe, or the thin tether of breath, or a name, or a day, a boundary, a theory, a bond– }

Notes on an Interview with Dr. Anne Foerst

Q. "What exactly do people do at this laboratory?"

A. "We are trying to build robots that are social and embodied."

(As if I'm an abbreviation of something else, something I can't know. I look out over this frozen sea and can't tell where land begins, if there is land. Shore is a distant idea. In this frozen world I can't know which step will take me from land to sea or back again. What appears as land is instead a floating ice shelf. I raise my arm, I open my eyes on so much whiteness, and cannot . . .)

Q. "Why is a theologian here in this particular laboratory?"

A. "When you build a humanoid you must think about the cultural and spiritual dimensions. What do you build into them? And what are the ethics here? Why should I treat someone else like a human, with dignity, when it is just a mechanistic thing? Yet I can benefit from doing just that.

One question we often discuss: What will happen when robots cross a threshold of development where you can't switch them off anymore? When does a creature deserve to be treated as intrinsically valuable?"

(Those first weeks in the forest I lay on leaf-moist ground, my voice different from the birds', and this difference confused me. I didn't know what I was. Yet I'd glimpsed your hands before you fled, knew mine looked like yours. I couldn't know then how you'd made me out of pieces of dead things, discarded things—only sensed I was something embodied whose one clear task was to continue to exist. Back then I had no words for what I felt and yet I felt that. What's resemblance? What does it mean to belong or not belong? Isn't resemblance or its lack often misleading, more complex, subtle, tricky, than we think? I look out on this stark sky, this white land the color of loneliness, or—)

Q. "When do *you* think a robot should be treated as intrinsically valuable?"

A. "Those who build it must decide, since they won't be blinded by fears of the seemingly human qualities of the machines. They will know what is inside them. The builders could become the creatures' strongest advocates. That moment is probably fifty years down the road."

(But who isn't blinded by fear? And you who knew what was inside me, did that knowledge make you any less blind to what I am? After all this time I don't even know whether to say *who* or *what* I am. If I could see inside my body, into my own cells, would my mind be any less mysterious to me? The mind deeply private, largely hidden even from oneself. So how could you begin to know me?)

Q. "What makes these robots so advanced?"

A. "They are embodied. Intelligence can't be abstracted from the body. In previous attempts abstract human features were programmed into a machine: chess playing, language processing, mathematical-theorem proving. But we feel that the body—the way it moves, grows, digests, gets older—is inseparable from how a person thinks. These robots have body feelings similar to ours. They experience balance problems, sensations of friction, gravity, and weight."

(This heavy body I carry with me always, these awkward, baffled limbs.)

Q. "Is this robot a she?"

A. "Robots are its. But I think of it as *she*. Only when you treat the machines as if they possess our social characteristics will they ever get them. In this laboratory this is what we believe. You need to create that circle."

(I can see no circles in the ice—)

Notes on Time

(The more I think of it the more it perplexes me—)

Aristotle asked, "What is time?" And answered, "It is the measure of change . . . but time is not change itself, for change may be faster or slower, but not time."

To Epicurus it was an "accident of accidents."

To Democritus, "an appearance presenting itself under the aspect of day and night."

And, of course, Heraclitus wrote, "You can't step into the same river twice."

"Everything will eventually return in the self-same numerical order, and I shall converse with you staff in hand, and you will sit as you are sitting now, and so it will be in everything else, and it is reasonable to assume that time too will be the same."–this from Eudemus of Rhodes

(Eudemus speaks in a comforting voice. He sits beside me on a bench, staff in hand. There's no past or present or future on my skin, but something else I have no words for. What does it mean to be a living thing? The garden flares, shivering its fragrant blooms. Is this where I've been all along? Each mind a curious, uncertain space, able to grasp so little of what is.)

Aristotle said, "Whether if mind did not exist, time would exist or not, is a question that may fairly be asked; for if there cannot be someone to count there cannot be anything that can be counted . . ."

(How limited I am, even with this large and lumbering body. A speck, an ignorance, a something made of matter, wondering, unwise. So how can I grasp time?)

When I think of Bernardino Telesio's view, time seems almost lonely: it exists by itself, and can exist unaccompanied by motion.

To Giordano Bruno, change is a necessary condition for the perception of time, but not for its existence.

Einstein said, "For us physicists the separation between past, present and future is only an illusion, although a convincing one."

(Last night I dreamed I sat at a wooden table on which there was a bowl of fruit, a writing pen, a notebook. On the notebook's cover was the letter *C*. I wanted to open it and read it. When I looked down I had no hands. My arms were the silvery rose-white of fish underwater, stumps that ended in healed, imperfect seams. There's so little I can know or touch or even think, and yet it's there. And what if you hadn't believed you thought me into being? What if you had sensed that maybe I existed all along, that nothing you could do could make or unmake me? That Time is stranger than we thought. That Time itself, not you, had made me.)

Descartes believed God by his continual action re-creates the body at each successive instant. Time, therefore, is a divine process of re-creation.

(But if there's constant re-creation isn't there also constant crumbling, de-creation, and I myself a relentless conflagration, though I can't see myself this way. Inside of me, a crumbling and a burning always—)

What of this idea called space-time? In 1908 Hermann Minkowski proclaimed, "Henceforth space by itself, and time by itself, have vanished into the merest of shadows, and only a kind of blend of the two exists in its own right."

(This feels so much less lonely, less disturbing, than Telesio's view of Time that exists unaccompanied, always and ever by itself.)

Yet Santayana said, "The essence of nowness runs like a fire along the fuse of time."

(*Now* seems less and less a solid entity to me, and time more a series of shifting, intersecting planes. Tenses fall away, the nowness. Claire picks up her pen, opens her notebook, raises her hand, starts to write. Where is she? And when? From what place do I watch her? From what time? I can almost touch the crispness of her sleeve, or the wet ink, each page a fractured, beating thing.)

According to Stannard, "In four-dimensional space-time nothing changes, there is no flow of time, everything simply *is* . . . It is only in consciousness that we come across the particular time known as 'now.' "

And for Grünbaum, "Events simply occur . . . they do not 'advance' into a preexisting frame called 'time.' "

(Could it be true what I've read—that there's no physical experiment that can distinguish among a state of rest, a state of constant velocity, and a state of gravitational free fall?)

A "Block Universe" is the idea that time is somehow laid out in its entirety all at once—a landscape made of time where all past and future events exist together.

(I've felt this but have had no words with which to say it.)

Lloyd wrote, "For the Quinean, what differences we see between past, present and future pertain to our limited mode of access to reality."

(Would that mean the buildings of imperial Rome still stand—it's just that we, caught in the net of the present, can't see them? And that the buildings of future cities already exist, though we can't see them either?)

And Weyl, in 1922: "The objective world simply *is*, it does not *happen*. Only to the gaze of my consciousness crawling upward along the lifeline of my body does a section of this world come to life as a fleeting image."

(I'm sitting on the bench with Eudemus. It's morning or afternoon or night. I watch his blue-veined hand curl around his staff. And I'm on the table where you made me. And in the forest alone, scavenging for food. I'm almost touching Claire's hand. I hear her slippered footsteps on the stairs. Her face is young then older then young again. Over and over Socrates is born, lives, dies. Zhuangzi dreams himself a butterfly. Or a butterfly dreams itself Zhuangzi. The sky's dark or not, the water calm or not, the snow fallen or not. My footsteps on ice, my tracks in the grass.

I can't know what the physicists know. How there are more than four dimensions, such things as defy our habitual ways of thinking. Borges wrote of time: "It is the tiger which destroys me but I am the tiger." Where is he now? And you? And Claire's hand on the page, all this ice I feel inside me, and the night, the day, the measurements we use: millisecond, second, minute, hour . . . season, eon, era . . . as if such things *could* be measured, as if there weren't this fire in the skull, and in that fire a hand, perplexed and burning, reaching through it— }

❨ ICE DIARY ❩

I'm now far north. Archangel. Salt winds from the White Sea mix with naphtha and lignite from the shipyards. Sea ice cracks and groans, breaks on itself, breaks farther. So much whiteness violently dividing. Then stillness: ice locks in around the ships, seals them like footprints left in wax, or pharoahs, mummy-wrapped, trapped and burning inward. For months each hull's a secret violently kept, volatile and cryptic. Shore lights flicker like something slowly starving.

If I still had a voice, if I could speak. But who would I speak to even then? These notes as if written in invisible ink. And the taste of blood in my mouth, or is it the memory of . . . And those bushes where I hid . . .

This morning I found a single stick ornamented with Chinese glass beads. Also a Kufan coin, a blurred list of provisions, a pair of oilskin breeches, a cap. A harsh quietness in them like the silence of those ice-locked hulls. Something helpless in them too, as if as they lay there in the ice they felt unremembered and remembering, unconnected yet somehow still connected—but to what? (Though of course I knew they could feel nothing.) Where did they come from—what lost ships?

But so many years since . . . And inflamed from blinding snow . . . And so far from . . . But I don't want to think about that now . . .

Even this town's frozen through. Stone walls still stand though most of what they guard's long vanished. A few abandoned fortresses, a monastery, the mouth of the Northern Dvina nearby.

If I could see behind the shuttered windows—hands moving and changing even now—but I don't want to see such things again, want only to leave. It's said the more you draw toward true North the farther it recedes. Still, I want to feel it.

This sting of salt. This shocked and changing emptiness of air. No trace of seabirds, wolves. Slaves built the canal here. Soon I will go farther.

Why when I close my eyes do I see a woman's hand floating in black air? Often now I see it. One of my books says it's not great events that incite the mind, but the slightest things that twist and batter us about. That slight, delicate hand, the uncertainty I feel each time I see it. But whose is it? And why does it come to me? Why would a mind need to see such a thing? Why would mine?

Protagoras said there's nothing in nature save doubt. And Nausiphanes said that of things which seem to be, nothing is more existent than the nonexistent. Parmenides said there's nothing certain except uncertainty. I don't know. But I look out on this ice-locked harbor and think of the ice inside my mind, how little I can know of anything.

Barriers. Snow blindness. Doubt.

How will I get to a place where even these closed shutters don't exist, where even the icebreakers don't come?—no human face for miles, no human hands.

Augustine wrote: "Hear how it glows. Smell how bright it is. Taste how it shines. Feel how it glitters," then said we can't do those things. But this quiet glows, acrid smells from the saltworks glitter then grow dull. It's almost night now. But what's *now*? Time shifts back and forth—sometimes I open my eyes onto old wooden houses, mica works, monasteries, fisheries, at other times the same land's deserted. None of my books has explained this to me, or even said that it happens.

(And those bushes where I hid, all the books I once read there. But I won't think about that now.)

Wind quickens, glows, stark as the place inside my mind where I hear nothing, remember nothing. Sometimes your face is gone from me, then I feel almost peaceful, but that never lasts for long.

(And if touch were bearable . . . or memory . . . or the voice of . . .)

Archangel Monastery's high walls have seven gates, eight towers, black cannons still embedded in the stone. It once housed over three hundred monks, and hundreds of servants, artisans, peasants, lived on the surrounding grounds. In the scriptorium, hands drew in colored ink, birds, animals, and flowers. Those hands must have wanted to leave something beautiful behind, though the land's desolate, and the blue-painted ceilings with their little gold stars have peeled, are badly faded.

Each time I think of going farther north, I consider what I'll leave behind. Illuminated books where letters turn into animals and birds alight on those letters (such things I hope to still hold in my mind). But also faces that might remind me of yours, or even mine. Gestures. Eyes.

"Taste how it shines." "Feel how it glitters." But something in me obliterates everything, keeps only this cold—its one clear syllable with its frozen walls.

Where do you end and I begin?

When I opened my eyes that first time, did you find in my face faint traces of the paths your hands had stitched, small declivities in a landscape made of flesh? Did you feel again the taut pull of thread as you blended one dead part with another, fastened one sallow patch of skin onto another?

Now I walk alongside the harbor wall and think of Mikhail Lomonosov, author of the world's first treatise on icebergs, wonder why he was imprisoned for a year. A fisherman's son, he was born near here in Kholmogory in 1711. In his father's shack he hoarded the few books he could find, vowed to study in Moscow even if it meant traveling the whole way on foot.

We are "feathers in a raging fire," he wrote.

Wrote, "words that contain the vowels *e, i, y,* and *u* in their first syllable should be used to depict tender subjects, while those with the vowel sounds *o, u,* and *y* coming later, are fit to describe things that cause fear."

What words, then, would I use for you? Or for that hand—delicate—which comes to me so often now in air?

(And if it's true we're born into reason and language, but are we? If attitudes are pictures, or . . . And what are "tender" subjects?)

"A cold fire envelops me," he wrote. "The icy oceans are burning."

(But there can be no proof of . . . And so few traces of who anyone has been. Is a voice a thing that flees, then vanishes? I want only to read.)

Lomonosov believed in the fluidity of bodies, that although the universe is stable, what dwells within it isn't isolate or unchanging. Nothing's purely itself but exists in relation to others. When an object moves another it's transferring its force to the one it touches, so nothing's ever really lost.

If you could have seen me in that way, believed my existence diminishes nothing, subtracts from the world exactly nothing. (And my voice long fled . . . this vague fever I feel . . . this sense of shame even now.)

I look out on all this whiteness. The frozen port he saw as a boy. Did he think he could walk over snow all the way to Moscow? Where will I travel to, and how? If true North's unreachable–but I don't believe it's unreachable. What will I find if I get there? What vowels rise in my mind, the tender ones, the harsh?

Why do I even speak these things to you? You who I never see and never will.

Lately when I close my eyes I see only this: a woman's white sleeve, her hand moving across a page, writing. The hand leaves steady markings in its wake—light chestnut-brown or black or darker brown. Sometimes it crosses out words, sometimes whole sentences, builds fences of *x*'s, drops ink stains on the page. Sometimes it turns the paper to the side, writes over and across words already left there. Or it halts as if netted, a sudden clenching of the tendons at the wrist. The first few times I could see little of the page but now that's changing.

Each night I wait for it—that white sleeve gathered at the wrist, that small determined hand. I read what it leaves:

> Tonight I'm remembering Snow Hill. They called me Jane then, not Claire. Mother and Godwin never once called me Claire. Cold nights under flimsy blankets—as if that very name, Snow Hill, was seeping into the walls and through my bones. The square where the public executions were held stood barely 100 feet from our front door. The year we arrived (I was 9) they hung Haggerty and Halloway for the lavender merchant's murder. 28 people were trampled and suffocated in the crowd. Mary and I barely slept, thinking of that crush of feet like cattle's hooves, and all those faces suddenly unable to breathe, mouths useless holes. Afterwards I walked down the street alone, past the milliner shops, furriers, coffee dealers, wondering what strange creatures we are to inflict such things on ourselves. Minds contaminate themselves and actions grow ruinous. I feel this in myself—ruin prodigious and luxuriant as plant-life. It flourishes, this crumbling, this destruction, and yet there's also—

> It was around that time I searched through Mother's things for my birth certificate. But it seems there's no record of my birth or baptism. Some say she was put in a debtor's prison shortly after I was born (so was I in that debtor's prison too?) then relieved and set free through a charitable subscription. A few years later she met Godwin. I've no name for my father. Maybe it's better this way.

> Snow Hill—I still feel its coldness in my bones, and how after a while I wanted only to leave. Though I loved the books on the shelves and sometimes the eyes that watched me, the eyes I watched back. How watching is a kindness and a shackling both. The chain of it, the net, the binding. And I remember, above the doorway, the stone face of Aesop reading.

Seawater ice holds my weight when I walk, but black ice is thin, can't be trusted. Sometimes I don't know which one I'm on. The wind's a fist in my mouth. I bend down, huddle on the ground, try only to breathe. Or I come back inside, say her name to myself: Claire. Air.

Why do I wait for her?—that hand and the walls of ink it builds and leaves.

Claire. Air. Care. Clear. Claire.

At first glance the hand's delicate, but I see now the finger bones are strong. Lately she comes before I even close my eyes, that hand lingering in the air and writing. Forty degrees below, sixty degrees below. Her white nightdress thin, yet she seems to feel no cold.

Her face not visible to me. I never see her face.

We were four children from four different fathers. Mine unknown. Charles's unknown (though he and I had the same mother). Then Mary whose mother died when she was born, and whose father is Godwin. And Fanny, who was older, seven when we met, daughter of Gilbert Imlay—but I don't think she ever really knew him. So that even though Fanny and Mary shared the same mother they have different last names. And they always seemed so different—Fanny quiet as if carrying a secret dulled and locked away behind her eyes, a drowned girl staring out. That girl slowly turning, adrift in brown water. William was born later, so in total we were five.

Maybe this is why I love ruins, feel almost peaceful when I visit them—however strange and adamant in their otherness they are, I'm returning to a place I somehow know. We were fractured from the start—waves hitting a brittle rocky shore, a bowl of patched fragments. So how could we just be kind to one another, alert to one another (each with our own jagged edges, our damage). (And staring out from Fanny's eyes the drowned one lost in the muteness of water.)

Sometimes I secretly followed Mary to St. Pancras graveyard, watched her sitting by her mother's grave. Her face turned from me. The back of her head a small night I saw but couldn't enter—

Sometimes she leaves whole sentences and paragraphs, other times just scraps. Once she lit a corner of the page. I watched it curl and burn until only a few words remained:

find no

and

awaken   strong against   Fanny   without.

(I think of your lost face, the way you left me. So much lostness in one single skull.)

I keep dreaming of snow, I don't know why. Last night for instance, Hadrian was ordering snow-lions built all over Rome. But I've never even been to Rome. And how could snow-lions survive beneath the Roman sun? He said he wanted them because they were impossible, that if the people loved him they would find some way to make them.

When I woke I remembered we're in France.

For weeks we walked and plotted in the Charterhouse Gardens—Shelley, Mary and myself, making plans to leave England. Godwin suspected nothing. But there's danger even in certainty (maybe, even, especially in certainty). As we crossed near Calais a storm rushed the boat. Everything reeling. A strange look on Mary's face, like someone walking through a house they sense will soon burn down but no one believes them. At the time I had no words for what I saw. Her skin much too white, her hands shaking.

Today a Swiss gentleman asked Mary and Shelley if they ran away for love and they said yes. Then he asked me. "No," I told him, "I came to speak French."

Mary and Shelley sleep and I watch them, their limbs intertwined, his fingers moving in her hair. Our beds are dirty, we have little money. Mary carried a small locked box with her all the way from England. I don't know what's inside. We walk for hours each day and none of us has a watch.

Mary and I still wear our black silk dresses. We're heading toward the Alps at the Swiss border. Nights we find cheap places to stay, eat milk and sour bread for supper. Why does she carry that locked box when it's so hard to carry anything at all? Shelley says we'll get a mule soon. Then we can take turns resting as we travel.

Skinner Street—it's far away now, Snow Hill's far away. But I dream of snow-lions, I dream of Hadrian impetuously giving orders, so how far have I come? ~~I don't know what freedom is I~~ The Madame at the inn warns us of Napoleon's disbanded soldiers, says they're roaming and pillaging. Urges us to turn back. But there's finally peace here and we want to see it.

Her hand stops, replaces the top on the ink bottle, puts down the pen, folds the paper, slips it in the drawer.

Her face hidden as before. Her name on my tongue an amulet or wish.

The whiteness of her sleeve before she leaves me.

"Magnetic needles always skew slightly east rather than purely due south," Shen Kuo wrote in the eleventh century, in China. (As this North in me also leans, grows errant, is odder and less stable than I thought.) Every night for three months he observed the course of the polestar, and three times every night for five years recorded the changes of the moon for his *Celestial Atlas*. In his *Dream Pool Essays* he explained how the magnetic needle compass could be used for navigation. It's said he was the first to identify true North.

(If I could talk to him, if he were here. But these distances in me, immeasurable, without markers.)

My book says he was an astronomer, mathematician, pharmacologist, botanist, encyclopedist, diplomat, general, hydraulic engineer, inventor—also a finance minister and governmental state inspector. He was Head Official of the Bureau of Astronomy, and, at one time, Assistant Minister of Imperial Hospitality. He improved the designs of the armillary sphere, the gnomon, the clepsydra clock, the sighting tube. How could he be and do all those things? The way this ice goes on in glaring sameness makes it all the harder to imagine such multiplicity within one single life, one brain, one being.

It's said after his father died he withdrew from the world in mourning for three years. Once, out of a deep mysterious sorrow, he attempted to drown himself in the Yangtze River.

(As Claire's hand's mysterious even as I read the things she leaves.)

Only six of his many books survive. Even his tomb was destroyed.

Did *Dream Pool Essays* even exist, or is it, like *Inventio Fortunata*, heard of and talked about but maybe never seen? And what of his *Record of Longings Forgotten at Dream Brook*, in which he wrote of his youth in the isolate mountains, has that been lost too?

When I focus my eyes they're met by raised white ridges, low white plains. Whole stretches barely touched by human thought. Cape Flora. Cape Mary Harmsworth. Bell Island. Alexandra Land. White Island. Teplitz Bay. This archipelago with its hundreds of ice-covered islands. "A glacial prison," one called it. But another said, "The most beautiful place on Earth." And others: "the edge of the world," "a circle of mysteries," "a sheer blank," "a longing."

(If touch were possible . . . If I could understand resemblance . . . Or are objects made of thought as well as matter?)

Now, here and there, airstrips, military installations, wooden huts, radar stations, abandoned makeshift camps, a graveyard. Every now and then the sound of fighter planes landing, taking off.

(Shen Kuo, is this what you dreamed of?)

I wait to see the northern lights, remember how Payer described them after being ice-locked for two years: "Waves of light drive violently from east to west, but are they shooting downwards from above or upwards from below? Rays move fast as if racing each other. In the center is a sea of flames. Is it red or white or green? It seems to be all three. Everyone stops moving. It's impossible that such violence isn't accompanied by an equally violent sound, but we hear nothing. Then just as quickly as they came, they vanish."

Are thoughts a form of violence? And human wishes seeded with a hidden violence?

I look out on this white ice, wait for something to destroy itself in me, immolate and fly past itself in me. I hear light waves, icebergs, flames, fighter planes practicing maneuvers overhead. But not your voice in my mind. Not your wishes or the way you left me.

Mary's writing a story called "Hate"—I don't know why. We walk most of the day, sometimes ride in a diligence, but we hardly have money for such things. At Nogent and St. Aubin the houses were rubble, the people left so poor by the war they just laughed when we asked them for a place to stay. Soon Mary will be seventeen.

She's writing in an oblong notebook bound in red leather with a broken metal clasp. Some of the pages burned at the edges. Writes the name *Mary Jane Clairmont* on the inside front cover. Crosses it out. Turns the page, writes *August 13, 1814*. Turns it again: a pencil sketch of a face. On the next two pages there are words in someone else's hand: "Lasciate ogni speranza, voi che entrate" and "Nondum amabam & etc., (August. Confess., Bk. III, Cap. I)."

Has it been hours, days? Her hand continues writing:

But sometimes Ixxx sometimes I don't feel bold though I don't say it. We walk through narrow streets of old towns, past buildings black with age, the sky black with rain, and I don't understand what freedom is . . . and yet I want to understand. Then the land opens up again but even the rocks in their wild freedom seem bare and awful and I didn't want to ever think of them that way. They rise over each other, jut against each other. I don't want to return to Skinner Street, not ever. Those rats that ran over my face at the Inn where we first slept, I still feel them. Even now they run through my mind, and in my mind Shelley says, Stop thinking, it's good to think but not the way you think.

Why must there be an immense chain thrown across the barrier-valley between France and Switzerland? It's attached on both sides to the highest mountain peaks in times of War. Ugliness cast over the land. These scarrings we bring to the land. Yet they had a revolution, they tried to make themselves free.

I want to see the Alps.

I tell Mary and Shelley my name's Claire now. Only call me Claire.

Shelley's hurt his ankle so we walk more slowly. Immense forests on all sides—

Trapped in ice for two years the Russian ship *Saint Anna* drifted northward for 2,400 miles. There was no coal or wood left for heating. Little food. For light and some warmth they burned bear and seal fat mixed with machine oil. The navigator, Albanov, and a few crewmen, finally set out by sledge in search of land, traveling for ninety days over ice and glacial rock to reach Cape Flora.

(As I wandered from you from the start, though I had no place in mind to get to, only knew I was alone. You'd looked at me and fled.)

Of the ones who remained on board no trace was ever found.

Albanov kept a diary: "I have severe pain in my eyes and write only with great effort. The route is so difficult we managed only two and a half miles in spite of our efforts. Last night there was thick, freezing fog. Understanding the movements of pack ice doesn't make it any easier to cross. I have been having persistent nightmares. I dream there are only two of us left. But every few minutes I walk over to my sole companion who's busy digging in the ice and ask about a third. I am sure there is a third. When I wake my legs are swollen and painful."

What have I wanted from this North? Albanov dreamed of Christmas dinners, plates piled high with fruits and steaming meats. He dreamed of music, dancing, warm blue sea.

He craved darkness: "This dull light makes one's eyes so terribly painful. Only in complete darkness does the pain gradually abate, allowing me to open my eyes again."

What do I crave? Not the darkness you left me in. Not the sense you must be beside me in that dark.

If I had been permitted to remain in silence, and fled away and climbed some rocks—no one watching or caring what I did—& so on and so forth from step to step—xxx maybe then . . . but the words burn and crowd too close to one another and everything's anarchy sometimes, no King of me no steady Queen—I wake in the night wondering what I belong to, what to name myself, where I am.

I'd like to know what a Pack Horse is. I'd like to know why this stove doesn't work. Shelley says we have to travel back to England because the stove doesn't work and we're cold but that makes no sense. I thought I'd never see those cliffs again. Didn't want to see them again. Every side of me shut sometimes.

At first I thought the Alps were white clouds. Then I saw they were really the Alps—peaked and broken. Everything's clean in Switzerland. Everyone suddenly hospitable and cheerful. We asked a Swiss man why everyone seems so happy, "Ah it is because we have no King to fear! When we have paid our rent to the Seigneur we have nothing to dread. We don't even have to take off our hats to him." But it's impossible to find a wild and entire solitude, the people multiply, the land's too lush and easily tamed, no spot's deserted.

Inside the mind so much is hard and unmeaning. Every side of me shut sometimes. And myself without government. So be it. My self without. I would like to know what safety is. I would like to know what freedom is. I would like to know why Mary sickens often, fevering and weak, as if she's finally left a blackened town but then must go back around to it again, and no boat can take her farther.

So much becomes suddenly harsh and afterwards. I must study my Greek, must learn the four tenses of the verb <u>to strike</u>—Must buy new shoes.

The faint watermark—*WT*—floats on each thin page, then disappears beneath her chestnut ink.

The navigator, Albanov, had visions as he walked: "The sun is a ball of flames. It's torrid summer. I see a port. People are strolling in the shadows of the high harbor walls. Shop doors are open. Peaches, oranges, apricots, raisins, cloves, and pepper all give off their wonderful scents. The ground steams with heat. Persian merchants are offering their wares."

"We're all sleepwalkers."

On July 5, after walking for nearly three months, he writes in his journal that Nilsen's dying. "He can hardly move, has lost the power of speech, mumbles only with great difficulty." Then his attention turns to a huge block of floating ice "on which we spotted two large walruses and one small, about the size of a cow." Then back to Nilsen: "He's no longer responding, stares with a glassy look. We construct a makeshift tent out of some sails, wrap him in our only blanket."

Then: "Sunday July 6, As we expected Nilsen was no more than a corpse this morning. Remarkably he did not display that terrible waxen pallor that makes the face of a corpse so ghastly. His features were calm. We wrapped the body in the blanket and carried it by sledge as far as the next terrace, roughly nine hundred feet. Not one of us wept for this man who had accompanied us for months, shared all our dangers, fatigue, and hardships. What does this say of us? What have I become? Nilsen has disappeared. His hopes and everything he lived for no longer mean a thing."

Have I headed north not to feel, as Albanov came to believe he couldn't feel? He mourned this in himself. "What does this say of us?" "What have I become?"

In my sleep I hear Albanov talking to Nilsen though Nilsen isn't there: "We heard the calls of countless birds winging their way overhead, but our snow-blinded eyes weren't able to see them."

For weeks she doesn't come. My days emptied of her, of anyone. On this map I've found: broken land-masses marked by black letters. Mt. Misery, Novaya Sibir, White Island, Savina, Black Cove. Two islands called: *Existence Doubtful*. This world hidden from itself, mysterious even to itself. The blue arrows must indicate the directions of the currents. (Haven't I sought such arrows in myself?—but little has come clear.) Then cordoned off in a rectangle in the lower right-hand corner:

> **PHYSICAL CHART OF NORTH POLAR REGIONS 1897.**
> By J. G. Bartholomew, F.R.S.E.

What did J. G. Bartholomew, F.R.S.E. think as he wrote in *Existence Doubtful*?—he who most likely never saw a single place he charted.

"Our veiled, damaged eyes," Albanov wrote.

"Only the darkness helps. Sunlight is too painful."

"Suddenly I spot some tiny yellow flowers. Imagine, after all these years! When I get closer I see they're only rocks."

"The brighter light is giving us violent attacks of snow blindness. Even close objects appear as if seen through muslin. Sometimes we see double."

(If I could see intervals as well as objects . . . If intervals are shapes in their own right, then were those shapes around the bushes where I read the contours and forms of my own hiding?)

"The sun blinds us even at night in our tent, coming in through every crack and slit in the canvas."

In the weeks before Albanov left, Captain Brusilov stared through fevered eyes. "In his delirium he looked like a skeleton covered not with skin but rubber. He would ask whether the horses had been given hay or oats. 'What horses are you talking about, Georgii Lvovich? We don't possess a single horse. We're in the Kara Sea, trapped in ice, aboard the *Saint Anna*.' 'The horses over there,' he'd reply, 'the ones nuzzling Nurse Zhdanko.' "

(Claire read of a woman, Eloisa, whose eyes were covered by a veil. Even here, in so remote a place, a security veil of sonar and electric eyes monitors enemy aircraft traversing airspace that's divided, owned.)

———◆———

I thought words could train me to see better, but often it seems they just throw a scrim over everything. Even my name shifts around, I call myself Clare, then Clara, then Claire, can't decide. Still, the banks of the Rhine are very beautiful, the river itself more narrow than I would have thought. Sometimes when I read it's as if my eyes finally have a place to go to for a while where my sight feels clearer. I don't think about how after I close the book the words will come back and maybe drown, or flap and hurl themselves against each other, and how the mind's like discord in music. I heard Mary talking to Shelley about my "blind manner." I keep thinking of the Duke of Gloucester's eyes, that his eyes were torn out, and yet a separate tenderness came after. Somewhere this road still continues—xxxthough Shelley says we have to turn back.

What of my own eyes? Why did you give them to me, what did you want them to do for me? "The orbits of the eyes," Goldsmith wrote, and each day my eyes open to this sky, to her hand that comes when it pleases. My eyes rapt within force fields not their own, obedient to laws not their own. "The Sight of the Mind differs very much from the Sight of the Body," but I don't think I can tell them apart. "The blind's visions are visions of touch," Bain wrote, so isn't touch a form of seeing? My eyes cast chains over everything until nothing I touch with them seems free. So isn't sight a builder of prisons, and watching a form of taking prisoners? Once I came across the term *eye-sorrow*. Though I don't know exactly what it is, I've often felt how seeing's somehow sorrowful at the core. Guns are used to sight. The center of a flower is called its eye. Why would I have thought I could find a place where my eyes would seek nothing, my mind nothing? Even here: electric eyes on the airstrips spot and track hostile traffic. Albanov would have known a boat can't "walk in the wind's eye," that the calm at the center of that eye, though quiet, is also desperate. I think of the eye of a furnace, painted eyes on prows of ancient ships—

I wonder who left this copy of Nansen's *Farthest North*? Spine broken, green cloth binding torn, it's inscribed to: *Josiah L. Hoale, from his aff grandmother. December 25th, 1897.* I look through the index: Arctic thirst; Bacteria in ice-water; Bandaging; Books—longing for; Clothing—deplorable condition of; Cloudberry flower; Dogs—harnesses, kennels, killed by bears, killed by their fellows, paralysis in legs; Eclipse of the Sun; Head shaving; Homeward; Ice—first meeting with, rate of formation, white reflection from; Journals—difficulty of writing; Moons, remarkable; Musical instruments.

And: Poppies; Red Snow; Shoes; Shrimps—vomited by Arctic rose-gull; Snow blindness—cases of; Sun—disappearance of; Telescope; Watches—run down; Wounds, Wrist-sores, Yugor Strait.

xxx but the joy, too, sometimes—the xxxxx and again I think how the
mind's like discord in music. ~~But it's impossible to find a xxx~~ it's impossible to find a wild and entire solitude, or one name to belong to

xx

then I go downstairs for breakfast (today we begin heading back) and Mary
doesn't want to look at me I don't know why. Shelley says I was sleepwalking again, that in my dream the stairs were rushing water there was no way
I could get down. He says that's what I told him but I remember nothing
xxxx so what's seeing when I remember none of what I saw? What's
knowing? So many stairs unbuilding themselves inside my mind. Horace
said the soul is at fault which never escapes from itself but how can it
escape from itself? Ruins everywhere . . . and that chain across the valley.
Chains of black hills at Maas-Sluis. Yet I want to see everything, no
vanishing line noxxx xxxx and nothing making concessions to anything
else. I would see the coexistence of all things. The near coin and the far
moon—

Not those stairs of rushing water   not the way they wouldn't let me go
down—

Church Street, Nelson Square, 41 Hans Place, 1 Hans Place, 13 Arabella Road, so many new addresses. And Mary so often unwell as she lay in her bed those months after we came back, waiting for the baby to be born . . . and now this . . . I don't know how toxxxand sometimes it seems even thinking's a cruelty

Dear Fanny,

I'm in Lynmouth. They sent me away. I came here the week after Mary's baby died. She's sad all the time now. The baby was born too early. They never even gave it a name. Sometimes I just lie here and think: it had no name. Those twelve days she lived without a name and now when we remember her what are we to call her? Or do we say: "it"? "It" was born too early, "it" died. I turn each chilly idea over in my mind while nearby the sea moves like a higher mind that understands it's incapable of knowing. Jessamine and Honeysuckle twining over my cottage window, but I'd rather see the London soot, anything angular and hard.

Today, I don't know why, I was thinking about how you always mis-spell afraid—you write "affraid." Two f's in it as if doubling its power in some way, and I'm sorry we didn't take you with us when we left for France, you think Mary and Shelley despise you but they don't. But there's this look of fright in your eyes, something breaking in you bit by bit, but maybe I'm mistaken.

You told me you didn't think I'd ever be able to live alone. But I feel an almost violent tranquility. I distrust the surmises of our minds, Montaigne wrote. And here it's as if all surmises have fallen away, I'm wonder and error and uncertainty and no one watches or criticizes or worries. As if I'm not even a Claire or Clary or Jane or Mary Jane anymore, but nameless or . . . Not hidden away but not seen either. Two ridges of mountains enclose the village. If I walk up the hill near Mr. Foote's I can see the whole valley. When I read a book a voice comes close to me and knows me. I wonder if you feel this too?

What are you reading? Are you feeling stronger? If you and Mary are both sad I don't know how I'll ~~but you always seem sad.~~ Remember what Ovid wrote?—"When eyes behold eyes in pain, they become painful themselves."

I think of your eyes.

Your sister,
Claire

Claire wrote of ruins as *a place I somehow know . . . so how could we just be kind to one another . . . each with our own jagged edges, our damage.* Are icebergs ruins too? They carry inside themselves pebbles, boulders, dust. I never knew they concealed so much roughness, that beneath those gleaming surfaces such damaged, displaced dark lies hidden. (I think of the Chinese stick I found in Archangel.) Under whiteness and light, so many ruined worlds.

Each time I see them, I remember her white sleeve, her hand leaving jagged letters that only even hint at who she is. But what of her face I never see? Her face. Her faces. Why do I make her plural like that? She signs her name so many different ways, as if there's no one name to belong to. To have so many names, has that made her almost nameless? Is there something in her that feels, like me, unnamed?

Fanny, I'll write more later. There are silences in us which I fear will never be broken. Sometimes I think what I know of you is your small French watch, your red pocket handkerchief, your brown-berry necklace and your purse. Such things as you lay out on the table at night. I'm ignorant and worse.

This milky midnight light. Icebergs drift through a white veil. Whiteness of her sleeve, of absence.

When I lie down, pieces of Nansen's index drift like icebergs in my mind: Books–longing for. Dogs–paralysis in legs. Journals–difficulty of writing. Moons–remarkable. Wind-clothes. Wounds. Wrist-sores.

I distrust the surmises of our minds, Claire wrote to Fanny. More and more I trust within my mind almost nothing. In my dream Nansen's paralyzed dog keeps trying to stand but its legs are useless twigs. I watch it though it hates being watched. It tries to hide itself, turns its face to the side. It wants somewhere private to die, but there's nowhere private in the ice.

When I wake I feel ashamed.

Nansen felt he had no choice but to feed the weaker dogs to the strong.

Why do I want to tell her these things? And of books that are longed for, journals that are hard to write.

(And myself hidden. No mask to tear from my face.)

I wait for her hand, then see the dog lift its eyes one last time, ice-locked and dying, thirteen months from solid land.

When her hand returns it's not writing. She's holding, instead, a letter from Fanny, spreads it flat on a wooden surface in the sun.

Dear Claire,

Papa has given me this space of paper to fill & seal. He says you and Mary and Shelley have gone away to the Continent again. There are such silences in me even as I write you. Something lost inside me & I don't know how to say it. Sometimes I'm not even affraid anymore as if I'm looking at myself from a great distance and so feel no need to be concerned. Everything over-with in a way. I try to speak plainly but understanding obscures and buries itself. I wonder if you feel this too, though you're not like me, you're bold, and I'm sure Mary and Shelley think me timid and a laughingstock, Mamma has told me so. The Creator shouldn't destroy his Creature but he does this all the time—I shouldn't dwell on such things and I do, but that doesn't mean I'm foolish. I don't know what I am . . . The other day Mr. Blood, brother of Fanny Blood, stopped by to see us. He gave me many particulars of the days of my mother's youth before Godwin. He hadn't been in London for 26 years. How can the world feel so desolate and deserted when it's so full? For a few hours I felt as though my mother was with me, as she had been with Fanny Blood in Lisbon in those few days before Fanny died after childbirth. I felt such happiness, so strange to feel happy . . . I know you think Papa is <u>cold</u>*, but he just seems that way as he worries about money. I can assure you he speaks of you with kindness and interest. Ever since Mt. Tamboro erupted it seems the whole world has grown cold. Dust everywhere blocking the sun. And such rainstorms and hail. They say the harvest will fail, that there'll be food shortages, maybe even famine. I'm not sure where you are—in France? In Switzerland? You say you are too intolerant to enter into society but it seems to me you're always going about, whereas I live in a solitude that . . . but I can't explain myself, and I wonder if the famine will come and where you'll be. Why does the mind grow ashamed of itself? I'm affraid you will dislike this letter, I've been rambling, but I write to you without disguise.*
Your Sister,
Fanny

If I could see Claire's face I might know what she feels. But I see only her hands folding the letter. I don't know where she is, what year it is, how much time has passed since she last wrote. It seems she's not in Lisbourne anymore, has traveled.

Nansen wanted his ship to get trapped by ice far out at sea, so when the ice drifted northward or even south it would be dragged to places no man had ever seen. I have no ship, this ice can't carry me. Yet I feel I've reached the farthest pole. No faces anywhere. Only the mind's isolate and perpetual movement—Ambiguity, silence, instability, exposure—

Dear Fanny,

It's rained almost every day and there are violent storms. We stay indoors for many hours writing stories. Mary says she can't think of an idea for hers but that's not true, I see her filling pages. I don't know what kind of thoughts to send you. Montaigne wrote that he hoped to become ashamed of his mind, and you ask in your letter why does the mind grow ashamed of itself, but I don't want to feel ashamed of my own mind. I want thinking to be free even if hunted by calamity, even if at times it makes of me a violent, desperate creature. Montaigne thought by withdrawing to live in complete solitude he could set his mind free. But his thinking couldn't steady itself, it became like a runaway horse, that's what he said. It presented him with thoughts "irregular and unmeaning." "I put them on paper," he wrote, "hoping in time to make my mind ashamed of itself." I wonder, did he really believe this?—or did he love his runaway horse more than anything. His books all runaway horses, the fraught and unstable extremity of sight . . . Didn't he love, in a way, thinking about Bertrand du Guesclin, who died at the siege of the castle of Randon, and how after, when his men had been defeated, they were forced to carry the citadel's keys on the dead man's body. Or of the uses of thumbs and why they are cut off. Or of Cannibals and Monsters, "this child just fourteen months old with a single head and double body, diverse limbs hanging and dangling." "What we call monsters are not so to God, who sees in the immensity of his work the infinity of forms that he has comprised therein . . . nothing whatsoever exists that is not in accordance with Nature." If we could believe in the infinity of forms, Fanny, not pull back from the infinity of forms. I think he loved letting his mind travel into extremity, every harsh or mysterious territory, no matter what. If we could do this, Fanny . . . I don't know when we'll return from Switzerland, if ever. There is much to say I won't put in a letter. Everything is different from what I expected. How are your eyes, are they better?

Your Sister,
Claire

If it's possible the mind can live unashamed of itself, and the "infinity of forms" be felt as a kind of goodness . . . If "nothing whatsoever exists that is not in accordance with Nature" . . . If all this is true, then how might I think differently of this body you gave me?

When I try to think of this my skin goes cold. I see only ice, distrust the "surmises of my mind." Thought isn't comfort. Still, if everyone and everything is patchwork in some way, am I all that different? If the soul is error (but is there a soul?) . . . If, as Plato said, chance produces more beautifully than art, and the mind's true movement is irregular, uncertain . . . then what's beauty, what's ugliness? Is there a clear line between the two?

Even so, I can't imagine heading back toward warmer land. And Claire will never look into my face, never know me.

Every now and then flocks of murres, auks flying in a northerly direction, a line of black wings.

As if in transcription.

(But there's so much tracelessness in me, in anyone.)

For long stretches Claire keeps no diary. I dream the cold silence where the pages would have been.

Architecture of oblivion, its drifts.

My cold hands barely moving.

In this cabin: rotting food crates half-buried in snow. Cans of peppermint drops and biscuits. Bunks scattered with torn clothes. Broken sledges, harnesses, frying pans, spoons.

Such fragile traces.

And always the question of who they were, what happened to them, did they suffer, did they die in the ice?

So many ways the mind tries to climb itself, but can't.

Swansea Oct 9

Clare,

You'll never read this—I'll burn it shortly, the light going down over the bay, an inward silence widening. Sometimes in my mind I ask how cold, sometimes I see miles of wooden fence posts. Sometimes I sit and think of a machine I would call a Difference Engine that would solve many things, perform many complex computations. Always I relate my story very ill in any case. I try but can't construct the outer. Something other is more present to me, in me, but I don't know how to say it. Why do we try to know one another? I don't mean to be coy. Only that we lived in the same house, ate the same breakfasts, walked the same walks, were mostly frank with one another, and still there's something icy and impersonal in us and between us, between anyone. I thought I didn't mind but something in me can't get used to it. As if I were a monster fled to the woods and mocking voices were speaking from the trees. This is how you make laudanum: take a basketful of withered poppies, pick out the heads one by one, pierce them with a sewing needle then set them in a

crock near the stove for the opium to sweat out. Mix the extract with
sugar or alcohol to make it easier to drink. I think of inanimate matter,
I think of descending shades of gray. I dream of someone—woman or man
I can't tell—looking into my eyes and fleeing. But that's not important. It's
this waking-time, all these gray or sunlit days. They'll say I'm visiting my
aunts . . . Families must present themselves "in the best possible light."

       Your Sister,
       Fanny

THE CAMBRIAN

SWANSEA WALES, SATURDAY OCTOBER 12 1816

A MELANCHOLY DISCOVERY was made in Swansea yesterday. A most respectable-looking female arrived at the Mackworth Arms inn on Wednesday night by the Cambrian coach from Bristol; she took tea and retired to rest, telling the chambermaid she was exceedingly fatigued, and would take care of the candle herself. Much agitation was created in the house by her non-appearance yesterday morning, and in forcing her chamber door, she was found a corpse, with the remains of a bottle of laudanum on the table, and a note, of which the following is a copy:

I have long determined that the best thing I could do was to put an end to the existence of a being whose birth was unfortunate, and whose life has been only a series of pain to those persons who have hurt their health in endeavoring to promote her welfare. Perhaps to hear of my death will give you pain, but you will soon have the blessing of forgetting that such a creature ever existed as

The name appears to have been torn off and burnt, but her stockings are marked with the letter G. and on her stays the letters M.W. are visible. She was dressed in a blue-striped skirt with a white body, and a brown pelice, with a fur trimming of a lighter colour, lined with white silk, and a hat of the same. She had a small French gold watch, and appears to be about 23 years of age, with long brown hair, dark complexion, and had a reticule containing a red silk pocket handkerchief, a brown-berry necklace, and a small leather clasped purse, containing a 3s. and 5s. 6d. piece. She told a fellow-passenger that she came to Bath by the mail from London on Tuesday morning, from whence she proceeded to Bristol, and from thence to Swansea by the Cambrian coach, intending to go to Ireland—We hope the description we have given of this unhappy catastrophe will lead to the discovery of the wretched object who has thus prematurely closed her existence.

Fanny,

I keep thinking of how you ended your note with "forgetting that such a creature ever existed as"—and then no ellipses, no period, no other words, nothing, everything fallen away. That cliff of who you were (and yet I didn't know you) overhanging only empty space. Nothing in the world more silent than your leaving it. Nothing in my brain more silent. (I know you're no longer alive and still I write to you.) And when I see your words fallen away (the stark blankness beyond them) I know there's an unsigned in me, something monstrously broken and unnamed. ~~Though you said I was bold xxx you said I was xxx~~ *But why did you call yourself a creature? When you began your note you called yourself a* being *(I almost feel your breath on my cheek as I write this) but you ended it with* creature, *as if you felt you were no longer human, or . . . I don't know, but it chills me. The blank space after "as" chills me . . . The newspaper account says you burned your name. But if you could have seen the runaway horse as beautiful, or, not beautiful maybe, but as something to be wanted . . . If you could have*xxx*Sometimes Shelley uses such pretty words, I hate that prettiness: "the sweet season of summertide" or "and gentle odors led my steps astray," "violet buds and bluebells," "the pale stars of the morn." But you died in a strange room, told them at the inn you were on your way to Ireland when you knew you never intended to get there, hadn't even brought the money, so why should I like pretty words? I don't think you liked them either. But then other times I see on scraps of paper or in notebooks other things he's scribbled: "In hating such a hateless thing as me," "You hate me [?were]," "The stream with a [leprous] scum," "You were injured—& that means memory," "a people starving on the untilled field," "chains & chains & chains." Those words more brutal and more true. Did you feel you were a hated hateless thing? I don't know why I write unless it seems like speaking to you though I know this is foolish. No hour on the earth is safe. So much of what living is—Concealed—*

Your Sister,
Claire

Claire folds the page from *The Cambrian* in fours, presses it tightly, slips it into a drawer.

Fanny, I'm not well. My mind always keeps my body in a fever. Godwin wouldn't let any of us go to your funeral or retrieve your body—your grave's a pauper's, anonymous. I'm going to have a child. By a man who, were I to float by his window drowned, all he would say would be "Ah, voilà." If it's a girl I think I'll call her Alba—the a's that begin and end it form a kind of gentle symmetry, a circle. (Then I think of that soft "a" in your name, that maybe something that soft grows too afraid.) But in my mind I feel something else, something like "slash this, slash that"—that this is what thinking is and there are so many sharp edges in me now, so many cuts and gashes overall. And I can't anyhow

~~sky, precipices~~   ~~(I see my own weakness)~~   ~~nevermind~~

~~the~~

~~and that I will never be able to~~

I remember after Mary ran away and you weren't permitted to see her she sent you a lock of her hair and you kept it in your drawer. It's late now. Why do I still write to you though I know you're no longer alive? Is it my way of slowly getting used to your not being here? Or am I delaying the idea that you're not here? The blunt fact of it. (I don't pretend we were even close.) Your hard, skinny body, your bones. The away in you, in anyone. The apart.

Nights I lie awake imagining chromosomes breaking inside me, suddenly estranged from what they were. Insurgencies, counterinsurgencies of thought. Scorchings. Retaliations.

I remember the notes you left behind. How they went over every step you took to make me, the discarded parts you collected from the graveyard, even the fevers you suffered as you built me.

I keep those notes in my knapsack, though I wish never to look at them again.

Months now since I've seen a human face.

"And he who studies himself will find in himself much discordance."

Fanny,

Mary visited today. She brought a few pages she found in your drawer (Godwin finally allowed her back into the house). I wouldn't have thought this of you, that you kept notes, made sketches. Even just a few. No one knows but Mary and me. Not even Shelley. In this one, here, the pencil line's so faint I can barely make out your shoulders' slope, your head with the face turned away. Why did you make the face turned away? The paper's so small, barely 2" square. As if you were already disappearing . . . Maybe time's different from what we think and we get only glimpses, we think it moves forward but it doesn't, just allows us in at different places. Maybe there's no continuity of space or time after all. So where are you then, and why? You with your face turned away. These faint traces you left that say however softly: I was here. Which is different from: am known.

This, too, Fanny, you left behind:
August 1, 1816

Mr. Booth says it's peace that has brought calamity upon us. But what hope
is there if Peace is Calamity? The foreign ports are shut, manufacturing
drastically cut back. Millions left to starve. That's what he says. He says
26,000 men are unemployed in Shropshire. Workers drag coals in immense
wagons without horses all the way to London and are turned back. So they
give the coals for nothing to the poor. Mr. Owen says he has a plan, but
how can he expect the rich to give up their possessions and live in a state of
equality with others—this is too romantic to be believed. His plan says that
"no human being shall work more than two or three hours every day; that
they shall all be equal; that no one shall dress but after the plainest and
simplest manner, that their slaves shall be Mechanics and Chemistry." But
why does he use the word "slaves"? I wish I were not a dependent being in
every sense of the word. Claire and Mary and Shelley all far away. Why am
I always so affraid? And Godwin always worried about money. I know Mary
used to sit near our mother's grave—but I could never do that. Too affraid of
what I'd feel there. Mary writes and asks about what old friends I'm seeing,
but I see no one. When I look at the page my eyes blur though the doctor
says it's not my eyes but my mind. So cold since Mt. Tamboro erupted.
What I write I write to no one.

And this:
August 7, 1816

A watch and some books arrived today from Mary. I'm not used to this
kindness. I would like to visit <u>Venice</u> and <u>Naples</u> one day.
And finally, this (no more papers left in your drawer):
5 a.m., Sept. 9, 1816

I record here my dream: Mary was visiting, and Clare. Someone was
complaining that vials of poison had been scattered on the moor, that this
should be looked into. Then we were all in a room with many large
machines. Soon we each lay on a bed by a machine. The machines seemed
to have an odd authority, as if they knew us. Mary's leg was taken off and
given to me. My arm was removed and a machine clamped it onto Clare.
Other body parts were exchanged. But even though our body parts were

being exchanged I still felt different from them, and alone. There was no blood. How would Godwin recognize us? And how would Shelley know who Mary was, which one? When I tried to speak I didn't know whose voice would come out of my mouth and this frightened me. There was a drowned woman too who was brought in and she, too, exchanged body parts with us. A man had cut the white dress off her and hung it in a closet. It was dry and unspoiled as if newly cleaned. I looked over at Clare or was it Mary? I was suddenly very hungry. But if I asked for some toast I would have to hear the voice from my mouth and so said nothing.

That's all, Fanny. Nothing more left.

"A cold fire envelops me," Lomonosov wrote. This is what I feel when Claire's hand doesn't come, sometimes for days, sometimes weeks.

I know she's going to have a child, but nothing of where she is or what she's feeling. Not who the father is or if she loves him. (Her hand's left no trace of this.) Will she care for the child alone?

(And you who made me in secret, and abandoned me in secret.)

Fanny's voice a shut place now. And Claire, where is she? Will she come back?

The revving of engines on the airstrip. Fighter planes practicing maneuvers overhead.

Fanny,

I'm thinking today of the plainness of things. The plain <u>facts</u> of things. The burnt corner of the note you left behind. Your small gold watch. Why do people have to turn such things into symbols? Make them <u>mean</u>? It's strange enough to breathe and to have eyes. Just to look and to have eyes, and that we will be gone (as you're already gone) and others will appear, and this cottage in Bath where I've come to have my baby will be here with its faint smell of wood-rot and wisteria. The cracks in this table, this frayed sleeve.

Pitcher. Chair. These objects I touch daily. The little weed that smells like mineral oil—I don't know what it's called.

Soot.

Loneliness.

Skinner Street. St. Pancras.

For weeks Shelley knew I was going to have a child, but neither he nor I told Mary (she has a baby of her own now, William). Now Mary knows and I think she's not pleased with me. Shelley's drawn up a new will, left money for me and the baby. On the way here from Geneva we stopped at Chamonix where Shelley wrote in Greek in the inn's guest book "I am a lover of mankind, democrat, and atheist." All that feels far away. Amid the thousand thousand lines of human life branching and intersecting in endless and infinite directions, I think now there's not one that leads to safety.

Lately I remember those long hours at boarding school with my French books when I seemed both I and not I as I read in that other language and sometimes thought of home.

I don't know how to think about what home is.

Awkwardness.

Breath.

The word "if." My shoes in the corner. The word "despite."

Claire writes to Fanny of objects she touches each day—a pitcher, a chair. What do I touch? Ice. Can opener. Boots. The Chinese stick I found at Archangel. Knapsack. Stray pages picked up here and there. In one of my books: "The mind's aliment is wonder, search, ambiguity."

Sometimes I see mountains and islands over the ice, then the light changes or the temperature drops and they're not there. Yesterday I watched for an hour a white Moorish city of onion-domed temples and walled streets. Is my voice also a mirage that crumbles and drifts off?

•

My affections are few and therefore strong—the extreme
solitude in which I live has concentrated them to one point and that point
is my child. We sleep together and if you knew the extreme Happiness

So Claire has had her child and is happy . . .

But this cold has many turns in it.

Olaus Magnus made this list:

Cold burns the eyes of animals and stiffens their hairs.
Cold makes wolves fiercer.
Cold makes hares, foxes, and ermines change color.
Cold causes copper, glass, and earthenware vessels to break.
Cold causes damp clothes to stick to iron if they graze it.
Cold causes nails to spring from the walls.
Cold makes lips stick to iron as if held in indissoluble pitch.

•

When she wakes I hold her and there is no cold in me, no
broken place. Is it possible that— ~~I am still however(nothing)~~
~~any creature must~~   ~~but then~~
To feel such consent in myself   I wouldn't have guessed it

So many places the northern explorers were sure they saw didn't even exist. They drew them into their maps—mirages, though they didn't know it: Crocker Land, King Oscar Land, Keenan Land, the Barnard Mountains.

and now unlocked from these strictures of

The maps were revised again and again. (So many gashes in me as I think of her arms, how she pulls the child in.) Each time, the mapmaker believed he was writing in the final answer—

Fanny,

Why is it I still talk to you—to you more than the living, or so it often seems? As if pressing my lips against an ice-shelf. Yet there's a comfort in the things that come to mind when I imagine you listening in the extreme ardor of your solitude. I've been told I must give up my child. First she lived away from me with Mary and Shelley and the Hunts in Hampstead. Then I came down from Bath and was allowed to live nearby. Finally in March Mary and Shelley and the children (William and Clara and my Allegra) and I moved to Albion house together. People think I'm my child's Aunt.

Little holds still in me, so much is clash and tremor, and I don't want to lose her but I×××

> What stays in place, finally, what is secured?—is anything?

> January ice. February. March wind batters the door, strong as instinct—

Even my child's name is a thing that shifts. First: Alba, or the Dawn (why couldn't I just leave it at that, let her be the dawn?) Then she was Clara Allegra (but did I want my name in hers?) Now she's Allegra.

Nothing's still or held in safety.

On her christening certificate her father has "no fixed residence." She is his "reputed" daughter.

In London last October I saw hundreds of vagrants lying about the streets, half-naked and starving. Sometimes the Night Officers brought them to the Lord Mayor's Mansion house, as many as 300 at a time, where their cases were "examined," whatever that means. I dreamt of them last night, I don't know why. Over and over someone kept saying the price of Bread now is extremely high.

××× all these rules we have and strictures. And if you fall out of what's expected, they punish you, Fanny,×××and I don't want to be married, never wanted it, don't believe in marriage. Anyhow he doesn't want me. And the vagrants in the streets . . . that they must be "examined" . . . so many laws to fall through, and Propertius said ivy grows best when wild and birds wing most sweetly without teaching . . .

I study my child's pleasure all day long. (what rules will consume her, what laws?)

They say for her sake I have to send her to her father.

I have no words for who I'll be without her. I should sign all my letters Unsigned. Or sign them as I once signed those to her father who would never, anyhow, reply: Cl___ Cl___, the blank unsaids as much a part of me as anything—

I see her signing her name on different pieces and sizes of paper. Where is she? Is she in various places, writing at various times? Her name shifting as this horizon line shifts (I see luminiferous stalks, but what could grow here? They turn into towers, a caravan, armored men wearing helmets of ice.):

Clara   *Mary Jane*   *Yours, Clare*   *Claire*   *Cleary*   *Clari*

Clara Mary Constantia Jane Clairmont (they'll put this on my gravestone)

I know Mary wrote in her journal: "absentia Clariae,"—she's glad to be rid of me

Write me as Madam Clairville, Poste Restante . . . I have taken the name Clairville as you said you liked the name Clare but not the mont because of that ugly woman

Then she's:

Unsigned

Then:

G.C.B.

(a mystery as to why)

Then:

address me as E. Trefusis

(also a mystery)

I wish to give you a suspicion without at first disclosing myself. I am an Utter Stranger.

More and more I go out alone. Mine is a delicate case, my feet are on the edge of a precipice. I am your own affectionate Clare

Ever quite affectionately, Clara   *My dearest Albe's Affectionate Clare*
Unsigned

Again:

Unsigned

I have unloosed myself from the trammels of custom and opinion. Most often I feel quite alone and hope you will think sometimes of me without anger & that you will love and take good care of the Child.

Fanny,

We're in Milan, Shelley and Mary, their little William and Clara, Allegra and myself. We traveled past the Alps, past mountain torrents in the valleys. Near Mt. Cenis snow at the road's edges was as high as our carriage. This comforted and excited me—that alien landscape where I could become something other than myself, anonymous, unnamed, no need to hide from anyone or pretend I'm not my child's mother. Where I could be a machine of flesh pulsing around a chainless core, a creature foraging, exploring. Cascades of ice hung in immense masses from the tops to the bottoms of the Precipices! A stream flowed between two snowy banks. We passed some Alpine bridges.

The Descent was beautiful—

Sometimes I'm quiet as a bird roosting in the night. Sometimes the Operations of the Mind are so strange to me I might as well be a piece of metal or wood. Then I know I'm afraid. But mostly I feel alive with my child. Shelley writes of being "entangled in the cold vanity of systems" but sometimes, when I forget I have to give her up, I can almost feel those systems fall away—myself finally outside them—

Mostly I jot down the mundane details of my days:

Sunday April 12th: Play chess with Shelley in the evening.

Monday April 13th: Walk in the Morning. In the Evening go to the Theatre of the Marionetti. Play at Chess. Read the Life of Tasso.

(Often I try not to think . . . I know what's coming . . . I wait for my child to be taken—)

Read Locke. Read Davanzati's Tacitus. Read Berrington's History of the Middle Ages. Very pleasant Evening.

I write in my journal, but all the while the creature in me forages through ice and deep snow. Waits for what's coming. Sleeps where? Tries to hide itself where? And then here and there, suddenly, as out of nowhere, the black acid of bare branches, a bare rock.

I wanted to come to this cold place where your face would be ash to me, or less. But now when her hand doesn't come, or comes only briefly, the eyeless glare of ice almost frightens me; I think of crushed ships, all the men who wrote journals no one would read, and sought an elsewhere they could never find.

The Barents Sea. The Kara Sea. White Island. Mt. Misery. Cape Mary Harmsworth. The small islands called *Existence Doubtful.*

Cape Allegra. Cape Clara. Cape Wonder. Cape Ruthless. Cape Abandonment. Cape Custom. Cape Longing. Cape Remain.

Dear Fanny,

Sometimes I feel I'm on a frozen Sea. My map's torn, and anyhow I feel stupid even looking at it since it depicts the sea in gradations of soft blues and greens but the water around me is a rigid, violent white.
~~*to never return to*~~   ~~*and there is no reason*~~

          ~~*at once captive and eruptive*~~   ~~*nevermind*~~

The map's suggested route toward land is laid out in lines red and broken—

Fanny,

Allegra's in Venice. She was taken from here the day after my birthday. I'm 20 now.

I write this to you as if a human voice makes sense. As if words are beads strung orderly and sanely. But I think now the mind's all edge and precipice. It has no grammar but itself. I don't know how to—

 ✗✗✗ and the cruelty of   ✗✗✗✗✗   ~~and no way to begin to~~

Such twists and turns, Fanny, such slashings overall—

Custom is its own punishment. The <u>within</u> cracks and buckles, stutters, rallies, fails. I dream of conflagrations nightly. I think of the cleft of de-creation embedded in every sentence, every breath. I think angrily of Logic's ramparts. Noun this, noun that. Subject, predicate, verb, verb.

We line them up so neatly, ~~but they're not, and the mind . . . ✗✗✗ and my own thinking . . . and what hides inside each word and in between them~~   (and how could I have let them take her?)

I dream of liberty.

I think now there's no privacy of the mind. But if I could have it would I hear a truer grammar? Not this yes yes I must and order order order follow done. Always at a sentence's end a period or question mark. But how many thoughts happen in that way, end precisely in that way—And does each thought even have an ending at all, or should we call whatever happens then something else, something we have no words or punctuation for? I can almost feel the punctuation marks crumbling, balance crumbling. Everything more skewed and wavy. Haphazard, rough, but it still makes a kind of sense. Nothing balances anything. Nothing exactly matches anything else. The abyss inside each word even as I write you—all I know is that it's cold. I walk on rigid ice floes of linked words that keep me, in their brittleness, from what? They're white as coma.

Fanny. Allegra. Each one of you adrift on your broken ice floe, alone.

(she is so small and I let them . . . how
could I have let them?)

And I with no verbs to clamp onto you, seizing.

I watch from my white shore. At least there's that. But there's little I can see . . . really almost nothing . . .

Maybe it's good that I can't seize you . . . (but what of Allegra?)

In my mind the fires claw so high, climbing and spitting.

Uprisings   Guillotines   Slaves

Flesh/Property

You, Fanny. And Allegra. You. Her. You. Are you bound on your ice floes or unbound? Or bound, unbound, at the same time? And what grammar is there for that, what ways of saying? ×××I have no . . . . So many walls of words when I think that I can't reach her—

She's writing in a small notebook of Italian red marbled paper. Rome, 1819. Inside the front cover, a list of Italian coins:

> Gratze, Soldi—Bajocci—Grani—
> Lira, Paoli, Carlini, Piastra Francesconi
> Centisimi, Pezzi.   Ducati.
> Quattrini

She writes

> Guardi

then erases it (I watch her do this but can't know why she wants to).

Then:

> Ne le me voglie ognor stringe e rafferme a cennit altrui (in my desires I am always pulled to and fro by someone else).

Is she thinking of Allegra? Or of Mary and Shelley? Or of Godwin, or Allegra's father? Or of all of them and more?

Below, notes for a book on Italy:

> On the Manners and Customs
> On the (Belle Arts)↑Pictures and Statues↓
> On the Music and the State of the Opera

Then:

> Letter for Bologna   Passport   Blk. Silk Stockings & Shoes   Ivy Leaves

(I wonder what this means)

> Palazzo Verospi   Al Corso Roma

Why does watching make me feel more *seen*? As if a chain, not rough but tender, not enslaving, links me to another. How the parts of that chain, though rigid in themselves, combine to move flexibly and freely. I know that she hates chains (she wrote this), thinks only of the ones that fetter and restrain. But her hand moves through the air, linking one letter to another, one sentence to another—a good chain—until her voice becomes visible, an almost-nearness.

Fanny,

If I could have just one lock of her hair . . . or, no, that's not enough. In Bagni di Lucca I rode a horse so fast the world spun away and when I fell I was glad. Nothing but blackness, cold and unfeeling. But first, right before I fell, my brain flashed with white light. All the trees in my brain were what thunder would look like if thunder could be seen. Then I had to stay inside for many weeks, but I still saw the white trees in my brain—that poisonous, unsparing light. (I think of you on the bed in Swansea—laudanum coursing through you—good shoes still on, and your silk stockings, your good clothes . . .). Herculaneum, Vesuvius, the Bay of Baiae, Paestum, Pompeii—When I could walk again I saw them. But what does it mean to be in the world, to walk through the world? Even through ruins? I want an unchained mind, I want ✗✗✗✗ And I feel more and more that there's as much distance, if not more, between the places within ourselves and the distance between one person and another. Everything various, unhealed. Coded spaces, spaces cast apart and cast away, irretrievable, inchoate, choked: all this inside one mind. And I can't✗✗✗✗ but then I think I must try . . . ✗✗✗ I see the scorched trees again, the white light✗✗✗✗✗ and still each day comes and goes.

After ninety days of struggling over ice, Albanov was flooded with fever-ish dreams. "I hear angry voices outside, someone's trying to break down the door." "Colonies of walruses, crouching in silent contemplation, drift past on floating ice-chunks, then I see their heads are horses' skulls."

He finds the remains of an old camp. A large boulder engraved with the words *Stella Polare*. A wooden cross, painted red. Shreds of dirty, mildewed cloth. Crates and boxes buried in ice. "It was like digging up the ruins of Pompeii." Inside: spoiled powdered eggs, pemmican, sausage in sealed tins. The name *Ziegler* embroidered on red silk. Cans of spoiled coffee and oats. Pharmaceutical jars. A drawing of a dogsled.

"Konrad wants to set out for Bell Island. I'm too weak but he says he'll come back for me. He's left some quinine tablets and food but I'm not hungry and it's hard to swallow. How many days has he been gone? Why would Nansen refer to sea-ice as a fisherman's net? Where's the icon of Nicholas I carry in my pocket?–I can't feel it. Nature doesn't want the presence of man. I thought when you're alone you're free but every-thing's splintering. Konrad comes back, he's sobbing. It was impossible for him to get to Bell Island."

White trees flame inside Claire's brain. And Albanov lived all those months in a whiteness like those trees she can't stop seeing. My own brain in those first hours after you left me, didn't it try to scorch back into oblivious white flame, until there was nothing left of who you were or where you went to, what you did? But something in me kept thinking (though I had no words and can't remember what such thinking felt like). And Albanov kept thinking, Claire keeps thinking.

See the temple of the Sybil   Read Dante (Purgatorio)   Read Locke

Trees white and unsparing—and still each day comes and goes—

February. Pisa. Though she writes in her journal almost daily, for long stretches she doesn't mention Allegra. Instead she takes notes on what she's reading:

Read Paine. Letter to the Abbe Reynal. Rights of Man—"It is the faculty of the human mind to become what it contemplates and to act in unison with its object."

If I could see the workings of my brain, would I see them change when I think of you instead of her? Does my mind become a different, harsher mind? As Albanov shivered, fevered, walked on ice then couldn't walk, as he dreamed of sunlit cities, plates of food, did his mind merge with that ice until it remade him as its own?

Paine's Rights of Man are a monument to the plain and sensible idea of Liberty. And for this glory he was repaid by being refused Burial in any of the Americans' Church-Yards.

Whenever such examples fall my way I remember Southey's "Man is the worst of all animals and it is a disgrace to the Oran Outang to be compared with him."

Shelley and I walk on the Argine. Later he goes to Livorno. Read more Paine: General Clive used to destroy his prisoners by shooting them from the mouth of a cannon.

I dream I'm in Damascus. I don't look like myself. I'm covered in black cloth. I'm walking on a dusty street carrying water in one hand and fire in the other. The water doesn't seep through my fingers and the skin of my other hand's unburned. The Ambassador asks me why I'm doing this. I tell him with my fire I'll burn Paradise, but I don't know why I say this or what it means, and I don't know what I'll do with the water. I start to feel my hand burning, it pains terribly, the skin's blackening, almost melting, though none of this was happening until the Ambassador asked his question. When I wake Mary says I was sleepwalking again, is angry.

A✗✗✗   Alle

The day is rainy. Write to Shelley. In the evening the Opera. La Cenerentola. Many Masks.

Her hand's moving slowly—I'm not used to this slowness—as she jots down details of her days, an invisible stone strapped to her wrist. Does she daydream of Allegra?:

Drink tea in Casa Silva. Write to Mrs. Pollock. The weather becomes rainy.

But when she takes her reading notes the hand moves rapidly, scrawls rows of slanting words across the page:

From Locke's ESSAY CONCERNING HUMAN UNDERSTANDING:

*"Extreme disturbance possesses our whole mind . . . allows us not the liberty of thought"

(but all that matters is liberty of thought)

*"Not content to live on scraps of begged opinions"

*"If thou judgest for thyself I know thou wilt judge candidly, and then I shall not be harmed"

(but the world is largely made of harm)

*"Whatever it be that keeps us so much in the dark to ourselves"

(as I'm in the dark to myselfxxx I haven't even seen where she lives, and why didn't I . . . and how could I let her . . . so much dark in myself so muchxxxand what does that say of me?xxxand Mary grows restless)

*"Because man is not permitted without censure to follow his own thoughts when they lead him ever so little out of the common road"

(I didn't want to be married . . . Didn't want to give her up, yet I told myself "it's for the best," so where was my liberty of thought? I'm complicit, custom's slave, a shackled and defeated thing. Fanny thought I was brave but I'm not.)

*"To be in the mind and never to be perceived"

*"So wholly strangers"

Fanny,

When I read Locke I feel almost comforted. As if he were looking into my mind, loosening the chains in my mind. "Extreme disturbance possesses our whole mind . . . allows us not the liberty of thought"—I read that and feel seen. *And then I think, if I can let myself think about that, then maybe I can find some liberty of thought after all. Maybe disturbance, if recognized and not flinched from, can lead somehow toward liberty, not away . . . the way Arctic ice is said to heave and break before it loosens and moves free. But then I close the book and remember how Thomas Paine was put on trial for his thoughts: "Certain False, Wicked, Scandalous and Seditious Libels Inserted in the Second Part of the Rights of Man." And I think of Allegra far away.*

~~and the instability of~~ ~~and a mind ashamed of its own being~~ (though Paine wasn't ashamed) (and yet they shunned him for this thoughts, wouldn't allow him proper Burial)

How does Understanding turn inward, make thought truly its own?

(You lay down on that strange bed and gave your mind away to the laudanum. You wrote again and again the word "affraid." And Allegra can't possibly understand why I'm not with her.)

Why do the workings of a human mind have to frighten and threaten other minds? Why must I keep my thoughts about my child silent?

This is the last day of Carnival. We drive on the Lung Arno with the children. Masked.

Fanny, I'm reading Locke again. I wish you could have read him. Instead we kept ourselves awake so many nights—remember?—frightening each other with stories like those of Virgilius who was condemned to be burnt for asserting the Antipodes or in other words the Earth was a globe habitable in every part where there was land. He was killed for that thought only. As if we had to prove to ourselves that thoughts are dangerous, our minds—moving—dangerous, even, maybe, murderous (would we have been Virgilius or would we have been the ones who murdered him, or both?).

But Locke says: "a supposition of the mind of something otherwise." (He doesn't flinch from that "otherwise")

And Fanny, he says: "How the very nature of words makes it unavoidable for many of them to be doubtful and uncertain in their significations." (but you were afraid of your doubt, and it made you feel ashamed)

He says: "So many parts of ideas which are not visible in action." And: "is not settled or certain."

"The great disorder that happens in our inability to penetrate the real."

"We have our understandings no less different from our palates." (I think this might have comforted you)

And: "Lost and unknown when clothed in words."

Soon we'll move from these rooms to other rooms at the Piano of Casa Frassi, closer to the Arno, where Shelley can have a study of his own. It's been a cold winter. But what are these words as I write to you?—"Lost and unknown when clothed in words," Locke wrote. Shelley fills notebook after notebook, as if coming to a truer life on each page, as if finding—what?—on each page?—he writes upside down, sideways, every which way. But when I write there's always something lost and unknown that I can't find. Sometimes I look at my journal and it's a cliff broken off and whatever I might have meant, or tried to mean, is in the air past where it stops. All the instability, all the movement of mind, the waves and currents of my mind, fluctuations, uncertainties—I don't know how to say them I don't know how to, not in words but all I have are words, what kind of clothes are they what kind of covering and of what? xxx And Locke said, "is not settled or certain" and wrote of our "inability to penetrate the real." I feel this all the time, Fanny, like the snow blindness we read of as children. The snow blindness we feared.

Must sleep now. Will read more tomorrow. Light rain.

When Sherard Osborn's expedition went in search of Franklin's ships, they carried ice saws ten feet long. They thought they could protect themselves by cutting huge holes in high glacial ice, then inserting their ships for shelter. All around them floes and massive icebergs collided. But even vigilance has limits. In those narrow passages the ships were thrown over on their sides.

Nothing's still or safe, Claire wrote to Fanny. In my thoughts I move among walls of shifting ice, massive barriers of breaking ice, carry in my hands the weight of ice. I don't walk along a riverbed like Claire, or dream I'm in Damascus.

This ice I carry in my mind, does it harm or protect me, or both? "Lost and unknown when clothed in words," Claire quoted Locke. This question's a cloth thrown over a wonderment I have no other way of saying.

How else can I know Claire but through her words? That hand filling pages in air, pages she sometimes even burns. But if words keep her "lost and unknown," if, in the end, they're a covering and little more, then does my vigilant watching mean almost nothing? There's no way to draw close to her and know her.

Locke wrote of "our inability to penetrate the real." But I want to know who she is, it matters to me who she is. What if words *are* the real, not just a covering, or clothing?

Still, Locke wrote, "to be in the mind and never to be perceived." So is each mind a shut, secret place? Is this, in the end, what it means to be alive: to be in the mind but never truly perceiving or being perceived? Do words cover over that one fact—its icelike core—or try to? Still, if words are only cloth, that cloth is intricate, intriguing.

If words are as much concealment as anything, and myself far from her or anyone, how could I have thought you might know me?

Each time I read the words she leaves, even if I distrust (and I do) my own mind (Locke said we "are in the dark to ourselves") something in me wonders, waits, listens.

Fanny,

There's this <u>place of fade</u> in me, I don't know how else to put it. Where I go away from myself, from everything, or it's as if there's an <u>away</u> in me, vast lake or shadowland where I'm drowned for a while, thin cut of light among a larger, grayish dark.

I do my chores, I sweep. Sweep this, sweep that. I concentrate on the swish of the broom. The back and forth of the stiff bristles, a metronome or clock, but with more swerve, more yielding. As if to bring me back, that steady motion. Ash, dust, paper, insects, hair.

I put things in my mouth. Chew bread, chew olives, cheeses, lemons, bits of cake. Thinking all the while: salty, bitter, sour, sweet. Thinking, <u>this is</u>, this thing in the mouth and down the throat. The press of it, the texture. That it's real and I'm in the world where a tongue tastes what it's given and a footstep makes a sound. Where there's a floor, a table, metal, wood-grain, dirt. But I can't feel it, not really. Each word grows strange, as if shedding itself inside my mouth. As if, were I to speak (but I don't speak) my voice would be a strangled, mutant thing. As when a word's said over and over until it makes no sense, or makes an other, farther sense that travels toward a denser, farther air part breathable, part not—stare stare stare stare stare stare stare. Like that. The stars in it and stairs and are's and air and the emptiness it climbs and how it can't wholly climb it after all and so falls back into itself hammering and hammering, but at what?

Salt. Sweet. Bitter. Sour. Salt.

I didn't know how the mind travels so far from itself. And the hands— ignorant creatures that need so much to <u>mean</u>; to have a purpose, a task; that need to <u>act</u>.

In such a <u>fade</u> the words go out of my mind, and I'm webbed in a gray light where once I was Claire and once again I will be Claire but not now, not quite, so what am I, and you, what were you when you also felt this as I think you did, a grain of salt placed on your tongue, sharp, edged, and then (stare, star, staircase, stanchion, stain) it dissolves and you're nothing, but not bodiless either, not quite that.

Who would choose to come here? Wind blows at the speed of sixteen feet per second. Huge ice-fields lock and batter. (Lock. John Locke. Unlock.) Still so many came, they chose this.

Nansen had this dream: "I've finally reached home but feel ashamed because I can't give any account of what I've seen. I've forgotten everything."

As if ice could lock the mind, lock language, make of the tongue a frozen, helpless thing. (Some days I feel the ice inside me harden even farther, the white of erased pages. When I sleep I have no dreams, no hands across a page or bright domes on the horizon.)

Nansen recorded another dream: "People ask me what it was like among the drift ice but I forgot to take accurate observations. I just look at them in silence."

"So wholly strangers," Locke wrote. "So many parts of ideas which are not visible in action."

Yet sometimes I feel almost happy, locked in, locked apart, where no human mind can find me. As if it weren't odd to be solitary after all, though each day I still wait for her hand.

When Nansen reached home, did he enter a loneliness deeper, more intricate than any he'd known or could explain? He who in his dreams couldn't speak of anything he'd seen—

———————

"Lost and unknown when clothed in words"

Fanny,

I keep thinking of Locke's "to be in the mind and never to be perceived" and "our inability to penetrate the real." Keep thinking if I could have facts, plain facts. And live safely in those facts. But do facts ever seem plain, or even safe at all? (My child away from me is fact, your death in Swansea, fact.) Salt is composed of the metal sodium & of a green air called chlorine. Soda is composed of the metal sodium and oxygen gas. Those are facts, I suppose, plain facts. But so, too, is the way straw's put before the door of a dying man so he won't hear the rolling of carriages going past. And the water in Lake Asphaltites contains bitumen which will take the bloodstains out of cloth. And Caligula adored his horses but hid his men in the woods where he fell on them and butchered them as enemies so in Rome and the Provinces word could spread of his great victory.

Even so I try to think of facts but then I think, "It was fear first in the world made gods." I think of the power of what we feel.

The other planets no doubt have other elements than ours—if a sufficient degree of cold could penetrate the air above our Earth it would freeze to a white mist, but on Saturn where the cold is more intense this doesn't happen so its air must be made of other elements than ours. And might iron, which is here the hardest metal, there be the softest, and would it serve in a thermometer as quicksilver does here? I go to my books, I try to think about what is, but even the nature of what is seems very strange and changing.

and I fail in the very tenderest

Mary asked Henry Reveley if we could borrow his Encyclopedia while he's away in England. Now Shelley walks around reading a great quarto Encyclopedia with another volume under his arm.

I read Rights of Woman and Letters from Norway. Read: "He who keeps his grief within his own breast is a cannibal of his heart."

Read: "O Monster! Mixed of insolence & fear/ Thou dog in forehead, but in heart, a deer!"

Is that what I am, Fanny? Is that what anyone is?—xxx

Her hand's working very hard to obliterate the words:

I find it strange

First she covers them with x's, then dark lines:

I find it strange that such a hatred should.

She stops. I don't know what she's not wanting to say.

Then:

Clara died in Mary's arms~~. . . . and if Mary hadn't been traveling to where I. . . .~~

~~Died in the hall of an Inn where they were waiting for a doctor~~

~~But I can't Fanny, write itxxx~~

Her hand crumples the paper.

I wait for what seems several hours, then:

Discord! ~~dire sisterxx of the slaughtering power,~~

M   ~~Book IV, Iliad~~

F—

xxxxx——

The date doesn't matter. Time is an odd otherness. (So long since I've written.)

This is what I want to say: I didn't know when I was sitting for that stupid portrait, or visiting the Colosseum, its arches and recesses like so many caves, its thorn trees in blossom, that all the while the Tiber marshes were growing stagnant in the heat, the malarial mosquitoes breeding.

William fell ill with a high fever. Convulsions for days and then an exhausted silence like a lidless eye. He died on June 7th.

Mary's face now Arctic and extreme. Planes of injured, shifting ice.

There's an Arctic in me too. I step outside into the heat, the grassy walks, wildflowers growing from the ruins, but vast ice fields build in me (they've been building for some time) and they feel neither hostile nor astonished nor kind. I cross thin sea ice, wind scraping my face. Ice so fresh it's not even dusted with snow.

She writes:

Augu

then stops. Leaves two blank pages. (She's come almost to the end of her notebook. Will she come back to me after this? I get afraid she won't come back.) (What is it she doesn't want to say?) Then:

Received		Paid—		
August 1		S—	P—	C—
43⁻4·4	Clasp	0	5	0
	Shoes	1	4	0
	Ties	0	1	4
	Muslin	0	4	0

The next two pages are missing. Did she write on them then tear them out?

Then:

Fons tua quo fugiens delapsa est
    Lympha? Quid undis
Tot factum? Quonam est ustus abe ?
    igne liquor?
In lacrimas abii totus: quodcumque
    liquoris
Mi fuit, omne hausit jam cinis
    Agricola.

(Ye streams of the fountain,
    why have ye fled?
Where is all the water gone?

What fiery sun has exhausted
    the ever-running spring?
We are exhausted byxxxxx

"Slaves be by their own [compulsion?] in mad game
break their manacles & wear the name of
Of Freedom graven on a heavier chain"

≈ ♏ (she scribbles this quickly)

And:

Comedy: a picture of Human Nature worse & more deformed than the original (Aristotle)

~~Aeschylus, Prometheus Bound~~   ~~thou all producing Earth, and thee,~~
~~Bright Sun~~

That's all. Her hand lingers for a minute. She closes the notebook and is gone.

Who would choose to come here? These were their ships:

the *Terror*
the *Erebus*
the *Half-Moon*
the *Ayde*
the *Gabriel*
the *Michael*
the *Mermaid*
the *Moonlight*
the *Saint Anna*
the *Sunshine*
the *North Star*
the *Fox*
the *Hecla*
the *Griper*
the *Fury*
the *Advance*
the *Jeannette*
the *Polaris*
the *Fram*
the *Neptune*
the *Alert*

What would I name mine? The *Mary Harmsworth*? The *Clariae*? The *Absencia*? The *Locke*? The *Shen Kuo*? The *Clairville*? The *Unsigned*?

Fanny,
Mary shivers all the time now. I think of places in the Arctic: Great Slave Lake, Repulse Bay, Icy Cape, Obstruction Rapid. Then of all the vast stretches that have no names—those most of all.

So many hands moving across their secret pages:

"... a weariness of heart, a blank feeling. Always it is night now," wrote one whose ship was stranded in the ice.

And another:

"October 12th Wednesday. One hundred and twenty-second day. Breakfast, last spoonful of glycerin and hot water. Dinner, willow tea. We can't move against this living gale of wind. Last night I dreamed I was wearing a breastplate of ice."

"October 15th Saturday. One hundred and twenty-fifth day. Breakfast, willow tea and two old boots. Buried Alexy in the afternoon. Laid him on the ice of the river, then covered him over with slabs of ice."

And:

"Everything is blurred, sometimes doubled. I dreamed I looked everywhere for my dog. He'd slipped away before I could harness him. I called and went peering around the hummocks. Finally I left camp without him, certain I'd seen his good face for the last time. Empty ridge upon ridge of ice-pack before me. Then he reappeared and looked at me with consoling eyes. I meant to whip him but his eyes disarmed me."

And:

"I'll probably never see you again. You should know I saw a red poppy breaking through the snow. How is this possible? Also white shifting shapes, like arches. Whether land or light I couldn't tell. Mostly there are no forms anymore, no cumbrous reality–only this odd glow I've gotten used to and which nonetheless irritates my eyes so that now I'll stop writing."

Fanny,

I'm staying up late, writing down these lines from Heraclitus—

"Everything gives way, nothing stays fixed" and "Homer was wrong in saying, 'Would that strife might perish from amongst gods and men.' For if that were to occur, then all things would cease to exist."

Do you believe him, Fanny? Do I?

Such cold air tonight, even here. There are reports that Parry's ships have found the Northwest Passage—

Casa Baldini

    Via del Giglio
       Passato Santa Maria Maggiore
Inghilterra   Via Valfonda
Casa Frassi   Casa Bojti, Firenze
Pisa (Shelley & Mary)   Casa Galetti   Casa Silva

Her hand comes and goes, writing addresses on the inside front cover of a newly bought notebook.

Then:

rich in nothing but deformities

(but why would she write this?)

And:

ashamed of

(I remember how Montaigne wrote of wanting to shame his own mind. As mine often feels ashamed, though it's not clear to me why). Again, she breaks off.

Then:

Dream of Allegra. She was on the road from Ravenna to visit me.

    Animation which is the Child of Liberty   In the fifth mystery we see
      and then we don't see

        Io non piangeva si dentro [m] impietrai (I did not weep, so stony I
        grew within)

the ~~wild~~ world abounds in uncertainty and dispute

I try to know where she is, wonder if I'll ever see her face, try to scrutinize her fragments of thought. Why do I say "fragments of thought"
instead of thought itself? Why look for completion, steadiness, uniformity? How much has that to do with the true workings of the mind? Why
shouldn't her thoughts break, swerve, mix in with silence? Just as I see her
hand, never her whole body, yet that hand's an entire being in itself,
clothed in words, but only partly.

Fanny,

I don't know how to think of time anymore, what it is, what it isn't. I used to picture it always moving forward, unified, strong, a relentless progression. But it feels fractured to me now, sharp with broken bits and edges that clash and intersect, refusing pattern. Or not <u>refusing</u>, exactly—maybe that's too willful a word—it's more that pattern is irrelevant to what it is. As if there's no clear past, present or future, but something constantly disintegrating and re-forming itself, a place not quite a place where objects and faces live and flourish and don't live and don't flourish and miss each other, meet, and miss again, intersect and part, stay and disappear, reappear. Always this crumbling and reassembling, my brain raw where it touches.

All these things, then, together, Fanny: Mary has another baby boy named Percy Florence. Virgilius is condemned to be burnt for insisting the earth's a globe, habitable in distant parts. Lead mysteriously floats on Lake Asphaltites which smells acrid and is the color of the sea. I move to Florence, Shelley pays a family to board me. Berkeley denies the existence of matter. I have nightmares about Allegra. In one we walk in the Boboli gardens among terraces, small evergreens, statues, fountains. She's crying because she has a deformity. She won't tell me what it is. Augustine writes, "The world was made not in time." In the square a beggar crawls on all fours and politely salutes a barefooted washerwoman carrying a bundle on her head. Keats dies. Parry hears the ice floes groaning.

And still I use the word "now" as if it's somehow sewn into my skin—or is it a fire on my spine?

Rain. The pocked surface of the Arno shining—

Fanny, ever since I wrote to you last night I've been thinking about the word "or"—

I think of the "or" in order, terror, fortress. It seems there are so many alternatives inside each single word and feeling, each idea (so are we wrong, then, to think of them as single?), that there exists no singular direction in the brain, not really, but many directions conversing with each other, wondering against and in and through each other. Or and or and or. "As if she were still here, or," "or if I hadn't agreed to," "or had she known beforehand that," "or if I hadn't told him," "or if safety existed," "or hot as I am there's this chill in me also."

Or if I didn't look like this. Or if my voice hadn't vanished. Or if you hadn't made me. Or if Claire could see how I watch her. Or if sledges didn't break and dogs go blind. Or if they had a better map. Or had they not gone there. Or if ice didn't kill. Or if there were no such thing as distance.

I wake from a dream of Claire's hand turned to ice.

She writes in her journal:

> myself a stranger on the earth to whom nothing belongs—and having no permanent township on this globe.

Writes:

> language tied by laws.

And:

> Shelley writes to me, "Poor M begins (for the first time) to look a little consoled." Then writes that he misses me—misses "your sweet consolation, my own Claire." (yet he sent me away, they both did)
>
> That word "console"—it's meant to be calming but why do I feel something isolate inside it?—a place where I, where anyone's, alone. "This greef is crown'd with Consolation," Shakespeare wrote, but I wonder. I remember a tale in which pilgrims were consoled by a star created to guide them on their journey—but that seemed sentimental. Nothing guides anyone. What does Smeaton mean when he says that one misfortune becomes a consolation for another?~~And Allegraxxxand I can't~~ I don't understand how that's so. And in Shelley's notebook: "Earth can console." He likes to use that word

Her hand stops, closes the notebook, disappears.

Parry's ships wintered over for three months in Winter Harbour but couldn't get past the ice to the west. For three months they barely saw sun: "From half past nine till half past two, the sun afforded us sufficient light for writing but for the rest of the twenty-four hours we lived, of course, by candlelight." Even the men's breath was dangerous. It froze on beams as they slept, then melted in the coal-fired heat of day, mildewing the sheets. Eyelids stuck to the telescopes' eye-pieces. Fingers froze onto sextants. By mid-October deer and ptarmigan disappeared. They saw wolves, clearly starving, and a single white fox. "The sea is now entirely covered with one surface of solid, motionless ice . . . the rapidity with which it builds has become so great as to cause us to spend several hours each day cutting it. Three to five new inches of ice in twenty-four hours . . ."

Claire turns in her sleep. She's dragging an anchor over the ice to the beach, thinking this will secure the ship when the ice breaks up in spring. Then she thinks: this won't work, I have to think of something better, but keeps dragging it anyway.

Fanny,

I've read that were one magically able to move at unheard-of speed, it would be possible to travel to someone else's future but not your own. You're always in your own present. Even so, there's something subtle and supple that moves through the nerves and makes them wonder. The mind's a finer body. I want to believe this, though we live in perplexity ever. I feel so cold tonight, and Mary's far away—so many planes of broken ice inside her. Shelley says she feels consoled but I don't know. It's late so I'll stop, will write more later—

How easy to lose track of this North when I picture her in her room somewhere in Italy, though I've never seen her face, don't even know what part of Italy she's in. Where is she? Florence? Pisa?

———•———

{Allegra}

but it is lost to me now
that animation which is the child of Liberty

~~the this makes deformity~~   a monstrous deformity in me

                                            and am ashamed of the

~~{monstrous} monstrous but {already}~~

                    by my own blindness I have fallen

drowning with the waves closing above our heads we are lost in the ✗

♒♏

                                  ✗

Mary,

I'm not used to being apart from you. Weeks now, and I still unpack my boxes slowly. There's been much rain. The banks of the Arno are like those of the Rhine, but of a much softer character. I'm learning German. I translate from Phaedrus, walk in the Boboli gardens with Louisa and Annina. Every now and then I don't think of Allegra, so what does that make me? Then I remember the Hoppners complaining of her "perpetual coldness." How she has grown so quiet. I dream of it often now: your face crusted with ice, my own also. Shelley walks with a warming fire in his hand. I hope the baby's well. Someone said today the French are so polite they call a robber "an enthusiast of what does not belong to him." So, we are all robbers—

(Your) ✗
Claire

Her hand's so often fevered now, or so it seems. (There's almost nothing I can know for certain.) She's in her room, but how can I know what to picture? Is there a window? A desk by the bed? What books is she reading? Once she wrote *Calderon* then crossed it out. Wrote *Rousseau*, crossed it out (I remember your room, though I want never to think of it). Her hand as if seared by a warning mark, and burning:

I yearn to be made beautiful with one kind action
~~but I gave her away I~~
    This deformity of mind   this   as if nature had set a warning mark
        upon me
~~beware of still water~~   ~~the tranquil surface tempts~~xxx
                   or is it that we are atoms   ~~xxxx~~   reeling
we are atoms in a dream   and are made into voices
                creating and destroying, undisclosed

Recipe for an Ague . . . from Dr. Warren

1 Oz. of the best red Bark.
1 Nutmeg grated.
1 Table spoonful of beaten blk. Pepper.
1 ____ ____ of coarse sugar.
To be mixed with Syrup of Poppies into an Electuary.

A large Tea Spoonful to be taken immediately and then repeated every half
    hour

That the whole quantity may be taken in 24 Hours—

Half the quantity for a Child—

Who would choose to come here?:

"I brought with me Spurr's *Geology*, also *Anna Karenina*. Unless a man has lived apart for a long time he doesn't know what he's talking about when he claims he wants to live solely with his own thoughts. I was grateful for any sound, even, for a while, the howling of wolves."

~ ~ ~

"Maybe our worst piece of luck was the loss of our sewing kit. We couldn't repair our clothing, though Broenlund fixed his boots with a nail. The rest of us descended the glacier in our stocking feet. Hagen died on November 15th."

~ ~ ~

"In my little hut I gave names to the different utensils, and often found myself babbling to my teakettle and the pots and pans."

~ ~ ~

"I'll never forget my joy at the return of color."

Sometimes Claire's hand disintegrates with an almost-gentle abandon before me. As if just to stay in one place is too much of a weight and she's found a way to drift from her fever, break free. But mostly her hand stays trapped in solidity, leaving words like heavy weights on the page. She writes *deformity* four times in one day, writes *monstrous* four times the same day. (What would she think of me? I who am "monstrous," "deformed," though you meant to make me beautiful.) If I could read to her, soothe her with books, though how would I reach her, with what voice?:

> "Loveliest of what I leave behind is the sunlight,
>   and loveliest after that the shining stars, and the moon's face,
>   but also cucumbers that are ripe, and pears, and apples."

Or:

> "I am a flood: *across a plain,*
> I am a wind: *on a deep lake,*
> I am a tear: *the Sun lets fall,*
> I am a hawk: *above the cliff,*"

How much of what I'd read could truly comfort? "To speak is pain but silence too is pain." How could she find comfort in that, unless there's comfort in what's true?

I close my eyes, remember the northern explorers who gave names to their utensils, felt joy at the return of color. I wait for her to return.

Fanny,

Whose laws am I obeying, whose habits of syntax, custom, thought, even as I write to you here, now, alone in this room in what I would like to think of as the privacy of my mind—What swervings and interruptions go uncaptured, what breakings, stutterings of thought? What does syntax cover over? This grammar I've drilled and drilled into myself, isn't it also a stifling, a blindfold, an Emperor, a platoon? Doesn't it partly build a closed world? How much do I keep even from myself within this orderly progression we've been taught to think of as thought? But thought's an odder creature, Fanny—wounded, struggling, raw

blooms of the Boboli gardens   Allegra's hair
*   no & no & no*
*   the small gold watch on your wrist when they found you*
your silk handkerchief   clasped leather purse   those narrow paths
~~and affect nothing being bound~~

So what is Liberty? My hands so often as if bound. These hands that have minds of their own, thinking that they touch Allegra's hair then startle back to this wooden desk, this pen. There's liberty and the appearance of liberty, so Locke said.

Civilization gradually increases and we call this liberty. But it's not. We're given license but it can never be a substitute for liberty.

I feel how language stiffens, tied by polite agreement, laws. So our words have all the gloss and finery which license can give, and are as far from the free, natural movements of liberty as East is removed from West, though both are visited by the Sun—

. . . real liberty never (will) can exist but with simplicity . . .

If I could touch its frightful preciseness—   If I could come near—

~~that rough and generous discordance~~   I think of the softness of your
dress even as your body stiffened   your smooth most secret hands

Today I see her hand as usual, then her whole arm, her shoulder white in her white nightdress, a glimpse of her neck, the dark back of her head. I never thought I'd see this much of her. It's as if as she grows more alone something in her becomes more visible, though I'd have thought the opposite would happen.

Mary I'm still not used to being apart from you. I don't know how
I'll . . . and Dr. Bojti and his family are perfectly nice, I walk with them and
read and continue learning my German but something in me isn't well and I
think I can be a governess someday go far away but everything's far away
since Allegra, I'm a coward and worse. Misgivings aren't reason. I don't know
what's "reasonable." I feel my actions as monsters. Myself a fiend inseparable
from myself. My mind dark—as when black vapors hover over the parent
marsh. In his first Canto Tasso wrote, "My heart has been made wise through
love, and ~~sadness~~ suffering has made a path to Wisdom." But I don't think
this is so. If Allegra suffers what will it give her? Doesn't suffering take away,
deform? It's not so bad for us, we're older. Sometimes it seems all the world
rises up against the world—

𝑥

~~a ruined temple with one remaining pillar~~

and (natural because)~~and Nature without restraint~~

~~because real Liberty will never exist without simplicity~~

𝑥𝑥

~~Disturbers of the State and of the established order~~

Still unused to seeing this much of her, I watch her shoulder, the back of her head. She's a volcano wrapped in a cloud, a hand of flame struggling in white ice—

If Parry comes back from the Northwest Passage I wonder what words will mean to him, if speaking will even make sense anymore, or will he carry a silence like drift-ice, or a silence, even, like Fanny's

Then she's writing backward. I wonder why she does this, and why now:

Thursday Nov. 16th. A Rettel morf (A) Yellehs—Od emos Namreg Sesicrexe. Osla (a Elbaf) Selbaf morf Surdeahp.

Friday Nov 17th. Od emos Namreg Sesicrexe. Osla Selbaf morf Surdeahp. Ni eth (gnineve) Gnineve Li Rongis Inailiug semoc.

Saturday Nov 18th. A Rettel morf Yellehs—Klaw tuo htiw Aniloap. Krow lla yad.

It's such a strange language, suddenly, when backwards. Each letter wrenched from its quiet hour. As if she's reached another shore, something rising nameless and unclothed inside her. Then she raises her hand, closes her journal, thinks (I imagine this, but what right do I have to imagine what she thinks?):

it's time to sleep. What would it mean to be free? I'm atoms in a dream yet I love as if shackled. I need to find some way to get her back. Captain Hely writes of being "monster-ized" but who isn't "monster-ized." Shame. Emahs. Am. There's no steadiness of mind. It's late, must try to sleep

When Albanov was rescued after months of struggling on the ice (a small ship, the *Saint Folka*, picked him up), did words still make sense to him, could they capture at all what he'd seen? He wrote an account of his journey, published three years later as an appendix to a small hydrographic journal.

He suffered from "a disorder of the nerves." Spent time in a military hospital in Petrograd. An acquaintance found him a job in a mapmaker's office. Years later his employer remembered, "He was clad in a shabby coat, his face thin and nervous. He was mostly good-natured and obliging, but had a strikingly unstable temper. A word or glance could throw him into sudden desperation."

Five and a half years after his return, Albanov was still trying to raise funds to go north in search of the *Saint Anna*.

"I dream the wind tears the ice I'm lying on from shore and carries me out to sea where no one can find me."

"I can feel no sorrow for Shpakovsky."

"Shpakovsky, Lunayev and Nilsen are ill. I put them in the sledge, but then I see their heads are horses' skulls, so why am I trying? When I wake I don't know where I am."

"I repeat the word *sledge* until it means nothing."

"I find the words *we, us, together, want,* painful and very confusing."

_____

Fanny,

Who would have thought there would be so many Russians in Florence? Often I spend my evenings at Casa Boutourlin, house of Dmitri Petrovich Boutourlin. He likes to speak to me of Moscow—of the Great Fire of 1812 in which his entire library was destroyed. That library had been among the most famous, the most vast, in Russia. Now all that's left of it is a catalogue with green marbled boards and a gilt spine, published in Paris in 1805.

His poor health has brought him here. Sometimes he walks me through his new library—shelves of thousands upon thousands of books he's collecting (there are now almost 7,000) but he says it's like walking through a blizzard—he can't see them, not because of his eyes, but because of what he lost in Moscow. He can't make his sight focus on the letters on the spines. Everything goes white, unfocused. As if he has a kind of snow blindness, a pain in the eyes that makes them sting in a whiteout of cold fire. When he walks into the parlor he can see again. He can see clearly in the gardens, the streets, the sitting rooms, the halls, anywhere but there.

I'm learning many things. The fire swept through the city leaving almost nothing.

As you left almost nothing. The cold white of you, the fire.

So, Fanny, today I visited him again, Count Boutourlin, and he talked more about the Moscow fire. As if he could see it right before his eyes as we sat and drank our tea. Or, no, not right before him, but as if it was locked partly away as in a vault (if fire could be locked away) and he could look at it without being burned (yet sometimes he seems to almost burn, and he has this problem with his eyes).

He told me that on the day Napoleon's army entered the city, most of the Muscovites had already fled. Most taking nothing. The sick and the ill left behind. One soldier said of that day, "We heard only our own footsteps. It was that quiet. The absolute stillness frightened me much more than gunfire. For a time we tried to reassure ourselves that the citizens were in their houses secretly watching."

Why is there comfort in being watched, Fanny, even if in secret? And there IS often comfort in it. As I imagine myself watching you, and imagine, too, that sometimes you watch me, even from your ever-absence. If I could watch Allegra . . . but sometimes my eyes are like Count Boutourlin's, I can't hold her face in my mind . . . can't watch over her even in my mind.

He went on to say the fires started on September 14th, but were small and scarce. Then on the 16th a hurricane blew in, spreading strong winds across the city. Soon the stores in Red Square were on fire. Imagine. The Kremlin was burning. Burning logs rolled through the streets, embers whirled, cascaded. Bell towers burned, their bells breaking loose and clanking through gutters. All the old beautiful buildings destroyed. Carved faces falling onto ruined columns. Dmitri's library gone. Paintings gone. Churches, diaries, domes, hospitals, gone. 25,000 wounded Russian soldiers in the hospitals died.

The Count read to me these words from Philippe-Paul de Segur, Napoleon's aide-de-camp: "Everyone was silent. We accused ourselves. We could not look at each other. We were an army of criminals who had destroyed a beautiful city. Then we learned it was the Russians themselves who had set the fires."

Napoleon said, "To annoy me they burn their own history, the works of centuries!"

Who burned the city, Fanny? Maybe it was both the Russians and the French . . . the hand of desperation, the echoes from all those vacant rooms.

Then Dmitri wanted to walk through his new library. I held his arm as his sight grew dim, as if he were walking through a fiery white wind that pressed against his cheek then spread to his whole face, pressing even harder on his eyes—until it made of his features a white cast to be left among his books and shelving, a hard white shadow of who he'd been—

I close my eyes and remember Claire's account of Dmitri Boutourlin's eyes, how they don't work right in his library, and it pains him to see. Everything gone white, occluded. How it's his mind that causes this, not his eyes. Then I imagine myself snow-blinded like Albanov. For three days and nights he stayed inside his tent, wore bandages over both eyes. Any light, even a sliver, was too much. His snow blindness stained the world red, not white as I'd have thought. As if snow and ice had caught fire and that fire lived inside his eyes. Now when I think of Claire I see her hands tinged red, her nightdress and writing desk, red.

I've read the cornea has no blood vessels of its own; nourishment and protection must come from tears and liquids in the chamber behind it. I wonder if you knew this when you made me—that two such vulnerable, transparent lenses have to carry us into all color and form, as if they weren't fragile . . . as if . . . The more I think of it the stranger it becomes, that such fragility secures us to the world.

So it's the fragile that enables. The fragile that makes possible what's seen.

If you could have seen even a small part of me as fragile, would you have acted as you did? If you, like Montaigne, had mistrusted the surmises of your mind . . . And what happened to your eyes when mine first opened? Did they become a site of harm, a longing for snow blindness, a wound? Or were they suddenly weaponlike, or . . .

I sense your breath, your hands moving over me again. I feel the soft bandages over my eyes. It's worse than loneliness. Your touch the red grit of snow blindness. My eyes trapped in an inwardness I don't want or understand.

Mary,

Why does fever bring such vivid dreams? I dreamt a child fell into a Well and that when I thought all hope was lost of getting him I turned around and you'd picked him out. Then Mrs. Williams, having said something imprudent against the Ministers, was tried for high treason, found guilty and beheaded. The little Boy Medwin died of a Worm Fever. Fanny stood a long time on a cliff, thinking. Clock bells kept tolling from a distant city.

As if something is always lost inside the mind and in fever burns forward and is felt—

I'm not used to being apart from you. I keep thinking of Allegra. That she's cold. What am I that I read the Voyages and Adventures of Fernand Mendez Pinto when she's cold?

Count Boutourlin tells me many stories of Russia. How the night before the Emperor Paul was killed he signed a letter exiling eleven hundred to Siberia. His killers took care to leave no visible marks on the body so it would appear he died a natural death. For years he'd sent exiles, chained to each other two by two, in carriages to the north. Often one died but was kept bound to the other for the duration of the weeks-long journey.

I think of the Emperor's body. How the wounds weren't visible. Sometimes I think of us like that, white and smooth as statues hiding a commotion of earth, tossed insides roughened, dark.

I've heard, as you must have, that Patras has fallen into the hands of the Greeks with the slaughter of 10,000 Turks.

And in Tripolizza they slaughtered 22,000.

Each night before sleep I see Allegra's face from the side. Then she turns to me and her eyes, though open, are blind—

Sometimes this ice is a vast rib lifted from a vanished body. Or it's the distance between one mind and another, one thought and another. The distance between memory and breath.

Shen Kuo spent his life charting the minutest changes in degrees of distance. But how does one measure distance in the mind? I was sealed from you from the start, the chambers of my brain as far from you as any star.

Today I found a canister with this list inside:

Herewith the daily allowance per man for seventy-one days:
10 ozs. biscuit
9 ozs. pemmican
1 oz. sweetened cocoa powder (being enough to make a pint)
one gill of rum
3 oz. of tobacco to be served out to each per week

That's all that's left of them. Who were they? Did they die on their journey or reach home?

Dear Fanny,

I dreamed last night Moscow was filling with snow, and as it snowed great fires were spreading. But instead of tamping the flames the snow only fed them. You were there, and Mary, and myself. We were hot and cold all at once and none of us could speak. Bells from fallen towers dotted the streets like burial mounds or grand Egyptian heads. Count Boutourlin's books were piled on a street-corner, the black print eaten by flames, crumbling back from sense and thought and law into some vast, unmeasurable whiteness. I wanted to say it was time to walk in the Boboli Gardens but my mouth was ice and anyhow I couldn't see you or Mary anymore. I remembered those special chocolate biscuits we ate as children and decided I must go look for them—I wanted to give one to Allegra—then I woke.

Now that I've seen more than her hand—the slope of her shoulder, her arm, the back of her head—it feels odder than ever when she doesn't come. As if she'd been slowly drawing close (though I know this wasn't so) only to pull suddenly away, vanished as the masked women in Florence at Carnival who wear black dominos and hoods. Or is she a dangerous secret I can't know fallen far from where my mind can find her? Then—

I am truly uneasy for it seems to me some time since I have heard any news of Allegra. I fear she is sick

Her hand moves fast, then slows, more deliberate:

I studied my German again today. Nothing can be stronger proof of the force of a language than when the same word can evoke so many linked yet varied meanings, as in Geist, pronounced Guyst. From this comes our Ghost. In German it means Soul, spirit, Essence, force, mind, intellect, divinity—

The Germans say, "That man has no ghost in him." They say of a poor wine, "This is an unghostly wine." They say a person can be Rich in Ghostliness. That a person of wit possesses Ghost.

(Each day I wait for her to come to me, to ghost me.)

One often hears in speaking of a man, "Ach! Er ist ein geist!"—Oh, he's a very Ghost!

And there are other words:

Zwei is two, & ein is one; therefore sich ensweien or sich uneinswerden have the same meaning; that is to "two oneself," or to make oneself two; or to "un-one" oneself; that is, to be no longer of one and the same opinion as another; to quarrel.

To "un-one" oneself . . . strange word. Though Claire says it means "to disagree, to quarrel," in my mind I assign a different meaning—what I've wanted to say for so long though I've had no word to say it: if I could have "un-oned" myself, become no longer solitary, apart; if you hadn't fled from me, or even if you had, if I could have spoken to another, learned to live beside another . . .

She folds the paper, returns it to the drawer. Her hand closes the window, pulls shut the white curtain, is gone.

Often as I walk over the ice, watch Claire, or read, or eat my supper, wash my face, I can't imagine who I'd be without this loneliness. If I could "un-one" myself, and yet.

When John Ross was rescued after two years alone on the ice, the kindness burned him. He'd become used to being given up for dead, putting on his hard wet socks, being hungry, talking only to himself. Does the familiar become a kind of comfort, and what once was comfort almost seem a form of violence?

Afterwards he wrote: "I'd been brought back to life and civilization from the borders of a distant grave. Long accustomed to a cold bed on hard snow or a bare rock, I could no longer sleep amid such comfort. Each night I'd leave the bed that was so kindly assigned to me and seek out the hardest chair I could find. I don't yet know if time can reconcile me to this sudden and violent change . . ."

Fanny,

I'm so used to you not speaking. As if in silence you can stay near me without being hurt by whatever it is the world wounds with—misunderstandings, calamities, language's prolific and intricate betrayals. Your mouth a firm shutness. Your hands folded, still.

and I am truly uneasy   I have not seen her for over two years and
    fear she is sick

She's opened her journal—scrawls swift cross-outs, ink blots, x's, the word
destroy, like so many storm-tossed ships:

~~I have not~~ xxxxx   xxxxxx

~~Dear Mary~~   ~~Dear~~   ~~Dear F~~

~~Fanny~~ *I*   *I fear she is*   *painful and unprotected*
that he threatens to put her in a convent   *that you threaten to put her in*
   a convent   ~~*that you*~~ xxx

I beg you do not   *and I could never see her*   ~~*would destroy forever*~~

would destroy   *& to banish her forever from her native (land by making*
   her unworthy)

you (have it in your power to) may destroy me   *have destroyed (my*
   own feelings)
but (you cannot) your power cannot   ~~*destroy*~~
               the feelings of nature

      resolve to be   *destroyed in*

But (I) as I will   *will not be destroyed*   *Allegra whom I nursed day*
   and night that first year

There is no person on earth who will give me notice of her well-being
   she is delicate and can't tolerate
the cold   ~~*can't tolerate*~~ xxxx

~~*Such beautiful creatures almost never*~~   *and has grown quiet and serious*
   as if old

~~*I can't*~~   *but were I to stay silent*   *the promise violated*
I don't know how to address you in terms fit to awaken
        cannot now think what to sign myself   *cannot sign*

In eighteenth-century China, Yuan Mei wrote of the "impenetrable north" as a bastion of ice between the known world and another. If you go far enough, the sky's "the color of tortoiseshell," clouds spew black hail. "Nowhere in that region are there any bushes or trees, nor is there any coal or charcoal." Nameless monsters rise from black ice. If you hold a torch to your clothes "the most delicate fur of your sleeves won't get singed."

Is this how the sky seems to her now, brown and shut as tortoiseshell, all Earth a frozen place where she no longer can even sign her name?

After the ship *Advance* had been ice-bound for three years, the captain and a few remaining men set out on two small boats and sledges to find land. Traveling for months they saw no one. Then one day they came upon a man seeking eider. One of the men called out to him, "Don't you know me? I'm Carl Petersen." But the man seeking eider called back, "No. You can't be. His wife says he's dead."

Claire doesn't sign her name, and Carl Petersen, who spoke his name into the air after so many years locked in ice, didn't hear it back. The man wouldn't say it. Just "he" and "his." "His wife says he's dead."

(And I who have no name. And you who didn't name me.)

Yuan Mei saw the ice as a place of annihilation and namelessness, a way "too terrible to traverse." Though he said there was a cave if only you could find it, and on the other side two statues thirty feet high—one a man riding a great tortoise, the other taming a serpent with his hand.

Fanny,

While walking with Count Boutourlin in his library earlier today, I began to fear his blindness is contagious, that over time it will afflict me too. I know this is ridiculous, but as we walked and I read the spines of his books out loud as he increasingly likes me to do, my eyes began to blur, a white film spreading over them soft as the "a" in your name. If I told Mary she would say this is just another "wild project in the Clairmont style"—that I'm running away with things, making trouble. And yet, I could feel a coldness coming into me, its white namelessness spreading. Or I was a mountain of ice—or was it salt?—but a mountain that could see, and a chisel was chipping away at me until the air whitened and thickened with all those particles set loose from what I was. I had no choice but to look through them—everything filmy, unclear. If Allegra's put in a convent it will be almost impossible to get her out. My claim is bare and obvious, yet amounts to almost nothing. There's a woman I met here who's six feet tall and is reputed to have disguised herself as a man so she could study medicine at Jena. But we're not like her, Fanny. Or—am I?—or could I be? Sometimes I wake with your name on my lips and I want to say, Fanny, no, you need a stronger name, not those soft sounds that you have now—that fragile "f" like a feather, that gentle "a"—but something more fortress-like, more hard. Allegra's delicate; I would take her to the Baths of Lucca. That day when she was christened Clara Allegra at St.-Giles-in-the-Fields, I heard my name go into her, mysterious and sharp. Mary's Clara was christened that day also. The knife of my name going into them. The air cut by that sound. Yet that "C" in Clara, when recited as part of the alphabet, sounds not like a cut at all, but indistinguishable from "see." As I see her now before me though I haven't set eyes on her in years. As I see you. Still, so much ice and salt fills the air, its whiteness spreading—The loss of you. The cold fact of where she is.

Blake saw the North as "Obscure, shadowy, void, solitary."

To Olaus Magnus it was a region of "demons, unspeakable derision, diverse shapes under the Seven Stars."

In the Chinese *Mountain-Sea Classic* it is a land of "deformed ghosts . . . over sixty days' travel from the kingdom of Kiao-ma." The few people who live there dress in dirty deerskin, eat from earthenware dishes, have mouths on the tops of their heads.

To the Anglo-Saxons it was a place of "souls with bound hands."

Fanny,

The town's called Bagnacavallo. That's where the Convent is. Just north of Ravenna. A small place of towers and old walls surrounded by fields of tangled vines. But what does it matter if I picture it or not? The winters there are bitterly cold. My mind's wonderings mean nothing, my picturing changes nothing. In the now-irrelevant and alien territory of my mind I see walls she looks out on each day. The wall surrounding the courtyard is 30 feet high.

Locke again   *and Locke*

allows not the

and keeps us so much in the dark

(she's only just turned 4, the convent demands double fees as she's several years younger than the youngest others)

and allows not   *allows not*

and

lost and unknown   *when clothed*
in words—

For the first time I see her sleeping, her arms wrapped around her head, the long sleeves of her nightdress white against white sheets. Are the convent walls building behind her closed eyes, and Allegra behind them? Walls thirty feet high, then higher, walls of white stone. Wherever she looks there's a labyrinth of walls, their quiet like this ice.

Fanny, I can't see her face anymore. As if this earth and its human processes have fallen from me, or rather I from them. Or I'm a stone disintegrating on the ground while the wall I wasn't needed for grows stronger, more imposing—

When the ships *Erebus* and *Terror* failed to return after six years away, a newspaper noted the "strange and unspeakable solitudes of the lost . . ." "We are bound to warn our readers that it is scarcely possible that provisions sufficient for three years can by any economy have been spread over five." Yet it was awful to think of crewmen and ships "so utterly annihilated that no trace can be discovered at all." Rescue teams searching for years found nothing–no glove, no log, no piece of hull, no tin of food, no bedding.

(I can't see her anymore, can't . . .)

Only once, a small copper cylinder which might have been used as a marker was sighted on some waves.

Fanny,

It's spring in Bagnacavallo. But in my mind I see snow falling onto fires as in Count Boutourlin's accounts of Moscow. I see walls of ice and ice that drifts and splinters. I see a face that's not a face, features unreadable as fire.

When the Goddess of Consolation came to Boethius alone in his prison cell she spoke of the tiller and rudder by which our world stays fixed and secured. She stood so close he could describe the woven cloth of her robe, "perfectly finished of the most microscopic threads and of a cunning manufacture." I can hardly imagine. But he saw it so clearly he could discern the Greek letter pi woven into the hem, and at the top of the gown a theta, with a ladder-like structure leading from one letter to the other. But the robe was torn, Fanny, "The hands of certain violent men had ripped this same robe and had carried off such scraps as each one could."

Even so, her right hand still held her books, and her left her scepter. And the ladder was still there to be discerned.

All day I think of Boethius locked in his cell, finding on the robes of the Goddess of Consolation a way to climb, rung by rung, from one letter to another, one feeling to another.

She came to him gently: "Do you know me? Why don't you say something?" Then gathering the cloth of her robe, she lifted it softly to his face and began to dry his eyes.

"Your eyes are clouded with the cataracts of the human world."

"I nursed you, did you think I'd abandon you?"

"Why are you crying? Why do your cheeks run with tears?"

Then: "You have ceased to know who you are. This is your sickness. You have wandered away on your own. Your lamentations glow white-hot. Though you prefer to think of yourself as driven out, it is you who have done the driving—for such power over you could never have been granted to anyone else. If I am to heal you I must find you in the dwelling place of your mind."

With this she fell silent.

How have I driven myself out? Into this frozenness, this severity I think of as your very being. I inflict it over and over on myself where I dwell in the unforgiving whiteness of my mind. Yet each day I bring another's life close to mine, and watch her hand move across the page, so what does that say of who I am? Liberty can exist only in simplicity, Claire wrote. If I feel my voice stripped to the very core, and feel her voice not as clothed but burning from the very core, am I any closer to liberty? I still see those walls strong and imposing in her mind—

Fanny, if I could touch one frail rung on her gown would it crumble? If she came to me . . . if that ladder were . . . if that cloth with its many folds and fine threads . . . But I won't let myself think it. No. Boethius was deluded—a desperate man about to die. Still, she "gently put her hand" upon his chest. She brought to him an "unassuming silence." She didn't flinch from the fevered workings of his mind.

~~Dear F~~   no   ~~Fanny, I~~   no   xxx *the walls are so high I can't feel you anymore, can't—*

not even you—   In the secrecy of my mind I   and there's no place for   and suddenly alone and apart

the walls grown so high and so many   (you in your never-here, yet you were here)

these walls in me so stiff and ladderless   and of such stone as can't be crumbled

such quietness swarming   such rips of distance   ice, ice

And always this inexplicable feeling that I will never see her again—her face lost behind walls and fevered—

Must steal her away   must climb somehow some ladder   must find some scheme or wager

Shelley writes to me of the "thoughtless violence" of my "designs." Says, "it seems to me that you have no other resource but time and chance and change . . . Come and look for houses with me in our boat—it might distract your mind."

But Boethius couldn't leave his cell, he couldn't "look for houses." Locked away as he was, he asked the Goddess of Consolation many questions.

"Ask me whatever you want and I will answer you," she said.

Mostly she answered him with questions: "Would you for all that just waste away in your own mind?" "Is a happiness that will withdraw from you valuable even so?" "Do you think that a man's power amounts to anything if he cannot ensure that what he can do to someone else someone else cannot do to him in turn?" "Can you define for me what a human being is?"

Then she told him, "Fate is the arrangement that inheres in the things that have motion, the unfolding of order in time."

Until after much talk, she seemed finally pleased, "I have been waiting for this condition of mind in you."

This condition of mind . . .   but the walls are so high and so many

     and the somehow-knowledge that I will never see her again   I
    cannot   and yet

would kidnap   would deceive   would—   xxxxx

So quiet now. My hand on the page a powerless, too-quiet thing—

"Can you define for me what a human being is?" the Goddess of Consolation asked Boethius. I stand in this frozen world and ask myself that question. Austerity, precarious chance, a desire for order—all these live and grow inside the mind, but how can I answer her question, how can I . . .

And starvation, slavery, cold. Sacredness and fire.

There is a tale in which a poisoner's tears are sharp as glass. But Boethius's tears weren't hard, she wiped them from his eyes with her soft robe. That robe had been torn, it was damaged, so even she who was immortal wasn't free from harm. Even so, she came to him and comforted him, healed him in the "dwelling place" of his mind. Or maybe she didn't heal him exactly but rather led him to understand that his suffering wasn't ugly, I don't know.

I came so far north to not think of such things. Yet more and more they seem the only things worth thinking. Claire's hand. Those too-strong walls. The ice she feels. The volcano Hecla erupting in a land of cold.

I'm in Pisa now with Mary and Shelley. Strange how even when the mind's in danger, deeply harmful to itself, cutting and cutting, there can be this outer smoothness over everything. It's as if some steady hand were drawing me, making of me something I'm not.

They want to distract me, I know. They don't want me to think of all those walls.

~~but if actions are monsters . . . I see black vapors over the parent marsh . . . and the eye is scarcely quick enough to follow . . .~~

If my hand were the one to draw her, placing her firmly in the world . . . But when I think of you in your laboratory, trying to make me into what you believed I should be, I feel no desire to draw anyone. I wouldn't know how to in any case, and couldn't, far away as I am and other. She wrote of the commotion of earth inside a statue, so even if I gave her a statue's calm smoothness, I'd only be covering (as Locke wrote of words) who she truly is.

———

Mary and I sit all afternoon reading and studying, our tables piled high with books. I'm translating Goethe's Memoirs. Shelley works alone in another room. He no longer uses sugar in his tea, it's produced by slave labor.

They sit there as if the world were calm, but what is safety? Quietness is composed of what, covers what? (She doesn't mention Allegra.) I see the back of her head in the white room, and her white sleeve, how as she writes her hand grows less steady.

"You have ceased to know who you are," the Goddess of Consolation said to Boethius. But isn't the mind largely hiddenness and error? Yet she led him closer to the "dwelling place of his mind," cautioned him gently not to "waste away" within his mind.

———

April. Mary's pregnant again. Shelley's having a boat built, he plans to sail it in the Bay of Spezzia come summer. I try to watch him with calm eyes as I know this is what he wants of me. The courtyard here is filled with flowers. If I were to say to them "in this painful activity of mind" they wouldn't look up, the flowers, which is why I watch them, which is why I talk to them, which is why . . . but then I pull back and go inside.

And Boethius was mute when the Goddess of Consolation found him. She wanted him to be able to speak again of what he'd seen, to talk of all he'd learned and thought and felt, to remember who she was and that he'd known her.

Boethius is dead. Executed without witness. I see his empty cell. Stone slab of bed. Barred window. The Goddess of Consolation promised she would accompany him to the Land of the Dead but I don't believe it—I think he's alone wherever he is. Bones. Emptiness. I can't help what I see. A name carved somewhere on stone. Even though she wiped his eyes with her robe, even though she spoke to him with kindness.

I think of Allegra's face all the time now, though Mary says it's better not to speak of it. Of how I can't see her, can't look into her face ✗✗✗this blindness I feel ✗✗✗ and Gloucester was blinded but a strange tenderness came after✗✗✗ then sometimes her hand suddenly flies into my mind—

✗✗

✗✗✗✗ can't concentrate ✗✗✗ must concentrate, must

Of Archilochos we have not one single work entire and most of the context's fallen away

Sometimes what's left is just one word: Recompense. Plums. Or a few brief, broken lines:

]so[

I then, alone]

I would trace these fragments like a hurt and beautiful face. Her face.

Did Boethius read the Greek poets, did he translate these lines as I do now?

Her face far from me.   (so close)   Fragment 243: "Lips covered with foam."

Can't concentrate. Must. Must concentrate—

The book. Must look at the book. Must ✗✗✗✗✗✗

Archilochos's mother was a slave so they say. He, a native of Paros, so they say. First half of the 7th century B.C. Killed by a man named Crow in a battle or a fight.

"Wandering hungry,
Wild of mind,"

"Here the papyrus is torn," says my Greek book. "Here it is too tattered to read." And the Goddess's robe was tattered, ripped by violent men, and still she came or did she? Did she stand in Boethius's cell, or in the coldness of his mind?

Allegra's face, her warm breath in my breath. The inexplicable feeling that I will never see her again—

I watch her reading as if she's on an icebound ship, though she's in a white room in Pisa with Mary and Shelley. She turns pages as if words could, could what? She in such danger . . . and so quietly . . . What does she find in those pages? Does her mind feel less endangered, less alone?

On the second Grinnell expedition, the surgeon Isaac Hayes carried three books in his clothes bag as he trudged for an entire winter over the ice. "Never had I valued books as I did then, three small books that I came to love well during that long winter."

For his Arctic voyage of 1818, Captain John Ross arranged for a shipboard library of twenty-five books, and in 1850, Captain William Penny stocked his ship, *Sophia*, with eighty.

When I first came here, I thought I wanted to get away from the human world. Yet I seek Claire's shoulder, her hand, still wonder if I'll see her face, turn page after page wherever I can find them. Pages of human thinking, human want. So what does that make of this solitude in which I live?

Some ships carried their own printing presses. There were pages printed on red silk, and thousands of tiny "balloon papers," "cylinder papers," "bottle papers," held for a while then cast off into the sea. There were pages imprinted with delicate lyres, and others embossed with a Tuscan ornamental face. Ink froze on the rollers. When paper grew scarce they still wanted to see words, printed them on handkerchiefs and their own shirts. On linen and wash leather. On whatever they could find.

They read by lamplight through the merciless winters.

———◆———

Wednesday: Read Schiller. Thursday: Read Adonais. Went with Countess Tolomei to buy linen for Mary. Read a Canto of Purgatorio. Translated from Phaedrus. Dreamt this night that S. had been to Bagnacavallo and had returned bringing Allegra to me. When he came I was watching ants on the pedestal of the statue of Ceres. The Chinese proverb says "the wise man fears calm." Saturday: Read Anastasius. Read Cabale und Liebe. Sometimes I dream the pages have eyes of their own and look at me and watch me, but then Shelley comes into my room and tells me I ought to be more gentle with them and careful as they're fragile and quite blind—

Fanny,

Most of the time I don't write to you anymore, I know. Just write in my journal or on scraps of paper. My mind far even from you. Always I see the convent walls and her face behind those walls.

Even in my journal I keep obliterating things. Write them, cross them out, make them unreadable. Scribble series of nonsensical letters over the words.

~~I've tried in vain to~~

Both the Bojti's children are sick with the measles, but already improving. At least their faces are real in front of me. I haven't seen Count Boutourlin for many weeks.

At this time of year a white fog covers the whole city of Florence. It's so thick you can't see a tree five steps ahead.

Shelley wrote, "Do not think my affection & anxiety for you ever cease, or that I ever love you less although that love has been & still must be a source of disquietude to me."

Some nights I dream many dreams though I don't want to. In one I'm in Pisa, a violent Earthquake's expected (I remember you wrote of Mt. Tamboro, how cold the air got after).

Who was it that wrote, "There is no country, faith or sacred cause but passes eventually into slavery and walls"?

Your Sister,

On their ships the men wrote on linen and wash leather, on handkerchiefs and their own shirts, on whatever they could find, so mustn't
words have been of some comfort to them? Why else would they have
bothered?

But she's scribbling over almost everything she writes, destroying each
word with brown ink:

"but I am bound upon a wheel"

no letters   write to M   write to S

Under the reign of Philip Augustus Poetry was inserted in an official list of
"futile & Criminal Arts"

"You do me wrong to take me out of the grave—"

through her robe not vices but kindness   but if I could feel her if

Shelley tells me "to temper myself to the season" refers to the "thoughtless
violence of my designs"

But what does he think he××××

                              and destroy and scatter the

Why do I even bother to write on these pages? Still, I get up or lie down
and words come into my mind I don't know what I'd be without them
coming into my mind. But where is she in all of these words?   I can't
find   can't find her in words

All this obliterated, thickly darkened, drowned on the white page.

They're huddled in the other room. We've come to this half-ruined house by the sea, in Lerici—Shelley insisted we come here, and so quickly, our furniture's not even arrived, everything's in boxes. I hear their muffled voices through the door: termites gnawing in a wall. Mary, Shelley, and the Williamses, all here. When I walk into the room the voices stop. I know Allegra's dead.

~~Fanny, I,~~

~~No, not you anymore~~   ~~not anyone~~

"Little slow fevers," they say. Consumption or Typhoid.

How invisibly harm passes from one being to another.

Tracelessness Convulsions

~~and the ladder on her robe . . . no~~

~~Fanny, I,~~   x   ~~no~~

Sound of the sea lapping and lapping. Sound of a stone inside the mind.

May. I tell myself it's May. But she died in April. So all those days after her death, and I didn't know she was dead, I got up and got dressed and ate and went to sleep and she was dead, and I ate and laughed and translated Goethe and it rained or didn't rain and I went with Edward and Jane to look at houses but none were "quite right" and I ate and slept and read and she was dead. April 19th she died. Her eyes looking at what, her hands holding what?

The nineteenth-century British traveler Lucy Atkinson wrote of the North, "as I headed through it I felt I was bidding farewell to the world."

Another said he had come "to a strange planet. I wouldn't have thought it part of our globe."

And another: "reality is thinner here than anywhere else."

Curzio Malaparte saw "a frozen lake with a whole cavalry regiment of horses dead in ice that had set in one moment of Arctic nightfall."

An old riddle describing an iceberg goes: "The monster came sailing, wondrous along the wave, it called out its comeliness to the land from the ship; loud was its din; its laughter was terrible, dreadful on earth; its edges were sharp. It was malignantly cruel . . ."

But Rabelais had Pantagruel, at sea in the Arctic, suddenly hear lost, frozen words all around him (the words from the dead of great battles), which he plucked from the air. They thawed right in his hands—alive again and warm with blazing colors, changing shapes.

But how can I accept that for almost two weeks her death was kept secret. Shelley kept it apart in his brain. It was a hostage he held in his brain. And my brain couldn't tell, couldn't see it.

What's a mind then, what's thinking?   What does it mean to know something, or . . .

(her face in fever, her face changing then stopping, draining white—)

And the Goddess of Consolation said to Boethius, "Absolutely every fortune is good."

"But how can that be?"

"Concentrate. You see, I think adverse fortune does more good for mortals than favorable. The latter, in the guise of happiness, only sweet-talks empty lies, while the former is true, and reveals her honest instability through change, whereas the latter binds tight the mind."

But my mind couldn't see, couldn't know, was bound tight as any, still is.

I don't want her "honest instability" . . . and her robes are torn anyway, the violent men tore them—

They've embalmed her body, have sent it—where?—to be buried. No one will tell me.

The sound of the sea. The sound of a stone inside the mind.   The sound of watching nothing.

Shelley says that he saw her, a naked child rising with clasped hands out of the sea.

But I see nothing.

Waves   Absences

In that white, final bed her eyes closed on what? Her hands, clenched or open, reached for what?

What if Boethius's ladder, the one he saw on the robes of the Goddess of Consolation, just hung in the air, no words beneath or above it, connecting nothing and nothing?

Is that how Claire thinks of it? Her hand unmoving wherever she is. Now if I glimpse her journal at all, I see only blank pages. (Does it matter where she is? In Lerici? Or has she left there?) Has she been given a lock of Allegra's hair, any keepsake at all? If she lies where curtains puff in and out in wind, does that wind feel unreal to her, irrelevant, some remnant from an abstract, distant world?

And the ladder I climb when I think of you, doesn't it connect only nothing to nothing? Or am I lying to myself? Do I climb from my face to your face then back again, baffled, empty-handed, or from my silence to your silence? Do I climb from your hand's first touch to this vanished Arctic sun? Or from the word *made* to the word *alone*? From longing to longing and back again?

"You have ceased to know who you are. This is your sickness," the Goddess of Consolation said to Boethius.

Now that Claire has vanished (but will she stay forever vanished?) now that her hand no longer comes, I feel that ladder shuddering in air. I barely balance on the narrow rungs. My knees shake, it sways but there's no wind. The horizon line's uncertain.

Even now I feel your hands on my skin. A faint touch like the last light on a deserted battlefield before night begins to focus and come on.

In her sorrow where is she? And if sorrow's a place, are its borders silent, sealed off?

Does she stand on a ladder of ash, and sway as the ladder sways? Does she climb from her name to Allegra's then back again, from the sea to the top of a high wall then back again? From absence to absence? Or does she stare like a statue that can't know it's on a ladder at all? Does she climb from powerlessness to powerlessness, from skepticism to anger and then back?

If grief is a place and absence a place, and solitude with its many burning walls . . .

And I, and she . . .

I never see her hand anymore or her white sleeve.

Did you stand on your ladder in air? My eyes horrible to you from the start (yellow, blurry, dull), my very being horrible. Were the ladder's rungs crumbling, were they ash? How could you step off them, and into what?—

All those times she came to me behind my closed eyes or in front of my open, waiting eyes, I didn't hear her speak, yet I forgot she wasn't speaking, each word vivid, present as my breath. As if I were hearing every word inside her brain as she wrote it, each pen-scratch, each footstep, every feeling she had of safety or danger. Now a quiet fire spreads inside my brain. My heartbeat's too loud.

Is this what Franklin heard when he realized he'd never return? This stripped, peculiar quiet, present as anything. This colorless burn. The ones who walked barefoot over snow, having lost even their shoes, is this what they heard? And the ones who lay final and shivering in their frozen clothes.

I feel the quiet of you too. That colorless, lost place in me where once I almost knew you. No hand alights. I lose myself in whiteness, air.

Fanny,

Why do people want to write down their lives? Why did I ever do such a thing? That journal I kept, the last page is just a date, then blankness. If we burned our words, wouldn't that make a truer picture of the mind?

I dreamed of you last night. You had no hands or feet, but smooth pink stubs completely healed, and you said they didn't hurt (I couldn't hear your voice yet in the dream I knew you said this. How does a person hear without hearing?—how did I hear your voice without your voice?). You were revolving in some sort of air, near earth but not touching it. Still, very close, just a few feet off the ground. The earth untouchable to you and yet your eyes took everything in. I never thought I'd dream of you again. Never thought I'd want to write your name or even say it in my head. Everything over. But you've come back. Or, rather, I've come back to you. Or both. I've felt an odd calm since Allegra died. I'm in Lerici, on the Bay of Spezzia, in the house called Casa Magni. The same house where they told me. I'm surprised I can stay here but I can. These past weeks—I don't know how to speak of them—I found in silence a home but it was as if that home was burning. And yet I could live there. Herodotus said we trust our ears less than our eyes. But I trusted what I heard, which was nothing, or nothing I could use.

I watch the tide moving in and out of the bay. No walls in it, no man-made laws.

Mary lost the child. She hemorrhaged terribly and almost died. Shelley put her in an ice-bath to save her. She's sad all the time and I don't know how to . . . ✗✗✗she says she hates it here, it's too wild, the waves threatening to flood our ground floor . . . I don't mind them, Fanny, but she . . .

Shelley's boat's almost built now.

I write these things as if I'm still alive, as if I have a stake in the world.

The quietness so loud now. I hear it more than these waves breaking against rock—

Though she's writing again she doesn't open her journal, just picks up scraps of paper wherever she finds them. Writes to Fanny on the back of Mary's old accounts:

Washing–3–
Lent Paolo–9–
Washing–4–
Doctor–3–
Baths–4–
Washing–1–7 7

Writes again on the back of Mary's reading list:

Geographica Fisica, Samson Agonistes, Tales of the East, Horace's Epistles, Remorse.

The journal's shut tight in the drawer like the quiet she keeps to herself while she speaks and is helpful and smiles in the house by the sea.

When she finishes writing, she holds the paper to a flame. I watch her do this night after night. The *F* in Fanny disappearing, then the whole word, the whole page of letters burning. (Why can I never see her face?) Liberty can't exist apart from simplicity, she said. Is she trying to set herself free?

White curtains blow in and out. Even in darkness, white sound of sunlight, the sea.

Dear Fanny,

Night after night, feeding these pages to the flames, your name to the flames, I think of how words are an odd otherness. Us but not us. "Out of the bitterness of my mouth," wrote the Psalmist.

Shelley and Edward Williams are missing. They sailed from Leghorn on the 8th. Now Mary and Jane have left to find out what they can.

a water cask bobbing on waves   x x   *a small coracle dinghy but no trace of   no word of*

*and not secreted behind walls like Allegra   not bound by heavy doors with
locks and bolts and yet the harm even so the moving sea*

     So even liberty is a prison ✗✗✗✗✗✗   *and* ✗✗✗✗

*The boat itself was top heavy, rigged like a frigate though extremely small   "a
winged miniature" someone called it, I can't remember who   squall
on the water   squall of words inside the mind*

When I close my eyes the watery surface is blank—

The navigator, Albanov, spent years pleading with Admiral Kolchak to launch a search expedition for his ship, the *Saint Anna*. Then suddenly, in 1919, he disappeared.

On a paper scrap he'd written, "But where could my ship be? Always this cold . . . That polar bear I saw dragged itself for miles on its front paws alone, both hind legs broken, spinal cord injured. I found twelve bullets in its flesh. If the ship is still intact somewhere, but what supplies would they have had?—six pounds of meat powder, two of dried apples, three tins of condensed milk. How long could they have lived on that? I find the word *lost* very painful."

For years he seemed to have simply disappeared. But he'd been blown apart in a munitions explosion at a train station on the way to see Admiral Kolchak; the body was eventually identified from a briefcase and a severed leg.

"Can you define for me what a human being is?" the Goddess of Consolation asked Boethius. "Your eyes are clouded with the cataracts of the human world." "Would you waste away in your own mind?"

I think of her questions as I watch Claire's hand holding her papers to the flames, and as I see in my mind's eye Albanov's words, the ones that pained him, and his briefcase, still locked, beside the torn body.

Fanny,

When the letter arrived I opened it as Trelawny had instructed. It was from Roberts, informing him two bodies had washed up on the shore. Shelley and Edward Williams. Mary and Jane in the other room, still waiting. (. . . all those weeks Allegra was dead I didn't know she was dead . . . this thin lock of her hair, this stilted miniature portrait I hold . . . Trelawny said I must watch for any letter that might come—open it and read it.)

> *it's festa tonight. There's dancing and singing from the village—*

How can I walk into that room, how can I tell them?

> ~~*And the Goddess(no) her robes were torn(no) her robes didn't exist*~~

Dear Mr. Hunt,

I assure you I cannot break it to them, nor is my spirit capable of giving them consolation, or protecting them from the first burst of their despair. Give me some counsel, or arrange some method by which they may know it. Their case is desperate in every respect.

Ever your sincere friend,

Clare

These are the never-returned:

John Franklin, who vanished with his two ships and all his crew in 1845 while trying to find the Northwest Passage.

Ross G. Marvin, who traveled with Peary to the Pole but died on the trip coming back. Some say he fell into an open lead, others that he was murdered.

George W. De Long, whose ship, the *Jeanette,* was sunk by ice in the Bering Strait. He and his crew escaped in three smaller boats, traveling the Lena River, but one boat was lost, and De Long and the remaining crew starved and froze to death after reaching land.

James B. Lockwood, who assisted on the Lady Franklin Bay expedition. After reaching the highest altitude recorded at that time, he died of starvation.

Charles Francis Hall, who went out in search of Franklin, and mysteriously collapsed on his last journey.

Henry Hudson, whose men mutinied and lowered him and his son into a lifeboat to drift out into the icy sea.

And so many others, their names lost or bundled together into the general category of "crew."

Fanny,

The watery surface so blank now. It's July, but I feel ice in me moving and breaking. Shelley walked with a warming fire in his hands. Last August on the morning of his birthday, we rowed out into the harbor. He said to me (but I can't recall why we were speaking of such things): "If I've erred it's on behalf of the weak, not in conjunction with the powerful." There were seabirds diving here and there, the sun just up and rising.

6 towels	Mary. Those marked ✗—S has read also:
2 neck cloth	✗ Letters from Norway
3 Tablecloth	✗ Mary, a Fiction
2 pillow cases	✗ Political Justice
1 flan pett	✗ The Monk—by Lewis—
	✗ Sorcerer. a novel.
	✗ Thaliba
	Emilia Galotti
	✗ Barrow's Embassy to China

Fanny,

It seems so much of what makes us who we are comes not firsthand, not seen with our own eyes, but from a distance—events learned about, heard of, and we hold them in our minds in silence (as I hold you). Alter them, construct them, break them down. Turn them over and over alone. Distance laying claim to whole tracts of who we are . . . The brain schooled and netted by such distance. Things happen apart from us and we make them our own. Our history. The texture of memory, breath.

Allegra, Shelley . . . they're never coming back (their deaths at a distance invisible and wholly real).

Trelawny ~~said~~ came yesterday ✗✗✗✗ He said first there was no sign of anything. Then a punt, a water keg, some bottles on the shore. No other trace for seven days. Until, near Via Reggio, a body washed up, and then another was found three miles farther on near the tower of Migliarino. Shelley and Williams. No sign yet of their sailor boy, Charles Vivian.

Shelley's face and hands were fleshless. ✗✗✗✗ But in one jacket pocket there was a volume of Sophocles, and in the other a book of Keats's poems, pages doubled back.

Mary said Trelawny was kind not to try to console her—that would have been too cruelly useless.

The medieval author of the Ancrene Wisse instructed the anchorite sisters not to look down at their pure white hands but to dirty them each day with the soil that would one day be their graves.

If the mind can be stained and soiled by what it knows, by what it's <u>forced</u> to know, I feel mine so covered now, so saturated, as any pair of hands xxxxxx

So why do I still see so much ice in my mind (not this dirt I think of daily, this dirt I feel covered with and stained by) though I know if I placed my hand on that ice just one time the skin would burn and stick and the fingers freeze—

For a long time she doesn't come. Then one day I see a page (it looks like part of a journal, though I thought she no longer keeps one—*Fanny why do people think to write down their lives?*). It says only: *Sunday May 7th at three or four o'clock.*

Another day I see: having {lost every object of} buried here every thing
   {may the eye}

   {relieve the eye}   Appennines darkened   black clouds

Then:

   Head.

   a Large

   Medicinalräthin.   Alessandro Manzoni.

            author of the Conte di Carmagnola

       fiss—1 fedelin

              fidelin

   Angella

All very strange, what could she be thinking? I see all this but not her hand.

For a while when I started to glimpse more of her, her shoulder, her arm, the dark back of her head, I thought I might one day see her face. Now that feels foolish.

I don't know where she is. Or why her hand is lost to me. Except that grief brings with it great quietness and absence (this I know from when you left me). It takes the mind away from the mind. Abducts the world from the world.

If I wait will she come back? But how could I not wait? Isn't it this waiting (I think of all those times I saw her hand) that links me, such as I am, to the world.

It's a small volume of Russian manufacture bound in brown leather. On the inside cover, some Russian words, and Mary's addresses. She's in Moscow. (How long since I last saw her?)

———

Teusday

(she always misspells Tuesday)

May 12–24

(but there's no year next to these dates)

I have long resolved to keep a journal again and so today have finally provided myself with a book.

When I first came here there seemed no power in myself to keep me alive (every gust of wind recalls Lerici)

I spend half the day not sending letters. Few here know who I am.

Her hand's moving again. Her sleeve white against white curtains in what looks like a small attic room. Her head turned from me as always. There's a lit candle on the desk but she doesn't hold her pages to the flame.

Mary,

I'm in Moscow. I suppose I'm only continuing what Trelawny called my "compulsive emigration to the North." A year since I've written you . . .

Three years since Shelley's body was burned on the shore.

Sometimes Trelawny's still standing in front of me, explaining what happened. How three white wands had been stuck in the sand to mark where the body was, and still they had trouble finding it when they returned. How Shelley would have loved the place—not a single human dwelling in sight. And how Trelawny felt he was no better than a dog or a wolf as he tore the "battered body from the pure yellow sand that lay so lightly over it." I wonder if you hear those words coming back to you unwanted and unasked for as I often do. Just the way he told us. And how he went on to describe the portable furnace stoked with wood; the difficulty of fully incinerating a corpse out in the open . . . wine, oil, salt making the yellow flames jump up and glisten . . . how the heart didn't burn and he reached in and took it . . .

Sometimes that man, Roberts, the one who found the boat, is standing in front of me. He shows me a trunk filled with Shelley's books and clothes. Tells me they found a hamper of wine that Shelley bought at Leghorn, the corks partly broken; wine and sea water mixed in together. He reaches out his hand to me and in it are two memorandum books of Shelley's, perfect, undamaged. Then he points to a pile of books at his feet, tells me he's cleaned them—mud had glued the pages together.

I work as a governess. Yesterday I taught the children about Lavoisier's system of Molecules and the experiment he tried with roses. A red rose washed with muriatic acid becomes perfectly white. Then, viewing it through a microscope, you can plainly see how the molecules which had been lying one way when the rose was red, have been decomposed and now in the white rose are lying quite another way.

I think of such rearrangement often—

Sometimes your name turns to air inside me. Mary. Air. The "M" dropped off and the "y" fled away. And my own name, too, mostly now just air. Or not quite that, maybe, but what are we now, the two of us? What were we then? This snow falling heavily as I think of you, as I so often do, even though you've had no word from me for so long.

Tonight I see the dark window behind her, white curtains pulled back, and for the first time since I've watched her she looks cold, a blue blanket thrown over her nightdress as she writes:

Smirna in Russian means gentle. "smirnyi"—quiet, peaceful, from <u>mir</u> peace
(I say this to myself every morning but don't feel it)

~~Dear F~~

and a {thin} veil before the mind   and all things which destroy

(Shelley gave me his shawl, it's all I have left of him)

Her lost face always her lost face   a table in the wilderness   this
seclusion   shipwreck of mind

I see so many unhappy people I can't complain of the singularity of my fate

Then:

There was a well-known drink in Greece from Homer's time onward, the
<u>kykeōn</u>—it was made by stirring barley and grated cheese into a cup of wine,
and since these couldn't dissolve the whole mixture had to be kept in
motion until it was drunk. Heraclitus says our world is like this drink.
Existing things aren't at rest. Strife is the nature of the world. So justice IS
strife.

always the waves at Lerici   the wind at Lerici—

The window whitens a little, fills with swirls of snow. Her hands—deliberately, slowly—fold a piece of paper into quarters, then eighths. She writes *M. Gambs* on the outside, lays her head on the pillow, tries to sleep.

All night the same dizzying dream: You're washing my cells in muriatic acid like Lavoisier's rose. I feel them rearranging themselves and their directions. Then I'm looking through a microscope, taking notes, as you took notes on me. What, precisely, am I documenting? Does it matter if the cells of the white rose are different from the red? Why does it matter? No one has explained this to me. Still, I feel I should take notes as you did. Then I'm standing on a great plain of ice. Your hand, warm as breath, is nearby me, though I see no trace of you. The air's perfectly clear.

On Parry's second Arctic voyage, the ice grew so vast—icebergs two hundred feet high, pancake ice and bay ice—he decided to winter over near Winter Island. "One day a very beautiful ermine walked right up onto our deck, though we were over four hundred yards away from land."

With so much pared away he believed he saw more clearly: "In the firehole kept open in the ice alongside us, multitudes of small shrimp rose and cleaned—in the most beautiful manner—any skeletons to be found there. The bones, turned the color of salt, were wholly smooth. Each day I watched this cleansing as if it were a ritual or prayer."

As each night I watch her planning her lessons in her attic room, snow filling the window, thickening on the sill. Sometimes I wish she could see me or that I still had a voice with which to reach her. But maybe it's better that I don't. Parry watched from his separateness the ermine walking, shrimp whitening and cleansing the bones, and not one gesture passed between them, not one breath.

To pass the months, Parry's men asked for an evening school. Almost all of them could read a little; some could even write, though they'd long been out of practice. Mr. Halse superintended the classes on the *Fury*, and Benjamin White, a seaman who'd briefly been to school, became the schoolmaster on the *Hecla*. By Christmas day, there were "sixteen copybooks filled by men who, two months before, barely knew their letters."

Mary,

I stay up late thinking about my lessons, planning what to teach tomorrow. Sometimes my mind drifts back to the books we shared, those hours we spent reading in so many different rooms, in Italy, in England. That big table in Pisa piled high with books where we read and talked and studied while Shelley was writing in the other room . . .

Do you remember Sappho's poem that ended, "But everything can be endured because"—There was nothing after the "because"—whatever had been there had been lost.

I prefer Sappho's line the way we have it with its brokenness, its silence. Isn't it the silence that feels true, the not-knowing?

Let me know how you are. Past midnight now, the snow still falling . . .

Fanny,

I didn't know you would come this far with me, and yet—

We live among things that destroy us yet we still exist. There's no escape from the scrutinizing misconstructions and efforts of the mind, though all I wish for now is quiet. Your mind alien to me, finally, as mine would be to yours were you alive, as mine is to Mary's and hers to mine, as anyone's is to anyone else's.

I think you would hate this sprawling city. Its streets narrow and twisting, still pocked and ruined from the war. Numerous trains of slaves walk about the houses. Not much thrives here, even the fruits are grown out of sight in the hothouses. They give you black bread and bitter coffee, and imitate the French endlessly. If only they would consent to be Russians!

Far away, Mary writes in a book she calls her Journal of Sorrow. It has no drawings or reading lists in it anymore, she says what she keeps now is a book of silence. Each night I write in my Journal of Ice and Snow, if I were to name it, though I feel no impulse to name anything.

Sometimes when I sleep I see a bone the color of salt in front of my eyes. Just a single clean white bone.

But I'm not a shadow as Mary says she is. Russia has a million soldiers and at least ten and sometimes fifteen in every hundred die from dreadful conditions and malnourishment. Even now when there's no war. Why think of the world as otherwise? Why should I think of my hardship as larger or more important than it is? And anyway Heraclitus believed that the world is made of strife and we are wrong to think otherwise. Sappho wrote, "to a single sapling most of all do I compare you." So there's that too—those words that draw the mind and somehow calm it—

xxxxxxxxxxx <u>Notes</u> for <u>Possible</u> <u>Ideas</u> for <u>Lessons</u>

~~How the eye xxxxxxxx~~

* How the eye works   the character of light and color—

            if Allegra were a color, and Shelley a color . . . if those
            colors were vanished from the earth, and they are

Erasmus Darwin suggests this experiment: "Place a circular piece of white
paper in sunlight. Cover its center with a smaller circular piece of black silk.
In the center of that place a still smaller circle of pink silk, and in the center
of the pink one a smaller circle of yellow silk, in the center of that one a
smaller one of blue silk. Look steadily a moment at the central spot, then
close your eyes, place your hand an inch in front of them so as to prevent
too much or too little light from passing through the eyelids, and you will
see the most beautiful circles of colors, different from the colors of the
mentioned silks."

Fanny,

*The window's dark. I can't see the snow. I don't see Erasmus Darwin's colors.
Only my face ridiculously staring. Soon it will be spring and I'll go with the
family I work for to the country, to Islavsky, where the River Istra flows into
the Moscow River through deep woods. I'll plant a garden there with Dunia,
help her build a dollhouse. When I speak it's as if my voice comes from
another's mouth. There are so many balconies here, if it were warm we could
walk out on them, one after another. Pascal said that the center of the universe
is everywhere but its circumference nowhere—*

If you who made me had given me lessons as Claire gives lessons, what might you have taught me? It's summer. We sit beneath the trees at Islavsky, near Stone Mountain, by the banks of the River Istra. You're not disgusted when you look into my eyes. I don't mistrust you, though I know I was made differently from others. Maybe you begin with Heraclitus: "Men who love wisdom should acquaint themselves with a great many particulars."

"So," you say, "let's look at Leonardo. He observed minute particulars with great care. Look at his drawings, his studies of anatomy. Of birds and the precise workings of their wings. Of the veins in an old man's leg compared to the veins in a young man's leg. He asked what is the difference. Of the chambers of the heart, the fetus in utero. Of the larynx, the thyroid gland, the muscles that, in motion, create gestures. He rendered Leda's head from various angles on one small piece of paper—face bowed, eyes cast down, then her braid seen from the back. He made designs for flour mills, canals, engines. When peasants brought him shells and corals from the mountains, he worried over their meaning for twenty-five years. How had they gotten so far from the sea? What did that say about geology and the history of those mountains?"

You speak and I listen. We examine his architectural plans, mechanical devices, renderings of tunnels, cords, knots, levers. We recall how he bought birds in the market only to open their cages, set them free.

But then whatever it is that enslaves and disorganizes my face creeps back into me. I don't want to hear your voice. Don't want to see your hands turning pages.

"Can you define for me what a human being is?" the Goddess of Consolation asked Boethius. I would pose this same question to you beneath the trees at Islavsky, by Stone Mountain, not so that you'd give me an answer, but in order that you might ask this of yourself.

Fanny,

Now that the snow's gone, now that we're not in Moscow but at Islavsky, you'd think I'd feel warmer but I don't. It's odd, this cold, and I remember Mary's face after Clara died and then William, the way she turned Arctic and extreme. This wind like the waves at Lerici—Church bells echo village to village—

I have a friend here, Hermann Gambs, he works as the boys' tutor. In our spare time he teaches me history, science, philosophy, astronomy. So I'm learning too, not just the children. It makes it bearable to be here. We walk on Sand Hill and Stone Hill. We walk by the granary and in the woods by the Moscow River. He writes poems and signs them C. Clairmont, I don't know why.

Lately I don't think about my name, or the way I used to have so many names.

We gather strawberries, we go to the dairy. I give lessons from 9 to 4. ~~but this fault {renders} renders~~ There is an extreme narrowness in myself I would walk out of. The children like me to read about Captain Sir John Ross's Arctic Voyage and Parry's first Voyage in the Hecla and Griper. They marvel at the presence of red snow, the amateur plays performed on board, the newspapers they published when iced-in. Also that the crew saw the Croker mountains clearly though they didn't exist. All this excites their minds.

But what of our minds, Fanny, yours and mine? What does it say about us that you've followed me this far, still follow me, that I still speak to you in this way . . . I'd never have thought it. Last night I stood on a fragile ladder of rope. It hung in the air, a thin and fraying thing, so how could it support me? I didn't know where I was—in Italy, Moscow, Snow Hill? I saw no identifiable doors or roofs or streets. And the air itself was hurt, but how can air be hurt? Everything scorched by the withdrawing countenance of itself. When I woke I thought of you though I don't know why.

It's said that on Parry's first voyage he reached Melville Island, that his ships broke clear of the ice—

It's winter again. She's back in Moscow. She writes in her journal and also on pieces of lined paper, making notes for lessons. Sometimes she leaves both on the desk, moves back and forth from one to the other:

Hatred between the Greeks and the Trojans a commercial hatred

Possible lessons: reign and death of Charlemagne   Caesar's
calendar   Marco Polo's
        journey to China

Then:

Lerici—which will always float across my mind, shining in my dark history

      I have forsworn sleep in Russia   Never did I sleep so little—

(S's face)   (if our sky were scarlet, not blue)

but there was scarlet fever in the village. We left Islavsky. Dunia had become very ill—I went to her at 8:00 and didn't leave her until 5 the next morning when she died. All night her chest grew more oppressed, her cheeks a burning pink. I held her upright to prevent suffocation. At five in the morning the doctor came with orders to apply leeches behind the ear and sinepismes of mustard on the legs. But she died too soon for this. She was the same age as Allegra. She was dressed in white, laid out upon a table. Tapers and tall candelabras burned all around. On her face the yellowness of death. All the peasants came to say goodbye. The doctor said we could have saved her if we called for help sooner. But it seems doctors always say that. ~~In the room all was light but the And Allegra so long dead now~~

Fanny,

The snow's come back. I hate it, but maybe it's better than the warm winds I felt all summer, the way Lerici lived in them. M. Gambs often talks of the immensity of the universe. Our sun, he says, along with 65 other suns (but how could he, or anyone, come to this precise calculation?) revolves around another sun whose size can barely be imagined. And another sun, a third one, exists beyond that . . . So we are nothing, really, each one of us. Specks, but much, much smaller even than that. Yet still pierced through, still xxx—

For the first time she turns her face in my direction, though of course she doesn't see me. I see brown eyes, the vague, changing contours of her face, her small closed mouth. But soon it's as if she's pulling away (or is it I who draw back, but why would I?), a small brown-haired woman wearing a white nightgown, pressing her hands against a window in a room minute as a dollhouse, so remote I barely see it. If she were to take out her journal and write, how could I even see the words? And yet she's turned toward me . . . as if it were possible . . . as if . . . For a moment my voice almost presses back into my throat. But it will never come back into my throat.

When she turns away, the pen and paper come back:

the hazard of my eyes, Newton wrote to Locke   the disintegration of forms

Madame Pomikoff says the Russian state is governed only by a coffin and a name

Mary says she's a shadow now

There's no one here to whom I can speak freely. As if a waxen black seal were over my mouth (but maybe it's of no importance, I don't know that I want to speak to anyone anyway. And they'd be appalled if they knew I was Godwin's daughter, a "free-thinker"). Today I called at Lenhold's and found a letter from Mary. Got into the carriage to read it. I remembered that night we looked out over the water and sensed Shelley wouldn't be coming back. The water itself and itself as far as we could see. A blank, unthinking thing.

Franklin, Lockwood, De Long, those lost explorers, what did they see in their last days? A loved one's hair softly floating? A face watching from behind a white veil? A wondrous city? Bowls of ripe fruit? One delicate pink foot dipped into water? An envelope addressed in their name? Or maybe shoelaces, metal screws, a spoon, a piece of twine—something useful they once had and wanted back. Whatever it was they saw—out of their own desire, out of the mind's extremest need—did they reach out, try to touch it? As silence touches silence, and snow, snow.

Mary,

Snowfall again. "Mad with introspecting joy" I sometimes think to myself in these hours I spend alone, but what does that even mean?

I've been reading the northern explorers (the children I teach like this, though lately when I give my lessons I feel far away, as if I were on some ice shelf and the children on another . . . I'm fond of them and am trying to change this). Often they felt someone else's presence behind them when no one was there. Or tasted a taste so distinct they were sure there was something in their mouth. But in fact they'd eaten nothing. Or felt a length of soft hair brush their arm, or heard, out of the whiteness of ice, a sudden clear song or a voice speaking straight into their ear.

What I feel now is unsparing distance. I think of how strange it is that this heavy, lumpy substance which is the body can produce such a thing as thought. I'm stamped by a tenderness I don't understand. Everything far from me. And still I feel this tenderness—what is it? How is it possible to feel both things at once?

Mr. Ichebaiff said last night that Schlegel has proved no nation can civilize itself. Now that Dunia has died, I go among various households giving lessons, I can't remember if I told you. When I think of you I see your face but never hear your voice. On my skin the mysterious pressure of what's vanished and what's stayed. Writing to you, it's as if my hand doesn't belong to me but is a stranger's and I watch it move across the paper with such purpose. The brown ink making a path to you, but not.

Inside this metal box, loose pages from a journal, or are they unsent letters? Holding them is like holding the utter loneliness of the body.

Oct 6
"I walk each day and try to make the walks seem different even though nothing in the landscape changes. How else can I stay sane? I could walk 150 miles to the north or 300 to the west and not see any notable difference either way. Lately I've divided my route into the stages of Marco Polo's travels; I've wandered now from Venice to China. Or I move back in time, watch the slow pulsations of the Ice Age. Or I speed the centuries until ice surges in a zigzag from New York to California, obliterating all but the tallest peaks. For centuries there's nothing but obliterating ice, then it melts and the whole earth turns ocean."

Nov 7
"The silence of this place is as solid as any sound and merges into an indescribable *evenness* along with the dark and cold. This evenness fills the air with a sense of unchangeableness; it sits across from me no matter what I'm doing."

"I'm getting absent-minded. Last night I put sugar in my soup, and tonight I plunked a spoonful of cornmeal mush onto a board where the plate should have been."

Dec 14
"I think I am close to going out of my mind. A sense of rolling vacancies everywhere. The notion that I'm dying won't leave me. Still, there is something animal and automatic in me even now."

When I first began to read these, I expected to sense whoever wrote them hovering at the edges of my body, a shadow crouching when I crouched, sitting when I sat, pacing behind me as I paced. But he's as far from me as anything. We stand on either side of an unbridgeable gap. Though the *evenness* he writes of floods into this air, finds me.

Mary,

I remember how even as a girl you kept a place inside your mind where you touched the "distant inequalities of ice." Felt its dominance, its shifts. Now, in Moscow, I feel I'm at the farthest Pole.

I cannot xxxx *(and even the trackless wilds no longer*xxx*)* xxxx *is this how the mind comes to itself finally, is this how* xxxxx

The snow falls and falls and I read accounts of the North (the children still like this). "Only the cold is real," writes one. "Beneath the aurora the snow is different shades of silver-gray, not white as one would imagine," writes another, and "were it not for my lame shoulder I should be making better progress."

M. Gambs says man is a disastrous and discordant atom among the greater elements. But aren't elements also embattled? Do you remember how as children we'd say And Morning's a Rose and Day's a tulip, and Night's a lily, and evening's like Morning again a Rose, singing out our perpetual chain of flowers. Your mother long buried in the ground by then—so of course you knew better than to believe in such a pretty chain. Fanny and I and the others, we also knew better. And in Naples when we saw the gray upright columns of the shattered temple—

xxxxx*And still this snow. So much of it. Your face so far from me. And your voice.*

One explorer wrote, "Then something approaching gratitude flowed into me, my lantern was still working." And another: "Though I have no appetite I'm forcing myself to eat. I've begun to read again. The temperature is minus 50."

The windowsill's piled high with snow. Sometimes it seems all this whiteness is covering my name, that I no longer have any name . . . xxxx *still, I look out on the snow, its broken lines falling sideways and into me (though how could they fall into me?) touching me like something I listen for but only partly understand—*

Ever since Claire turned to me I've been wondering why I was able to briefly see her face, and why, after I glimpsed it, she suddenly seemed distant. Mostly she comes only in pieces—a hand, a white shoulder, the dark back of her head. Some pages of her journal but not others, some letters but not others. Maybe this is all one person can know of another, as close as one person can ever get to another. When she wrote "mad with introspecting joy," I wondered if I was mis-seeing, or if she'd made a mistake, the way she always misspells *Teusday*. Yet the more I think of it the more it makes a kind of sense.

Fanny,

Remember the freed Roman slave Epicharis? She went into a silence where no one could find her. ~~This snow now, this~~

X   XX

She'd been part of a plot to end the corrupt rule of Nero. When it was uncovered, Natalis denounced his friend Piso and implicated Seneca; Scaevinus named Lucan, Quintianus, and Senecio. Lucan implicated his own mother.

But Epicharis said nothing.

*I think of silence often now—mine, yours, Allegra's, Shelley's, Mary's. (The silent "h" in ghost, the silent "s" in island.) How it cuts into each word—lives in my eye, a thin splinter. Often here it's 20 or 30 below. I walk among the houses carrying my lesson books, my pencils. Inside the rooms such chattering, such loudness, everyone getting on each others' nerves, but sometimes I feel moments of serenest calm out in the cold as I walk between one house and another. If I spoke openly and said what I believe, if they knew of Mary and Shelley and how we'd lived, they wouldn't want me here, wouldn't want me near their children—*XXX ~~wouldn't~~

I wonder if Epicharis felt the silence pressing down into her flesh, then strong and metallic in her throat, or did it live solely in her mind?

Often I feel a door inside my throat slowly closing, though I speak barely anything aloud. Inside each word so many chains and conflagrations—

Fanny,

Sometimes Italy floods back into me and for a moment I'm not cold. I never know when it will happen or why. ~~Not the walls and the horrible sea but the~~ Then the cold comes back and I think of all I don't let myself say✗✗✗

M. Gambs says there's a painter in Spain who lives in a world of silence and vibration. His house is outside Madrid and he paints directly onto the plaster walls. In his 70's now, he no longer titles his paintings. Once he boasted about being the King's painter and of all the money he made, his fancy carriage, etc. But then something terrible came into him—illness, two wars, the sound of self-enclosure.

M. Gambs described the paintings, or at least what they're rumored to be. Ever since, I've been seeing one of them almost constantly—on one brown/gold wall, a dog's head occupying only a very small corner of the picture peers over a dark hill of—is it sand?—and it's struggling not to drown, not to be drawn completely down and under. Small head at the edge of the world—You can't see the body or paws, only the way the head strains upward, so much dirt and vacancy around it, so much✗✗✗—

So little can be explained. ~~In this intense cold I,~~   ~~in the intense cold of~~ ~~✗✗✗ I,~~

M. Aconloff wants me to read Hannah Glasse's The Art of Cookery Made Plain and Easy with his daughter. He found it at Gualtier's bookshop, and thinks it will be an "entertaining" way for her to improve her English. And M. Amfeld wants me to start Matouschkin's Journal of his Travels to Asia with his son. So you see I'm quite busy.

✗✗✗ But Fanny, that small dog-head at the edge of the world—its one visible, wide-open eye ✗✗✗—

~~Epicharis who would not speak who would not~~

~~and died rather than speak~~

LESSON:

THE SILENT LETTER IN ENGLISH:

Examples of the silent "b": climb, numb, comb, debt, subtle, plumb
      (as there is a numb place in me, a speechless debt and silent climbing)

~Examples of the silent "g": though, light, gnaw, gnarled
      (the "g" in Allegra isn't silent . . . but I feel the silent space of her, the
      "g" in light that's her body, her voice . . .)

And on and on, through all the letters . . .

Silent "s"–island, silent "p"–psalm, silent "u"–guest, guilt, guide, dialogue,
      tongue
      (my tongue a ghost of what it was . . .)

~~

And there are silent combinations

There are few rules to learn, but <u>presences</u>—one can learn the <u>presences</u>—

(silence embedded in any question, any wish, in my wrist as I write this—)

Fanny,

*For hours I've been trying to compose my lesson on silent letters, but it's as if
Epicharis IS each one of those letters and stands now in so many words,
determined, irreproachable, fierce. Stands there and stands there. She's solid
and intact while sounds whirl around her—Whatever they do they don't
matter to her, can't penetrate her at all.*

She can't speak, won't speak—that part of her is over now, she knows this. Think of the "h" in hour, the "l" in talk, in calm, the "n" in column.

When I went in my sledge to the Kaisaroffs earlier this evening, I felt for a moment suddenly nowhere, that the earth is composed, if only we could feel it, of molecules of nowhere . . . Then M. Kaisaroff opened the door and I was suddenly back and Moscow was a somewhere again and words came out of my mouth as if they had no silences inside them, as if Epicharis, as if she had not . . . xxxxxxxxx

M. Pomikoff says there are rumors that Constantine will refuse the Russian crown, that he intends to resign all his rights. It's late. I have to get up early to finish my lesson—must get up to xxx I'm thinking of the silence in "leopard," "have," "give," "weave," "fasten"xxxxx must finish my—
xxxxxxxxxxxx must finish—xxx must—

As she builds her lists of words, I think of how you're like the silent letters they enclose, wedged inside each thought I have, each cell. I feel the faint vibrations at her throat—but how can I feel this when she's so far and other?—as she says into the air to no one

none, none, none,

then

climb, ghost, thought, enclose. Island, island, island. Answer is ghosted, whole, ghosted.

I read her lips as she does this. The silent *h* stands with rigid, upright back as once you stood near me wondering what features to add next, what aspect of my being. Did you suspect you left in me a frightening silence, some gap, desolate, uncontrollable, unsolved, unfinished? Was that partly why you feared me?

So how could I know you? How could you know me?

Fanny, the night's very still. The depth of winter. The doctor came today. It hurts me to speak and my chest hurts. With Alexander dead the serfs won't be freed. Nicholas has had himself proclaimed the new Czar. Already there are many arrests.

Why is it I speak to you when I speak inside my mind? Not once to her, never to her. Though her hand brings me so many words—*thought, light, thistle, Wednesday, meant.*

She's lying in her narrow bed. It seems she's too tired to write, throat and chest convulsive with coughing: I see this but don't hear a sound. Her hands are much paler than before.

She takes out her journal.

  charged with snow and the desolate,

she writes, then:

  invented by tenderness

(I wonder what she means even as I sense it's true.)

  My journal has been a long time interrupted. I am increasingly quiet inside. And the precariousness of   in Greece Mavrogenia is a heroine, says she will only marry a freeman   that you must fight for your liberty   she's armed, leads her own band of followers in the uprising

Then:

  This snow burying itself in itself. Dr. Jenish came again today, gave me the Lives of Saints to read, says it passes the time ✗✗✗✗ ✗✗✗✗✗✗ but the waves breaking at Lerici, the wind at Lerici ✗✗✗✗✗✗✗✗ and this muteness I feel in my throat and in my brain, I think of it as white, I don't know why. The shawl Shelley gave me, the one thing I have left from him. I wrap myself tighter. He walked with a fire in his ✗✗✗✗✗✗✗✗✗✗✗✗✗✗✗✗✗

  Fanny, Mary, no, I feel such muteness in my mind. I read of Saint Drugo. Also known as Saint Droux or Saint Druon. All is broken off in me now, all is and the waves at Lerici the rough shore

  He's the patron saint of muteness. His well-born mother died at his birth and at 18 he became a penitential pilgrim, then spent 6 years as a shepherd. He seemed to find peace in this, but it wasn't peace he wanted and he set out on his pilgrimage again. He suffered a disfiguring injury. The book won't say what it was. I think it must have been something with his face, that something monstrous happened to his face . . . like the man I saw years ago in London whose face was red scars criss-crossing where his eyes and nose had been, and lopsided darkness for a mouth. Saint Drugo built himself a narrow cell, ate only barley-bread and ashes, hid himself away for 40 years until his death.

The doctor says my eyes are inflamed. But it's my throat that stings: I think of the words I can't say and the waves at Lerici the wind the boats the shore at Lerici xxxxx What would Shelley think of it here?—Innumerable arrests and imprisonments, a "third section" of secret police to monitor "subversives." Today at Kazan University they suspended the study of anatomy and astronomy, calling them "impious."

Saint Drugo is also the patron saint of coffee and coffeehouses, of sickly and homely people, broken bones, and shepherds, cattle, gallstones, orphans. Shelley would have smiled at this, said something mocking. Such a clatter of voices in this house, always such clamor. When I wrote my lists of silent letters I didn't think for some reason of my own name, Claire, the silent "i" inside it—

Sometimes I imagine standing over you as you lie on the couch in that dim, shuttered room where you made me. You've got one of your fevers— it seems you're always having fevers. A "cold shivering" you murmur, pulling the blanket up over your shoulders, bunching it around your neck. (As Claire shivers in fever, and I feel helpless as I watch.)

Every season's battling inside you—you're burning and freezing, shivering and red with sweat. From time to time you write in your notebook. "I can no longer observe any outward object with the faintest pleasure," "but I resolve to remain silent—I'll tell no one of what truly troubles me," "exploded systems and useless names."

I stand there, a dark and beating heart.

Beneath all those fevers, was there a North inside you too, vast miles of silence as far as you could see? I don't know what to feel as I think this. My thoughts freeze: I look upon you as if you're an object encased in museum glass. Your head sarcophagal, exotic as a pharaoh's. Each path to you buried, useless, uncertain.

Smirna means gentle   quiet, peaceful, from <u>mir</u>, peace

and enlivens what seemed to be dead   but how is that possible?

     fight and gain your liberty, Mavrogenia said

Χ Χ

Psammeticus wandered much and a long while alone   then we go to
the garden to gather black currants

          we gather strawberries we go to the dairy   this snow
this hot snow   I can't count the number of balconies at Islavsky there
are so many   I stroll with Marie Ivanova from one to the other

~~All~~   ~~Allegra~~

I don't want to be ashamed of my own mind

Her fever's building (the locked silence in my throat is building). She closes her eyes, wipes her forehead with a cloth. Does she think of Boethius even once? Does she feel a hem in air, or only coldness?

(If my voice weren't lost, if she could see or hear me. But what comfort could I give even then?) And the ones who were trapped by ice for so long, the ones who survived, what did they think as they struggled and waited?:

"I decided I needed strategies that would make me capable of a protracted and profound self-containment. To keep myself focused, I imagined a pair of surgical scissors cutting hundreds of red dresses into two-inch strips."

"The air filled with a profusion of sounds—I was convinced they were real: the soft whirring of motors, of electric batteries and switchboards, the ticking of many clocks. Delicate, methodical sounds. They were of subtle, varying textures, and spoke to me of some sort of allotment, containment and order. No one could have convinced me they weren't real. When they suddenly vanished from my ears I grieved for them for days."

"I'd think of place-names. Resolute Bay. Arrival Heights. Focus my mind on them. Cape Walker. Sheerness. Good Hope. I'd dwell even on Great Slave Lake and Icy Cape. Anything precise, specific."

"I felt Wilson's arm on my back though I'd lost him in the blizzard weeks before. Whichever way I moved the arm moved with me. Always that weight, a drenched heaviness like cloth retrieved from a river. I never got used to it, though I came to accept it—that arm a rough peninsula across my back, turbulent, unsoothed, remorseless."

As I feel her arm on me now, though she's far away, has never seen me.

These weeks of fever—~~Mary, Fanny, no~~ these weeks of ✗✗✗✗✗✗ the mind can't be perceived, not really. How will I save enough money to leave here when I can barely give my lessons? ✗✗ I remember the molecules were rearranged when the red rose turned into the white. M Kaisaroff says I must go to the Baths of Toeplitz, near Dresden, that she knows a family that will take me. But I ✗✗✗ and the waves at Lerici ✗✗✗and the snow ✗✗✗ and when I wanted consolation most . . . ✗✗✗ Stratagems. Concealments. Such clamor in these houses, yet the household slaves stand in silence, they don't dare answer or answer only in the blandest terms. I must plan more lessons. Dr. Jenish says I can't stay in this cold, I won't get better. I don't know if my sickness is of the mind or of the body and I feel embarrassed not knowing. Silence comes to me more and more—it's silvery, a kind of metal. I must plan my ✗✗✗ When the Princess Montemiletto told us of being trapped under her ruined villa after the earthquake and hearing pure, utter silence for the first time in her life, she spoke of it as horrifying yet her face conveyed a certain enjoyment, even an odd peacefulness and wonder ✗✗✗ ~~and immolating one's own wishes or~~

LESSON:
PUNCTUATION

~~Modern punctuation was designed to clarify syntactic structures rather than to indicate breathings. Along with the printing press came codifications of spelling and capitalization.

> but what of all that isn't codified & can't be—in me, in anyone—
> and this precariousness I feel, this ✗✗✗

> and the waves at Lerici the shore the wind the rocks at Lerici

> Allegra, Shelley

~~For a discussion of modern punctuation, look at Ben Jonson's English Grammar (1617)

. . . this snow all around me . . . such hot snow. Boethius was alone in his cell the whole time, wasn't he, she didn't come to him not once not really she didn't speak to him at all ✗✗✗✗✗ he made it all up he needed to make it up ✗✗✗ the walls so high and so hot now and this snow all around me white-hot ✗✗ the ladder wasn't there—there was never a ladder there—or maybe there was a ladder after all maybe she came to him maybe ✗✗✗✗ and her robes ✗✗✗ and on her robes there was a ladder but this snow is so hot now these high walls

Pushkin's friend Chaadev says this is a time of madness, says about this country: "what have we ever created, we Russians, what have we ever invented?" Says Russia stands outside of time without past or present or future, "an orphan cut off." Calls all Russians, "nomads" in their land, "strangers" to themselves. The Czar has placed him under house arrest, doctors visit him every day. Pestel and Ryleev have been hanged in the courtyard of the Fortress. Volonsky's exiled to Siberia for 20 years of hard labor while his mother accepts a new diamond brooch from the Czar, and says of her son, "I only hope there will be no more monsters in the family."

Mostly there's silence. Arrests in silence. Thoughts in silence. Disappear-ances in silence. Everything violent, intransigent, difficult, unresolved, covered by this whiteness, this hot snow, these fevers I feel, but if I left here . . . And anyway everywhere's a jagged splinter in the eye in one way or another, and it's not bad to feel it, the splinter—If the reconcilable's a cloister, a jail, then I don't want that cloister, that jail ✗ ✗✗✗✗ I should plan more lessons. I should ✗✗✗ But how can I make corrections on their papers, what is a correction anyway and this snow so hot now these walls I haven't the least idea how to ✗✗✗✗ and the snow and the

Dr Jenish says rest, just rest. But I feel this splinter in my eye and the snow so hot so thick and Boethius felt the soft cloth of her robes she held it to his eyes but what if she wasn't there ✗✗ what ✗✗✗ if ✗✗✗ Allegra, Shelley ✗✗✗ I don't need the ladder but there's this splinter in my eye ✗✗✗ this splinter that enables me to see ✗✗✗ and the snow's an envelope burning . . . who wrote on it who sent it . . . inside it, and inside it burning xxxxxxxxx

and the waves at Lerici and the

Fanny, Mary,

My fever's broken. Moscow's still covered with snow. In winter all distance turns inward, differentiation vanishes. I need to grow strong and healthy like I used to be. I don't understand how tenderness invents itself but that it does. "Lost and unknown when clothed in words," Locke wrote, yet this is the only way I have to reach you. Each day I mount a stranger's stairs. The world is closed in silence to me—I've told myself this again and again, but maybe I'm wrong. Think of what the Northern explorers felt when color flooded back into their world. Still, so many of them never returned, or returned only partly— damaged, sullen, numb. For four years I've lived among strangers—xxxx I thought consolation was what I needed but now I don't know. I keep thinking I have this splinter in my eye and at first it bothered me, the way it interfered, black line through every face, each wall, each door. A caught piece of turbulence lodged inside my sight forever—

but it's become just a part of seeing and I find now I don't mind it

What's wholeness anyway—and why did I formerly think of it as something to be prized?

Remember the ruins at Luna, how we loved them

The other night I dreamed a pair of surgical scissors was cutting our red dresses into strips

it wasn't a bad dream   that's what amazed me—it wasn't bad at all—

the floor all covered with those strips, a mess of red—

I think of you   there are so many conflagrations of mind   so many xxx
   I don't know how to say it—

XX

(turbulence/ruin)

more and more I feel myself climbing a rope of turmoil and peace, each rough strand inextricably bound to the other, intertwined with the other—

know that I think of you ✗✗✗

the two of you wherever you are

the last consolations are torn away—

{ Notes }

Notes on Perplexity

(When I go to Google and type in this word which seems to mark the place you've left me in, this word I want to understand, there aren't so many entries after all. There's a perplexity that has to do with statistical models of speech recognition. There's a Perplex City, which seems to be a game. "Perplex City's greatest treasure has been stolen . . . Explore Perplex City through websites, emails, texts and live events. Find the cube and claim $100,000 reward." I do my research where I can. I forage, hunt.)

So I'll begin with Socrates, that "self-stinging stingray."

He stung himself with questions:

"For I am not free of perplexity when I make others perplexed; but I am more perplexed than anyone."

The meanings of the most common words crumbled under his tongue.

Euthyphro said, "But Socrates, I am simply unable to tell you what I think, for whatever we put forward goes around and around and refuses to stay where we place it."

(The way the woods I slept in those first nights now sleep and stir in me, their shudderings and complex shiftings, small breakages shot through with slippage, doubt . . . No stillness in me, no shelter I can touch or trust.)

(Yet maybe there's a kind of shelter after all in the way things shift, turn ripe with possibilities, uncertainties, the mind un-tombed, the puzzles ever-changing.)

A question is a site of astonishment. "Why has not the universe been used up long ago and vanished away?" Aristotle asked.

And Gertrude Stein: "What is the wind what is it." "How many windows are there in it." "What is the difference between ardent and ardently." "To smile at the difference."

(Boundaries blur. A question mark seems too solid, too intact a thing. What's *suppose,* what's *comfort,* what's *else* and *elsewhere,* what's *other,* what's *difference,* what's *alone?*—each word ripping through itself like water, or brain waves in minute vibrations, curving, casting out. I remember plastic models of the brain, perplexity etched into their crevices from the very start.)

"The human mind stands ever in perplexity," wrote Emerson. "Thoughts walk and speak and look with eyes at me . . . and make all other teaching formal and cold."

(I think of you in fever. The more you tried to understand, the more your thoughts bent down beneath that weight, thin lantern-skins flickering. As now, the winds inside me shock the leaning trees, the smallest storms inside my brain releasing . . . Mind's a perilous place, it knows how each horizon crumbles.)

"And there shall be signs in the sun and moon and stars, and upon the earth there shall be distress of nations in perplexity at the roar of the sea and rolling waves . . ."

"O Lord, increase my perplexity concerning Thee!" wrote Ibn 'Arabi in the thirteenth century.

He wanted to be guided by bewilderment.

There's another prayer: Let me be undone, unsewn, disrupted.

For perplexity disables the will, disables tyranny.

Ibn 'Arabi retells the story of Noah. Only those who refuse the ark are truly holy. Having turned their backs on the ark's rigid structure, they choose to die instead in the vast waters, the multiplicity that perplexes (as God perplexes): They drown "ecstatically in the wider seas."

"Perplexity lifts the servant out of his servanthood, causes everything to shimmer and change."

To be perplexed is to wander truly and well. There's no single destination to arrive at.

(And yet sometimes I wish for a clear answer, a something that consoles the mind. Maybe the sea can console, how it's not one single thing but wave upon wave building and dissolving, the way a face wanders through itself all of its life, the quiet deluge of it streaming. Still, some nights when I can't sleep, or days I think of you, or days I'm frightened by my thoughts, the needled wings inside my fingers, my heart . . .)

Augustine ended his *Confessions* with a puzzle: the last word he chose, *aperietur,* meaning "will be" or "shall be opened."

Those who later transcribed his text altered its ending to "amen," as if to shut that perplexing door he had left open.

Disquietude. Perplexity. The words: "perhaps," "will be," and "shall be opened." Endless space . . .

(Some nights I dream I'm in the sea. Cold slits of light ride miles of viscous black. The water's full of doors opening and shutting, soft fins or lungs that somehow function underwater. The burlap sack I wear, stitched with every letter of the alphabet, bulges out from my body then flaps back then bulges out again as the letters begin to disintegrate and then drift off, drift away, until I'm alone and drowned but still breathing among the many scattered letters, each gash and sway of them traveling far from the built systems, the built world . . .)

Notes on Dr. Joseph Vacanti and
Dr. Robert Langer

Dr. Joseph Vacanti directs the Tissue Engineering and Organ Fabrication Laboratory at Massachusetts General Hospital. He is also a professor at Harvard Medical School.

Dr. Langer is a professor at MIT. He's known for his "highly profitable engineering successes," blurring the lines between engineering and medicine. He won the 1998 Lemelson-MIT Prize, at $500,000 the largest single cash prize for invention in the United States.

They are considered the "fathers of the field of tissue engineering."

In their lab, they have grown a human ear on the back of a hairless mouse.

(That hunchback, that winged creature in a cage . . . four-footed, unable to see itself or know, as I didn't know.)

Specially bred to lack an immune system that might reject human tissue, the mouse nourishes the ear, which is composed of human cartilage cells distributed throughout a scaffolding of porous, biodegradable polyester.

(And if a mind could be bred not to reject?)

(Yet how it breeds desolation even as it thinks this—)

When the ear has fully grown it's removed from the mouse and transplanted in a human host.

The cells re-create their proper functions, blood vessels attach to new tissue, and the scaffold melts away.

(But there's that shadow-sense of how it came to get its shape, its beginnings in a cage.)

They have not yet been able to grow human nerve tissue.

They hold many patents. Dr. Langer alone holds over three hundred licensed to over eighty companies.

Their patents include No. 5,759,8305770,193, and No. 5,770,417. These are available for viewing online from the Patent and Trademark Office, Washington, D.C.

Advanced Tissue Sciences, a biotech company in La Jolla, California, has licensed these patents and is preparing clinical trials.

(But what profit was there for you who made me?)

In an interview Dr. Langer mentions a possible collaboration with MIT's Department of Earth and Planetary Sciences to control the weather. His only criterion for a project, he says, is that it be done in a reasonable amount of time and have a reasonable impact.

(Reason is a fragile wing. I feel such perplexity when I try to reach and catch it.)

He and Dr. Vacanti met in the mid-1970s as young researchers in the lab of Dr. M. Judah Folkman.

Their lab has produced a wide range of body parts—cartilage, bone, ureters, intestines.

In 1986, while standing in shallow water at Cape Cod, Dr. Vacanti noticed the seaweed's branching networks. It occurred to him to seed cells along branching scaffolds like theirs.

(I don't know if they have families. I don't know what they like to eat.)

They are in search of "elegant solutions."

Dr. Vacanti has seen many of his pediatric patients suffer.

(That he would want to do good, want to heal what can't itself heal . . . This I can understand. Was there something in you that you also felt the need to heal?—a powerlessness, some sense of wrongness? Did you think that making me might cover grief with power, cover fear with willfulness, control? But what if you'd believed that a flaw—in you, me, anyone—could be beautiful in its way? That irregularity can be beautiful, lack and damage beautiful? Always I've had to ask myself these questions, have lived within these questions . . .

And what of how cells, experiments, methods for building new tissue, become property and the division of property—profit, loss—immense wealth amid squalid poverty? How to think of the idea of ownership, the idea of being free?)

Notes on Marco Polo

⟨ The more I think I'm finally certain, the more uncertain I become. Even as I hold you in my mind, does this mean I truly know you? I glimpsed you for an instant, then you fled. So much of what I thought was knowledge knots and then undoes itself. I map the routes of you—customs, motives, patterns, cruelties, fears; your face afloat in me in sleep. ⟩

In 1298, in a prison in Genoa, Marco Polo dictated his account of his twenty-four years in Asia to his fellow prisoner, a writer, Rustichello.

They called their account *A Description of the World*: "Here you will find all the greatest marvels and the great diversities . . ."

The book is also known as *The Travels of Marco Polo,* and *Il Milione* (*A Thousand Marvels*).

Of the 150 medieval and Renaissance versions known, no two are exactly alike. No copy of the original exists.

In the "F Text," considered the most reliable, the book is sometimes referred to as "my" book, sometimes as "ours."

⟨ I picture them in their cell, two strangers become friends. Rustichello writing in Franco-Italian, asking, "What did you see?" Marco leaning close to him, saying with the confidence of one who has seen many things and so knows the diversity of the world, "In the Baku peninsula there is a fountain which jets oil in great abundance, not good to eat but good to burn," and "In the province of Cathay is a sort of black stone that is dug from mountains where it runs in veins. When lighted it retains fire much better than does our wood. It gives heat through a whole night and the next morning." When they tire, they lie down on the hard floor, and if Polo has spoken of a city with twelve thousand bridges, they walk among those bridges, waves slapping stone arches, gold light on the water. ⟩

In 1271, when Polo was seventeen, he set off from Venice with his father and uncle on a journey to China. There they spent the next seventeen years. In 1275 they arrived at Shangdu, gaining entrance to the summer palace of Kublai Khan.

Although Polo describes in detail what he saw, there's much silence in his book: he's quiet about what hardships or illnesses he suffered. Quiet, too, about whom he might have loved, why he returned to Venice, how it felt to live so long among strangers.

It was the world and its wonders he sought to capture, not the workings of them on his mind.

(After twenty-four years away, once home again he must have also felt a stranger. All those deserts in his head, hills of white salt, lanner falcons, horses with hoofs so hard they didn't need to be shod, a ruby the length and thickness of an arm ... What is belonging? What is a home within the mind?)

His book, though popular, was considered mostly lies.

No Chinese or Mongol documents prove he was ever there, or even mention him in passing. He's not mentioned in missionaries' letters, or in other travelers' accounts.

Still: "In this city of Kanbalu is the mint of the grand khan where mulberry leaves are steeped and pounded to make paper like cotton but quite black." And, "There is a regulation adopted by the grand khan, both ornamental and useful. On the sides of public roads trees have been planted to mark the road's curve even when covered in deep snow."

Sometimes he refers to himself as "I," sometimes as "he."

He chose to serve the khan, didn't live among the Chinese people.

He never learned Chinese, never once mentioned chopsticks.

But "perceiving the grand khan took pleasure in hearing accounts of whatever was new to him respecting the manners of people, he endeavored, wherever he went, to obtain correct information on these subjects, and made notes of all he saw and heard."

{ How did his fellow Westerners feel upon hearing there were civilizations unknown to them as grand as or greater than their own? Over the years miniaturists added grotesque illustrations to his text: men with faces sprouting from their chests, for instance, as if what's distant, not one's own, must be, by its very nature, threatening, horrible, wild. }

{ I was ugly to you from the start. How could I have shown you what I am? }

{ If I'd had my Rustichello, would he have helped me tell you what I've seen? He looks into my eyes. "What then?" he asks. "What did you see then?" After I tell him and we tire, we lie down near each other, then he walks with me through the forest I described, foraging for berries, purple sweetness spreading on our palms. He links his arm in mine, the sun faint through veils of leaves. }

In the early fourteenth century, Francesco Pipino, a Dominican friar, was commissioned to make a Latin translation of Polo's text. When any reference to the Muslim religion appeared, he added his own adjectives: "wretched," "abominable," "wicked," "insane," though none of these were in Polo's text.

In 1392, Amelio Bonaguisi, having been sent to oversee an isolated village, decided to "pass the time and keep melancholy away" by transcribing Polo's book. Afterwards he wrote, "What he speaks of could be true, but I don't believe it. In the world one finds very different things from one country to another, but these, it seems to me, are things not to be believed, though I've enjoyed copying them."

In 1621, Robert Burton imagined a journey in which he would discover "whether Marcus Polus the Venetian's narration be true or false, of that great City of Quinsay and Cambalu, whether there be any such places . . ."

{ But I think Rustichello didn't doubt him. All those days and nights together. Maybe he encouraged the embellishment of a detail here or there to heighten the dramatic impact or move the story forward; he'd been a writer of Arthurian romances, after all—though truly, Polo doesn't attempt to tell much of a story. Mostly he coaxed out details, "Tell me, Marco, how the pepper trees are cultivated and the indigo's prepared." They built their kingdom of words, so different from their prison walls. }

So:

"The Tartars have the best falcons in the world. Also they drink mares' milk which they prepare in such a way that it takes on the qualities and flavor of white wine."

And:

"Sin-gui is a large, magnificent city, the circumference of which is twenty miles. The inhabitants manufacture great quantities of silk, not only for their own consumption, all of them being clothed in silk garments, but for other markets as well. They have among them many physicians of eminent skill who can ascertain the nature of disorders and apply proper remedies. There are also persons distinguished as professors of learning, or, as we should call them, philosophers. On the nearby mountains rhubarb grows in the highest perfection."

Over time, there were those who doubted less. William Marsden wrote in his introduction to *The Travels of Marco Polo,* published in London in 1818, "Mr. Henry Browne, who for many years filled the situation of Chief of the Company's Factory at Canton, assures me that he has seen enormous pears like those described by Marco Polo, from the province of Fo-kien, the bulk of which equaled that of a moderate sized wine decanter." From this edition on, the book has stayed steadily in print.

Now you can buy *Marco Polo: A Book of Wonders,* a facsimile edition with eighty-four illustrations, for $9,150.00. There's a species of endangered sheep called the Marco Polo sheep that live in China and along Afghanistan's Pamir Mountains. The Marco Polo Hotel chain offers "welcome to a legendary blend of Asian hospitality and Western innovation, in the tradition of our thirteenth-century Venetian namesake who was perhaps the first truly international explorer to be welcomed to the east." The ship, *Marco Polo,* has been "built with a strong ice-strengthened hull that makes her perfect for Antarctic expeditions."

After his release from prison, Polo lived his remaining years in Venice. He married, had three children, tried money lending, set up small business deals, sold musk.

Among his possessions when he died were: a Buddhist rosary, the silver girdle of a Tartar knight, a gold tablet from the khan, and sendal, a type of cloth, from Cathay.

Pietro, the Mongol slave he brought back, was to be released, by the terms of his will, upon his death.

At sixty-nine, he lay on his deathbed. According to Jacopo D'Acqui, "Because there are so many great and strange things in his book, which are reckoned past all credence, he was asked by his friends to remove everything that went beyond the facts. But Marco Polo replied, 'I have not told half of what I actually saw.' "

("Ah Rustichello, I wonder where you are. Why did we lose touch all these years, all these years live apart without speaking? Your arm's linked in mine . . . it's evening . . . we're walking among bridges . . . our wavering reflections. When we wake you'll ask me to tell even more. So I'll tell you of the land-wind so hot that those who survive it must be immersed up to their chins in water-filled clay vessels. I'll tell you of the city of Changanor, which means White Lake and is covered with hundreds of swans. I'll tell you of oxen nearly as tall as elephants, and of the softest white hair of camels, the enormous dock on the Kara-Moran River that can accommodate fifteen thousand ships . . .")

He died on Sunday, January 8, 1324.

Notes on Leprosy

At Lille the leper carried a small horn to warn of his approach.

At Arles he sang "De Profundis" to warn others of his presence.

In France the leper was required to wear gray or black embroidered with the red letter *L*.

Henry II of England and Philip V of France preferred the afflicted be strapped to a post and then burned.

But Zhuangzi wrote of the wisdom of a man who was "mutilated" and had "lost all his toes," "who neither preaches nor discusses, yet those who go to him empty depart full."

And Confucius said, "It is not the outward form that is important."

This was after Duke Ai of the Lu state had come to him with this report: "In the Wei state there is a leper named Ai Tai To. Though he's physically loathsome, the men who live near make no effort to be rid of him. Women even dream of being his concubine. He never preaches at people but puts himself into sympathy with them. I offered him a post which he reluctantly and sullenly accepted. Then after a very short time he went away. I grieved for him like a lost friend. What kind of man is this?"

{ I, too, wonder, what kind of man? Did he mourn his outward form, or did it mean little to him, even nothing? How might it have led him to sympathy, kindness? His body a question asking what's ugly, what's loathsome, what's beautiful, what's valuable, what's not. He lived within a kind of silence, kept his own counsel, went away without explanation—No clear summary of who he was. }

Accounts of leprosy are found in the literature of ancient Egypt and India. In the Berlin Papyrus, there's a reference to a case as early as 4266 B.C.

Often the leper was used as a symbol of sin, evil, moral lack, corruption: "lepered with so foul a guilt." And: "ye lepers ... of ye saull," "sinne leapered age," "Leprosy'd with Scandal," "The Leprosie of Sin."

{ Did you fear the horror of what I was, or what you believed me to be, would spread to you as well, a mad secret festering then bursting on your skin? }

In the medieval Mass of Separation, a leper was summoned to the grounds of the church, then sent away forever: "I forbid you to enter churches, or go into a market, or a bakehouse, or into any assembly of people ... I forbid you henceforth to go out without your leper's dress ... I forbid you to touch a crossing-post before you have first put on your gloves ... I forbid you to wash your hands in a spring or a stream ... I forbid you to go through a narrow lane lest you should meet someone ..."

{ That word *forbid*. Such bars on it, such locks and shackles. }

{ If you could have forbidden me, what might you have said? "I forbid you to read books or to go out into the world which doesn't want you, I forbid you to think of me, I forbid you to seek any comfort in another. I forbid you to wonder why I made you or who I am or where I've gone to. I forbid you to speak to me. I forbid you to show your yellow eyes." }

In Leviticus it is said, "Now whoever shall be defiled with leprosy ... shall have his mouth covered with a cloth ... and he shall dwell alone without the camp."

{ I dream my mouth is covered with white cloth. When I try to speak only muffled sounds come out, animal and cryptic. I'm covered with dark fur, I'm hiding in a cave, my eyes peer darkly forward. Later I'm behind a row of bushes. There are piles of books, but when I pick them up my lips go numb, my throat festers, fills with blood. }

Nearly nine out of every ten of the infected never show any sign of the disease.

{ If I hadn't shown who I am ... but how could I not have? This lumbering body, black lips, yellow eyes ... Yet Ai Tai To showed who he was, and the others didn't shun him. }

In advanced stages many don't feel pain, heat, or cold and so suffer from wounds that go unnoticed.

(Odd to think about that particular form of suffering—suffering from what one *doesn't* feel.)

Many eventually go blind.

Leper colonies were located on islands or in remote areas. In the Middle Ages such dwellings administered by a Christian order were called lazar houses, after the parable of Lazarus the beggar.

(And yet they had each other . . .)

Bartholomaeus Anglicus enumerated leprosy's various causes: the bite of a venomous worm, unclean and corrupt wine, highly spiced meat "as of long use of strong pepre and garlyke," melancholic meat, coitus, the conception of a child in "menstrual tyme." "Lepra cometh of dyvers causes . . . for the evil is contagious, and effecteth other men."

Those in whom the disease lay dormant for more than nine months were issued a "quiescent certificate," then allowed to return home. This rarely happened.

(I carry my begging bowl and clapper. I hide my face behind my hood, kneel outside your gate in sunlight, don't hold out my hand, wait for you to pass. I don't want to come in.)

In 1847 Dr. Cornelius Danielssen and Carl Wilhelm Boeck published their *Atlas of Leprosy,* a color-illustrated volume of changes that occur in human faces.

For years they kept detailed notes: "Duration of illness—4 to 5 years. Suffered great pain during shepherding, principally early in Spring whereupon the illness broke out in the form of many blisters on his feet. Both corneas are scarred. Eyebrows gone, facial skin evenly infected and thickened, purplish-blue hue chiefly on the brow. Many small reddish-brown nodules on the hands and feet. Much lack of sensation."

In 1873 Dr. Armauer Hansen of Norway identified the bacillus now known as *Mycobacterium leprae.* Shortly afterward, leprosy was renamed Hansen's disease.

Today, a single dose of Rifampicin, Clofazimine, or Dapsone can kill 99.9% of the bacteria.

Only half of those who are ill have access to these drugs.

(It seems there are so many forms of prison, slavery, deprivation.)

(When Ai Tai To wandered off, he didn't say where he was going. Hands numb, feet blistered, toes mushroom-shaped and sore, he walked out of the known world, leaving the state, power, privilege, behind him. Did he go to where no one would look into his face, where he wouldn't meet, not ever, the face of another? Where he fed himself from trees, streams, maybe a small garden? What I think of most isn't the deformity of his face or hands or feet, but the silence that accompanied him, the lack of explanation. The silence that he left behind.)

{ DREAM OF THE RED CHAMBER }

Dear Father,

I write to you from a small village northwest of Peking, at the foot of Xiangshan Hill. Of course you'll never read this. It's over 3 years since I left without saying goodbye or letting you know I'd be leaving and where I might go (I hardly knew myself). Most likely you think I'm dead.

My home is made of mud bricks and the roots of reeds. The roof is thatched straw supported by branches of cypress and pine. When I wake I see their inscrutable language arching above me, rough and lovely. My floor is dirt. The house is all one room.

In spring the dust-storms blow in. "Shachenbao" they're called. They cover everything with a fine pale layer of grit. Streets, houses, tools, utensils. Animals walk as if veiled, their eyes red and swollen. Many stumble pathetically through the fields or spill into the streets, bumping into carts and doorways. In fall the round leaves of the smoke trees on the hill turn a brilliant red.

Maybe if you hadn't tried so hard to keep me from books I'd have come to love them less. I've found, hidden in a wall of my house, a rolled sheaf of thousands of pages written in black ink, mostly in a careful yet vigorous hand. I spend my days reading it, wondering what it is and how it got here. It's divided into 120 sections, and as far as I can tell, 80 are written in one hand—the hand I just mentioned—the remaining 40 in another. There's red writing in between the lines, and some at the tops and bottoms of pages, some in the margins. A curious thing. I've started to wonder if the writer died part way through and another took up the brush to finish his work. Or perhaps the writer grew too ill to hand-write it himself, and so spoke it from the plain straw mat that was his bed while another faithfully recorded his words. Or could this be a copy transcribed from an original now lost, or a copy of a copy?

I have no idea how long it lay hidden in the wall, or how and why it came to be there. When I read it's as if something torn in me stings slightly less.

Your son,
Henry Clerval

Clerval sleeps and I watch him from whatever this distance is that makes me what I am. My mind moves close to him, as if I could touch his sallow cheek. Always I love to watch him rising at first light, rolling up his narrow mat, spooning tea leaves into the pot to steep, then sitting down with his manuscript to read. Sometimes he washes his few clothes, hangs them on the line to dry.

I know so little of him, this man who was your friend and tended you through fevers. Sometimes I imagine him caring for me too, his kindness a mysterious wind against my skin. Maybe it's his aloneness I've come to love, how he moves within a world of silence, and in that silence there are words, his hand so often writing.

The writing in his notebook is clear and small and clean:

> There's a certain consolation, perhaps, in patterns of thought, as though they are intricate muscle fibers, networks of living tissue all their own—

> Ever since that strange man, Morrison, told me of Lady Su Hui's *Xuan Ji Tu Shi,* I knew I must come here (though truly I wanted to come east for as long as I can remember). It's a poem composed of 841 characters woven into a five-colored tapestry and arranged in a perfect square. Reading it, there's no need to start at the beginning or move straight to the end. Instead, it can be entered anywhere. Any cluster of characters forms a living pattern, a poem. It's said there are at least 3,752 possible poems within its borders. What would it mean to get lost in such a place? Or would being lost become an anachronism, an impossibility? One coherent place leading to another coherent place . . .

> Of Lady Su Hui little is known. Some speculate she composed the poem to win back her wayward husband. Many say she succeeded. Sewing those patient, intricate patterns must have taken her many years.

> I'm not a sentimental man. I don't imagine her in her chamber, longing for him, late 4th century A.D. Patterns are radical desire. They are, perhaps, an expedition.

> And so I'm here. Yet oddly I no longer wish to find that poem. I've found in the wall of my home a sheaf of pages. My expedition has already

taken an unexpected turn. Often before falling asleep, I imagine the lonely man who wrote them, his scaffolding of blood vessels and bones a shadow-grid over my own.

That strange man, Morrison, who I first met by chance on the street in London, and who taught me Chinese, I wonder what he'd think. When he first came here, he dressed in Chinese costume, wore a fake pigtail, let his fingernails grow long. Spoke only to his Chinese tutor, avoided contact with the wealthy, read Horace, Pope, and Dryden while translating 26 books of the Old Testament into Mandarin. Now he's back in London, having founded a language institute, wearing a gray suit, a fellow of the Royal Society.

I want never to leave here.

I have only just begun reading the pages I found in this wall—

Each day I wake to them, as if, like Lady Su Hui, they'll show me a pattern I can enter, a place where, no matter how much I wander, I'll somehow not get lost—

When you fled you left your laboratory notes behind. Though I carry them with me, mostly I have no desire to see your handwriting in front of my eyes (it pains me to see it). But once, as I unpacked my few things in the woods, a note from Clerval slipped out from your papers, and I read it:

My friend, I know you're suffering and wish there was more I could do to bring you comfort. I still worry about your fever, though I know it's much better. I worry about the tremor in your hands, the look in your eyes I find troubling but hard to describe, the way you stay always alone (though I myself mostly prefer to be alone). Sometimes I think you've mistaken my tenderness for a kind of frailty, some central flaw, an inability to face the harsher aspects of who you are. But I'm less foolish than you think. We've known each other from before I can even remember—an intimacy such as ours becomes almost a separate creature, composed of cells we can't see or hardly fathom. Maybe in some ways we are simply each other's native tongue. Caxton wrote in Sonnes of Amyon, "It is sayd, that at the end a frende is known." I don't believe this. I understand you're unknowable to me. Still, I'd have liked to comfort you. Now I've decided to go east—it's what I've wanted for so long. I've told no one, just you. I wish to live out my life among books, even those written in a language I don't yet understand. I plan to find a teacher in London, then make my way to China. I hope never to return. Your friend always, Henry Clerval

I hadn't known a human being could sound like that. He used the words "comfort" and "tenderness." He called you "My friend." Nights I'd lie in the woods thinking only that I wished I could see him, and wondered, if he saw me, what might he think? Would he flee from me like you did? But he wrote those words . . . I imagined him not fleeing.

Now I watch his slender fingers turning pages, the way he's careful with each one, and a feeling almost of peacefulness comes into me.

Sometimes I imagine he left that note for me, not you. And that, along with *Sonnes of Amyon* (I have since read many books) he also knew this line from Turner, "rais'd by the Comfort of The Sunne to water dry and barren grounds."

Clerval rubs his eyes idly with his hands, gets up for a cup of water or to make tea. He's been reading for hours. Mostly he stays very still, as if the words coming into his eyes demand of him great stillness, the way a harbor needs to be calm for its ships. Often he goes nearly a whole day without eating.

———•———

Already noon-light streams in from the small window. I feel like I've been in my chair for a few minutes, but it's been hours.

Never have I read such a curious book. As if the pages were turning to vapor in my hands—I can't get a proper hold. Every time I think I've found a steady voice to guide me, it complicates itself, fractures or leaves and is replaced by other voices (though it's true the first voice eventually comes back).

The first chapter begins: "This is the opening chapter of the novel. In writing this, the author wanted to recall certain of his past dreams and illusions." This is written in the same hand as the paragraphs that follow, in which the author, now speaking in first person, says, "Though my home is now a thatched cottage with matting windows, earthen stove and bed of straw, this shall not stop me from laying bare my heart."

So who's speaking? And why this shift from third person to first? (This book seems to have many beginnings.)

I've learned the author is Cao Xueqin, who exiled himself to the outskirts of Peking. These papers I've found in the wall are one of several handwritten copies of his novel, though no two are exactly alike.

Some say he wrote all the pages himself. Some say he found a rough version of it on a stone and spent ten years studying, transcribing and rewriting what he found there, revising it five times before he died, his work uncompleted. Others say he wrote 80 chapters, and the bookseller Gao E got hold of them and wrote the rest, setting the whole in moveable type, then publishing it to great acclaim in 1791.

It's called the *Dream of the Red Chamber.*

Interspersed throughout the text are signed commentaries by as many as ten people. In my copy, the one who writes the most is Red Inkstone.

Yet some say Red Inkstone is really just another name for Cao Xueqin. Could this be?

Who was the solitary man who wrote day after day about the fate of a neglected stone? Who saw the smoke trees turn red on the hillside, the dust whirl in from the north . . . Who had not one name, but many. And no clear date of birth (1715? 1724?) or date of death (1762? 1763? 1764?). Who lay on his straw and dreamed of a child who vanishes during the Festival of Lanterns, never to return. Who dreamed of conflagrations, absences, illnesses, betrayals, the corrupt power of the state. Who transformed himself into a novel and the commentary on that novel—a labyrinth, a web, a puzzle. Who insisted he wanted only to bring pleasure, as he ate less and less, and slept on his rough mat, and grew a stranger to the ones who'd known him.

Long after Clerval packs up his reading for the day, slipping the pages back into the slit in the wall where he stores them, I linger over them in my mind, read the working notes he's left on his table. As if they could bind me to him, myself, anything. Or are they harbors where the ice has finally melted so boats can set sail from them again?

Today he translated this passage:

> "When Nu Wa-shi fused the rocks to repair the heavens, she took 36,501 stones of enormous size from Wu Ji Peak among the Da Huang Hills. She used 36,500 of these, and then the one solitary stone which she rejected as useless was thrown to the foot of Qing Geng Peak. Strange to relate, after its ordeal the stone acquired spiritual understanding. It was conscious. It lamented in shame and distress day and night, desolate that it had been rejected. With its magical powers, it could expand or contract, move and change shape, but nothing could heal its sorrow as it lay on the ground no larger than a lady's fan."

The stone falls to earth in the form of a boy, Jia Baoyu, who's born with a piece of clear jade in his mouth. It will suffer and be changed. It will feel human hands on it and kiss human mouths. But what is it, really? Is it a stone, a boy, part of each, or neither? Should I call it "it" or "he"? I think of its solitary fall, how the others were used but it wasn't used.

Some say that stone is no other than Cao Xueqin who called himself a "useless wretch," yet wrote of "the waving willows, the bright moon, the fresh breeze of morning," and said, "these are still mine." Who, as he turned from the world, still wanted the world. But maybe even that can't be assumed.

Last light. Clerval finishes his bowl of noodles, washes his dish. Soon he'll sleep on his straw mat as once I lay on mine, wondering if you'd come back, then knowing you never would.

Cao Xueqin, who were you? Each day I translate your pages. I sleep and dream I'm a stone found in the mouth of a newborn boy. I dream I'm the stolen girl sold into servitude who when asked years later, aren't you the daughter of _____, can only shake her lowered head and say, "I can't remember." I'm the young nun from Water Moon Convent, and the maid stirring ashes in her mistress's hand-stove. And I'm old Gardener Ye, designing acres of artificial mountains and lakes, pavilions, rockeries, balustrades, all for one wealthy family. I'm the shamed servant girl who drowns herself in the well.

And I'm none of them. I walk among them in my mind, a stranger, a cipher, a man helpless as a doctor writing prescriptions that don't work. Often in your book someone is mysteriously ailing, unable to eat, fading for no earthly reason—the pulse weak, but why? A girl crouches among pomegranate petals, crying, scratching at the dirt with a hairpin but I don't know why. Another buries peach blossoms in the garden. So many private rituals and sorrows—pieces of paper hidden away, paper that's written on then burned or crumpled, paper passed from one stealthy hand to another.

Many think you saw all this as a boy in a rich household with vast gardens where you lived.

But the mind travels far from what it's thought of as itself, from anywhere.

Often you point out there are parts of the story you won't tell: "With that he left, but where he went does not concern us." "The rest of the room need not be described in detail."

So it's as if I have blinders on even as I translate. Even in my clearest moments I must look through a thickening mist.

And still I follow you into that house, that garden, that world with its wealthy family and nearly a thousand servants. I think of you sleeping on your straw mat by the end. Poor. Maybe even in this house where I found these pages. Here in this small village where animals stumble blindly through dust, and my hand trembles from tiredness.

"The rest cannot be recorded," you wrote. And: "easier to unravel a skein of tangled hemp than to recount this." "The rest of the inscriptions cannot be recorded here."

Even among so many, many words, this sense of what's not knowable, not shared—

Sometimes I train my breath—rhythmic, slow—to match Clerval's own. But it seems his body's turning into words, there's no way I can stop it. He translates all day, his hand cramping, ink trailing fine lines on the paper, leaving blotches on his wrist and palm.

Last night I was a stone the size of a sparrow's egg found in the mouth of a newborn boy. I was iridescent as clouds. The boy wore me on a string around his neck so wherever he went I went with him. It was strange to be thought beautiful, for everyone to want to touch me. Yet I didn't feel at ease. I was a stone that had fallen to earth, but from where? I couldn't remember. Then it seemed the stone wasn't me but Clerval. He felt such sorrow at not having hands, there was no way for him to translate. Then Clerval was also Claire, or was he Fanny or myself or Mary—or were we all a tangled braid of hemp, each bound to the other, inseparable from one another?

Still, I remember that feeling of not being ugly, and how so many hands reached out to touch me.

Clerval   Claire   Claireval

Father,

I've just returned from Canton. Why do I even tell you this? Why do I write to you at all (though I won't send a single letter)? You who wanted a practical son, a businessman, someone who would move among well-appointed rooms, not this mud and brick rectangle with its uneven dirt floor.

In Canton, a second city of water exists beside the one on land. (This is the kind of place I dreamed of as a boy.) Nearly 300,000 people live on boats, their entire lives spent on canals and rivers. There's always the hush of dipping oars and steering-sculls—a faint, continuous breathing beneath the other, broken sounds.

The ones on water are despised by those on land. They're never allowed to draw near shore.

Almost everything on land has its counterpart on water. Doctors practice from slender sampans, barbershops drift by. Police boats arrive with shrill calls from conch shells. I saw a whole world of businesses thriving on water—fleets of oil boats, rice boats, boats carrying sugarcane and bean curd, boats hauling salt, crockery, clothing, others filled with flowering plants.

(As I write I can almost feel you drifting away. You always grew impatient with my stories which you found frivolous, indulgent. I should get back to my translating, I have so many pages left to go, over a thousand . . .)

But I'm thinking of the leper boats, hundreds of them filled with the afflicted who marry, beg, have children, grow old and die out on the water.

Outside the city, there's one leper village on dry land, a walled enclosure on the edge of the graveyard called Silent City. There, the afflicted make ropes out of cocoa-nut fiber and bring them to the rope-market to sell. I don't know why they're allowed to go there but they are. Some of the wealthier ones buy wives from healthy families. And there are many children in the village, some afflicted, some not. I still see an almost-faceless woman with a broken rice-bowl begging for money. I see the slave girl who was told by her owner that if she kept a silver coin in her mouth her new owners wouldn't suspect she was diseased. But of course they found out and threatened to drown her in the river.

When I was making my way east, I made a friend in Italy, a leper. About that, Father, I'm not willing to speak to you.

Still, I thought of him in Canton. I think of him when I get up in the morning and when I go to bed at night. I think of him when I translate and when I dress and make my tea.

It's said that lepers don't suffer any pain, only numbness. Often a paralysis of the face ensues. The body dismantles itself bit by bit. And yet the mind, what of the mind?

It's late now. Time to stop. No need to sign what I won't send.

My Friend,

By the time you read this I'll be dead. There's a man here who'll make his way to China within the next few years. He's agreed to take these letters to you. I think often of that day when you passed accidentally through the gate near the tower in which I live. There, in the garden, you extended your gloved hand to me before you left. It had been fifteen years since I'd felt, even through cloth, another's touch. I still wonder why you weren't afraid.

You had come to see the ruins of the 15th century castle where René of Chalans is said to have starved to death his wife, Marie of Braganza. Hunger Tower it's called, and many claim to see on dark nights the white-clad figure of a woman holding a lamp between her hands, but I think this is nonsense.

The hospital of Saint Maurice still supplies me with food and books and clothing. A messenger comes once a week to drop them off. Other than that I see no one. I tend my garden and read.

I wonder what you've found in China. That day you took my hand and we talked for hours, two strangers, when you asked me to write to you, I refused.

There's something called the "Mass of Separation." Do you know of it? It's a medieval mass spoken by a priest and performed at the site of a leper's dwelling. This is part of what it said: "I forbid you to touch the rim or the rope of a well, I forbid you to share your house, I forbid you to touch any child or give anything to a child, I forbid you to eat or drink in any company but lepers, I forbid you to leave your house without your leper's costume or your bell."

Still, I write to you. My garden's doing well. But I think it's too pristine—no one walks in it but me, there are no signs of the offhand, irregular life of another, a twig dropped idly or by accident, a piece of scrap paper, a shopping list's ripped edge.

I want only to speak plainly to you. I don't know if I'll know how, or even what I mean by "plainly." I feel a distrust of words, a strong dislike of them even. Isn't any word an embellishment and covering over of something more precise and starker? Mostly I distrust myself. I think of you—

Your Friend

Clerval returns his letters to the shelf, pours himself some tea. He's not hungry, only tired. He straightens his papers, lies down on his narrow mat on the dirt floor, tries to sleep.

_____village

My friend,

Sometimes it seems almost everyone in this book I'm translating is falling ill or suffering in some way. So many of them are young and live in a beautiful garden and still they get sick. The boy, Baoyu, endures many terrible fevers and hallucinations; at one point he falls into a coma, lies unresponsive to any herbs, drugs or charm water. And Daiyu, the cousin whom he loves, is often racked with nightmares. She lies on her couch, too weak to sit or eat, her face turned to the wall. There are many prescriptions and remedies but they rarely seem to work. When Baoyu loses his precious jade for a while, things only get worse. He grows deranged and Daiyu dies. But even before that, as if each life were either the incarnation or the result of a faltering dynasty, a corrupt system that must re-make itself in greater understanding, so many of the young ones suffer: Baoyu's closest friend, Qin Zhong, dies of a sudden fever, the dismissed servant girl, Qingwen, "a mere nobody" as one of the household staff calls her, grows quiet and wastes away; dying, she gives her long fingernails as a keepsake to Baoyu. Jinchuan, the misunderstood maid, drowns herself in the well. "Don't take it too much to heart," the woman who wrongly accused her is told. "Just give her relatives some silver for her burial and you'll be doing all a kind mistress could." There are numerous bad omens as well, "The begonia at the foot of the steps was thriving, but then for no reason its branches withered."

Still, there are good times. They walk through the garden with its pathways and pavilions, its flowers with such untranslatable names as huona, shifan, luyi; and willows and hanging lanterns. They write poems, drink heated wine, watch operas. They dress in luxurious silks and cover their windows with rare "soft-mist silk" that comes only in four colors: light blue, russet, pine-green and pink; from a distance it looks like smoke or mist. And they eat many delicacies: lotus-foot cakes flavored with fragrant osmanthus, pine-kernel rolls, pigeon eggs, sweet and savory pastries shaped like peonies and swans.

Throughout there's a sense of precariousness, unease; this never ceases. I feel it beneath my skin as I translate, a wing slowly turning, a muted, threatening wind.

I write down these lives and think of you. How you kneel and weed in your garden, and pick up each weekly package left by your door. How you speak to no one. Always to no one. I don't want to believe that you're dead. Each night I hold one of your letters in my hand. Wooden carts clank along the street, and every now and then there's the sound of a bell, crickets chirping from their bamboo cages. I wonder what you hear. Church bells? Children playing outside your garden wall?

The more I translate the more the world grows strange. The author I'm translating, Cao Xueqin, often interjects into the text a sense of withholding: "the rest need not be enumerated here," or "no more of this," or "but we can't know all that he was feeling." So I've increasingly come to feel the silence embedded in each word, and I go to sleep and wake up with that silence, that presence of the unsayable—as you and I are unsayable—among all the many words.

Your friend, as ever,
Clerval

My Friend,

Month by month the sensation in my hands grows weaker. Sometimes when I pick up a cup it clatters to the floor. I no longer know with what firmness to grasp things, how to gauge the correct pressure brought to bear. Maybe I shouldn't write of such things, but I said I would speak plainly, and if I spoke only of the beauty of my garden I wouldn't be speaking to you at all.

Yesterday after my morning's weeding I read parts of the Purgatorio again. Virgil rinsed the dirt from Dante's face and plucked a smooth green reed from the soil (as Cato had instructed) which he wound around his pupil's waist. Such a tender gesture, small and clear and simple, yet somehow I hadn't noticed it before.

"And there he made me clean," Dante said. The mud was soft, the reed supple. So much ugliness behind them. Then they saw how the proud must carry great stones on their backs, and not walk upright but creep doubled over, and how the envious are the color of a bruise.

I don't dream much, but that night I dreamed I wore a medieval leper's costume and carried a wooden clapper. My hat was brown and wide-brimmed; a piece of gauze around its rim covered my whole face. When I looked through it everything was inscribed with fine, minute hatchings. I didn't mind them, really—it was as if I was looking through a microscope's lens, everything more specific and enlarged—the only bad part was that it all seemed slightly unreal, removed. With each step I shook my clapper as was required.

But the odd part was that, as in old illuminated manuscripts, a holy man came near to heal me (he had me kneel before him as he reached out with his right hand to place two fingers on my head) but I got up and walked away. Why would I do such a thing? Why wouldn't I have wanted to be healed?

I think of you in China. I wonder what species of flowering plants you're seeing, what names they have for them, what uses they might be put to, medicinal or ornamental. I wonder what kind of house you live in and what you do with your days.

From my window I can see a long white chain, its links soft and unbroken. Tomorrow should bring a little rain, which will be good for the garden.

I think of you with fondness.

Your Friend,

Clerval sits at his desk barely moving, head lowered, mouth closed, his friend's letter beside him. What would I see in his eyes if I could see them? When his hands begin to stir, he gently folds his friend's letter, turns his face to the window, wipes his forehead, starts to write:

When I first began translating these pages, it didn't occur to me so many characters would suffer from the cold. After all, there are many luxurious flowers in the garden, such a sense of what is <u>tended</u>. Yet the Lady Dowager's servant brings her a hand-stove as she sits in her black sedan chair sheltered by a black umbrella, or reclines on her kang. Daiyu writes, "Snow covers the broom of the monk up on the hill," and coughs ceaselessly, can't stand the slightest chill. Each day she drinks a tonic of bird's nest boiled in gruel. It's made from the purest snow-water from Moon Crescent Nunnery; she can't tolerate anything else, and she never eats cold things. " 'There,' Xueyan said with a laugh, 'that will carry away her illness,' and with a pair of small silver Western scissors clipped the cord tied to the reel. The kite drifted away until soon it seemed no bigger than an egg, then dwindled to a speck like a black star . . ." But Daiyu doesn't get well. The narrator comments, "The longing to be close ends in estrangement." Snow falls and falls. They move through rooms called Pear Fragrance, Happy Red Court, Bamboo Lodge, but all the while something shivers deep inside them. All the while the Great Waste Mountain that Baoyu fell from as a stone casts its shadow near them. "The jade hairpin is broken, the red candle cold," is the answer to one riddle.

> on Beggar's Bridge the crowds of poor standing, sitting, crawling, holding out their hands as I pass, my hands in my pockets, my white hands—

> Father, what would you think of all I see?

<u>WORKING NOTES FOR DRC:</u>

~~the name Zhen Shiyin is a homophone for "true facts concealed"

~~the name Jia Hua is a homophone for "false talk" (Cao Xueqin is very fond of such names)

~~there's a practice in which rich families pay poor families' sons to be priests or monks in their stead in order to ward off evil

~~the following lines that Daiyu recites are from "The Western Chamber":

> What a riot of brilliant purple and tender crimson
> Among the ruined wells and crumbling walls

So many books inside this book. I wonder what my friend in Aosta would think—

Aosta, May 31

My Friend,

When you were here and we sat face to face for those few hours, you asked me to speak of my illness and its history but I refused. But yesterday I wrote to you about my hands, and today as I sit down to write I'm thinking about the lepers of Gloskar.

The island was desolate. "Small and lonely," many called it, and in November 1651, it was chosen as the hospital site for the lepers of Aland. About sixteen were taken by boat to their new home: two cabins alongside a cattle byre and bakehouse. The warden's house stood some distance away.

The winters were very harsh and the cabins very quickly began to fall apart. There was no money to fix them. Cattle walked on snowdrifts high as roofs, and trampled the roofs of sheds to pieces. About a third of the patients died every year, most between November and April, and every year new patients arrived. Each year they petitioned Aland's sheriff for firewood but were refused. Instead, they uprooted the island's juniper bushes, used them until the land was bare. One day some set out in search of wood on other islands but their boat became trapped by ice floes and capsized. Somehow they managed to get back home and in milder months used the boat to ferry their cattle to pasture on outlying islands. They'd tend the cows each morning and night, then return to the island with fresh milk, the one thing they could manage for themselves.

(As I write this, I think of the way we're so anxious to picture their skin, their hands, whatever deformities we associate with this illness, but their voices are silent. Silent even to me who shares their disease. Why don't we think of their voices? Of what they said or what they read. Of a hunger that felt like any other hunger. Or of their names. Or of what they did hour by hour with their days.)

The warden pleaded to be released, but the authorities wouldn't allow it. Finally, after five years, the hospital was closed. Imagine the remaining patients traveling in a wobbly chain of small boats over the sea. They were taken to another, farther island where no one spoke their language, where they understood nothing at all. The warden wrote to the king of Sweden, "I carried out my service in frost and cold. In autumn and spring I was often trapped in sea-ice. Thus have I now become an ailing man."

I think of their voices. Of the way I can't hear them. The way I can see the ice floes, cattle, roofs, but not a single individual face, not really.

Last night it rained as I thought it would.

Your Friend,

Clerval hunches over his writing table making lists of medicinal herbs he hopes to someday send to his friend. *For my leper,* he writes, and then, *but why do I say "my" and with what arrogance, what presumption?* Then crosses it all out. *But I don't know his name, he never told me his name*

He writes to his friend who has no name, or no name he can know, and I live out my life without a name. Sometimes I still marvel that you gave me no name, though of course it makes sense—I was nothing you wanted.

The window's darkening. He's writing *Daiyu* over and over, then crossing it out.

Daiyu   Dai   yu   die/you/I   I/You

Then:

> I want to know what happens to Miaoyu, the young nun from Sakyamuni Convent who calls herself "The One Outside the Threshold." She lives in poverty, keeps to herself, refuses to shave her head, gives plum blossoms to Baoyu. Widely read and well versed in the sutras, she's come to the capital to see the relics of Guanyin.

> There are so many people and stories in this novel it's hard to keep track. Still, when I lie down I think of Miaoyu and how she holds herself apart, refers to herself sometimes as "The Odd One."

> My Friend in Aosta, could he also sign his name "The One Outside the Threshold"?—he who must never pass his garden walls.

I think of the violence inside the word *threshold*. "To trample, to tread," my book says.

To enter a house one must cross a threshold, so is there violence in the very entering? As there's violence in the many thresholds of the mind . . . Those first days after you left me I grew afraid of my thoughts as I watched distant windows, human shapes lit and shadowy behind them, sometimes touching, sometimes not.

What thresholds does Miaoyu keep herself away from in the world and in her mind? If she stays apart from Baoyu's world, if she won't step across *that* threshold, are there still others she must cross?

Is it possible never to cross or enter at all?

(She keeps her hair long, lives in poverty, stays to herself.)

"The One Outside the Threshold." I'm nameless. Could that be my name?

<u>from Chapter 17—</u>

"If not for this hill," observed Jia Zheng, "one would see the whole garden as soon as one entered, and how tame that would be."

My Friend,

I've been reading Marco Polo's Travels, *also known as* The Description of the World. *I who travel nowhere travel in this way. Sometimes in my mind I walk up to your door, raise my hand to knock. If it's winter when you read this, do you carry in your wide Chinese sleeves the tiny brass stoves I've read of? Do you hear the bells that hang from the necks of donkeys and camels laden with goods: bags of rice flour, tea, and the hard compound of clay and coal dust made up into tight balls that serves as fuel? Have you seen the great stone pagoda thirteen stories high, its four doors facing north, south, east and west that can only be reached by long ladders? At night when you dream, what country are you in? Or have such boundaries and categories dissolved—shape-shifted and redefined themselves in ways I can't begin to know? (My garden walls, my weekly package at the door . . .)*

Marco Polo wrote his book in prison. He dictated it to his cell-mate Rustichello, their voices traveling back and forth, weaving, diverging, intertwining. I think of those four walls that meant so little and so much. There, not there.

Though I'll never hear from you, my friend, tell me of the open-air cook shops, of the Monastery of the Azure Clouds, its temple with 3,200 small gilt images inside. Tell me of the old men kneading brass balls in their hands, of paper lanterns, and of the houses of the poor where there are no lanterns, only wicks floating in bowls of dirty oil.

The Mass of Separation decreed a leper must have "a hood and cloak, his own plain shoes, and clappers." He should have "two pairs of sheets, a cup, a funnel, a small knife and plate." He should "never go through a narrow lane lest he might meet someone."

Though I carry no clapper or bell I often hear one as I walk. I feel the rough hood on my forehead, the weight of the cloak on my shoulder-bones, my arms. The garden path's very still in this sunlight. Not one petal has fallen onto it today. Not one leaf.

I think of you with affection—

Your Friend,

......If I had a wooden clapper, a hood . . .

Iron Threshold   Steamed-Bread   Luminous Clouds
Temple   Convent   Studio

Pear Fragrance Court   Wasp-Waist Bridge

PRESCRIPTION (from chapter 10)

Ginseng	.2 oz
Atractylis (clay baked)	.2 oz
Pachyma cocos	.3 oz
Prepared Ti root	.4 oz
Aralia edulis (cooked in wine)	.2 oz
White peony (cooked)	.2 oz
Szechuan selenium	.15 oz
Sophora tomentosa	.3 oz
Cyperus rotundus	.2 oz
Gentian soaked in vinegar	.08 oz
Dioscorea from the Huai region (cooked)	.2 oz
Genuine Tung-ngo glue (prepared with powdered oyster shell)	.2 oz
Corydalis ambigua (cooked in wine)	.15 oz
Dried licorice	.08 oz

Take with seven Fujian lotus seeds with
the pits extracted, and two large red dates

Clerval puts down his pen but leaves the paper on the table. *Corydalis ambigua.* I wonder what that is, the shape and color of its root, its stem?—ambiguity built into its very core.

"Admitting more than one interpretation or explanation," my dictionary says of *ambiguity,* and "of double or several possible meanings." "Of dubious classification or position." Isn't that like me?

It also means "being on the boundary line." I remember Claire asking what liberty is. She didn't want to be ruled by boundaries, didn't want to be ashamed of her own mind.

And there's: "wavering, uncertain in tendency or direction." As your face remains uncertain to me—an underwater face—drifting, mysterious, undisclosed.

My Friend,

My mind swarms with soft mud and supple reeds, cattle walking on roofs, harsh winters of Gloskar—everything you've written me. Though I mean never to leave here, and know I'll never see you again.

My days are simple. I translate the Dream of the Red Chamber. In the evenings I write letters that I'll never send. To you, and a couple to my father. Sometimes I travel.

You write of the clear path in your garden. In the Dream of the Red Chamber there are often many petals on the ground: "strewn with balsam and pomegranate petals" reads one passage, and elsewhere there are peach and plum blossoms, fallen rose and azalea petals. One day, near Seeping Fragrance Lock, Baoyu comes upon Daiyu gathering up whole handfuls of petals, burying them in the ground. "I've a grave for flowers in that corner over there," she says. Another time, walking in the rain, he hears crying and peers through a trellis to see a girl kneeling among fallen rose petals, digging with her hairpin in the dirt. "Can this be another absurd maid come to bury flowers like Daiyu?" he wonders. "She must have some secret preying on her mind. She looks too delicate to be out in this rain." Often in this novel people do small ceremonial things in secret: bury flowers, burn minute scraps of red paper, write words in the dirt, cry while handling delicate keepsakes wrapped in silk.

I've been thinking about one passage I just translated. It's from Zhuangzi, whose book, in chapter 21, Baoyu has been reading. It's called "The House Breaker." I'll write some of it out for you below:

> "Confuse the musical scales, break harps and lutes, stop the
> ears of good musicians, and all men under heaven will learn
> to hear for themselves. Dispense with ornaments and colored
> patterns, glue up the eyes of the keen-sighted, and all men
> under heaven will learn to see for themselves. Destroy
> quadrants and yard-measures, throw away compasses and
> squares, cut off the fingers of old deft artisans, and all men
> under heaven will learn skill for themselves. Burn tallies and
> seals and the people will revert to their natural simplicity.
> Break measures and scales and they will no longer quarrel.
> Abolish all the sacred laws of the world and the people will
> discuss things freely."

So you see, my friend, I wonder what Zhuangzi would think about your cloak, your hood, your clapper, the sound it makes inside your mind.

It's dry as dust here. Each day I wipe from my pillow a fine layer of grime.

Your Friend, as always,
Clerval

When I think of the way Clerval and his friend hold and comfort each other in their minds (even though they never speak, and Clerval won't even send his letters) I wonder how it feels to be welcome within the mind of another, to believe another's mind will take you in. What if Locke was mistaken and words aren't a covering, a cloth made of wrongness?

Sometimes lying awake, I feel a pair of small hands beside me, lingering, waiting. How can I explain this? Yours were large and harsh. But these are more like the hands of the sad servant girl in Cao Xueqin's book, or the girl who was kidnapped and can no longer remember her name. They're waiting, but for what? I think they want something to lift up to the eyes of the body they belong to, something I can give them, but I don't know what it is. And those eyes—would they be partly trusting and willing, partly not, like Clerval's friend? Then my chest tenses, my eyesight goes wavy, the night's suddenly cold again and vacant.

Aosta, June 23

My Friend,

I confess I think much about my left hand these days.

*Do I speak to you as from behind a hood, a cloak, and in my hand a
warning bell, a clapper?*

*Do you listen to me as from behind a wall where the air is safe, your
breathing safe?*

*If you'd stayed here would you have come to fear me? Would I have
recoiled from you, preferring the petty study of this festering burn on
my left hand that troubles me because I can't feel it at all or figure out
when or how I even got it?*

*When I first wrote to you my pen didn't hesitate along the page; I
didn't worry over what I was saying or how. I don't know why or how
that happened. But now something else has come into me, a feeling of
recoil. I picture your face. Then I picture your face turned away. As if
I need for you to turn away. Why would I do this?*

*I think of my garden wall, of all the earth's many, many walls. Walls
with leper's windows, the Great Wall of China. I search for them in
my Atlas at night. Walls for protecting towns, for fortresses, for farms,
for fields, for keeping back the sea.*

*This morning I read the Purgatorio again. That passage where the
Envious sit with eyes wired shut, "eyelids pierced and sewn with iron
wires, as men sew new-caught falcons, sealing their eyes to make them
settle down." I think I was an envious person once. And yet, when I
think now of the people outside these walls, the ones I often envied
as a boy and for years after, I don't really envy them anymore. But
shouldn't my envy have grown greater, not less, given what's befallen
me? Shouldn't I want to be like them, want to take from them what's
theirs, resent them for what they still have? Yet I watch as from a
great distance, a place I'll never return from, a gap composed of space
and time. A tenderness, a certain feeling of protectiveness even, comes
over me—for the ones I think of and the small, vulnerable dailiness of
their lives. I once saw a woman with terribly skinny arms; the sharp,
elongated bones seeming almost to poke through, and I think of each
and every one of them like those arms—so easily breakable, so fragile.*

A MONSTER'S NOTES · 221

I want them to go to the market and be all right, to laugh with each other and talk over dinner and play with their children and go to their jobs and have celebrations and longings and dreams and plans and be all right. I don't envy them or hate them. I can't say if they just seem unreal to me now, part of something I can never touch or be part of again. I don't know. But I think of their fragility, always of their fragility, even the obnoxious and the rich ones, the ones I can't stand, the ones who eat too much and wear too many rings.

I shouldn't have written you about my hand. I wonder if you found that poem you spoke of when you were here, the one you felt you could wander in forever. The one the woman wove for her husband.

My garden is doing well.

Your Friend,

My Friend, each time I translate a prescription from the Dream of the Red Chamber I think of you. These prescriptions that mostly sound crazy but seduce me all the same with their promises of improvement or cure (I think of your hand now and wonder how you are).

But Zhuangzi didn't speak of cures. He said destroy, said throw away, said ~~dispense with, break, cut off the finger of the deft, glue up the eyes, destroy and throw away. He didn't say mend or heal or repair or build or straighten. He didn't say make orderly or clean or~~

I can't write this to you. Can't write anything to you.

"Destroy quadrants and yard-measures, throw away compasses and squares."

Destroy and throw away. Glue up the eyes. (but beneath my shut eyes your scarred face) (your scarred face still with me even if you need to turn away)

~~*and destroy*~~   ~~*and destroy*~~

Translation Notes for the Prescription Explained by Baochai to Mrs. Zhou in Chapter 7

"You must take 12 drams (?) of rain gathered only on the day called Rain Begins." (I think this is February 20th, must check)

"But what if it doesn't rain on that day?" Mrs. Zhou asked.

"Then you just have to wait. You must try the next year or the next."

My Friend, the day's over and I haven't written to you. I don't even know if you're alive. You write of tenderness, of fragility, of sewn eyelids, blinded eyes. Of the Mass of Separation, and of walls. I, too, sometimes dream of a clapper and a hood. I haven't told you of all the hands on Beggar's Bridge. You write of Virgil's tender gesture. Of Dante and Virgil walking together. I imagine us walking like they did. Where would we go? Would we speak or walk in silence, or both? I'm used to my straw bed now. I remember the narrow winding lane that leads to your house with its tower and garden. I remember how you said you never touched the

flowers you'd sometimes leave for the man who delivered your packages,
fearing you might contaminate him, but held them only between scissors,
then dropped them onto paper laid out on the stone steps.

I think of you—

Your Friend,
Clerval

I'm thinking about how Clerval's friend in Aosta dreamed he didn't want to be healed, didn't stay on his knees but got up and walked away. And for a moment—but why?—your face loses its power in my mind.

Each day I wait for Clerval, fear what I would be without this watching, my eyes emptied of his tired face, his hands, fingers gently smoothing his friend's letters.

He picks up another letter. It's late, he's worked all day turning characters into words. *Shan* is mountain, the surname *bao* means "to carry in the arms." There are so many nuances, complex histories, allusions—how can he ever get them right? *Qiao* means happy coincidence. *Ge* is boy. "Doesn't grass turn into glow-worms?" Daiyu asks, and he notes that she's referring to the *Book of Rites* which says, "Rotting grass turns into glow-worms." And what is this thing called *The Beauty in the Snow?*—it's a painting by Qiu Ying. So much to know and he knows so very little. I can see from his notes that often he considers giving up. But what would his days be without Baoyu and Daiyu, their pavilions, flowers, glowing lanterns, the many secret dramas, the servants who don't own their own lives, the meddling Lady Dowager, the decline of families and empire, scandals, thwarted loves, the prescriptions that make him think of his friend in Aosta? He knows he won't stop, that tomorrow he'll get up and look at the black and red characters in vertical lines down the page, and his hand will move slowly, horizontally, until his own page is filled, and then he'll move on to the next. All day until nightfall, and all the days he can envision after that.

Aosta, June 26

My Friend,

Do I write to you because you're at a safe remove from me? Because I know I'll never hear from you or see you? I've lived for decades with the daily knowledge of bodily contagion, but what of the contagion of the mind?—the danger of one voice answering another, contaminating, altering, needing another. Still, the recoil in oneself is inconstant, isn't it?—it surges forth, then slackens, gains force again then goes etc.

Now that you know about my hand, that my condition is worsening, I don't feel I need to hide things from you (though part of me still wants to) and I find that, at least at the moment, I don't resent that you know. Maybe because you're far away. Maybe because I know you can't tell me what you think. I don't need to live in fear of what you'd say. Nor can I be made uncomfortable by your possible desire to comfort me (which I would find painful and would very much dislike) if that were your impulse. Whatever your impulses are I can't know them. I comfort myself with this knowledge. So you see, my leper's hood, my leper's cloak, it's not that I've taken them off, it's not that I trust you or myself.

In any case, since I know you can picture my garden, let me tell you a little about my house. Though seeming completely isolated, it stands not too far from the Hospital of SS Maurice and Lazare and La Charité. I don't know if you realized this. It was purchased by order of the king and turned into a sanctuary before I ever arrived. I know little of the people who lived here before me as it's the custom to conceal their names, as my name is concealed. Some say they were a family by the name of Guasco, from the district of Nice. All of them afflicted with the same illness as mine. After the mother and youngest son died in Moncaliere, near Turin, the others were sent here. Soon there were only two survivors, a brother and sister. It's said they barely saw each other. They couldn't stand the sight of each other's loathsome affliction. Do you remember the part of my garden where a trellis is covered with climbing vines? It's said they met there from time to time, each on either side, to talk. The trellis kept them hidden from each other. Mostly the brother worked in the garden and walked on the terrace from which he could see distant glaciers, laborers in the fields. The sister mostly stayed in her room, or sat under the shade of the walnut tree when she believed her brother was indoors. It's said she died first, that he lived on alone for many years. I don't know if any of this is true.

In Aosta my tower is known as The Leper's Tower. But this you probably know. The whole house was constructed from remnants of the old Roman wall.

Often I watch the distant glaciers. When I look up from the proper angle, I can see Mount Emilius and Mont Blanc. I wonder what you're seeing now? Sometimes I imagine you hunched over your table, translating, in a house where you live all alone, and a feeling of tenderness comes over me, a feeling I don't really want to feel. And yet I think of you with fondness. Of those hours we sat in my garden. Of the way you asked me to write to you, though you knew I would need, at least at first, to refuse.

Your Friend,

My Friend,

*You write to me of your home and I wish that I could write to you of
mine. But I'm not sure what my home is. Is it this mud-brick house in a
dusty village half the world away from the place of my birth? Or is it, as I
often think it is, this book, the Dream of the Red Chamber, which I live in
day and night or so it seems. I move among its gardens, its pathways,
intrigues, its many words and seasons. I listen to Baoyu and Daiyu, and
to their relatives and servants as they go on with their lives. But really it's
all strange to me—I am, and will always remain, an outsider.*

*There's a character in the book, Miaoyu, a young nun who calls herself
"The One Outside the Threshold." I find it very beautiful that she calls
herself this. She lives in poverty in Green Lattice Nunnery and refuses to
shave her head, though this is the required practice among nuns. She
learns to read and write, teaches characters to the poor, but lives mostly in
silence. Her tea is made with rain-water and snow gathered from plum
branches she keeps buried in a jar. If a valuable bowl comes into her
possession she gives it away. Everyone calls her "eccentric." By the end of
several thousand pages she comes to great sorrow . . . but I'm getting
ahead of myself . . .*

*"The One Outside the Threshold"—could this be your name? You speak of
your leper's hood, your cloak, of the contagion of body and mind. You
speak of the brother and sister who walked in the garden, never seeing
each other's face. Of the ones in town who you watch as from an
unbridgeable gap, a separateness as strong as the Great Wall. You who'll
never enter their world . . . who won't cross . . . The opening's closed to
you. And yet to be "Outside the Threshold"—surely there's a kind of
opening in that. Miaoyu felt this. She walked the woods alone, wrote
greetings on secret pieces of paper she tucked into walls. Combed her long
hair. Didn't want to be like the others, to have what they had, to think the
way they thought. Would you think I leave out too much pain and conflict
in my account of her? Or that she chose and you didn't choose? I wish you
could tell me, that your face were here before me (though I know this is
something you don't want).*

I think of you, and of the garden we talked in, the garden you tend—

*Your Friend, as ever,
Clerval*

What if what's distorted isn't so much my body as the space between us, the silence between us?

Watching the movement of Clerval's pen across the page (isn't this how he talks to himself, and to another far away?) a harsh wind suddenly stops—something pained and pliant unfolds in an air that won't kill it.

Clerval lies down on his narrow mat. And Claire—does she stand at her window in the snow? The young nun who calls herself "The One Outside the Threshold," is she writing secret notes in the woods?

Last night I dreamed I tended plants behind a garden wall. I was watering, clipping. Then I looked up and Clerval was standing before me extending his gloved hand. But I couldn't bear to take it. How many hours had I watched that slender hand, loved the angular bones of his face?—and still I couldn't touch him. When I looked down, the plants had burned red lesions into my hand.

His cloak's on fire, the fire must be spreading to his hood, he must feel it on his face, how can he not feel it on his face?

He won't talk to me at all.

I can't understand why it's not spreading. But it looks like it's not spreading. Still, the fire—it's so close to his face, leaping near his face—

We're in Canton. Today's the Festival of the Consolation of the Dead. We walk among the living, stick-like, hungry, even the arms of the young ones wrinkled and knobby. Beggar-spirits walk among us—those who've died in wars, famines, far-off countries, at sea . . .

There are rows of booths selling everything the dead might need—hats and garments, boots, shoes, eyeglasses, fans. Sugarplums, furniture, gold and silver money, opium and pipes. There are pawnbrokers' stalls and stalls for the changing of money.

Why did I bring him here, what did I think I was doing, he who is so quiet in his hood, and unprotected—

He walks in his coarse brown cloak among Buddhist monks in yellow robes and scarlet mantles, and Taoists in green satin brocaded with gold, tortoise-shell combs fastening their plaited, rolled-up hair.

(And I forbid you ever to go out without your leper's dress, that you may be unrecognized by others . . . I forbid you to leave your house unshod . . . I forbid you to answer anyone who questions you unless first you turn your face the other way . . . I forbid you to go into a market or a mill . . .)

(I forbid and I forbid.)

(And it is thus mandated that the leper will be provided with 2 sets of linens for his bed, and 2 pairs of woolen stockings and woolen gloves. He will be provided each year with 90 lbs of grain, 50 of meat, 12 of butter and of salt . . . A watchmaker will be found to fix the watches of the unclean poor, and a coffin-maker to provide their coffins.)

Fire-boats are blazing on the river. Tall red candles line the bridges.

Why did I bring him here? What was I thinking? What could I possibly have thought I was doing?

The whole city a bonfire. His cloak, his burning cloak . . .

My Friend,

Today I'll tell you more about where I live.

It's still possible to see remains of the old Roman road on the plain that stretches beyond my house. On that road Caecina led 30,000 men through deep snow across the Pennine Pass. In 774 Charlemagne also drove his soldiers over it. After him came the Saracens, the Normans, then pilgrims bound for Rome, Tuscan soldiers led by a man who was called, I don't know why, the "White Hand." So what am I to make of this benignity all around me, this mild wind through my pear trees, the careful glass cabinets in the library, Studer and Escher's geological charts neatly arranged on the wooden table where I look up specimens— dark bluish-black striated with varied lighter veins, or those the color and sheen of agate or jasper—left by the former tenants?

But my friend, even as I write this, all of it feels wrong somehow, not in its facts, but in the question of where to start and where to go from there. As if there's nowhere to set out from where I can speak plainly as I've wanted. And feelingly, as I also want. Everything tinged with a bitter, twisted distance, and I don't know why. This air as if almost unreal. I can't feel your presence as I usually do, or what I think of as the tender, complex texture of your absence. I feel, somehow, nothing, and yet I don't want to stop with me coldly here and you coldly there.

So I must try to continue . . .

Maybe in my reference to the ruined road you'll infer my own body, my skin, or the grotesque marring of my face which by now, as is often the case, may have become little more than one large scar. I don't want to tell you if this is what I look like now. Here is my hood again, you see—right here in this letter. Do I ever take it off? If you came here would I even let you past the gate?

I speak of benignity, of this slight wind, my tended flowers, but when I think of that road, as I do several times each day, and of all the soldiers killed there, the calmness falls from me, the beauty of my garden falls—its quiet suddenly infiltrated, coarse, rubbed raw. Maybe it's easier for me to feel this about the road than my own body. I walk through my garden painting whitewash onto troubled vines, trimming back others, tending to potted oleanders and asters, but even then there's a violence inside me I can't name. Like the severe silhouettes on ancient coins, it's all sharpness, force and will, and allows no tenderness for anything.

I didn't speak of this during the hours we spent together. You seemed to think me a gentle man. I believe you were moved by my suffering and the quiet way I carry it. By my interest in books and art and in my garden.

Today when I first sat down I meant to write to you of the frescoes at Issogne. I meant to write of gentle, beautiful things. I don't know why I've written what I have. And on such a beautiful day. And in this light, this early warmth of summer.

I hope you're well, and translating as you wanted to.

Your Friend,

Cao Xueqin, I spend every day translating your book. In the evenings I write to my friend in Aosta, letters that I'll never send. Often I dream of you and this strange, elaborate world that came out of your mind and through your hands. No matter how much I translate I can never come close to you or know you. Your country will always be foreign to me even if I live here for the rest of my life. This I never doubt.

Still, there are so many things that draw me close even as I feel this unbridgeable gap. The practice of burning paper, for instance. When I was a boy I liked nothing more than to look at words on a page, their black curves, sharp edges or lithe, narrow spines. My father hated that I did this. But here, each morning the paper-collectors walk through the streets with large bamboo baskets, gathering any stray papers they can find. It's believed one must preserve anything that's written-on from being trampled underfoot: scraps with quotations from Confucius, maybe, or other classic texts. Even within households such fragments are saved and given to the paper-collectors when they pass. All this is carried to the temple where it's burned, then the ashes taken to the river, sprinkled on the water, swept out to sea. I've learned this is done in obedience to an edict of Emperor Kangxi who proclaimed there's nothing more precious on earth or in heaven than written characters. No fragment's too small to be committed to the sacred flames.

You walked with such a basket in your hands. How many years, or was it your whole life? I wish my friend in Aosta could see this world of flames and paper you collected, this world that is your book. (I save all his letters and read them one by one. Should I give them to the flames and then the river?) How weary you must have gotten. Yet you gathered each individual word, overlooked almost nothing, even as you insisted there were grave limits to what anyone could know of another person or the world.

Aosta, July 10

My Friend,

I'm told there exists in Norway an Atlas of Leprosy, or should I say it's in the process of coming to exist? It consists of painted studies of patients at St. Jorgens Hospital in Bergen. I think they have twenty portraits so far, and hope to have twenty-four, all in vivid color. Many are of faces, but some are of limbs and the internal organs.

I saw, long ago, some portraits of leprous patients. I won't say how that came to be, only that what struck me most was how old they looked, though one was a boy of thirteen, and another a young girl. I would never have guessed it, that they could be so young. Was the painter exaggerating? What I saw was a rough male face with nodules all over it, and a girl in a clean white bonnet, her neck and shoulders graceful, but her eyes were rimmed with lesions, her downturned face sorrowful and worn. I saw, too, a portrait of a thirty-eight-year-old man whose lopsided mouth was frozen in a grimace.

The man, Danielssen, who's compiling the Atlas, was himself sick and bedridden for several years with tuberculosis. I hear he still drags his leg when he walks. He's a doctor in Norway. He's traveled all over observing people like me—through Switzerland, Lombardy, Sardinia, Paris . . . And if he came to my door?—but he won't come. I know my tower is safe in that way.

I've heard rumors his hospital burned down last Christmas, that eighty-four patients were killed. But there's no way to confirm this.

Think of them without their hoods. Think of them painted or burning. Your silence is loud to me, the distance between us very loud. Still, I write to you. Is each face a hidden face, even the most brutally exposed?

I haven't written to you of the frescoes at the Castle of Issogne. I still mean to.

Can you hear the silence on this page—is it a lesion, or the smoothest, most undamaged skin?

Your Friend,

For weeks Clerval doesn't read any letters from Aosta, just leaves them in his stack tied with twine. His table's covered with papers—the name Cao Xueqin written alongside characters, working notes, newly translated sentences, questions. How can he forget about his friend? (I keep thinking of the way his hands held those letters with such care, and how, long ago, he wrote to you of comfort.) Then one day he leaves this on the table:

I'm reading the *Atlas of Leprosy*. It's a large book, maybe 3 feet high with stiff cardboard covers. I want to put it down but can't. The pages turn of their own will. I see them clearly in vivid color. The thirteen-year-old boy with nodules all over his face, the girl in her white bonnet. Then I see Baoyu's bare feet. They're horrible, ulcerated, the toes like mushrooms being absorbed back into the foot. He can't walk anymore. Cao Xueqin is very angry with me, says I'm ruining his book. My father says this too. He says I can't come into his library anymore, all I do is ruin things, and the paper gatherers won't come either so all the words will just stay on the ground to be trampled underfoot.

WORKING NOTES FOR DRC:

The Goddess of Disenchantment   Prince Who Shades the Sky
The Goddess of   ~~The Goddess of Leprosy~~
~~Goddess of Not Understanding~~   Bamboo ~~Cottage~~ Lodge
Hall of Respectful Reproach
Smartweed Breeze Cottage   Happy Red Court   ~~Goddess of Seclusion~~   ~~Goddess of Muzzled~~   ~~Goddess of Walls and Walled Gardens~~

In the chapter I'm working on, Miaoyu, the nun I like so much, is writing on small pieces of paper, signing them "The One Outside the Threshold," then leaving them in crooks of tree trunks, under rocks, between skinny branches, among low-lying flowers by the stream. This is what they say:

"on the moonlit bank, all that remains is the millet's scent"
"past Red Cliff the world is crooked, nothing remains but empty
     names"

"one flute in the distance"   "the winding path leads to a secluded
    retreat"
"the wild colt is muzzled"

I put down my pen, just think for a while of her face hidden among
branches (Cao Xueqin you made her but I fear someone's trapped her
in the woods, is hacking off her hair. Why do I fear this?)

~~and I forbid you to go out without your leper's costume and I forbid
you . . . and your clapper your hood . . . and if you~~ speak~~you must turn
your face from the one you are speaking to~~

        she's making loud sounds, animal sounds, shrieks, horrible cries

her chopped hair in zigzags all over the forest floor
                    ~~and I forbid you henceforth ever to touch a child and
I forbid you to go out, I forbid you to enter a marketplace or a mill~~

Then she's silent. The one in Aosta spoke of different kinds of silence.
Cao Xueqin, what kind is hers? (I think I know but I don't want to
know.) What kind is yours, or mine, as I try to hear you under all the
many words—

"The wild colt is muzzled." "Past Red Cliff the world is crooked, nothing remains but empty names."

(My muzzled voice, my absent, silent name.)

I hear Miaoyu's words as I walk. The air singed with burning paper, burning words—

~~not him~~   ~~not in Italy~~   ~~not in Aosta~~

~~not that garden not that Atlas of~~

~~not his face~~   ~~not that leper's hood not that cloak not that~~

My Friend, last night in my dream I couldn't tell which face was yours and which was mine. I had no name anymore or like yours my name was secret so how could any letters reach me? Then we were reading the Atlas of Leprosy, *turning pages of one distorted limb after another, one suffering face after another . . . and the words: cutaneous, macrophage, neural, corium . . . I wanted to stop but you wouldn't let me stop and I didn't want to leave you—*

Cao Xueqin, I think of you in a mud house much like this (or were you in this very house?) writing long hours at a wooden table. Baoyu and Daiyu are never really at ease in this world. And Miaoyu never felt she belonged. I wonder, did you also feel this? What exists of you is mostly rumor: that you painted well but preferred to make paintings of rocks, things no one wanted to buy. That you died before your book was finished, though you left notes for the remaining chapters in a sketchbook that's been lost. That when you were a boy your family fell from favor, its property confiscated. One document claims this is what was taken: "thirteen houses comprising 483 rooms, eight estates totalling 328 acres; retainers and servants of both sexes, 114 persons old and young; books, tables, chairs, a hundred odd pawn-shop receipts." Others claim this is wrong, the document's a fabrication. In any case, you lived in poverty by the end, your wine bought on credit.

I live with your face in my mind, and with another, hooded face in my mind. The two of you never speaking to each other, each knowing nothing of the other.

It's said you fell in love with an orphaned girl named "Lin" you weren't allowed to marry, as she was "penniless and helpless." That you had a breakdown after that much like Baoyu's and fell into a coma for four days. Afterwards you seemed distant, changed, came to live in this poor village. All this, of course, is rumor. I don't even know the precise year of your birth or when you died.

But what I think about most is how you showed your pages to the one called Red Inkstone (unless Red Inkstone is yourself under another name—I know some claim this—and you wrote these commentaries on your manuscripts in red ink, all by yourself). But if Red Inkstone wasn't you, this means you weren't just alone. He wrote between the lines of your text. You must have trusted him, as Polo trusted Rustichello.

(I think of the one alone in Aosta, in his garden.)

As I translate I see Red Inkstone's words stitching in among your own:

"yes, this is true, in daily life she loved to wear old clothes"

"I remember these past events as well, so sad and bleak, almost unbearable to hear"

"she was the flower-burying girl in the pavilion of the flower grave"

Who was Red Inkstone? Did you visit in this house, drink wine at this table? What made you able to trust him? Why did he choose that name to sign your pages? (How little of your book must be pure memory, even as he says he remembers.) Why do I think of Red Inkstone as a man and not a woman? Couldn't Red Inkstone be a woman? So many silences inside your silence, so many words—

Clerval looks out his window at the smoke trees turning red in the distance. Does he think about the silences inside each silence? The silence of Cao Xueqin, the silence of his friend in Aosta. I hear a silence too: each word I think to say to you too loud with a wrongness I can't name, yet underneath it, silence, and inside it, silence. And inside that silence, pathways I can't find.

(And my voice long fled. And the way I used to read out loud.)

Now he turns from the window, walks over to the table, unbinds the twine for the first time in weeks, takes another letter from the stack.

———◆———

(I didn't want to leave you)   (I couldn't tell which face was yours and which was mine)

Aosta, July 15

My Friend,

In my last letter, when I asked you to think of the leprous patients being painted (so exposed to the gaze and scrutiny of another, displayed for the use and interest of others) or the ones burning in the hospital fire, I wonder what violence was I trying to inflict on you, what scarring? My pain, like anyone's, inhabits me blindly. My pain, such as it is, knows nothing of me or my particularities. It feels only itself, is an engine purely of itself. I say it's "mine" but really it belongs to no one. Why would I try to fling it from myself onto you? Why would I try to hurt you in that way?

I warned you there's a violence in me different from what you saw in the garden. It allows no tenderness toward anything, is vivid as the numbness in my hands, or the rocky peaks I look out on each day: geological, persistent, cold. Yet I wanted you to think of those faces, I still want you to think of them.

That day I meant to write of something else, something beautiful. Does this mean that I find the leprous faces unbeautiful? The ones stripped of their hoods unbeautiful?—why would I even use this word and the categories it implies? I did mean to write of something else that day, it's true: the frescoes at Issogne. They're in a castle not far from here, one I visited as a boy in the days before my illness.

I wonder why they mean so much to me. Maybe even then I felt they possessed a clarity I lacked, a sense of the daily as uncluttered, unconfusing. As if the painter were speaking plainly through his brush. On the lunettes of arches in the entrance hall you can see a series of scenes from daily life: a tailor's workshop, a butcher, a pharmacy, a guardroom, a fruit and vegetable market, a baker's shop, a spice seller, a cheese-monger. My mind moves close to them but not to the saints with their miracles and wonders, never to those.

So often I feel a wounding or confusing silence (you know now how I myself can wound, or try to).

I don't know who the painter was.

I wonder how you are. Do you wear Chinese silks or rough peasant clothes? What language do you think in now? Have you read the great classics?

Your Friend,

Today Clerval holds sheets of paper much smaller and thinner than the manuscript pages, but the characters are in the same careful hand. He seems to stare at them for hours, his mouth softening, his fingers vaguely stroking the worn paper.

Cao Xueqin, I can hardly believe what I've found—mixed in among your manuscript, these loose, scattered notes in your hand, remnants and hints of who you were. Even as I read, I can't find my way into you, will never find my way into you. I know this.

Your words the heat spreading through the smoke trees on the hill. You must have lived in this house after all, looked out of this window after all.

TRANSLATION OF CAO XUEQIN'S 1ST NOTE:

Reading List: MARCH 1st through APRIL 3rd
The Doctrine of the Mean (Confucius) The Great Learning
(Confucius) The Hairpin and the Bracelet (by "Master of the
Moon Pavilion"—but what's his true name?) The Book of Songs
Yellow Emperor's Manual of Medicine
Mencius ("to have no fixed estate and yet to remain steadfast")

think about Palace of Cold Void   think about Baoyu's dream of
his double

    seven red embroidery needles   scented beads   fan-sheaths
                powder ink-stones

ask Red Inkstone to comment on Chapter 18. I think I'll call it Feast
of Lanterns.

TRANSLATION OF CAO XUEQIN'S 2ND NOTE:

Baoyu, Daiyu, Baochai, that sad servant girl Qingwen, the nun
Miaoyu, and all the many bond-slaves of the house are turning into
mist in front of my eyes. I see their backs growing smaller as they
leave, each one coarsely disintegrating. They walk and walk and I
can't stop them. Baoyu's walking along some shore I don't

recognize, he's near a boat and I call out, ask him to come back—can't he see the Rong Mansion's in ruins?—but the fog only grows whiter, thicker over the rocks, my bowl of noodles grows cold my eyes are sore but he doesn't stop to hear me. Nu Wa melted down the stones to repair the Heavens but I think they're not repaired can never be repaired I see the prow of a boat a shaven head bare feet the corner of a red felt cape but other than this only their backs growing smaller and smaller, all of my characters deaf to me their ears closed, eyes turned away, there are sea-birds, waves, but mostly this white mist, the contours of rocks completely hidden, the faint sound of waves in my ear-drums but no footprints in the sand at all

TRANSLATION OF CAO XUEQIN'S 3RD NOTE:

Hui Tzu said to Zhuangzi, "Your teachings are of no practical use at all."

Zhuangzi replied: "Only those who know the value of the useless can be talked to about the useful. You describe a big tree that's useless. But maybe it's you who are at a loss to know how to use it. Why don't you plant it in the Realm of Nothing Whatever and aimlessly tread the path of inaction beside it, or lie beneath it dreaming?

You tell me you have a gourd so huge it's useless. Why don't you tie it around your waist and use it to buoy yourself aloft on the waters where you can float to your heart's content amid the streams and inland seas?"

So why do I work so hard on this book? And why did Zhuangzi work on his?

TRANSLATION OF CAO XUEQIN'S 4TH NOTE:

I've given Baoyu a beautiful, moon-shaped face. But my own is ugly, too large, asymmetrical. My father often commented on this, I could tell I annoyed and disappointed him. In Nanking we lived in such luxury. Even then there was a terrible vulnerability I sensed underneath it all, so seemingly out of place amid the silks and delicacies, the many goods, the jewels, the servants. I know now we were still technically the Emperor's slaves, descended from bond servants of the Plain White Banner. We could be broken by him at any moment and lived well completely at his whim. But at the time I knew nothing of this.

TRANSLATION OF CAO XUEQIN'S 5ᵀᴴ NOTE:

These are the sounds from the street this afternoon: bells on the animals' necks, singing from carved wooden whistles attached to the feet of airborne pigeons, sharp splashes of street-watering, high-pitched crickets and larks inside their bamboo cages. When I first came to Peking, before I moved to this village, I spent weeks learning the many street names: Happy Sparrow Street, Picture Street (where they sold hand-painted scrolls), Monkey Street, Stone Tiger Street. I remember the sounds there, can still hear them to this day—blind beggars wailing and singing, sighted beggars also wailing, lined up on the beggar's bridge, crowded together like tossed, discarded rags. It was so different from the garden where I'd lived. The city was surrounded by walls.

TRANSLATION OF CAO XUEQIN'S 6ᵀᴴ NOTE:

Red Inkstone came today. I gave him another chapter. He said I'm putting too many dreams in the book. But that's part of how Baoyu comes to know the world and his own mind. These dreams often make him ill but also heal him. I don't know that I want to give them up.

My Friend,

A hot rain today, all day. The leaves in my garden have turned a dark green-black, wet and weighted down.

My mind moves once again to the frescoes at Issogne. This time to the fruit and vegetable market where large woven baskets brim with enormous green leaves and yellow squashes (strange to think of such abundance as my own body grows more severe, pared down, erratic).

I've often wondered about the curious pairs of shoes in the background, two dark, two light, that hang on a wooden rack behind the vegetable seller. Why would they be there? Unlike the rest of the market, they give me an odd feeling of heaviness. Maybe because they're unused and empty. Probably they're newly fixed or for sale, yet what I feel is a sense, somehow, of lack, something forlorn. So much abundance—piles of plums, grapes, long strings of garlic—and then those empty, hanging shoes.

I wonder what vegetables and fruits you're tasting in China? Certainly ones I've never heard of. I should look at Polo's book again, see what he described.

As a boy, when I first spotted lesions on my body they looked mild, innocuous, just bits of skin slightly darkened from the sun, my own modest and broken constellations. Over the years they slowly roughened and enlarged. Why do I even put this in a letter? And why now? I want to speak of the frescoes at Issogne, of the beauty of Issogne, to dwell only on that—a beauty I wish you'd seen, or that we'd seen together, though I wish you never to come near.

I wonder what you're seeing in China—how many kinds of azaleas and what colors, what ancient walls, and the rooftops of Peking, are they really a bright yellow?

This rain will be good for the garden. Some leaves will have fallen in lively and surprising patterns on the path. I look forward to seeing those tomorrow.

Know that I think of you with fondness.

Your Friend,

What if Clerval hadn't found Cao Xueqin's few stray notes? What if everything Cao Xueqin wrote, even his book, remained forever lost or hidden? What if the paper collectors had plucked it all from the street, brought it to be burned and strewn as ashes?

And these notes I keep, should I give them to the flames?

Mencius wrote: "To have no fixed estate and yet to remain steadfast." But Clerval's friend stays alone in his tower, that fixed and steadfast place, remembering the tailor shop, the market, the disturbing pairs of shoes. He writes to his friend, "I wish that we'd seen them together, though I wish you never to come near." I wonder if he wants to destroy his tower's walls or build them even higher, or both? And I, would I burn my walls if I could? Are these notes walls of paper I should burn?

Did Cao Xueqin burn most of his notes, and only these few survive? There's no way I can know.

What does it mean to have a home in the world?

My Friend,

*After reading your account of the Atlas of Leprosy, for several weeks I
didn't touch your letters. This isn't something I'm proud of, but it's so. For
weeks I had many bad dreams. As if words could be a form of contagion,
and they are. Words lesions, thoughts lesions, images lesions. Still you
come back to me, always you come back.*

*My fingers undo the rough twine. I look for you in the lines and markings
of each page.* ~~Can you forgive the way I~~

*I'm glad you wrote of the frescoes, how they speak to you of the daily life
you miss. Yet I sit here and see Danielssen dragging his bad leg. I see the
patients' ashamed faces as they're painted, the hospital in flames.* ~~I can't
tell you I don't know how to tell you xxxxxx~~

*It seems I translate all the time. It tires me though I want to do it. I should
be more alert when I write. Or am I writing to myself since I know you'll
never see this? Yet it's you I hold inside my mind.*

*In the chapter I'm translating Baoyu limps like your Danielssen. He's
suffered a terrible beating at the hands of his father. Though just a boy, he
walks for months with a cane. His face is also badly injured, burned by the
son of his father's concubine who knows that if Baoyu's out of the way
his own status will improve.*

*So you see the crumbling world in which I live, this world I put down on
paper every day. A world in which Daiyu's phlegm is streaked with blood,
where servants don't own their own lives, where Miaoyu, The One
Outside the Threshold, will surely come to harm. Where the rich live at
the expense of the poor, but isn't this just the history of the world?*

Baoyu learns these lines:

> *Naked I go without impediment.*
> *My sole wish now is to roam alone*
> *In coir cape and bamboo hat,*
> *And in straw sandals with a broken alms bowl*
> *To wander where I will.*

*Imagine Baoyu wandering off on his own, not limping, no longer needing
his cane. You asked me to think of the burned faces. I think of them and*

of the broken alms bowl, and the frescoes you wrote of with their small, clear moments of fruit, white cloth, measurement, and light.

I think of Baoyu's and Daiyu's love for each other. Of Daiyu's love of books. Of Cao Xueqin, and his friend, Red Inkstone, who wrote in red ink between his words. Imagine if we could do that, you and I . . . write in between each other's words . . .

Part of me still fears you. (All those weeks I stayed away from your letters.) In the lines Baoyu memorized the desire is not to be revealed, but to go off alone. ("In coir cape and bamboo hat.") And the alms bowl is broken. I wonder what you think of that?

Your Friend,
Clerval

Clerval translates all day, the sentences accumulating like lines on a map, rough pathways into his mind, or Cao Xueqin's. I follow Baoyu and Daiyu, the yellow roofs of Peking, Miaoyu leaving secret messages in the woods. But when his hand stops it's as if a fog rolls over the land wrapping them in silence.

I go out and walk, imagine I carry an alms bowl in my hands. To be alone and the alms bowl broken . . . if I could feel the freedom in that, understand there's a freedom in that . . .

Yesterday I came across a *kepper*. I wonder if you ever saw one? It's a rough wooden rectangle lodged inside a pony's mouth to prevent it from eating while hauling fresh-bound sheaves. It must pain the pony to have it in its mouth.

I kept picturing the pony's eyes. Then the eyes were Claire's, then Clerval's. The *kepper* pressed into their gums until they bled.

Everything was very quiet.

Later when I slept I had this dream, at least this is the part I remember:

(But why would I even tell you my dream? Why would I want to?)

Like Baoyu, I was limping, walking with a cane. Then I was bedridden. I thought if you could see me you'd realize I was weak, pathetic, couldn't hurt anyone, didn't want to. Then I wondered if this was true. Every part of me was sore, even my mouth, and I heard—from where?—the word: *kepper*. When I looked up you were at my bedside, and for the first time I had a name, you called me Black Jade. Then suddenly you were Claire. She was writing the word *destroy* over and over in her notebook. I told her that's the word Zhuangzi used, "*Destroy quadrants and measures.*" Yes, she said, everyone uses it.

Then I woke.

My Friend,

It's been nearly two months since I last wrote. The impairment of sensation now extends to my eyes. Not feeling is a strange form of pain, of difficulty. I'm told the ophthalmic portion of the Vth facial nerve has been affected. This is not uncommon. I no longer blink normally. Often I can't blink at all. Many nights when I sleep I no longer close my eyes. The cornea lies exposed and unprotected. So you see, I can't keep out the dust, or whatever else it is that moves through the air and towards us.

I've not forgotten about the frescoes at Issogne. ~~I'm ashamed that I~~

But let me tell you about something else today.

I saw something once that's come back to me vividly. ~~I have no other guide no~~ ~~and in the mind's roughness~~ ~~and not in tranquility~~

It's a simple piece of Attic pottery: a white-ground lekythos from around 450 B.C. Unlike the more common black and red ones (those you've probably seen), this one depicts no satyrs or maenads, no epic heroes involved in all manner of dramatic action. Instead, it holds a simple grave offering. In her cupped hand a young woman carries a small vessel like the one on which she's painted. With the other she holds a woven basket. She's bringing offerings to the dead soul who stands on the other side of the vase where she can't see him; he grasps his spear and shield. Her back is straight but not rigid, her elongated neck gently curved. She's wholly focused on one thing only, that the olive oil in the vase be brought to the one who waits but can't see her. Neither is able to glimpse, for one second, the other. As if all knowing were quiet, sealed off, all attachment quiet.

I suspect in writing to you now of this graceful vase, I'm swerving away from some violence in myself (think of the clapper, the hood, the ruins of the Roman road). I write of my eyes but then don't want to think about my eyes. Yet the scene on the vase is mournful, so maybe I'm circling what I feel, trying out what I might feel . . .

The olive oil would be unmixed, maybe scented with perfume from irises.

Should I rip up this page or should I let your hand touch this page? I wonder which way will win out?

When I sleep I don't see, I don't know my eyes are open.

Your Friend,

It's not even the end of his workday, but already Clerval opens a new letter, leaves the rough twine untied in its snake-curve on the table. This letter's different from the others—there's writing on both sides, and on one a slash mark through all of it. He starts reading the slashed words, then turns the page over, touches the words "Aosta" and "My Friend." Did his friend forget he'd written on the other side? Or did he want to send what he'd slashed but couldn't bear to say, the way I wrote my dream for you, though I wouldn't claim I wanted you to see it.

xxxxxI can't stop seeing the frescoes of Issognexxx my eyes won't close
xxxbut why is it so hot in here xxx Danielssen is limping I wish he
would stop why won't he stop why does he come into my room I don't
even know him he has no right to come in xxxxxxxxxxxx and I
forbid you ever to wash your hands in a stream I forbid you ever
henceforth to go out without your leper's xxx dress xxx and you must
not go outside your house ever unshod xxxxxxxx you must not xxx I
forbid and I forbid and you must not and I forbid

the hospital's burning all those faces in their beds are burning xxxx
and I command you not to answer anyone who questions you unless
your face is turned away and each will be given two pairs of sheets a
cup a funnel a small knife and I forbid xxx I forbidxxx Danielssen's
dragging his bad leg why must he drag itxxx you must not and you
must not his eyes blink he drags his bad leg he looks at me he blinks

Aosta, October 6

My Friend,

I had a few feverish days but I'm better. I think it was my <u>thoughts</u>
that made me sick. I couldn't stop thinking about what I must look like
when I sleep, each blank and staring eye wide open. Maybe I wanted to
hurt myself in that way, focusing as I did on what seemed to me a
horrible sight. At least no one can see me. But I see myself in my own
mind, and what am I to do about that?

I think about how the cornea is meant to be protected. How, like the
mind, the body needs a way to close itself off. These visible or secret
shelters of ourselves . . .

I'm still too tired to write much. I've traveled far, but I've gone nowhere. I think of Polo, of the soldiers on the Roman road. The world remakes itself in strangeness. Unshelters itself always. Even in my garden, my tower, even here.

Maybe this is why the brother and sister who lived here before me couldn't bear to look upon each other's face. They would have seen how far they had traveled from what they'd thought of as themselves, each other, the world.

Have you seen the elaborate temples carved into stone cliffs, and the many decorated statues inside them? Is it true that, unlike them, the Confucian temples are stark and nearly bare? I think I would like those best of all, though I know some call them cold.

I must stop now.

As Ever, Your Friend,

Cao Xueqin, I picture you and Red Inkstone, two friends hunched over a manuscript, looking into each other's eyes. Once he signs himself "Winter Night," I don't know why. But my friend in Aosta can't close his eyes, can't . . . and I'm far away from him. If I knocked on his door he wouldn't let me in

~~Working notes~~

Guanyin is the Goddess of Mercy ~~Goddess of the hood and clapper~~ ~~Goddess of eyesight~~ ~~Goddess of Lekythos and Issogne~~ ~~Goddess of locked doors~~

X

XX

Baoyu says odd things yet I find this makes him all the more believable.

Says, "Last night I dreamed the spirit of the apricot tree came to me to ask for a string of white paper money."

I wonder if Red Inkstone wanted this small dream taken out. Too many dreams in this book, he said.

XX

Goddess of the lame   Goddess of fires

My Friend, What words aren't weak and unconvincing against affliction? What intricacies or plainness of argument don't falter and collapse? I think of your eyes and XXX cannot XXX and now lost XXX each locked window bolted door
XX

Cao Xueqin writes of Baoyu: "His cheek was badly blistered but luckily no damage had been done to his eyes."

When Daiyu is ill she grows ashamed and wants no one to see her, turns her face to the wall.

I close my eyes and obliterate the smoke trees on the hillside. Open them, bring them back. Close, open, close. A child's game, but not. Then I'm looking out on the floating city of Canton. All that water one large eye that can't close.

My Friend,

When the Goddess of Disenchantment comes to Baoyu in a dream she hands him the manuscript book of twelve songs called The Red Chamber Dream. "Read this," she says, but also warns, "These songs are our laments for mortal people and worldly events, no outsider can truly understand their meaning. At first they will seem to you as bland as chewed wax." And in fact, Baoyu sees at first "no merit in these disjointed, cryptic songs." He's attached to this world of silks, swords and servants, the various flowers in his garden, delicacies carried on trays, teas brewed from the purest snow-water. (But you know this already from my other letters, the letters I don't send.) Still, he listens as the songs are sung, and reads the text before him.

(Why do I tell you this, my Friend? The Goddess wants Baoyu to look past this world of appearances, yet you can't stop looking even for one second— is there a way one can look at the world and still look past it? Do you close your eyes inside your mind? I think of you being forced to read the world over and over, and I wish I could . . . I don't know what comfort is anymore, I suspect I never knew. The Goddess calls Baoyu by name, speaks to him directly, but I, who have no powers or songs like hers, how am I to reach you? I don't even know your name.)

"Those who see through the world escape from the world," says one song. And another: "What remains of the generals and statesmen of old?/Nothing but an empty name."

But my friend, what of your eyes that can't "escape from the world" as the song put it? Your eyes that can't turn away? What of your hidden, secret name? You sit in the sun, or lie in bed at night, always with those wide-open eyes, but does something in your eyes turn inward? "You must realize the vanity of love in your dusty world," the Goddess tells Baoyu. So often in books there's this image of the world as dust and our needing to look past it. But it's real dust that hurts your eyes, the cornea stings and festers.

In many passages in Cao Xueqin's novel, Baoyu's encouraged to look through this world of appearances. At one point he's told the story of a wealthy man who goes to Shaozhou in search of a teacher. Finally he finds him in a monastery on Mount Huangmei where he takes work as a cook to be near him. Each day from behind the kitchen door he listens to the monks composing Buddhist gatha. One morning the most senior disciple recites:

> The body is a Bodhi tree,
> The mind a mirror clear;
> Then keep it cleaned and polished—
> Let no dust settle there

The man's hulling rice in the kitchen when he hears this. For years he's spoken almost nothing. But now he recites his own version of that song:

> The Bodhi tree is no tree,
> The mirror no mirror clear;
> Since nothing actually exists,
> Where can any dust appear?

The teacher hears this from the other side of the door, opens it, passes on to him his robe and alms bowl.

How little I know of you. Not even your name. Nothing in the mind is clear or clean or polished. And still I keep thinking of your eyes, that something hurts your eyes and they don't close. I lie in the dark, feel how my own eyelids shut as in gentle protection. As if they were another's careful hands. I don't know what's real in the world, this place of no-mirror. When I sleep I dream of Baoyu and Daiyu but not of the man next door or the tree outside my window.

"The Bodhi tree is no tree." You who I can't see, I think of how the eyes need shelter, even if the world (our world such as it is) isn't real.

Your Friend,
Clerval

Why does my mind return to you the way dreams return to the site of a fire? As now, Clerval returns to the letters describing the leper hospital, the atlas, the island of Gloskar—each page that gave him nightmares. He leaves his translation work untouched, barely lifts his eyes as he reads, rereads. When evening comes he doesn't open a new one but picks up his pen and writes another letter he won't send.

My Friend,

I never answered your question about the Confucian temples, if they're stark the way you'd like them to be. There's one not far from here, the Kong Miao, with beautiful old cypresses in the courtyard—the oldest trees in Peking. But I wouldn't call it stark. You approach through a large gate, then two sets of steps lead to Great Achievement Hall. Between them, on a huge turquoise stone, dragons fly through fire and water. Farther on there's another hall with large stone tablets engraved with the names of Confucian scholars, over 50,000 from three entire dynasties; also numerous steles on which Confucius' Thirteen Classics are engraved. There's a building called the Pavilion for Sacrificial Animals and another called the Well Pavilion. And others still . . . So you see, it's quite elaborate, though it was much smaller and plainer, I'm told, when first built in 1304.

Maybe somewhere far from here there's a starker, simpler temple. Often I've imagined it. A bare room of uninterrupted quiet (but is there such a thing as uninterrupted quiet?) with one stele or two propped against a wall. But what could the words on those steles even say? Maybe they'd best be left blank.

You have your tower and your solitude, though your solitude is never simple, I know. And in that solitude you want to hear about distant temples, their quiet resembling yours but inhabited by others. I, too, would choose the plainest temple, the plainest room. What if the words on those steles were indecipherable? What if there were no steles at all—

Your Friend,

Clerval

My Friend,

My mind wanders—forgive me. The quiet and solitude in which I live
is more and more a labyrinth where I turn one corner then another
not knowing what I'll find. I never know what I might come to next—
past or future, my own face or yours, the copper mines dug into the
hillsides, or the narrow, winding streets where I once walked—the
Rue du Foller, the Rue des Prisons . . .

I wonder about the brother and sister who lived here before me. Did
they visit the frescoes at Issogne? Did they go together more than once?
Did they think back to them years later, especially to the one of the
apothecary with its neat row of nineteen labeled jars lined up on a
shelf behind a man weighing medicine on a scale, his hand delicately
poised, as if a hand were a mind that could contemplate, assess, decide.
Did they wonder, as I do, about the man in torn clothing sitting in a
corner of the shop, using a large mortar and pestle. One foot is bare.
His left elbow pokes through his sleeve. His face is dirty. Why is he
there? The finely dressed woman, the only customer in the shop, turns
the other way.

~~I can't xxx and the corners keep coming, the turns xxx and I can't
xxx and if you~~

When you were here did you see the old Roman arch, the Triumphal
Arch of Augustus as it's called? It's visible from my window where it
frames a view of mountains and glaciers. But the thing that's always
puzzled me is that it's blank—there's nothing carved on it at all. All
the slaughtering and conquering that led to it, the wiping out of the
entire Salassi people (and of those not killed, 36,000 were sold as
slaves) and yet the arch is blank. How could that have happened? Even
its pillars are plain, not fluted. Why would there be no inscription, not
a single leaf or figure, not one word of triumph? Often I turn the
corner of this labyrinth in which I live and it's there, suddenly, before
me: that question of blankness, that arch of gneiss and quartz that
expresses nothing, states nothing, depicts nothing. Or is it the dulled
shadow of a prideful power? Or could it be a hooded face? Or a face
that has no features? Or is it a cold refusal to account? A summons at
once arrogant and sealed . . . I don't know . . . I only . . .

Forgive me, I xxxxxxxxx

After the sister died, did the brother remember alone? Did he think of Issogne?

And when he passed the walnut tree under which she used to sit . . .

xxx and when he passed xxxxxx

But have I told you that alongside some of Aosta's streets, streams of cool, fresh water from the mountains still run clean? Sometimes I hear them, though I'm told that's not possible from here.

I hope you're well. That you carry some warmth in your sleeves.

Your Friend,

I've said my mind returns to you, always to you. Yet the more I watch Clerval as I watched Claire, the more you start to fade, sometimes for whole hours at a time. When I dream I dream of the leper's eyes, not yours. I dream of those who'll never dream of me.

I say their names as I walk or watch or sleep: Claire. Clerval. (I carry my clapper, don my hood.) Claire. Air. Care. Clerval. Clear. Err.

Claire: Care:

I've learned that *care* has more meanings than I thought. It's another name for the tree called Mountain Ash, though I never thought that care could be a tree. It's an archaic term for a textile used for cloaks. It means to sorrow and to grieve, to mourn and to lament. It's mental suffering, and the expression of that suffering. Mourning dress is called the *cloth of care*. A *care-bed* is a bed of grief.

Yet care means less sad things as well: it's the "charging of the mind with anything," and is "regard arising from desire, inclination."

One gives care, takes care of. The shepherd "tends his fleecy care." A man stands guard "with watchful Eye Fix'd on his youthful Care."

As I fix mine on Clerval and Claire and Clerval's friend . . .

In the name Clerval, I also hear: to "err," from the Latin *errare,* which means to wander, stray, roam, ramble.

(How would I even have come to know their faces if I hadn't been forced to wander from the start?)

Birds "err upon their course." And: "He erred so ferre by strange londes that he passed the flood of Ganges." Clerval would like that line, having come to live so far from where he started. Men "erre Within the wildernesse." You erred within a wilderness of mind as I did, and still do.

When you first began to make me, didn't you set out on a course you couldn't possibly understand? Then I opened my eyes and you pulled back, became a rigid, frightened man. You found yourself in another wilderness where everything was frozen, and then it froze in me.

　　　　　the delicate tissue of　　　　　　　the vulnerability of
　If I could know your name

xxx

Baoyu's name means that which is most precious and solid. It's said to protect him.

"You referred to him by name," a woman from outside the mansion's gates accuses Baoyu's faithful servant, Qingwen.

"You should call him 'Young Master.' Using his name shows lack of respect."

"So I called him by his name, did I?" Qingwen replies, flushed with anger . . . "As for using his name, we've done that since he was a child—on the Empress Dowager's orders. At his birth didn't they have his name written out and posted up everywhere so that everybody would use it, for fear that otherwise he might die young? Why, even the water-carriers, night-soil collectors, and beggars use it. The more it's said the more he's protected. You don't have any business here—go back to mucking about outside the gate where you belong."

But I call you no name, I call you My Friend, I call you . . . I don't know . . . there's no name to protect you . . .

I want to say your name as Cao Xueqin said "Red Inkstone" and the two looked into each other's eyes

TRANSLATION OF CAO XUEQIN'S 7TH NOTE:

> Sometimes I start to get very cold. I fear for Baoyu. He has no interest in status, honors, official advancement. How will he protect himself? It's not up to me to protect him. I have to take him down this path. But sometimes I just want to stop, pull back, close my eyes, shut out his fevers, his wounds, the way he has to walk with a cane. His family's crumbling, their money and luck's running out. The dynasty's corrupt. Red Inkstone says I have to be accurate, not

pull back from what I see. Daiyu will die because there's no place for her in this world—she won't be allowed to marry Baoyu, it's not in the family's interest. She won't marry out of duty, her spirit refuses to be fettered—there's no one else she loves. She'll burn all her manuscript books. But sometimes I just don't want to write it, don't want to see it in front of my eyes

I remember preparing for the state examinations. Of course I was expected to become an official like my father. I read and read. But one day when I looked up my mind went black, then I saw in that blackness Zhuangzi's words, white as phosphorus: "Why not plant it in Nothing At All Town or in Vast Nothing Wilds?"—Just that.

My Friend,

But the brother and sister xxxx did they xx and if ~~but~~ It's getting cold now, the garden will get its first frost soon, any day.

What of the sister's empty room? How he passed it many times each day, though he'd always thought he'd be the one to die first—

And of those taken into the lazar houses it was written: "The leper brothers are to remain by themselves, and likewise the sisters by themselves. They are to have four fires a day as needed for which they will receive two baskets of peat. Every Sunday they are to receive ten white loaves, five for the brothers and five for the sisters. All are to work together for the house and allow no harm to come to it. They are to have a bier for carrying the dead."

~~In the harshness of~~ ~~but no form of attachment can~~ Often I think I wouldn't know you if I saw you again

In the foreground of one fresco, the butcher shop's barred window—

The man in torn clothes I wrote you of—he's wearing just one shoe and is off in a corner away from the others—~~what do the others think of him why do they let him sit there why is he there what is he doing?~~

~~I must close~~ I've ~~got to stop now~~

Think of the clear mountain water rushing alongside these winding streets—

Your Friend,

My Friend, in your last letter you started to write "but no form of
attachment can" and then you stopped and crossed it out but I've been
wondering, No form of attachment can—can what? and the suffering you
feel and this question of your open eyes

Zhuangzi writes of the "blindness of the mind." I feel this acutely in
myself. I don't know how to

I don't know how to write to you today

xx

Mon—mend shirt
Tues—buy more ink
        "qin" means "lute"
          ask Mr. Lin about the "torch of chaos and doubt"

TRANSLATION OF CAO XUEQIN'S 8TH NOTE:

A month of dust storms. I stay inside reading Zhuangzi. Only
Zhuangzi. Even indoors my lungs burn and my eyes sting. I've
caulked the window with rags. For over five weeks Red Inkstone
hasn't come. Animals walk with blinded eyes. Sometimes I dream
sand's falling around me faster than I can dig it away, I try to speak
but make only choking sounds. No sooner is the road cleared than
it vanishes. There are so many maimed, deformed people in
Zhuangzi's book. Some have only one foot, one is so bent and
crooked his chin nearly touches his navel, his left shoulder juts up
above his head. The leper woman fears she'll give birth to a child
covered with sores. Yet Zhuangzi finds beauty in all this. If a man is
cast aside he's useless and to Zhuangzi that's a form of freedom, of
goodness. "The cinnamon can be eaten and so it gets cut down, the
lacquer tree can be used and so it gets hacked apart." Better to be
useless. The man who's seen as undesirable, maybe he can become
free? No one wants or asks anything of him, or expects him to be
other than he is. I sit inside and listen to the swarming dust. Lambs
and goats stumbling and bleating.

Clerval's grown thinner, sometimes his hands shake. Now when he isn't translating he's reading Zhuangzi. Often he looks puzzled as he reads. Why can I see his face, often his whole body, whereas Claire came to me only in pieces, and mostly with her face turned away?

It seems what you thought of as my ugliness wouldn't have bothered Zhuangzi. What I've hated in myself he wouldn't have hated.

Clerval sits in his hard wooden chair for hours. Sometimes he speaks a few stories from the Zhuangzi out loud (I watch the small movements of his lips), or picks up his pen, translates a passage here and there:

> "One day when Carpenter Shih comes home after rejecting an old, rotting oak tree, it appears to him in a dream. 'You said I was a worthless tree, that boats made out of my timbers would sink, coffins quickly rot, and vessels break at once. But what are you comparing me with? Those useful trees, the pear, the cherry, the apple?—as soon as their fruit is ripe they're yanked around, torn apart, and subjected to all sorts of abuse. Their utility makes life miserable for them. But I—I long to be of no use, and though I almost died I've finally caught on.'
>
> "The tree paused, then continued:
>
> " 'What's the point of this—things condemning things? Why do you do this? Why did you bother to speak of me in that way?' "

I could ask the same of you, and of myself.

Maybe I'm like that oak tree and what you thought of as my repulsive form isn't so horrible at all. But that oak was part of the natural world—nature made it what it was. And I—I don't know if that's the case with me. *You* made me. If the workings of your mind were, in the end, a distortion of nature, a betrayal of and faithlessness toward nature, then what am I?

In any case the question holds: "What's the point of things condemning things?"

As you condemned me. As I condemned myself, and still do, wishing to be other than I am.

My Friend,

*It seems so much of what we take into our minds is random,
disorganized, haphazard. Why do I know about tallow trees, for
instance? I remember that they're tall xxxxxx and grow in China,
and that their seeds, when crushed and boiled, yield the tallow to make
candles. I wonder if you've seen them. This, too, I somehow know,
though maybe it's not true: on the road to the monastery of Tien-Dong
every 29th stone is engraved with a lotus blossom, and in that
monastery the monks wear mantles made of bits of fabric sewn roughly
together so that, however fine the cloth, their robes look like a
patchwork of rags.*

*xxx I've gotten afraid of the way my mind is interfering with xxx but
then why do I write to you xxx why do I xxx*

*But in truth I keep thinking more and more about the sister. It feels—
how can I put it?—that she <u>waits</u> inside my mind. xx And when she
sat under the walnut tree xxx and what did she xxx and did she read
there and which books? ~~I don't know why I~~ Her eyes, were they locked
wide like mine? Her room is xxx I've never stepped into her room. But
years ago I found a piece of paper crumpled in a crack beside her door:*

Of the two ointments recommended the following may be given:

Oil of eucalyptus	(15.0 ml)
Honey	(60.0 ml)
Cod liver oil	(60.0 ml)
Zinc oxide	(28.4 grm.)
Bis. Subn.	(56.7 grm.)

*If the pupil still does not dilate satisfactorily the following
subconjunctival injection may be given:*

Atropine sulphate	(0.016 grm.)
Cocaine	(0.03 grm.)
Distilled water	(6.00 ml)

What am I that I copy this out for you, send this to you?

~~monstrous~~   ~~unforgivable or~~

How quiet she must have been all those hours she spent under the walnut tree, such quiet she lived in. Her footsteps on the very stones my feet touch daily. More and more I'm drawn to her room, the brass latch on her closed door. I'm sorry ××× I didn't mean to ××× and of course ××× but I will try again later will still try ×××

Your Friend,

. . . The monks in their patchwork rags . . . and I a patchwork . . . and the workings of each mind a patchwork, each self roughly stitched as you stitched me . . .

My Friend,

For so many weeks I watched my mind moving away from itself, I don't know how else to put it. Even the air, which I often stared into for hours at a time, seemed more visible, less intact, inside it minute particles swirled and collided—small brightnesses flaring then flickering away. My mind, as I felt it, was several minds at once, clumps of cells, obsessive and enslaved, spinning tightly wound in their strict orbits, then circling farther outward. Everything breaking. I saw the frescoed bodies at Issogne become atomized—the objects were still there—baskets filled with fruit, shoes hung on the rack—but the people, the people, they were ashes, dust, swirling in an otherwise calm world. I lived within that breakage, and when I thought of you it was like looking through a dust-storm, your face a crumbling cage of dust.

That's over now. Even as I write I'm not making mistakes, as you can see. I'm not needing to cross out. But what am I to make of what overtook me? My eyes still remain mostly open, and they sting. There's no reason to hope this will change.

I think there's no known world. I don't know what awaits me. It's myself that shape-shifts, changes, grows errant, not the world.

The garden's less lush now. On one of the mountains there's a snow-peak shaped like a horn. When the sun sets one half of it glows rose, while the other half darkens. Looking at that slender horn of light, I think of Sordello leading Dante and Virgil toward Purgatory's gates. It's nearly sunset; the edges of the valley glow. He explains the Law of Ascent; that no one can go upward after sundown. "There," he says, "where the mountain makes a lap among its folds: that is the place where we may wait until the new day breaks." And of the souls nearby, Sordello says, "You can observe them from this rise and follow their actions better, singly and en masse, than if you moved among them in the hollow."

Is this how we track each other, you and I, from this rise which is our separateness, these ways that we're apart?

In the end Dante drinks from Lethe and the Eunoe, of course, and is purified and set free—"I came back from those holiest of waters new, remade, reborn," he says, "healed of Winter's scars; perfect, pure and ready for the stars."

So foreign to me, that idea of being "pure," of being "healed." I wonder what you're learning in the East? Or should I say unlearning in the East? This silence between us. Lit snow on the mountain. Winter's scar—

Your Friend

Goddess of the Walnut Tree

Goddess of Atropine Sulphate

Goddess of the Atomized

Goddess of the Rotting Oak

Zhuangzi's oak said of the fruit trees, their utility makes life miserable for them. Yet I sit here all day translating, trying to be useful. I don't know what to do anymore. My friend's eyelids aren't useful. But they come into my mind and I feel I'm witnessing something wonderful, exciting (is it awful to say this, and cruel?)—that in their uselessness they're somehow suddenly alive, the whole idea of eyelids suddenly alive. As if, though I've seen them my whole life, I've never really seen them before. My head aflame with thousands upon thousands of eyelids. Is my translating useful at all, do I even do it to be useful? I do it because I like the look of characters and letters, brown ink and black, the feel of paper under my hand. I do it because the word "oak tree" suddenly appears and then "subjected to" and Carpenter Shih walks into my mind and I look at him and not at my neighbor who's perfectly nice or this street with its covering of dust, or the man selling melons from his cart

My Friend,

But the sister. The walnut tree. The crumpled paper. I said I was calm, and I was—my mind no longer so many spinning, breaking minds. I wrote to you of Dante, Virgil, Sordello—I remember it all. I could write that to you, couldn't I?—I remember sitting calmly at my table. My letter was of the sunset, the hidden, purification, "being healed." I felt how the figures at Issogne had grown intact again, their graceful forms no longer atomized. I remember being grateful. I remember the feeling of Clarity. The simple beauty of a working hand. The working hands of the figures at Issogne.

I went into her room. It was yesterday, late in the day. I still feel the brass latch on my hand. I don't know why I xxxx What is intention what is sxxxx clarity what is wanting to know and to know what?

What is necessity   what is choice?   And of what is the ongoing astonishment of solitude composed? that astonishment so plain in its way, and daily, yet how can astonishment be plain?   xxx the mind's stalwart or delicate faithfulness   each tender detonation   I xxx

Her room was as she'd left it. Bed, desk, chair, a wooden dresser with four drawers, eight knobs. A bookcase beneath the sunlit window which framed the horn-shaped snow peak. How could they not have emptied the room before I came? Her clothes still in the drawers, and the little book she kept in which she noted the changes in the garden, what she was reading, reactions to medicines, a few poems she'd copied in her careful hand.

Why hadn't they burned all of her things? Taken them away? I touched the white sleeve of her blouse.

"And no more than eight healthy brothers and sisters shall live in the leper house to care for the sick. When either a sick or healthy brother or sister dies their possessions shall remain in the house, and their belongings shall be used by the remaining brothers and sisters and must not be taken away. They shall be used by the brothers if the deceased was a brother, and by the sisters if the deceased was a sister."

"No brother or sister shall pass out of that house beyond the bryde."

"No brother or sister may disclose, utter or betray any of the secrets of their house, and if, by due proof they are convicted of such, shall have but bread and water for thirty days."

What do you think of this trespass of mine? ~~I know I should not have~~ xxx On the old Roman Road, cruelty, brutality.

My cruelty more veiled and quiet, if it is that.

The white sleeve was smooth and soft like my lilies, or any new-formed leaf.

Your Friend,

~~My Friend,~~

I—I see you standing in the sister's room. You touch the white sleeve of her blouse, and I'm touching it too. Why do we need to inhabit another's gestures, another's mind? How does this happen? Why does the brain need to dream and imagine at all, to transfer, transpose, and sew, and layer?

on my fingertips the softness of a sleeve   not the roughness of this wooden table

I don't want to see or feel these things anymore. Don't want to think of the sister, the empty room, the white sleeve. If I could leave here for just a few days   xxxxxxxx   but where would I go? and with what money? xxx I—xx You think of the sister   you lift the latch, walk into her room and I?—I think of Daiyu choosing to die   I sit here translating her dying and sometimes it seems wrong—that I'm stripping a veil from her, peeling off her clothes that I have no right to xxx   that I xxx   "and no brother or sister may disclose, utter or betray any secrets of their house." But if anyone betrayed Daiyu, it's Cao Xueqin. He wrote her pain, laid it open on the page.

xx   x

My Friend,

I hold your letters and think of the sister, her white sleeve, her wooden dresser. I think of you standing in that room, then of Daiyu who is choosing to die. She knows she and Baoyu will never marry, and she's never felt at home in the world. Not even when she wasn't sick and coughing. She lies on her bed in Bamboo Lodge, feverish, cold. No one comes. Her illness is kept secret from Baoyu. She burns her manuscript book and the white handkerchief Baoyu gave her, then takes three sips of pear juice and dried-longan syrup from a spoon (why does she bother?). Says she wants to go home.

I translate all this as the light builds and fades, and I feel somehow traitorous, unclean.

While on my page the maids are laying out Daiyu's afterlife-clothes, you stand in the sister's empty room. I think of her fragile body, of the mind not wanting to be in it anymore. Her mind much like your eyes that won't close—relentless, unsparing, fixed in place.

I'd like to leave here for just a few days. I don't want to hear this much quiet.

Your words are eyes staring from each page. And the gaze inscrutable, though you say you want to write "plainly" and you do. It's been such a long time since we spoke. I can hear the crickets singing in their bamboo cages.

Your Friend,
Clerval

Clerval reads of the stones of the old Roman road, all the carnage that broke over them, and I walk among old stones, almost feel the seconds breaking over them, each with its brief and too-thin skin.

If I could go to Nothing At All Town what would become of those seconds, would they follow? And my clapper, my hood, would I still need them? Would each memory of Claire and Clerval, even you, break and flame out? Would I come upon that tree deemed useless by Carpenter Shih, its ruined leaves suddenly beautiful to my eyes, its battered trunk rough and peaceful where it leans?

But I'm not in Nothing At All Town or in Vast Nothing Wilds. I watch Clerval holding the letters, his sad face as he reads and rereads. His lips moving as he says out loud to no one, "the sister, the white sleeve."

TRANSLATION OF CAO XUEQIN'S 9TH NOTE:

> Red Inkstone still hasn't come. And the other one who signs
> himself Odd Tablet—I haven't set eyes on him for months. I worry
> I'll die before I finish this. But then I remind myself of Zhuangzi
> who'd see this worry as needless, as being caught within a "bitter
> thing." "Think of the story of Uncle Lame-Gait," he might say:
> "One day out of nowhere a willow sprouts from Uncle Lame-Gait's
> arm. 'Are you worried?' his companion asks, 'Do you resent it?'
> 'Why should I resent it?' he answers. 'To live is to borrow. You and I
> came on this earth to watch the process of change, and now
> change has caught up with me, that's all.' "

Aosta, Dec 11

My Friend,

My eyes sting, they always sting. Every day I go into her room. I remember the touch of your gloved hand. The way you weren't afraid. In her top dresser drawer, a small hand-mirror. Did she use it in the weeks before her death? Or did she wrap it in cloth months before (it was wrapped when I found it), then slip it in among the clothes she knew she would no longer need? Through a crack in the window the smell of the ironworks. Slowly I feel a leaving in myself, I xxx and it's not a violent thing though the quiet of it pierces and the solitude's slightly different from the solitude I've known these many years

Did I tell you my illness was never explained to me xxx the course it could take not explained xxx I didn't know that the lesions could be internal   in the throat for instance   the larynx   so that if I were to speak to you nowxx I mean if you were here if you were xxx but I'm glad you'll never be here and my voice such as it is   what's left of it is hoarse and shallow   xxx   xxx   I've thought much about what skin is—a boundary, a shield, a site of harm xx a pleasure   a raw stopping-place a starting-place a home   site where the hidden senses what's beyond it xxxxxx   expectant   visible   variable   unfree   I—

I didn't know of the categories: non-infective cases, quiescent cases, arrested cases, neural cases. Acute, subacute or chronic. With fever or without. With succulent lesions or without.

I still wonder what skin is. I've thought about it often as I said yet I still wonder. The smell from the ironworks grows even stronger in winter—

Your Friend,

My Friend,

You write to me of your old Roman Road, your arch with no inscription, the sister's closed room, the frescoes at Issogne, and trying to picture what you see, I also want to tell you what I see. But what I write I never send. I keep thinking of leaving here for just a few days, but with what money, and to where? Instead I close my eyes, lie down and remember. Strange what stays in the mind, what strays, wanders, erupts inside the mind. The narrow strips of pink paper pasted over the statues' eyes in the old temple near Snow Valley, for instance. What purpose did they serve? Some say they were used to protect the gods' eyes from the decaying temple walls until the day they could finally be repaired. Why do I remember this now? I remember also:

Large wild silkworms feeding on oak leaves. They produce the coarse silk known as Mountain Silk, the only silk that slaves are permitted to wear. Rice plants a few inches high being transplanted one by one to a large field. The bent postures of peasants as they worked. White storks outside Silent City. A dozen blindfolded oxen harnessed to six grindstones churning winter wheat into flour. Narrow streets lined with horn lamps, paper lanterns. The scarred foreheads of penitents at Kushan.

Why do I remember these things and not others? Last night I dreamed your eyes were covered with thin strips of pink paper—

WORKING NOTES FOR DRC:

~~~ the iceberg in the Goddess's Ninth Song is unexplained, but seems to refer to a family's suffering and fall

~~~ "Thirty-six ways to enclose a corner" refers to a treatise on cures by King Rong (I would have thought it easy, but it seems there's truly no way to enclose a corner)

~~~ the best guess for an answer to this riddle is "inked string"—what carpenters use for making a straight line on wood (though often it seems nothing in this book forms a straight line)

Red Inkstone: "If the person you were before reading and the person you are after is the same, then you haven't really read"

my friend's letters, his frozen eyelids, my eyes

My Friend,

~~then~~ xxx *over time when I grew worse the doctors said words to me and those words left cuts inside my mind—"infiltrative" "fibrotic" "trophic." I walked into her room it was too quiet I left I walked back in. Skin is quiet, thought quiet. I wonder if there are cases in which the face remains completely smooth, lesions limited to torso or limbs, so one could cover* xxx *and completely* xxx *just imagine it* xxx *nothing would show* xx *yet all of it still there* xxx *Sometimes I imagine they hand me a "quiescent certificate" which verifies I've tested negative for nine months. Then I visit* xxx *the faces of Issogne so smooth, unmarked in their mute world, just a few shadows here and there suggesting age or worry or the structure of the hidden bones* xxx *So many words inside my head: "rose-spot nodules" "evanescent erythematous rashes" "subcutaneous" "iritis" "exacerbation of" "atypical or typical of." I should stop now it's past midnight too late to have tried to write to you after all. The white horn on the mountain, I watched it for hours from her window* xxx *forgive me, I* xxx xxx *"intradermal" "subcutaneous" "chronic" "neural" "acute"*

~~My Fre~~

My Friend,

more and more I think about what skin is how it's meant to be protective and it is   but what of how it turns on itself, becomes its own madness?   something wildly wrong inside it (chronic reaction, subacute reaction) the sane receptive world of each fingertip suddenly insane   each palm suddenly insane   skin a living mind after all (treatment of, prognosis of)   nerve-fibers   blood vessels lubricating glands thrust toward the world unprotected ~~Ican't~~ *(and the faces at Issogne so flat, so without shadow) It's cold so I can't work in the garden like I used to and skin's both living and dead, a gatherer of knowledge that nourishes itself, replaces itself (intradermal, subcutaneous) often I think of the trust one needs just to live in it, carry it, accept it for what it is, this thing so easily cut or burned or damaged (neural anaesthetic, borderline, progressive)   I wonder how old the walnut tree is   all those books she read in its shade her lips slowly moving but no voice from her mouth her eyes on the pages no voice from her mouth no voice at all*

My Friend, I lie awake and think of what you wrote: "skin a living mind after all," and of how the doctors' words left so many cuts. But I can't even ask about your eyes, can't speak a single word to you xxxxxxx I live with the knowledge there's no comfort I can offer. This distance in which we live. ✗ *And I live with Baoyu whose skin is words, and the others whose bodies are words. I watch them struggle and none of the words I bring to them can save them, not even the characters that combine to mean "winged horse" or "sun"—*

Sometimes I feel my own body turning into words, my skin a living network of words—

TRANSLATION OF CAO XUEQIN'S 10TH NOTE:

Red Inkstone still hasn't come. Maybe he'll never come again. Lately I wonder what he'd say if I told him the one thing I've kept back—that years ago a monk came to me with my entire manuscript already written and tucked into his sleeve. "I was walking near Blue Ridge Peak," he said, "and found these words on a piece of jade. I knew if too many years passed the inscription would grow blurred, so I made a rough transcription myself, but need someone to polish and circulate it." He paused, then continued, " 'Go to the place called Mourning-the-Red-Studio,' I was told. 'There you'll find a man, Cao Xueqin, who'll take care of it for you—everyone else is too busy with their own advancement.' So I've come to you. Will you do it? At the very least it will dispel loneliness some rainy evenings under the lamp by the window . . ." Would Red Inkstone believe the monk was real? Do I? He handed me the pages, yet when I look down they aren't there . . . all the pages and scraps are in my own hand, and I cross out much in my confusion as I write, add and take away again and add . . .

Maybe I should just go back to Nanking. But who do I even know there anymore?

My Friend,

Don't think I can no longer be calm. I suppose I shouldn't have written of xxx I don't know xxx but sometimes my mind races xxx and I xxx I haven't forgotten the lekythos—that Greek vessel on which the souls of the living and dead are depicted. The ones who think of but can't reach one another. Theirs is in many ways a gracious, tender world. I still feel this. Didn't I write to you of all the townspeople outside my wall, how fragile their lives are and tender, that I'd protect them if I could, even the horrible ones, though of course I can't protect anyone, least of all myself. But I was saying about the lekythos, on that white-ground vessel, too delicate for daily use, though the dead one stands in the "ekei," the world of "there," and on the vase's other side the living one walks forward holding a long shallow basket filled with gifts, they're not completely separate. I like to think something could still pass between them, even though the dead one stares with blinded eyes, even though a grave stele stands between them. Or is there something much harsher I must face?

The walnut tree's bare now. The brother remembers and walks toward the sister on white ground. Many of those vessels were meant to be broken, left in pieces beside the dead one's stele (and the brother and sister . . . none may disclose the secrets of . . . her mirror wrapped in cloth). Isn't the mind, too, a collection of fragments?—moments of pinned hair, folded cloth, shoulders, loneliness, curved ankle, rim of shield. I lifted her handkerchief out of the drawer, unfolded it, smoothed it, put it back. What was odd was that it smelled of sun. But how could it smell of sun? Of being dried in the sun? So many years. The living brought libations to the dead, oil mixed with wine and honey. They also brought flowers, pomegranates, grapes, sometimes eggs and ribbons.

I hope it's summer where you are, I don't know why I wish this. I imagine willow trees, silks, ponds, tended gardens.

Your Friend,

Cao Xueqin waits for Red Inkstone who no longer comes, and for Odd Tablet who also doesn't come. Allegra didn't come back. And Shelley. And the northern explorers—Franklin, Lockwood, De Long—none of them came back. And you didn't come, though I waited, until absence was a skin, cold layers of waiting, scratches, scars.

Last night I dreamed Claire sat under the walnut tree in Aosta. She wore a white hood to shield her face which was covered with lesions. One of her eyes had frozen open. All around her the garden was in bloom: dahlias, pale blue gentians, Martagon lilies nearly five feet high.

"It's good not being cold anymore,"

she said,

"I don't miss Moscow at all."

I was sure she'd spoken, yet I hadn't heard her voice (not once have I ever heard her voice). Somehow I still knew what she'd said and that she said it.

"Skin has a subtle, secret life,"

she said,

"more than you know. I don't want a quiescent certificate, I never wanted one."

Then all I could see were the cuffs of white sleeves at her lap, her hands buried in the folds of her white skirt.

Aosta ~~Jan~~ Dec 16

~~My Fri~~

There have always been captives of one sort or another why should I be an exception—xx Skin is a secret the mind's imaginings wander through unguided. A testing ground a laboratory a field. Law speaks only angles into justice. My watchfulness is chained to who I am. ~~The sun is very bright today~~ I went into her room again today I always go in now it smells of sun but how could it smell of the sun? ~~Of clothes freshly drying.~~ In her notebook there are many blank pages and many half-filled, many break off in mid-sentence. ~~What is the grammar of~~ xx What is the grammar of thought that doesn't want to complete itself, that doesn't believe in completion? Plutarch wrote of the Athenians tattooing their Samian prisoners with the sign of their ship. But to reduce the body to one thing, the self to one thing, one single mark, there's such cruelty in that. My xxx skin grows more elaborate more complex becomes a new language there's no sovereign of xx belongs to no kingdom xxx there's no one it bows down to or serves no civilization no penal code or slave system it moves through branded with its single barren mark xxx but then the doctors' words come back: "interstitial fibrosis," "septic absorption," "atropine sulphate," "acid tartaric." "Treatment of." "Description of." On one page near the end of her notebook she wrote the words "radical joy."

Clerval sits at his table for hours not writing or reading, his stillness an impenetrable skin.

I miss the movements of his hands, his legs when he gets up and stretches.

How can I know what he thinks?

Hours pass, or are they days? What do I really know of him at all? I who've never even felt his gloved hand in my hand.

———◆———

the sun's almost set I meant to get up and work but I keep thinking about Aosta, the walnut tree, the Samian prisoners marked with the sign of their ship. Baoyu's skin turns to jade then back again to flesh then to columns of words then to jade again then skin that's smooth then intricate with scars and then it's fog. He seems to want to speak to me (all these months I've been translating I've never once heard his voice). Says, "What if my skin were water and nothing could mark me, think about that, think about Zhuangzi's Nothing At All Town and Vast Nothing Wilds—what would my skin be like there? Would I even have skin? Would I need to?"

Years ago, it must have been in London, I read that when the waters of the Hellespont impeded his army, Xerxes ordered his men to lash the waves 300 times then hurl a pair manacles into them.

Baoyu's skin is water then flesh then words then jade then water again then flesh. I translate it but can't control it. Dark now. Must buy more bean flour tomorrow. I wonder if my friend in Aosta's still alive.

xxxx   ~~wwww~~   xxxx

eyes blink all the time we hardly notice but now that mine have mostly stopped it seems so mysterious and odd this thing the body does   this way of interrupting   of disappearing

I lie here and look at the wall she's walking under the walnut tree I want to just blink for a second like I used to but the wall stays her walking stays

What is the blinking of an eye?

spasms   refusals

disruption and resistance built into the very core of sight

My Friend, I

I forgot to address you   forgot to mark the proper starting place of this letter

I remember the comfort of it—upper lid lowering, closing. Small rush of darkness. World gone, everything gone. So fast you barely notice. A hush, but visible. A pause. Such gentle obstruction. 3/10ths of a second, fifteen times per minute. 17,000 times each day.

The eye shuts much faster than it opens. Is it so eager for the dark? How the body needs to go into that darkness and not notice. And to blink is to elude, turn away. As if the mind can't stand to look for too long, all seeing shot through with involuntary contractions, the facial nerves programmed for refusal. I hardly used to register them at all those small rests so many times each minute those infant refusals but now I think of them and miss them she walks in the white wall the walnut tree grows, leafs out in the white wall it's been so long since I've gone away gone anywhere there's a China in my mind where you walk among ponds with blooming lotuses you pass wooden temples, ivory-carvers sitting in windows, baskets filled with rice

I wonder what skin is it is so many things so I keep wondering and I wonder what blinking is I think of you walking, each small resistance in your face each automatic convulsion so many times per minute

Each day the dark comes earlier but her room still smells of sun

When Clerval's friend wonders what skin is I picture Claire at her cold window in Moscow, her skin turned to snow. When he wonders what blinking is I feel her eyes staring at the window as she thinks, like Baoyu,

"What if my skin were water and nothing could mark me, what about that?"

But she didn't want to be water, she wanted to be human and still free, wondered if it was possible to be both. When the jade that was Baoyu fell to earth, its story was already written on its body. Claire isn't like that, or Clerval—I don't know what might befall them. My blinking makes small slashes all over their skin.

What slashes did your leaving make in me?

If all thought's insupportable and wild, is it a ladder that shakes like Claire believed? Is it a skin that can't heal? Once I believed you could have made it otherwise for me, but of course I was wrong.

Morning now. My eyes find Clerval's slender hand, graceful over pen and paper.

Translation of Cao Xueqin's 11th note:

> If the monk hadn't come to me those years ago . . . But did he really come? As it is, I've rewritten everything at least five times and arranged it into chapters, but so much was obliterated from the start, so much blurred or worn away, I often feel lost and worry I'm doing this wrong. Red Inkstone and Odd Tablet reassured me but now they've both gone. Sometimes I lie awake and feel that jade still up in the heavens all alone, shape-shifting and suffering, waiting for the monk to pick it up and inscribe its story on its body. It's as if it has eyes all over its stone skin and all of them are watching. I want to ask it, what will the world give you? What do you want from it? Are you sure you want to come here? Maybe you shouldn't come? Sometimes I think the stone is me, sometimes not. When I write it's as if I'm only making more slashes into what's already been slashed, burned, scattered. I wonder where Red Inkstone is.

<u>WORKING NOTES FOR DRC:</u>

~~ "zhen" means "real" and "jia" means "imaginary." In this book nei-ther exists apart from the other

~~ the Octopartite Composition, or Eight-legged Essay, was the core of the Chinese educational curriculum and the most important part of the official examination for over 500 years. This is the exam Baoyu takes in an effort to restore his family's good fortune.

~~ There are at least two titles for this book. "Hong lou-meng" and "Shitou ji." Cao Xueqin kept changing his mind. I wonder which to use?

ⅩⅩⅩ

My Friend, when I blink I think of what you wrote, how disruption and refusal are built into the very core of seeing. (are they also built into the core of thought?)   To live so uneasily in ⅩⅩⅩ *and we* ⅩⅩⅩ

I once knew a man who after an infection could no longer discern except by sight if he was sitting or standing or lying down. When he closed his eyes he couldn't FEEL himself in space, that he existed as a body in space. If he closed his eyes he simply crumpled to the floor.

Such quick darks I go into again and again. And you, who can't close your eyes—

and the hands for example and the eyes   I wonder what touch is   a
tenderness that suffers   such distances crossed and re-crossed   what
is touch when there's no skin to receive it   She walks in the garden
she isn't there but my eyes that won't close touch her my lips touch her
always I'm here among these walls   the smell of sun on her clothes
my memories of blinking   and my touching violates her doesn't it this
touching I do with my mind   she would turn from me if she could as
she turned from her brother stood on the other side of the trellis
and no brother or sister shall divulge the secrets of their house   nor
shall they pass beyond the bryde   nor utter nor betray   no brother
shall take his meals with a sister   no brother may loiter nor linger
near a sister   and I forbid you henceforth to go out without your
leper's dress   I forbid you to wash your hands in a stream or ever
touch another

but my eyes wander into her xxx   there's not even blinking now to
shut me in the dark and stop my looking   no spasms of refusal in my
face   my eyes on her skin which she believed a place of shame   in
her notebook she wrote "face beyond the face." Wrote, "this feeling of
tenderness so strong now, so what's a suffering that doesn't suffer?"
"How can I suffer yet not suffer all the same?"

What's touch when there's no skin to receive it . . . It seems much of my life has been this question. And the sister's "radical joy"—what did she mean? And her "suffering that doesn't suffer"?

When the Goddess of Consolation came to Boethius in his cell, didn't she speak of a suffering that doesn't suffer? Would radical joy be one thread of her torn robe?

aosta, dec?/jan?

if I could feel my hand hurt   I think she must have been afraid but how can I know she was afraid what is the mind of another the actuality of the reality of ✗✗✗ and not in tranquility ✗✗✗ and tenderly harshly   this numbness a presence in itself the arch was left blank, remember?   no inscription at all in China they carry stoves in their sleeves to keep warm   whereas in Gloskar cattle walked on snowdrifts high as roofs ✗✗✗ the patients uprooted the juniper bushes for firewood until there were none left "my service in frost and cold" but I have been to neither place have seen nothing much past my garden ✗✗✗ her face through the trellis   the actuality of the reality of I call you My Friend but look out on these mountains   the actual the real   window/horn of snow

Cao Xueqin, you end all your chapters with sentences like this: "To know what the outcome was read the next chapter." "To know how he made out, read on." "If you want to know what became of her continue reading." But you also wrote, "In the end, neither author nor transcriber nor reader will know what to make of this book." As I translate, the pages turn to vapor in my hands.

You called your working-place "Mourning-the-Red-Studio." I wonder why you called it this. Is this also where I live?

You wrote that in your book the real (zhen) and imaginary (jia) can't exist apart from each other. (each time my eye blinks it creates separations)

Soon Baoyu will head off to take the official exam. He's studied hard for months. If he does well he'll salvage his family's ill fortune.

Daiyu's dead. Miaoyu's been raped and abducted, all her hair shorn off. (I wanted to believe in "The One Outside the Threshold" and now I can't think of her and the notes she left without thinking she's come to harm)

Why did you paint pictures of stones onto stones? What did you think you were doing?

Over time you crowded your characters so close together it was hard for the red-inked comments to fit in. They migrated toward the margins, unsigned and undated—

Always before your birth date a question mark, and after your death date a question mark.

I spend all this time with you, I wait for Red Inkstone to come, even for Odd Tablet to come . . .

You wrote that the real is unreal and the unreal real. I spend all this time with you in this world whose existence you questioned and which you called Red Dust—

Clerval looks tired all the time. His back must hurt from so much sitting. He never gets up to look at the smoke trees, or nod to his neighbor, or buy melons from the melon cart. Papers are strewn over his table like all that snow Claire looked out on for so long.

———•———

Dream of the Red Chamber

A Dream of Red Mansions   The ~~Re~~ Scarlet Dream

Story of the Stone

TRANSLATION OF RED INKSTONE'S NOTES:

~~ Red Inkstone: "every phrase forsees the true way ahead, every word saddens one's heart. Reading this passage, I almost don't know what I am."   (my friend, reading your letters I almost don't know what I am)

~~ Red Inkstone: "Cao Xueqin, I visited the garden. Its terraces are nothing but piles of broken tiles now. Here and there pines still stretch out their branches; below them, the ruins of the vegetable beds."

~~ Red Inkstone: "I have made five copies of the pages you gave me. This one is for you, I will keep the others here for now. The end of the chapter seems to have been broken off or lost. Since you're ill, I have seen to repairing it as best I could."

~~ Red Inkstone: "but how will we come to a 'settled version'?"

~~ Red Inkstone: "There are many irregularities and chronological problems. I will fix what I can. I know you are weak now and in the end they are not so important. In the Nine-fold Spring of the other world, no one will care that, when Baoyu is 19, Chia Yun can't be old enough to be sold off as a concubine. What your readers will care about is her suffering. I hope you've gotten some sleep and that your fever has improved."

~~ Red Inkstone: "I have made five copies of these new chapters (my suggestions are few this time, and in red ink, as always). If you don't live to finish the book I promise I will see that it is finished."

~~ Red Inkstone: "and what if you don't ever come to a 'settled version.' Maybe that's not such a bad thing."

My Friend,

In between words and in the margins Red Inkstone writes his commentary
for Cao Xueqin. He writes of the ruined garden, of "irregularities," and
"problems," that there'll never be a "settled version" of this book. I hold
no settled view of you, of anything. Baoyu slips through my fingers.
Meanings build and crumble. I see your hand in numbness and in flame.
The properties of. The reality of/the actuality of. And in faithfulness to
what? How can I ✗✗✗ and finally. How are your eyes now? And your face,
has it greatly changed since we last met? (you wrote of a tenderness that
suffers). Ink, red and black surfaces, skin. This trying to take hold, but
slipping. Cao Xueqin writes into the text the word "pian"—"to deceive."
"Do not be deceived by the author"—this phrase recurs often, I don't know
why he does this. Words, crumbled bridges, vapor, scars. No grammar for
this. Thought's odd ferocities. I drink my tea. I listen to the crickets.

This cold wind's a ripped robe as I walk, or certainties dissolving in my hands if certainties could materialize and be touched. Red Inkstone wrote that maybe there could be no "settled version," and that maybe this isn't such a bad thing after all. Always I feel this, that there is no single angle or story to belong to. Your face and others' drifting from me, changing.

I don't know if Claire stands at her window in the snow, or if she dreams of Allegra (but how could she not dream of Allegra?). Does she stand on a ladder of ash? And you—I don't know where you went or what you thought that night you left me. Even my own skin's mostly alien, mysterious. The hidden cells inside my brain opaque and changing. And even though Red Inkstone wrote in the margins, nothing of what he said solved the questions left open by his friend Cao Xueqin.

My Friend,

This place I live in, I think it was once called Mourning-The-Red-Studio. So I write to you from a place of mourning and redness. Here your words revolve in planet-like obsession, a gravity that tugs and binds me: "acid tartaric," "atropine sulphate," "there have always been captives," "why should I be an exception," "spasms," "refusals," "a tenderness that suffers."

"Disruption and resistance built into the very core of sight."

What can I tell you? Baoyu's fallen into another coma. His teeth are clenched, his skin's cold, but his mind's traveling, vibrantly alive. A mysterious monk leads him to a desolate region where he comes to a dwelling with twelve cabinets, their doors partly open. These are the same cabinets he saw years ago in a dream (as you repeatedly return to her white room, her clothes, her notebook). Inside are twelve albums, but the writing's blurred. Only "pity" and "sighing" come through clearly. He doesn't know what to do with all those pages when he can only read two words. When the monk reappears he asks him: "Did you pry into any secrets here?" "Yes, I saw some albums. I tried to read about people I know, the ones I love who died and suffered, and those still alive, but I could only understand two words." The monk replies: "All earthly ties are bewitchments. Now you must go back."

As you and I in our own ways are turned back. The albums inscrutable, the print blurred.

What is blinking? A pulling away. A pulling back. Flinching built into the central workings of the face. Absence making its quick claim. Everything partial. Beneath the skin, whole tracts of hiddenness. The beggars on Beggar's Bridge at once visible and hidden. The sister's skin was shame to her and visible but what of the rest of her that wasn't visible?

I don't know if Cao Xueqin lived to finish his book. I don't know if you're alive. I write from this place of mourning and redness. I see your face through red light like the smoke trees in autumn.

I think of Red Inkstone's words to Cao Xueqin, "perhaps there will be no settled version."

Last night I saw Claire. She was standing at her attic window in Moscow in the snow.

"I don't want to be back here,"

she said,

"I liked it better under the walnut tree in Aosta. And why all this dwelling on what skin is, what blinking is? Do you think the Northern explorers would have stopped to worry about that? That Parry would have dwelled on that? They waited their snow blindness out when they had it, that's all. Waited and didn't complain. Though I suppose I dwelled on walls and ladders, so I'm as bad as anyone. Allegra's been dead a long time now. And Shelley."

"Why do you never think of Mary?"

"She suffered over you, but you hardly ever mention her."

"I miss writing in my notebook. When I speak—as I'm speaking now—I sound more harsh than I feel. I feel little freedom when I speak. I don't want to speak."

Waking, I felt lost. I remembered looking into your eyes when I first opened mine, how you flinched and turned away. I felt a coldness dry as dirt. No "tenderness that suffers," no walnut tree, no movement of a hand across a page. No album, no leper's dress, no marginalia, no red mourning, no name.

My Friend,

✗✗✗ *but nothing can prevent* ✗✗✗✗ ✗✗ *and I'm glad you can't see me, that I don't have to deal with your kindness or pity or whatever you might feel* ✗✗✗ *atropine sulphate distilled water* ✗✗✗ *when they first brought us here from Moncaliere I was frightened. I believe she was too. First our father died, then our mother and brothers. Just the two of us left* ~~and I forbid you henceforth to go out without your leper's dress~~ ✗✗✗ *Do you think there's a place of calm in the skin no matter what, something inviolable, untouched, and nothing can despoil it? So many years of not speaking. The mid-day bells at 11, not 12, as is the custom. Her footsteps on stone. My fear I would somehow make her worse. In the study, pieces of mica and gneiss from the hills. I lined them up on the table, pulled back the curtains, watched them glint.* ✗✗✗*But I was unable to* ✗✗ *and ever afterward* ✗✗✗ *from the beginning they kept our names secret* ✗✗✗ *packages of books and food on the doorstep* ✗✗✗ *"should not be in proximity to towns" "water supply should be adequate"* ✗✗✗ *"tenderness of nerves/presence of bacilli"* ✗✗✗ *I watched the unchanging gray in the distance: slate, gneiss, serpentine, schist* ✗✗✗

Mourning the Red Studio ~~The Stone's Story~~ Story of the
Stone   Mourning the Red Dream

<u>WORKING NOTES FOR DRC:</u>

"zhengmian" indicates the "surface of the text" while "fanmian" indicates the "meaning underneath," but why believe the two are separable or even distinguishable from each other?

Red Inkstone: "It's true my commentary is unsystematic. I'm sure many of my comments contradict others I've made in the past."

Red Inkstone: "Reading this, I'm reminded of the painter's technique known as 'bemian fufen'—whitening the background to bring out the foreground."

Red Inkstone: "Cao Xueqin, are you the stone? Are you transcribing the text that was written on your body in script so minute no one could see it?"

χ χ

My Friend,

If I could reach you . . . Baoyu's mind is traveling . . . When he comes back to the world he knows what he must do. All thought is approximate at best, he can see this. Yet he studies his books day and night, readies himself for the imperial exam. He remains in his "quiet room." He "never leaves the compound." (I think of you in your stone tower, alone.)

"Today is the first time you'll be entirely on your own," his mother says as he and his nephew leave for the exam. "Come back as soon as you're done and set my mind at rest." But even as she's talking, Baoyu's remembering a line from a poem: "He breaks through the first door of his cage." Then he wonders, How many doors does a cage even have? Do the first, second and third look just the same? Why would a cage need more than one door?

Yesterday I touched the barred doors of your letters, wondering how many. Wondering, are you nameless to me now or not, is your name in fact

Guasco, was she truly your sister? Did you come with her from
Moncaliere, and the others died, was that family you wrote of really your
family or is your mind in some kind of fever?

So many cage doors: "from the beginning they kept our names secret,"
"my fear I would somehow," "something inviolable, untouched." The
light's dimming fast, it's too late to continue—I'll tell you more about
Baoyu tomorrow—

her face on the other side of the trellis. How does a face bring
harm to another what can it possibly inflict on another why did I think
that even a look from me would hurt her that the touch of my skin the
thought of my skin on her skin could make her worse? Have I told you
her lesions were mostly internal? Some on her torso and arms but
almost none on her face. What is silence what is fear? Every now and
then words from a song we'd learned as children xxx her eyes always
lowered so why did I worry why did I need to turn away xxx she lived
as though alone as though she'd never had a brother ~~and shall not and
shall not~~   ~~nor shall they betray or utter~~   She in her part of the
house I in mine or in the garden. In her notebook: "In my sleep I hear
myself laughing, and the laughter grows redder and redder, a fire
made of sound, and spreading."

Clerval writes quickly these days. Though he's thin and frail-looking, his hand seems vigorous, the one part of him that isn't withering. As if his hand's a mind and that mind is traveling, filled with a secret, mysterious determination like Baoyu's.

zhengmian, the surface of the text,

he writes. Then,

fanmian, the meaning underneath. Inseparable, yes, that's how it is.

Then:

Her face, her red laughter, but how will I ever understand? Do I need to understand, do I even have the right to?

TRANSLATION OF CAO XUEQIN'S 12TH NOTE:

Red Inkstone would chastise me for dreaming of him. "Too many dreams in your book," he always says, though we haven't seen each other in months. But maybe this is my way of drawing him close. Or is he here and it's just that I can't see him through my fever? Am I ill at all? I don't know if I get up each day and work and write or if I'm sick in bed and only dreaming that I'm working. In my latest dream he's wearing a green silk robe like Baoyu's, but the cloth's turned into pages. I don't know if I'm Baoyu, Daiyu, Red Inkstone, or myself, or all of us at once. I don't know if the monk ever came and handed me a sheaf of pages. I'm struggling to read Red Inkstone's robe, I need to put the pages in some order. But the characters keep changing, moving insect-like in circles, then they're still as twigs, then withering, blooming.

My Friend,

Baoyu's arrived at the examination hall, determined to do well for the sake of his family. The narrator says, "Let us leave Baoyu and his cousin Jia Lan for the time being." So we don't see him take the exam; we don't know how long it lasts, what he's asked or what he's thinking. This is how I often feel with you—I'm almost with you but a fissure opens up and I see nothing. Still, I write to you of doors and cages. And though there's a wall of time and space between us, it's a peculiar wall that attacks itself at its core.

X

×××××   ×××××

×××   ~~The characters for "fake wall" are "jia qiang"~~

×××××   The Emperor Yuandi was told "Once you build a wall behind yourself all will be well." But a wise man said to him, "Your wall can never be solid enough."

My f Friend,

I'm very weak now.

She wrote in her notebook, "What am I if I can't be of use?"

"all these years behind walls"   "but what am I if I stay here useless?"

Wrote, "as if I myself am a wall and crumbling. No, I'm not a wall at all. I'm so tired of being kept behind these walls. How can he love his walled garden, how can he stand to walk there, does he walk and tell himself stories, pretend that he's free?"

Wrote, "The red laughter's come back again. A whole night of it spreading."

It's harder to get to her room now. ~~Th~~ My legs increasingly distant from my mind. I tell them "move" or "feel" and sometimes they do, but from a place unknown to me and to which I have no definable access.

She wrote in her notebook, "He keeps planting and transplanting. Some days I think I'll go mad."

Wrote, "His hands among the flowers. My skin as if pressed to a wall and eroding. When I walk the wall walks with me. When I sleep it sleeps with me."

"Is there some way to be of use? If not, then what am I?"

Sometimes I hear Claire's voice in the shore's stunted trees:

"Mary says she's a shadow now." "The hazard of my eyes."

The wind stopped as if suddenly blinded. Seabirds. Rain.

I touch:

ulceration, magnesium sulphate, trophic disturbance,

a hurt, unclosing eye. Touch:

"my legs increasingly distant from my mind."

The sister feels each wall move with her.

Allegra was surrounded by walls. And Claire and the sister touched so many walls.

And shall not and shall not and your leper's dress . . . must not utter . . . must not betray . . .

"There is no settled version."

I wonder how many times she heard the red laughter.

My Friend,

Baoyu's done with the exam but no one can find him. Not even his nephew, "In the hostel we ate and slept beside each other. At the examination grounds our cells were close by. We even came out of the exam together. But I lost him in the crowd at Dragon Gate." And your sister (but was she your sister?) felt the walls walk beside her, move, wake, sleep beside her. Her face lost to you, and her thoughts, where she stood on the other side of the trellis—as you are mostly lost to me, though you send me so many things—Issogne, ruined roads, red laughter.

TRANSLATION OF CAO XUEQIN'S 13TH NOTE:

Each day I grow weaker. I don't think I'll be able to complete my book. You'll find all my notes in the green cupboard. Everything's sketched out, though nothing, as you say, is "settled." I think often of the calligraphers who spend their entire lives practicing. Only at the end do they find their mind's and hand's true wildness. A wildness that's disciplined, severe. If my book is wild, contradictory, at odds with itself, I hope it's honed to its raw, unsettled core. The red dust is dry and astringent in my eyes.

I dream, though you've warned me not to: a traveling salesman brings my manuscript to a bookseller in Peking. Asks him, would you like to buy this, it's called The Story of the Stone. But the bookseller, Gao E, says the price is too high, sends him away, eats his lunch at his desk, does some paperwork, sells nothing, goes home. The next day the manuscript's on his desk. He reads it, then takes it to his friend Cheng Weiyuan, and says, "You should publish this." "But where does it come from, who wrote it?" "I don't know. A man left it the other day when I was out, I've no idea who he was or where he came from." Cheng Weiyuan reads it, says "It's good but what are we to do, it's not really finished, too much is rough, unsettled." "I'll polish it. Just give me a few months." The air turns red, and it's hard for me to see the two men talking. I can't hear them at all. Cattle walk by, red dust on their skin and in their eyes. Even the rice in my rice bowl is red. When I wake I think about Baoyu, how he never belonged in this world. I remember the abundant delicacies of my childhood— lotus-foot cakes scented with osmanthus, dumplings filled with crab. Our chopsticks were made of ivory inlaid with gold. All this while the peasants stooped and walked bone-thin in a namelessness I never questioned. I'm cold all the time. The heat cold, my fevers cold. I've left the green cupboard unlocked. There's no reason to lock anything.

My Friend,

Why should the lamp not disintegrate as I look at it? Why should the floor hold? Each moment is a threatened net of touch and sight and sound. I'm very ~~e~~ tired now. ~~I~~

I marvel at the mind's trust and linkages, how it believes the walls won't fall, how it waits for one sound to follow another expecting they'll connect to form words and those words will make meaning. It all seems suddenly so effortful, precarious, unlikely, even odd.

I write this slowly, wanting to make no mistakes. The garden's gray and brown.

There are sentences whose lesions are internal, as hers were largely internal (and yet she wouldn't show her face).

Is it true what I've read?—that a Chinese scholar's garden should take on an appearance that's "simple, emptied of desire and striving"? I wish I could have read Wen Zhenheng's "Treatise on Superfluous Things." I found only this sentence: "If one indulges in extravagant planting and colorful effects, a garden becomes a fetter, a mere cage."

(Her face hidden behind the trellis. Even her voice mostly hidden, and her hands.)

She wrote in her notebook: "He never leaves the garden alone. What if he didn't touch it for a week?"

Wrote, "When I look at the garden as though I'm already dead and nothing, it becomes more beautiful, more distinct."

"My eyes want to control what they see. But if I were dead and nothing . . ."

Wrote, "At first the red laughter was fierce but then it simply washed over everything."

"What is the color of laughter that's no longer afraid?"

I believe I mostly forget to sign my letters these days. I am still—

Your Friend,

. . . Your face red dust, your laboratory table red dust . . . your notebooks, your instruments, my face, your dreams and fevers, this body you gave me, this shore, these waves, this waking, this sleeping, red dust . . .

red laughter   red dust   as if she were a wall and crumbling

~~Goddess of~~ Crumbling   Goddess of

My Friend,

It's the fourth watch. The welcome-home banquet lies untouched. When word arrives that Baoyu's placed seventh among the thousands of exam candidates, his family thinks surely he'll come back. "Since Baoyu was fated to pass, he's bound to turn up." "Now that Master Baoyu has passed we're certain to find him." "You know the proverb—a successful candidate's fame spreads throughout the land."

Only his sister says quietly, "People shouldn't have anything unique about them. We thought it was good he was born with jade in his mouth, but such mysteries can't be understood. Maybe we never knew him at all."

On the page I'm now translating the narrator says "Honorable Readers, certain things are predestined and cannot be helped." He doesn't say this in a mournful way. I suspect you would be more skeptical.

Meanwhile, the Emperor restores the family's fortune. Their confiscated property's returned, they're reappointed to their official posts.

I hold your remaining letters—the stack so thin, not even a stack now, hardly more than a frail layer of skin. This frightens me.

In Shen Fu's "Six Chapters of a Floating Life," he explains that near is far and far is near. The landscape must create this illusion. "Thus do you suggest something which is not there," he says of placing low balustrades along the top of a wall to suggest the presence of a nonexistent roof garden. And "Thus do you conceal what is there," he says of a garden's bamboo trees and few rocks set just so to block the further view. The unreal lives in the real, and the real in the unreal.

As your voice lives in mine and mine in yours. As your sister's red laughter moves through me, though I don't know if she's your sister or if her clothes still smell of sun. I don't know if you're even alive—

My Friend,

and cannot ✗✗✗✗✗✗✗✗✗✗✗✗✗✗✗   ~~and cannot~~   ~~and~~
~~the burns~~

I don't know how or why she died what caused her death   ✗✗✗
*sodium hydnocarpate soft infiltration so many years and we went on
and on the two of us just living* ✗✗✗✗ *discomforts yes fevers lesions
sleeplessness yes but why did she die what happened and why do I
grow weaker? Infected burns on my right thigh but how did I get them
how long have I had them I don't know* ✗✗✗✗✗✗✗✗ *bone pain nerve
pain* ✗✗ *elbows and knees tender when they bend* ✗✗✗ *peripheral nerves
swelling under skin   glycerine   borax   gold salts   excision of
histology of   I still wonder about the Chinese gardens Qi Biaojia
wrote, "where it is level I introduce a little unevenness, where it is too
diffuse I tighten it. It is like being a good doctor"* ✗✗✗✗ *and what is a
"landscape window" it is said Li Liweng had one installed in his
Mustard Seed Garden but I don't understand I don't know what it is*
✗✗✗✗✗ *I remember her white sleeves divided into diamonds by the
trellis*

*She wrote in her notebook "He works in the garden but he must see it's
enclosed, doesn't he care that it's enclosed?"*

"but even in the most closed system might some freedoms still exist?"

Wrote, "irreducible core"

*Wrote, "Very tired today. I don't want to watch him weeding. I don't
want to see him bending down among those tall red flowers."*

Clerval pushes his translation work to the far side of the table, sits for a long time with the pages of his friend's still-unread letters. Doesn't pick them up. Sometimes he rubs them lightly with his fingers.

Soon there'll be no more letters left unread. I learned to live within that kind of quiet, I know about such things. Then Claire came to me, and Clerval, though never you. Or was it I who went to them? I couldn't touch them or be touched, couldn't speak to them or listen to them speak. Even so, a kind of tenderness began. Something within the harshness broke and opened.

Clerval eats his noodles, drinks his tea. Washes his pot, his cup, his bowl. Sits down again and reads about gardens, takes notes on gardens, as if he could send his notes to his friend.

———◆———

NOTES ON GARDENS

Ji Cheng in his "Yuan Ye" (17th c) The Craft of Gardens, writes that a garden "should make your thoughts travel beyond the confines of this world of dust"   (my friend, has your garden done this for you? I picture you planting, weeding, bending)

~~~

there are no fixed rules for garden design, only the essential principle that such a place must touch one's deepest being

~~~

a gateway functions as a surmountable barrier   (imagine, my friend, something surmountable, after all)

~~~

a moon gate offers the sense of distance   no space within a garden is too narrow to be shaped, thought about, used

~~~

different eras bring different fashions—windows shaped like caltrop flowers give way to windows shaped like willow leaves, yet each has its own particular beauty

~~~

one should feel a sense of motion within it yet be far from worldly con-
cerns   (did the scholar take care of his own garden, or did his servants
do it for him?)

~~~

a garden is the larger natural world in microcosm   all paths must lead
to quietude, humility (my friend, where has yours led you?)

~~~

let there be no single vista, no central point of view, all aspects will
reveal themselves over time and from differing angles

(Red Inkstone, again: maybe there will be no settled version)

NAMES OF GARDENS

Master of the Fishing Nets Garden   this includes the Pavilion for
                                         the Advent of the Moon, also
                                         the Ribbon-Washing Pavilion

Garden of Harmonious Interest

Green Vine Studio

Lingering Garden

The Humble Administrator's Garden

Garden of Perfect Brightness

Warm Garden

Outlook Garden

Lion Grove

Garden of Autumn Vapors

Could-be Garden

Thatched Hut of the Abundant Stars

My friend, what would you name your garden? Would you keep it secret, or would you tell me?

but no wall will ever be solid enough   and the red laughter through
the wall

> but the walls are so strong
> no wall will ever

My Friend,

*I feel the space of you growing narrower and narrower, walls closing in.
There are so few letters left so very few and I feel cold suddenly and
suddenly coldly afraid. "No space is too narrow to be thought about or
used," Ji Cheng wrote in his book on gardens. And one can build a moon
window, he said, a way for the distance to open and come in. Yet the walls
moved as your sister moved, they walked beside her. Now I feel them
walking beside me. They hover, press in. I can't feel the smoke trees on the
hillside or the way the distance opens.*

*There are no more notes of Cao Xueqin's to translate. Often in my mind I
hear Red Inkstone's words, "there will be no settled version." Of you,
myself, or anyone, our hours in Aosta, your sister, these months I've read
your letters. Something in me resists this even as I know it's true.*

*In Xu Yuan Garden, in Nanking, there's a guesthouse named Tongyin
Guan which means music-from-the-tong-tree. It's named for Bo Ya who,
almost 2000 years ago, played a qin made from tong tree wood. Legend
says he played more beautifully than anyone ever had. He traveled on
government assignments but went off alone whenever he could. One day
heading back from a mission he moored his boat among reeds. From
behind the trees an impoverished woodcutter stopped to listen to him
playing. When Bo Ya played of high mountains the woodcutter saw high
mountains, when he played of water the woodcutter murmured, "how
vast are the rivers and oceans." Whatever Bo Ya played, the woodcutter
never failed to understand. Though he'd lived for decades as a hermit, he
stepped out of the woods and the two became close friends. "Your heart
and mine are the same," Bo Ya said, promising to come back within the
year. But when he returned his friend had been dead for one hundred days.
At this news, Bo Ya smashed his instrument and never played again.*

*When I touch the door do I touch the same wood Cao Xueqin touched?
When I sit at the table is this his table? Do I wash my cup and bowl in the
sink that was his sink?*

You write that you feel cold all the time, that there are burns on your leg you don't understand. Your garden shines with red flowers. There are words that grow red inside my mind: excision, infiltration. Cattle stumble in red dust, our faces are covered with red dust. There's a garden near here named Sufficiency Garden. I wish we could go there, you and I. It's said that even the smallest garden path, if made properly, can form a path for the eyes that's longer than a hundred miles—

For days Clerval adds other gardens to his list: Lotus Garden, Half-mu Garden with its Chamber for the Appreciation of Stones and its collection of zithers. Garden for Solitary Pleasure, Hundred Plant Garden. There are paths, moon windows, the Hall of Cloud Shade with its roof that seems almost to float. Every now and then he rests his head on the rough table. There's only one letter left to read. What will he do after he finishes his friend's last letter?—probably go back to his translation work, but then what?

"Your heart and mine are the same," Bo Ya said. But I think Claire was right—there are walls within walls we'll never understand. Does she still stand at the cold window in the snow as she writes the word *destroy* over and over, and says to herself, *liberty of thought* and *silent letters*? And the Goddess of Consolation, did she really come to Boethius, or did he sit in his cell alone, touch his lips only to air?

Aosta, Feb 13

My Friend,

These burns on my legs don't go away I don't know how they xxxx photophobia ulceration hypopigmentation xx I dreamed they gave me a quiescent certificate but all it said was I must stay completely quiet not make one single sound not ever xxx I tore it up my legs were working I ran into her room xxx

She wrote in her notebook, "We live in accumulations of the actual with so little understanding."

"I dreamed I hacked at his garden wall for hours until it broke into 5,000 pieces. Then we were standing on either side of the trellis. I have to repair it, he said. No you don't, I said, but could tell he didn't believe me."

Wrote, "Can extremity nurture?"

"He moves things around as if it matters—why doesn't he look to the hills, let into his garden the feeling of hills?"

Wrote, "Sometimes he looks so small from my window, a crouching animal, unguarded."

xxxx If I had someone to read to me   If I could ask you about the Mustard Seed Garden and the Mustard Seed Manual that was written there but I'm glad, as always, you're not here xxxx

My Friend, there's only one letter left to read. I delay. I pretend I can send
you my notes on gardens, I make my lists of gardens

XX

FURTHER NOTES ON GARDENS

"Borrow from the view afar," Ji Cheng wrote. "Bring the vast external landscape into that which is contained and private."

(what do you take into your eyes?)

~~~

Each plant has its own history and associations. The plantain, for instance, is associated with poor scholars who used its large, broad leaves to write on when they couldn't afford paper or silk.

~~~

Each segment or "space cell" within the larger garden needs to be contemplated on and then named.

(I still don't know your name)

~~~

Having retreated from the world, Sima Guang wrote his encyclopedic work Comprehensive Mirror for the Aid Of Government (11th c) within the confines of his garden.

~~~

"For twenty years I continued to build the garden. I worked and sat and thought and worked and rested and thought but it was still not very good. When I returned from my post in Szechuan I gave my whole heart to the garden, I thought only of the garden." (Yu Yuan, 16th c)

~~~

My Friend, I'm still delaying. Will I ever run out of gardens to list?

NAMES OF GARDENS

Pavilion of the Roosting Red Clouds

Surging Wave Pavilion

Garden of the Foolish Official

Late Spring Studio

Winding Garden

Cool Spring Pavilion

Pear Garden

Plum Garden

Path of Flower Rain

Kiosk for the Watering of Flowers

With-Whom-to-Sit Pavilion

Five Star Bridge

Jade Peak Pagoda

Three Pools Mirroring the Moon

Always when Clerval comes to me, when I can see him, I love to watch his hands, his face, the opening and closing of his eyes, the tensing or relaxing of his forehead, his jaw. But now I'm almost tempted not to look. After he's finished reading, when there are no more letters left to read, will something rip itself in him as once, long ago, it ripped in me?

Aosta, Feb 17

My Friend,

In what ways does thought pierce itself destroy itself? Her white sleeve the smell of sun xxxx *and thou shall not   thou shall not and your leper's dress* xxx   *your hood your clapper   What laws govern leaving?* xx *atropine sulphate   acid tartaric* xxx *she said when she walked the wall walked with her   In her notebook she left many blank pages   the sores on my leg much worse now and I don't know why   I can barely   ~~I will try to~~*

I'll try to focus better. Be more clear. Will write more slowly. Maybe that's what the Master of the Mustard Seed Garden did, just calmed, slowed, talked to himself all those years he worked on his manual. I read that he named it Mustard Seed Garden because it was small like a seed, that modest plot of ground he tended. She dreamed of destroying these walls (she dreamed red laughter). I say she's my sister I write of her notebook quote from her notebook but what do you really know of her or who I am and how I've lived or if she even existed? I remember the touch of your hand through the glove in my mind I call you "my friend" I think of you daily xxxx

I don't want to become a "story" to you xxxx *Is anyone truly held or known or settled within another's mind? The man who'll bring you these letters if he can find where you live—I've told him that he must not let you set eyes on him or speak with him no matter what, he can leave them only if not seen. These pages are what you have of me as I have my thoughts of you, the idea of the warmth in your sleeves, your small house north of Peking, our hours in Aosta. ~~I can't~~*

You'll wonder if I'm alive or did I die, but what does it matter?

~~th xx The sores on my~~   the sores on my leg burn   she seemed so sad under the walnut tree and lonely   If I could hack these walls   but the

Master of the Mustard Seed Garden, did he mind his garden's walls?
Wars outside them, disunity, corruption ~~did he~~ ~~and thou shall not~~
if I could rip this solitude this quiet but nothing ever really rips it
three injections of 0.01 grams sepsis tourniquet local anaesthetic
xxx another snowfall last night her sleeves still smell of sun

Baoyu still hasn't returned. His father hurries home from his mission in the south, travels day and night by foot then boat. Near Piling Post Station it's starting to snow. Baoyu's father moors his boat, steps off toward shore, briefly wonders: If I could live as a recluse in the country . . . if I could tend my plot of land . . . forget . . . But he misses his son, is surprised how much he misses him. White air swirls. Cold seeps under his clothes. Then he sees something moving on shore, the shape of a man with a shaved head and a red cloak. The shape stops and deeply bows, turns and walks the other way. It seems almost to glide. Two other shapes appear and gently take its arms. There are no footprints in the snow.

At Piling Post Station the snow falls and falls. Baoyu's father stands in the secluded cove. Didn't the shape in the red cloak turn the way he imagines planets turn, beyond willingness or mind, undoubting. Something beautiful in how it turned. (My friend, I turn you over in my mind. What will I do with this silence you left me in? There's rice in my bowl but I don't want to eat it I should make myself eat it . . . One face on either side of the trellis . . . And Red Inkstone didn't come, or did Cao Xueqin not know that he had come?)

Baoyu walks and walks in his red cloak. Snow falls on his shaved head, his shoulders—

{ NOTES }

Notes on Agnes Martin

From the early 1960s until her death at 92 she painted grids. Why would she do this?

Often she titled them after nature but they were of the mind, the way it feels itself and thinks: "My paintings are not about what is seen. They are about what is known forever in the mind."

She was born in Saskatchewan, Canada, in 1912.

Her father, a wheat farmer, died when she was two.

⟨ I look at her grids, the steady and unsteady pressure of a human hand, soft graphite lines darker here and there, so thin sometimes as if about to break. The mind is an unsteady place. And yet it holds. I feel inside myself its mixture of fragility and chance. How mind is more than mind, outstrips itself somehow— ⟩

She said, "I was thinking about the innocence of trees and the grid came to me." "I have a very quiet mind."

She said, "Nature is the wheel. When you get off the wheel you're looking out. You stand with your back to the turmoil."

She titled her paintings: *White Flower, Words, Night Sea, Falling Blue.*

Why would she make grid after grid? And year after year like that? "Why do you make another?" a visitor asked. "I have a dream. I dream another grid."

⟨ Like the way I go over and over in my mind the place that is the mind. As these notes accumulate . . . these nets of . . . these grids, veils, traces of . . . these marks of being on the edge of or immersed in, or— ⟩

Each grid bears its own particular irregularities, minute fluctuations, intervals, exaltations. Yet how orderly they seem overall, each speaking to the others over space and time, as if to say, each of us is isolate and odd but not singular only, not just that.

(As I'm not just singular, after all. As a mind's patternings partly recognize another's.)

(She marked such minute gradations, zones of transitivity, of becoming, how did she do that? It's what you couldn't meddle with in me even as you made me—somehow it escaped—that grid of thought materializing, dematerializing, in this place inside myself I can hardly grasp or name.)

"When I cover the square surface with rectangles it lightens the weight of the square, destroys its power."

(I watch her fields of powerlessness float. They're strong in themselves and do no harm.)

In 1967 she gave away almost all her possessions, left New York City, drove in a pickup truck across Canada and the West. She didn't paint for seven years.

Then she settled in Cuba, New Mexico.

She had no studio assistants: "I don't know what they do."

She didn't own a TV.

(I don't have a quiet mind, but the thought of a hand moving across a surface sometimes quiets me. The way marks create a merging and dissolving, a setting out, a dissonance or peace, a flickering, a membrane, a rough bloom—)

She titled her paintings: *Untitled, Grass, Rain, Leaf, Wheat, The Spring.*

What is it that consoles?

She said she was painting joy. (I only partly believe her.)

She wrote, "I would rather think of Humility than anything else. She cannot do either right or wrong. She does not do anything. All of her ways are empty."

She died in a retirement community in Taos, New Mexico, on December 16, 2004.

Notes on John Cage

He believed there's no such thing as silence. "Until I die there will be sounds. And they will continue following my death."

Even in the most quiet moments: breathing, hum of electrical appliances, rustling pages, trucks in the distance shifting gears.

(When I couldn't speak, I *heard* the blood-taste in my throat, the fear inside my body, everything withheld, unsettled; Mary's hands holding pebbles as she waited, the tossed quiet of her leaving.)

He said, "quiet sounds   were like loneliness"

"I was a ground in which emptiness could grow."

All this is music.

Years earlier, he'd entered an anechoic chamber expecting to hear silence, but instead heard two sounds. "When I described them to the engineer in charge, he informed me the high one was my nervous system, the low one my blood in circulation."

After this he wrote his "silent piece," *4'33".*

The first performance was given by David Tudor on August 29, 1952. He walked out onstage, sat down at the piano, closed the keyboard's lid. After a period of time he opened it. This marked the end of the first movement. He did this again for the second, the third, his hands never touching the keys.

(There's so much sound in waiting and thinking, in stillness and absence, your face rising in my mind then disappearing.)

He said, "Everything we do is music."

"Wherever we are, what we hear is mostly noise. The sound of a truck at fifty miles an hour. Static between the stations. Rain." "I found that I liked noises."

(Was I noise to you, but noise you couldn't hear as music? As if such sound must be a wrongness, a crude disordering of thought and feeling.)

He sought no summations, built no walls.

(He found the beautiful in what's dismissed or overlooked as ugly. Found such terms, in any case, not useful. I look at my body and wonder: if I'm noise and that noise is part of the ongoing texture of the world, why must I think in terms of ugliness, beauty, aberration? Still I hide, never look in a mirror.)

His pieces include: *Cheap Imitation, First Construction (In Metal), Etude Borealis, Imaginary Landscape No. 1.*

He designed a prepared piano, placing screws, bolts, rubberized strips, and other objects between the strings.

(You worked to make the parts of me combine to form a new, amazing being. But I think you didn't want me new or different after all, wanted, instead, a replica of the known. Why must difference frighten?)

"If you think   you are a ghost   you will become a   ghost"

(I feel myself a ghost when I think of you, even after all these years.)

"Sounds need to come into their own, rather than being exploited to express sentiments or ideas of order."

(The living fact of my body broke all your ideas of order.)

An interviewer asked, "Why is there so much noise in *Variations V*? You used to be gentle, tender, how could you have become so violent?"

He answered, "What is a quiet mind? A mind which is quiet in a quiet situation? Let's say there are only a few sounds. Let's say they're loud. What shall we do?"

(If I was sound you thought you wanted then found you didn't want, did that mean you should choose not to hear me? Maybe I was the texture of your mind, the hidden noises and workings of your mind.)

He used the I-Ching to make pieces through "chance operations."

(I remember Plato wrote that chance builds more wisely than art.)

For one piece he used star charts placed on a musical staff.

In 1985 he composed *Organ2/ASLSP (As Slow As Possible)*. The first performance began on September 5, 2001, in Halberstadt, Germany. On February 2, 2003, the first chord was sounded. The piece is scheduled to take 639 years.

(Time builds, dissolves, re-forms inside me. Presences, absences intertwined, inseparable, conversing . . .)

"Nothing was lost when everything was given away." "I write in order to hear."

(These notes I throw to the wind . . . but what would I even hear without them? My rough scrawls on paper scraps, old shopping lists, torn pages. Even so I know so little.)

He was a lover of mushrooms, pointed out that "music" and "mushroom" stand next to each other in many dictionaries, though for him their link was random.

He won a mushroom quiz contest on Italian television in 1958.

Lactarius piperatus burns the tongue when raw but is delicious when cooked.

"beware of that which is   breathtakingly   beautiful,   for at any moment   the telephone may ring   or the airplane   come down"

(If I had said those words to you, bright shudderings I still hold inside my mind . . .)

He wrote: "we are getting   nowhere   and that is a pleasure"

He died in New York City, a few weeks before his eightieth birthday, on August 12, 1992.

Notes on Genetic Privacy

The Nuremberg Code states, "The voluntary consent of the human subject is absolutely essential." It calls the patient the "experimental subject." (What would you have called me?)

It holds that experiments must not be "random in nature." (Yet doesn't much that's beautiful and good arise from what's random? My mind spins as I think this.)

(In "consent" I hear "sent." You sent me forth into my self, my body, but that self was made of otherness and strangeness, in darkness and in shame. The experiment I was wasn't mine. I was sent into a foreign country, but that country's inside me, and I never meant to go.)

In October 1976, John Moore was diagnosed with hairy-cell leukemia.

After "withdrawing samples of blood, bone marrow aspirate, and other bodily substances," Dr. David W. Golde confirmed the diagnosis and recommended Moore's spleen be removed.

Moore signed a consent form authorizing the operation.

(Forms, signatures, codes—how far from what happened in your laboratory. Yet when I think of the doctor in his white coat behind his desk, and the patient on the other side, lost in the strange country of his illness, I think of all that passed between us. So much unspoken. So much before my eyes had even opened.)

On October 20, Dr. Golde removed John Moore's spleen. He'd made arrangements to keep it for his research, but Moore didn't know this.

He was using Moore's T-lymphocytes to establish a cell line of lymphokines for medical purposes. From 1976 through 1983, John Moore returned for additional visits at Dr. Golde's request. Each time he left samples of "blood, blood serum, skin, bone marrow aspirate and sperm."

(Strange to think how part of oneself can thrive, exist, outside one-self, can have a separate life apart.)

("The Truth, is Bald, and Cold—")

Moore thought giving samples was an ordinary part of follow-up thera-peutic care.

(How little we know of our lives. The mind sees but doesn't, knows much but also doesn't.)

His T-lymphocytes were "interesting" to Dr. Golde because they "over-produced certain lymphokines, thus making the genetic material easier to identify."

On January 30, 1981, Dr. Golde, his colleague Dr. Shirley Quan, and the Regents of the University of California applied for a patent on John Moore's cell line.

(Unlike them, you hid in shame what you had done. Should I respect the shame you felt? Feel tenderness toward the way you suf-fered, lived in secrecy? But what might have happened if I'd turned out as you wanted? What if you'd liked what you had made, hadn't felt ashamed, disgusted? That question haunts me.)

On March 20, 1984, U.S. Patent No. 4,438,032 named Dr. Golde and Dr. Quan "inventors of the cell line" and the Regents the "assignee." They would "share in any royalties or profits."

Biotechnology experts predicted a three-billion-dollar market for lym-phokines by 1990.

(More and more I trust in the bare facts of things, even if such facts are hard to gather and get clear. I want to grasp the facts of this, what happened. I want to let those facts—not my wonderings about them—speak.)

When he learned of the patent, Moore filed suit, accusing the doctors and university of interfering with his "ownership" and "right of posses-sion." He claimed a proprietary interest in any "products the defendants might create from his cells or patented cell line."

(Strange how the body becomes a thing that's owned, co-owned, disputed. How it's one's own but not—a generator of profits. Legalized, fought over, shared, unshared. What does it mean to be "oneself"?)

In 1990, the California Supreme Court ruled against John Moore.

Dr. Golde had, by that time, "negotiated agreements for commercial development of the cell line and products derived from it." He would be paid in exchange for "exclusive access to the materials and research performed."

(There's a silence in John Moore I can't get hold of. Not the part of him that sued, but that place within him where he came to know his cells were taken, grown, changed and sold by others and all the while he hadn't known it. Unlike me, had he been asked, he could have decided yes or no.)

The court ruled human cell lines patentable because "long-term adaptation and growth of human tissues and cells in culture is difficult—often considered an art." (And yet they were *his* cells.) Therefore, the cell line is a "product of invention" not a "raw material" of nature.

John Moore asked, how could he not own his genetic material? How could it belong to someone else?

(When you made me did you feel you owned me? Did you think of me as your *invention*?)

Justice Arabian wrote on behalf of the majority, "The plaintiff has asked us to recognize and enforce a right to sell one's own body for profit. He entreats us to regard the human vessel, the single most venerated and protected subject in any civilized society as equal with the basest commercial commodity. He urges us to commingle the sacred with the profane. He asks much."

(Yet it was the *others* who were profiting and selling. What would have happened if John Moore had sued to have his cells not sold at all, no profits made from them for him or anyone?)

Justice Arabian continued, "The majority view is not unmindful of the seeming injustice in a result that denies the plaintiff a claim for conversion of his body tissue, yet permits defendants to retain the fruits thereof."

(Sometimes it seems the same questions continually arise in different guises: What's privacy, ownership, slavery, freedom, what's choice? What can be commodified, what not?

I don't know what became of John Moore. I don't know if he's even alive.

Such an ordinary night, this night. I look out on the stone face across the way, stoplight flashing, slow line of passing cars. Familiar sounds, background sounds. Then I think, what's ordinary? There's so much that's strange within a single, ordinary day—look at what happened to John Moore, the otherness his body became without his even knowing. When the ordinary starts to seem frightening, what then? Or has it always been frightening and I just hadn't noticed, hadn't thought of it that way?)

Notes on Stelarc

He believed the human body as we know it is obsolete—distraught, over-whelmed by information and sensory data, inefficient.

His body was his exhibition space. He performed his ideas in Japan, Australia, Europe, North America.

He sought to "rupture the body's surface," examining it as an "extendable evolutionary structure enhanced by the most disparate technologies."

(My body is something I hide, or try to.)

He wired himself with electrodes and transducers in order to allow Internet data to be transmitted into him and activate his movements.

For his performance *FRACTAL FLESH* he developed a touch-screen Muscle Stimulation System which enabled remote access and actuation of a human body. "A movement that you initiate in Melbourne can be displaced and manifested in another body in Rotterdam."

(Even as I hide, the world comes into me and through me, as once your laboratory instruments probed beneath my skin. Radio waves, subliminal messages, electronic and mechanical vibrations, toxins, chemical pollutants—such fragile boundaries between a body and the world. Or are there any boundaries at all?)

"The usual relationship with the Internet is flipped—instead of the Internet being fed by human input, it constructs the activity of the body."

(I find this frightening. I wonder if he found it frightening.)

(Often in my nightmares I see you feeding data into a computer, though computers didn't even exist in your lifetime, waiting for the printout of my body, the information that will help you make me. Then I see some of my flesh is human, some constructed. Like the robot, Cog, my eyes are grayscale cameras, a microphone's mounted in my head. I've been designed for "rich, flexible, dynamic interaction." As I watch I feel my mind dissolving.)

Sometimes he performed with a robotic third hand and arm, or atop a pneumatic six-legged walking machine.

In 2003 he built a prosthetic head. (I remember Roger Bacon built a talking head. Albertus Magnus built a brass man.)

Once he implanted a mechanical device inside his stomach, then videotaped its actions, noting how "the hollow body becomes a host."

"The body reclines, pacified, to accept the implant . . . the machine mechanism dances within . . ."

(He sounds almost joyful, finds a kind of freedom in a future without body-feeling, but what's thinking apart from the body? How would I feel and experience what I think?)

"The body is no longer an object of desire but an object for designing."

"Machines will manipulate molecular structures, extending the body from within . . . They will inhabit and navigate cellular spaces."

Such future bodies will be "more complex and interesting," each no longer a "single entity" but "host to a multiplicity of agents."

(When I watched Claire and Mary and Clerval, wasn't it partly their quiet suffering that made them vivid, all the ways I couldn't reach or help them, the ways they were separate and enclosed?)

"Can a body act with neither recall nor desire? Can it act without emotion?"

"The body's complexity, softness and wetness are difficult to sustain . . . A hollow body would be a better host for essential technological components."

We live in a "zone of erasure."

The body will no longer be interested in "circling itself, orbiting itself, illuminating and inspecting itself."

It will become a collection place for efficient operational modules.

Think of a body that quivers and oscillates not to sadness, joy, heartbeat, lungs, circulation, but to the ebb and flow of computer activity.

{ I close my eyes: Clerval's hand moves from left to right across the page then back again, line after line of words appearing. Is he writing a letter to his friend? He warms some noodles, looks at the smoke trees out his window. Does he get dizzy for a few seconds when he stands? Does his hand suddenly remember the weight of a book, a pebble, a brook's cold rushing water he played in as a boy? How odd the way something in us remembers even as we don't remember—remembers without words. }

Notes on Eva Hesse

From 1964 until her death in 1970, she made sculpture from industrial materials: fiberglass, latex, rubberized cheesecloth, plastic, steel.

She didn't want her work to be beautiful. Of *Right After* she said, "Coming back to it, I felt it needed more, and that was a mistake, because it left the ugly zone and went into the beauty zone."

She had just been operated on for a brain tumor.

(Can ugliness be a form of beauty? Her latex panels look beautiful to me—each worn, damaged membrane slowly leaving but still tethered to the world.)

She wanted her work to be "non-work," to exist beyond her preconceptions.

Right After can be hung differently each time.

(When thinking, my mind goes this way and that, swerves, reconsiders, swerves again. But I pull back, as if I must create a single line of thought, stable, unwavering—that this is what's expected.)

"I don't ask that pieces be moved and changed, only that they *could* be moved and changed."

(Did you think control might make you safe? In your laboratory you sought so much of it. But what if you'd been more curious than frightened, though in your own way you were bold, determined? What if the result, my body, hadn't filled you with revulsion?)

A friend remembers: "She found some object on the street—a broken pipe or something—called it a 'nothing' and said she wanted to make 'nothings.' "

(If you and I could have seen ourselves as nothings, as not locked within the quantified, the known, the labeled, what might we have been to one another? Myself that broken pipe even now, scrap paper, crushed metal, fraying cord.)

In many of her pieces the latex is badly degrading. It oxidizes, weeps, turns brittle.

Some say those pieces are "beautiful ruins." Others that they need to be reworked to resemble the originals (but aren't the 'degraded' ones *still* the originals?). Some believe Hesse made a terrible mistake.

She said, "Life doesn't last, art doesn't last . . . It doesn't matter . . ."

"The whole issue of the unfinished is a living idea . . . something unfinished changes. That means it's in a certain way alive."

(I think of her making sculptures as she sickened. How they grew up around her—fiberglass forests; broken, aging windows; the sound of something mixing in with nothing.)

(Her hand as she sickened . . . That unstable, still-willful, leaving hand . . .)

For years *Aught* was kept in boxes. "The curators were afraid to take it out . . . The last time they exhibited it, a couple of days into the hanging it started to weep, that is, the latex began to drip."

An expert on latex explained it could drip just as easily inside the box as out. What was gained from keeping it hidden away? Hung once more, "for some reason known only to the latex, it remained completely, utterly stable for the whole two months on display."

In a small notebook she kept lists of words: "Aught—anything, in any degree or respect. Anything whatever; any little part."

(All those parts you found to make me . . . How you fevered as you arranged and rearranged. As if we inhabit a controllable, known world. But what if our world is mostly, and ever will be, unknown?)

She believed chance is articulate. After filling four latex and canvas panels with polyethylene sheeting, rope, and other materials, she hung them on the wall so the random falling and settling would show through.

Dying, she lay in her bed partly directing, partly watching, the hands of others. This was for her piece *Untitled* (*Rope Piece*) made of latex over string and wire.

⁄ There's a ripped beauty in the mind, a harsh tangling that wonders, doubts, falls silent. ⁄

⁄ I see I've left out her childhood in Germany—she was born in Hamburg in 1936—and how she and her sister were sent to Holland to escape the Nazis. I've left out her marriage and much else. Mostly I don't think about or feel those things when I look at what she made, but intersections of presence, absence, namelessness, the vulnerability and utility of form. ⁄

Her lists of words included: Sequel. Accretion.

She kept the business cards of: World Plastic Extruders; Joe & Manny (General Contracting of all kinds); Alfred Covered Wire; Toy Balloon Corporation; John Boyle & Co. (Outdoor, Industrial, Marine Fabrics); Paris Lighting Fixture Co.; Arko Metal Products, and AEGIS Reinforced Plastics. (Manufacturers/Consultants).

She died in New York City on May 29, 1970.

Notes on Albertus Magnus

He believed contemplation is the highest form of human happiness.

He asked many questions.

"Do there exist many worlds or is there but a single world?" "Does the sight of the pains of the lost diminish the glory of the beautified?" Of what is our intelligence composed? What is the distinction between truths naturally known and truths that are mysteries?

This was in Germany, in the thirteenth century.

(Those days when I read behind the bushes, the words lifted me over threshold after threshold yet I never moved. All those dirty pages found in gutters—even the ripped ones, those with missing parts, still posed their questions, and each question was a wound and partial healing: "The proper names of things are the rays by which we"—by which we what? Or, "Why is the race of man so timorous as to need to believe more in things that are not, than in things that are?")

He built a Box of Secrets. Three sides were lead, three gold engraved with the signs of planets.

(Mary also had a secret box. She took it with her to France when she ran off with Shelley. But somewhere along the way she lost it.)

Nothing much is known of his early education. Most who knew him thought him exceedingly slow.

(When I consider that word "slow," I wonder why it's used to indicate some lack or flaw. Clerval, translating, considered so many choices, ways of saying, pausing to wonder which was best, knowing there's never one that's perfect. Why shouldn't such choosing be slow? I think of the "owe" in slow—how feeling one owes the world an honest faithfulness, and trying to fulfill that, can be mistaken for malingering, distractedness, forestalling.)

When he was a child, a woman in white came to him in a dream. This happened more than once.

"She appeared to me again, her white veil stained crimson, the scent of vanilla in the air . . ."

One night she leaned close to his ear, breath warm against his skin and asked, "At what would you like to excel?" Cold dark air all around him, the others sleeping in the quiet house . . . "I would like to do philosophy." She told him she'd grant his wish, then whispered, "because you don't choose to study divinity, this will be your punishment: some years before you die you will forget, suddenly, everything you know."

He never saw her again.

(Did he think of her often after that, as I think of you? Did he draw that crimson veil into his mind, wonder how it came to be stained? Where had she gone? Would she ever come back? Why the scent of vanilla, not cinnamon or roses? If she ever came back to him— though he knew she wouldn't—would her veil be white, or must it always remain stained? Sometimes, unthinking, did he feel her warm breath at his ear?)

He built a brass man named Android. This took him thirty years.

It's said to have uttered sounds to him. He asked it many questions.

(Speaking to it, did he think of the woman in his dream, how she came to him and whispered, all the ways he wanted her back? In building it, was he trying to find her replacement?—though that idea's too reductive, straightforward, unlayered.)

His friend and former pupil, Thomas Aquinas, believed the Android was evil and had it destroyed.

Alone as he was, he continued writing books and teaching; took years paraphrasing the complete works of Aristotle for others to study.

Convinced that Aristotle had produced certain works now missing, he made them up himself.

(As I imagined writing in Mary's margins, amplifying, correcting. As Red Inkstone wrote among the words of Cao Xueqin. As anyone who reads leaves invisible markings in the margins as they wander among another's thoughts.)

His writings range over vast areas of inquiry: logic, mineralogy, psychology, metaphysics, zoology, meteorology, botany.

He paraphrased Euclid, Porphyry, Boethius, Peter Lombard, Gilbert de la Porrée, and Pseudo-Dionysius.

Legend claims one day he turned a snowy garden into a garden of green leaves and singing birds for an entire afternoon. (This I don't believe.)

"Do things exist in themselves or are they the constructions of our minds?"

The intelligence can accomplish "a summoning of the good." The essence of the human soul is its intellect.

In *De Mineralibus* he wrote, "The aim of natural science is not simply to accept the statements of others, but to investigate the causes that are at work in nature."

(I remember Aristotle wrote, "Memory is a form of investigation," wondered if Mary would agree. And myself a question, and everything I think a question.)

He believed in direct observation, rejected the notion of the music of the spheres.

He valued silence as an integral component of music.

(Mary, Claire, Clerval . . . all those years there was such silence as I watched, and yet I somehow heard them.)

He wrote about the sleep of plants, the origins of riverbeds, the character of light in the air's lower strata.

One day late in his life he suddenly forgot everything he knew.

Three years before his death, the archbishop knocked on his door and asked if he was there.

"Albertus Magnus isn't here," he replied. "He used to be here. He is not here anymore."

He died in Cologne, Germany, on November 15, 1280.

{ METROPOLIS/THE RUINS AT LUNA }

They're all gone now—Claire, Mary, Allegra, Clerval, his friend in Aosta, Shelley under the sea. I can't watch their hands move across their secret pages, or how they hold themselves in sleep.

I'm here in a city of neon and digital billboards, news zippers, vibrating pixels swarming to make faces. Vast terrain of glass and steel and blasted towers.

I don't watch Claire picking out her silent letters anymore, or Clerval folding his friend's last letter, putting it back onto the stack. I don't lean to hear the rustle of paper, the scratch of a pen across a page (though all that time I watched I could hear nothing).

I remember Lerici, I still see the ruins at Luna. And ice caps, lepers' hoods, Chinese gardens (how each section of a garden had a name, but I have no name).

In this abandoned building, the cold sea I crossed to get here still swells and withdraws inside my bones. And all those years I crossed—their silences are walls, lost countries.

Lerici. Archangel. The sea.

There's a sea, also, in this book someone left here. By the light of my bare bulb I read of whale calves feeding from their mothers even as harpoons rain down around them. Then: "But even so, amid the tornadoed Atlantic of my being . . . I still bathe me in eternal mildness of joy." Did Claire ever feel that, or Clerval?—how the waters aren't wholly terrible even as they fill with carnage.

I close my eyes, feel them through the skin of distance. Claire. Clerval. Their absences more loud than anything, louder, even, than yours.

Baoyu walks off into the snow. The Goddess of Consolation does or doesn't come. Claire stands at her cold window. Clerval sleeps with his head on the table, then steps outside to watch the smoke trees in the distance. His friend can't close his eyes.

Aosta. Cape Mary Harmsworth. Lerici. Issogne. Great Slave Lake. The ruins at Luna.

Outside: car horns, car alarms, buzzings and rumblings from things I can't see. The dark here glows and shudders. The birds don't sleep. Wires cross the sky.

Those years I watched Claire and Clerval, I wondered what would they think if they could see me? My black lips and yellow eyes, my odd proportions, all the signs of something botched, unwanted. Would they have run from me as others ran?

But here I step outside and it seems no one sees me. Not the hurrying ones, or the slower ones dragging a bad leg, carrying too many packages in their arms.

I don't know if I walk on the street or in my mind.

Back inside, I dust off rows of books propped up where the floorboards meet the walls, live awhile among the whale calves who "though surrounded by circle upon circle of consternations and affrights" serenely revel. They eye the whalers quietly. Beyond them lies the frantic wall of whales who know they're being hunted. But could the whale calves also know this? Can panic grow so deep it turns to a strange calm and stillness?

Above the nursing calves the water's almost delicate, unstricken. Whalers have a name for this, a "sleek," that "enchanted calm . . . at the heart of every commotion."

Claire's face. Clerval's. I felt that sleek-like presence as I watched. How there was a calm that bound me to others, that arose *because* I felt bound to those others, though neither could see me. And though I've lost them, like the whale calves that see the whalers yet look past them, I look past these walls and remember what I saw.

Cold in here. No heater. Sirens cut the sky. The windows glitter, cracked and damp above the rush-hour traffic.

Last night I met Claire in a dream. It wasn't the same as watching her, but grayer, more impoverished. It was strange to hear her speak:

"You left me standing in Moscow in the cold. What did you think you were doing? Why didn't you try to find me after that? Instead you took up with Clerval, got all wrapped up with Clerval. Maybe you're more like Victor than you think. You take such an interest in my walls, seize them for your own. But what do you know about walls? Allegra lived and died behind walls, but you, in truth you probably crave them . . . Look how you watched me all those years and not once did you ever try to reach me."

Across the street, a stone mouth's been blasted away. Nearby, on St. Marks Place, two limestone eyes can't close behind their iron grating.

I lie down on the floorboards, think of whale calves, try to sleep.

My book says a wall is "a structure built around a garden," "a site of torture," "a wailing place," "the steep portion of a wave about to break."

In my sleep, the whale calves circle far from the frantic wall of whales. What gentle bond holds them not in slavery but in trust, and is that trust a kind of freedom?

Waking, I take another book from the floor. Inside it Bartleby stares at the wall, barely speaks. He works as a clerk in an office on Wall Street, his small window facing a brick wall.

"Here is the money, you must go," says Bartleby's employer. "But he answered not a word," just stood there "like the last column of some ruined temple."

(And my voice long fled. And the things I thought to say but couldn't.)

He's been fired but won't leave. Finally he's taken as a vagrant to the Tombs where he dies curled up beside the courtyard wall.

The whale calves eye me unafraid—am I sure they're unafraid?—as they look into my eyes then past me while Bartleby's still breathing, his pale hands hanging useless at his sides. Does he sense the whale calves, too, though he can't see them? I can barely tell my breathing from his own as the whale calves circle even closer and still he doesn't see them, or does he sense them circling, nursing, looking past him in a calm, deceiving wonder. Those calves so vulnerable, their mild, unguarded eyes . . . Then suddenly I think of Mary, remember that first time I . . .

But I don't want to think about that now. Why must I remember that now?

For so many years I tried not to think of her, or thought of her only as Claire's sister, hazy as through dust storms or smog. I didn't want her to come back, but she's come back.

Dear Claire,

Now that we live apart and I don't see you face to face anymore, now that all but one of my children have died, and your Allegra has died, maybe now I can tell you, but why do I even want to tell you?

I was a girl when he came to me. This was before Shelley. Before France, Italy, any of it. I would go to her grave, sit there wondering what it would be like to have a mother.

I think I have a fever now I think I Truth burns itself up or goes suddenly, horribly cold; it seems there's no neutrality, no balance (though that's not what they taught us—I think of Socrates with his measured, steady questions). And when I try to feel what thinking is, it's not a series of faithfulnesses but of betrayals, treasons, crumblings. (Remember the ruins at Luna?) There's so much extremity in us, outside of us . . . and we call it the ordinary, we call it . . .

I have become a shallow

This is ordinary: I was a body coming out of another body that died. That died because of my body. This is ordinary: famine, oppression, slavery, carnage, misunderstanding, hatred, love, sun, hostility, squalor. Why do we think the ordinary is benign, why do we . . .

I would sit there like an idiot by her grave, waiting—for what? I was 8, then 9. Some afternoons, some nights . . .

Thought a violent thing to me, in me (though I kept this mostly to myself). I still feel this, that thinking is a violent act. The smoothness of skin a kind of lie.

When I heard rustling in the bushes, I wasn't afraid. I'd been sitting there for hours, as usual. He stepped mildly toward me, one large hand over most of his face, his head bowed above hunched shoulders.

But maybe I should stop this right now, say nothing more. I don't know. So why sign my name at all, and still I sign it—

Your sister,
Mary

But I don't want to think about this. Why must I think about it now?

I sit on the floor with my computer. I'm not sure what kind it is or how it works, I just found it in a trash bin, brought it back. If I can get the screen to light, the hum that means it's working, to begin . . .

The instruction manual refers to "troubleshooting," "finding information," and "support." (Isn't this the kind of thing you would have mastered in an hour?)

(Mary suddenly quiets as I do this.) (And Claire and Clerval, lost beings from another world.)

Modem. Cable. Control panel. Ethernet. FireWire.

Trackpad. Power button. Safety. Restart. Sleep. Cancel. Shut down.

Brightness controls. Volume controls.

I think again of Bartleby silently facing the brick wall, his hands pale and listless at his sides. As once, long ago, I also wouldn't speak, or rather, unlike Bartleby, *couldn't,* the words violently severed from my throat, and nothing I could do could bring them back.

Claire,

I sat there in St. Pancras graveyard. The end of summer. The River Fleet moving sluggishly nearby.

I don't understand stillness, I was thinking—I remember this clearly—thinking, what could be odder than stillness though it's everywhere? Rock. Bone. Knife. Death. Table. My brain ached as I thought this . . . I was 8 . . .

He moved very slowly, his chin pressed down and inward where it met his left shoulder.

This is the cemetery of St. Pancras, I said to myself, and St. Pancras is the Patron Saint of Children, but he couldn't be St. Pancras, his head's still attached, and he's too old. Yet he didn't seem like other humans.

Black lips and yellow eyes. Long black hair.

For weeks he came to me. Mostly he stayed hidden in the bushes, would speak almost nothing of himself. Not even when I asked. Read to me from books. Seemed to know who I was.

It's the ordinary that frightens—water, rock, stillness, absence, faces. Thriving gardens. Anchors. Skin.

For weeks I listened as he read.

And then this also comes back to me, a voice as from the graveyard—but *before* the graveyard—I can tell by what it says that it's her mother's, though I don't exactly hear it, it's more like shapes in air, though shapes more sensed than strictly seen:

William, my hands are cold—I'm writing this in my head so I know you'll never read it, I couldn't hold a pen if I wanted to—I know I'm going to die—The unfound of me the I told you "our animal" would be born today and she was— But there's something spreading in me I can feel it—It was all an experiment, wasn't it? I only ever wanted to be a continual experiment. They'll call it Sepsis or Puerperal fever. They won't let me nurse her, will say my milk is poison, put puppies to my breasts to drain them—You'll write the exact time of my death in your notebook, nothing more. You who have so many words—We thought we were going to have a boy, but we were wrong. So she's a Mary like me. Silence is a refinement on cruelty—A hawk's wing. A blade. A blank page. I didn't know chaos could be so serene—Delicate almost, but also fierce—When I gathered watercresses and thyme—Nevermind—My brain's on fire, I must go into the air—

Claire,

Remember when we kept our journals?—

"Tuesday 8th Letter from Fanny—drawing lesson—walk out with Shelley to the south parade. Read Clarendon and draw—in the evening work & S reads Don Quixote aloud."

That was October, 1816. Fanny died the next day. What was I doing when she died?—reading the memoirs of Princesse de Barreith? Drawing? Walking alone or with Shelley? Such ordinary things—

"Wednesday 23rd Write Walk before breakfast. Afterwards write and read Clarendon. Shelley writes & reads Montaigne—In the evening read Curt. & work—Shelley reads Don Quixote aloud." Days like that. Remember? But not a scrap of writing survives from the years I was a child. So much I didn't tell you. Yet I criticized you for being melodramatic, for your "Clairmont Style"— your conviction that some unworldly being was moving through your room disarranging things. And all the time I kept from you what I'd seen when I was 8 . . .

He stepped out of the bushes, partly shielding his face with his hand. He seemed a hurt presence. A presence somehow ashamed.

It's the ordinary that frightens: a plain white envelope, a sunny day in the mountains, reading, thinking, looking at a newborn's skin. The words: "infant," "Monday," "Leghorn," "July," frighten me.

When I was 8: stillness, trust, my own bed, thinking, frightened me.

I felt no need to turn from him.

I asked his name. "I don't have one," he said.

That seemed to me an extraordinary thing. I couldn't decide if it was wonderful or horrible, to have no name like that, yet to be a creature of language, a creature using words.

Why had no one named him? And un-named like that, did he know an aloneness much worse than my own?

He held a book in his hands. I could tell he didn't want me to look into his face. How does one calm another's shame? Then he stepped back into the bushes, head still deeply bowed, and started in a gravelly, hushed voice to read.

I thought she must have run away. When I stepped from the bushes she'd seemed calm, unfrightened, even curious, but wouldn't she have quickly reconsidered and then fled?

Back within the bushes' cover, I read out loud as I often did to calm myself. I kept many books with me by then:

"In France they have a dreadful jail, the Bastille. The poor wretches who are confined in it live entirely alone; have not the pleasure of seeing men or animals; nor are they allowed any books.—They live in comfortless solitude. Some have amused themselves by making figures on the wall; others have laid straws in rows. One miserable captive found a spider; he nourished it for two years; it grew tame, it partook of his lonely meal. But when the warden learned of this he crushed the spider. The prisoner looked round his dreary apartment, and the small portion of light which the grated bars admitted only served to show him that he breathed where nothing else drew breath."

~ ~ ~

"Loveliest of what I leave behind is sunlight,
    and loveliest after that the shining stars, and the moon's face,
    but also cucumbers that are ripe, and pears, and apples."

~ ~ ~

"We are not as hardy, free or accomplished as animals."

"Before begging it is useful to practice on statues."

"I threw my cup away when I saw a child drinking from his hands at the trough."

"The greatest beauty of humankind is frankness."

~ ~ ~

"I have just completed a forty-two-day voyage around my room. The fascinating observations I made and the endless pleasures I experienced along the way made me wish to share my travels with the public . . ."

After sunset, after the girl had gone home, her dead mother's voice would often visit, speaking to William or sometimes to her friend Fanny Blood, but never to her child.

William—I keep seeing those early years, all those letters now lost or destroyed— How as punishment my parents made me sit in a straight-backed chair not speaking for hours—Then the years in London when we lived among silk-weavers and offices—Years of failed farms—My father beating my mother—me sleeping like a dog on the landing outside their bedroom door—As if that could help her—At sixteen I met the Reverend Clare. His spine contorted, legs bent, he could barely walk—wore out only one pair of shoes in fourteen years—Was often sick—Was kind—Gave me books, taught me things. Brought me to meet Fanny Blood—So much hurts the mind but I only ever wanted to be an experiment, it was all an experiment, wasn't it? I never wanted a genteel life—

Later I'd see her hand in air clearly writing; brown letters quickly drying on the page.

William I must teach myself things—If I could lay aside all restraint, if I—What are girls allowed to learn in school?—needlework, music, dancing— Trivial things—I don't want to be anyone's wife—Jane Arden's father gave us a private lesson on globes. Taught us about optics and the expansion of metals—

Claire,

He read and I listened. The river rough and muffled in the background. Dull leaf-sounds rustling underneath his voice. My fingers picking at pebbles in the dirt. This was before "must go into town for pins/sealing wax/spy glass," before "buy mourning and work in the evenings," before "I am ill most of the time," and "the watery surface was blank." Before "~~at half past three nothing remained but a quantity of blackish-looking ashes mingled with pieces of white and broken fragments of bone . . .~~" I don't even remember why I crossed that out. This was before "my Book dedicated to Silence—"

I came to realize that some of what he read had been written by my mother. ~~In the extreme . . . in the mind's farthest corners . . .~~ I don't know how to explain this. Sometimes I glimpsed his face, but mostly not. A few times I found some scraps of paper he'd dropped in the bushes: "Clerval who's left for the east," one read. But I'm getting ahead of myself . . .

So many years since I've seen you.

Your sister,
Mary

I walk where Melville walked, try to forget her. But her small worried face keeps coming back, and her hands as if waiting.

Before she ever saw me, I watched her for days without speaking. Tried not to move, didn't want her to know I was there. Feared even a glimpse of me might harm her. But how would it harm her?

So why had I stepped from the bushes? Why had I begun to read?

William, Are you there can you hear me?—I'm visiting Reverend Price—It's years before I knew you—He's very excited for the Americans and their revolution but questions how they can truly succeed given their evil practice of slave trade. He tells me to question, always question, never stop—his voice halting and weak, he's not well—I must teach myself things—I have a fever I know I have a fever—How can the Americans contend for liberty when they themselves enslave others?—So much hurts the mind—Scars on a whipped back—Nameless-ness—Silence—Eyes forced to the ground, eyes not allowed to look where they want to, eyes that don't know how to read—

Then I'm in Bath's warm springs where the sick pass infections unknowingly to each other—this happens all the time—What if I've passed my infection to our daughter?—Isn't the mind like this too?—every idea infected by the unfought-for, the accepted—There's little freedom and solitude after all. Reverend Price writes to John Jay—I can see his hand moving— "It will appear that the American people who have struggled so bravely against being enslaved themselves are ready enough to enslave others." So many cages of action and mind. I haven't met you yet, don't know if I want to. I have a fever can you even see me—I want never to marry.

Claire,

One day he read to me from my mother's letters. But how could he have seen her letters? They were to the American, Imlay, Fanny's father. From before we were born.

She wrote of his "barrier-face," and called the child "our barrier-child." "You are mistaken if you think me cold," she said. "I am determined to earn money for myself—the little girl and I will live without your assistance—." Wrote, "I cannot sleep—" and, "Our little Hercules loves three things—to ride in a coach, to look at a scarlet waistcoat, to hear loud music—The child can't rest with anyone but me, yet I look out over the sea and everything is cold. To deaden the mind is not to calm it—You don't love me, I know."

I turned the pebbles over in my hands as he read. Years later, at Lerici, I'd hear in the sound of the sea his gravelly voice, though I tried not to hear it. How many years since Fanny died? No one ever claimed the body. That day I bought mourning clothes, standing in that awful shop I felt her beside me one last time.

Then a pained silence came into me.

But William I want to understand what Liberty is. I don't know you yet—I'm in the North—a place called Rusoer, houses crowded under cliffs, only wooden planks for walkways. What am I wanting? Sometimes I imagine Fanny Blood's still alive rendering her botanical drawings for Curtis's Flora Londinensis, *making her living that way. That she and I could live together—be happy—the Child and I sail back to England in the morning—*

Then I'm in France, it's winter. I'm watching the King escorted to his trial—The entourage goes silently through the streets, every now and then a drum rendering the stillness more awful. When night comes I can't bring myself to put out the candle—Eyes everywhere glaring, bloody hands—Yet I'm filled with admiration for the people and their revolution. There must be equality, no part of mankind left chained as to a rock—Milton called women "this fair defect/ Of nature." As long as we're called a defect, William . . . Our new daughter, will they call her this also? And what of the poor who are accustomed to being punished, often for merely just getting in the way of the rich?—This refined villain that is our artificial life—It's justice, not charity, that's wanting in the world. I don't know where you are I don't know if you can hear me—

Those days in the graveyard I read from whatever I could find—food-stained books lifted from trash cans, newspapers, stray pages left on benches:

"The Emperor Ling Ti, who reigned circa 170 A.D. felt that nothing was too good for his favorite dog. The animal, undoubtedly born under a lucky dog star, was given the official hat of the Chin Hsien grade, the highest rank of the time. The hat was eight and three-quarter inches high and ten inches in circumference."

~ ~ ~

"Yao, the famous legendary emperor of China's Golden Age, is said to have been born with eyebrows of eight different colors."

~ ~ ~

"Why is our fancy to be appalled by terrific perspectives of a Hell beyond the grave?—that Hell is here in the lash that strikes the slave's naked sides, in the poor too sick to eat their sour bread."

~ ~ ~

". . . although I hear people say 'Moses meant this' or 'Moses meant that,' I think it more truly religious to say 'Why should he not have had both meanings in mind, if both are true? And if others see in the same words a third, or a fourth, or any number of true meanings, why should we not believe that Moses saw them all?"

Claire,

Lord Dillon once said to me, "I'm puzzled because you seem in no way like your writings." But the outward is so little of anything. Those days in the graveyard why should I have been afraid? What did it matter what he looked like? And anyway his manner wasn't threatening, though sometimes his voice grew taut and I felt a kind of pestilence spread inside my brain, an acrid warning. As if he and I were all that was left in a world that had destroyed itself. Everything in ruins. The air a barren plain between us, and I felt a chill, a barrier, a recoil. Not wanting to be left only with him. But then he'd start to read again and the sense of plague would quiet-back inside me.

Do you remember that locked box I carried to France when Shelley and you and I ran away? Inside were the few scraps of paper from the graveyard, the ones he'd dropped in the bushes or the grass. I never knew if he'd left them on purpose. "Clerval who's left for the east" one said, and then there were these: "unable to endure the aspect of the being he'd created" / "inside his laboratory" / "oppressed by a slow fever" / "dejection never leaves him" / "that I might infuse a spark of being into the lifeless thing at my feet" / "this trait of kindness moved me."

And a few more:

"my life was indeed hateful to me" / "to seek one who fled from me" / "vast and irregular planes of ice which had no end"

The handwriting was large, dark, crude, as if written with a branch or twig.

Some nights I'd lie awake imagining a plague covering the earth, and I'd wonder why I couldn't stand the thought that he and I might be the last ones alive—why didn't I want to be left with him?—even though when I listened to him read, a comfort fierce as burning sand came into me.

Was I reading to myself or her? After a while I couldn't tell the difference, though I recoiled when I thought of the human world she was part of, that world that had recoiled from me.

If human contact had come to seem a form of contamination, and it had, and myself ugly in my own eyes when I considered what I'd glimpsed in yours, then the contamination I felt from books was less a disease than a blending of minds, conversations unfolding across centuries, weird impersonal probings, wonderings passed from one being to another, facts and syntactical combinations taking root in one being then another.

Over time I thought of you less, though I still feared I might hurt the child who, though motherless, must certainly have been beloved. She sat there sorting pebbles as I read:

"Man has been changed into an artificial monster, his faculties benumbed."

~ ~ ~

"There are authors whose object is to narrate real events. Mine, if I should be able to attain it, would be to tell of what is possible to happen."

~ ~ ~

"A Robin Red breast in a Cage
Puts all Heaven in a Rage.

Each outcry of the hunted Hare
A fibre from the Brain does tear.

Under every grief & pine
Runs a joy with silken twine.

The Beggar's Rags, fluttering in Air,
Does to Rags the Heavens tear.

Every Night & every Morn
Some to Misery are Born.

Every Morn & every Night
Some are Born to sweet Delight.

Some are born to sweet Delight,
Some are born to endless Night."

~ ~ ~

"Ivy grows best when wild; birds wing most sweetly without teaching."

~ ~ ~

"Be very careful, in painting, to observe that among the shadows there are other shadows that are almost imperceptible as to darkness and shape."

~ ~ ~

"Now I will tell you about the city of Kinsay. It has some thirty thousand baths, the water of which is supplied by fresh springs. They are the finest and largest hot baths in the world; large enough for one hundred persons to bathe together. The people delight in them. In that city there are also ten principal markets. Some contain pears weighing as much as ten pounds apiece, their pulp white and fragrant as a confection. And there are peaches in their season both yellow and white, of very delicate flavors. The natives are peaceful in character. They know nothing of handling arms and keep none in their houses. Every year they produce enormous quantities of salt which bring in a great revenue; also great quantities of sugar and silk. The trading of these keeps them in comfort. But now we will quit this place and speak of other cities . . ."

Claire,

I kept imagining that he and I were the only ones left alive. His gravelly voice a spider's web which instead of viciously entrapping created against the air a refuge of intersecting lines, a kind of dwelling. I lived within that voice, its stories. And still I couldn't stand the thought of being left with him. Sometimes I imagined hurting him, seeing him cry. ~~Why does the mind disfigure itself why does it~~ . . . *Imagined telling him I hated his voice, his yellow eyes, that he was a disgusting aberration of nature, nothing anyone could ever love. I'd picture his shoulders heaving as he sobbed. Imagined throwing a stick at him or stones. For a while this comforted me. But why would the thought of hurting him comfort me? I waited each day for him to come—*

Beneath the threatening thoughts a calm so pure nothing could rip it.

I told myself I didn't care what she was thinking, just wanted to calm myself with books, didn't mind if she listened. But more and more I imagined the words traveling to her as I read, surrounding her like the whale calves' sleek, or a loose shelter of breath. Is it possible for beings to breathe and think in proximity to each other, hear the same books, think the same words, and for nothing bad to pass between them, nothing harmful seep in?

She sat barely moving, fidgeting a little, face down-turned, eyes as if cast inward. But her mother was different, her voice, though it was sounds without sound, or sound transposed into form—even now it's hard to speak of what it was or how it came—was a small storm or fever with no body to belong to:

William, Who will take care of my daughters?—I won't see them grow up—I remember my room behind the castle walls. The field outside called Ghost's Field. I worked as a governess. At night read pamphlets and books. Knew I must educate myself—Began to write—What is mental comfort, how does it come into the brain? Joseph Johnson let me live above his shop in London. I was frugal, spent nothing on furniture or clothes—Fuseli called me "a philosophical sloven." I was 29. Remember how after the poor in Paris marched on the King and Queen demanding bread, walls went up all over England?—and ditches, hedges, to protect the great estates—I only ever wanted to be an experiment—it's justice not charity that's needed. I never wanted gorgeous words. Wanted language stripped. Plain as undraped windows. Such hatred of the poor—hatred of what suffers and what's other. Thomas Paine wrote, "Man has no property in man." "This is an age of Revolutions in which everything may be looked for." No stillness in nature or the world—

Claire,

Sometimes I'd imagine I was the only one left alive, then try to feel whether I'd miss him. That hidden, companionable voice . . . all the stories he brought me, the ideas, the ways of thinking. The buildings around me intact—mansions, palaces, libraries, hospitals, hovels, all of them empty but still standing. And I washed up on the narrow shore that was myself, only myself. There was no hope of finding anyone alive, the plague had wiped everyone out, yet I went into a painter's shop and with paint and brush left messages on walls— "Friend if you're alive come find me in ____." (though I had no friend in mind). I wrote messages on paper scraps, left them on benches, tucked them into windowsills and doors.

At those times the words I'd heard him read out loud came back, but scrambled, rearranged for this new world emptied of all human breath but mine:

"To have been born emanates from thought itself"; "each outcry almost imperceptible"; "each damaged design."

I'd lie in my bed like that, thinking. Then I'd think how it might feel to be like him, alone behind those bushes. Was he angry? Scared? What did he want what did he dream of? And what to make of the world when every impulse is infected with recoil?—

I started to wonder if she wanted some glimpse of me again, some sign beyond my voice (I'd guarded my face when I stepped out, kept my eyes and mouth largely hidden) but couldn't bring myself to step forward, was perplexed I'd ever done it to begin with. Felt angry at the thought she might want this. Every now and then, searching eyes through the bushes, hands very gently parting branches, though mostly she stayed to herself, didn't try to see me.

Still, I read and she listened:

"Isabelle de Montolieu was born on May 7, 1751, in Lausanne, Switzerland. Author of the novel *Caroline de Lichtfield* and translator of Jane Austen into French, as a child she knew Jean-Jacques Rousseau. In her tale *The Canary of Jean-Jacques Rousseau* she describes visiting his tomb, and finding at its foot a small box containing a stuffed canary and a manuscript by a child named Rosine."

~ ~ ~

"Personal size and mental sorrow have certainly no necessary proportions. A large bulky figure has as good a right to be in deep affliction, as the most graceful set of limbs in the world. But, fair or not fair, there are unbecoming conjunctions, which reason will patronize in vain,—which taste cannot tolerate,—which ridicule will seize."

~ ~ ~

"Caroline wrote the letter to Count Waldstein, but ripped it up many times. Finally she gave it to him with shaking hands. She didn't mention his twisted appearance, and had always showed toward him the deepest respect and what he wanted to believe was affection. Nevertheless, he knew she couldn't bear to look at him or be near him; she was asking him to let her go. Years later when she returned of her own free will she was surprised to see that his body, damaged since birth, had mysteriously healed itself. From that day on, they lived happily together, reading and talking by the fire in the evenings."

~ ~ ~

"I was born in the year 1632, in the city of York, of a good family, though not of that country, my father being a foreigner of Bremen, who settled first in Hull ... Being the third son of the family and not bred to any trade, my head began to be filled very early with rambling thoughts. My father, who was very ancient, had given me a competent share of learning, as far as house-education and a country free school generally go, and designed me for the law; but I would be satisfied with nothing but going to sea ..."

William, They're storming the Bastille—The revolution is finally beginning—Then it's years later and Robespierre's saying, "Terror is nothing other than prompt, severe, inflexible justice."—Everything turned ugly, harsh—Hope and goodness poisoned at the core—I'll never hear our new daughter speak her first words—The mind injures itself resists itself—So much twisting and turning in me now—But the people fought for justice, wanted justice. I lived under the Law of Suspects—Fled Paris for Le Havre where a wall held back the sea. Even then my carriage full of books—Signed my name Mary Imlay—Everything blood-soaked. Thomas Paine was in prison, a white X on his cell door for execution but the guards didn't see it and passed by—So many chains again and walls nothing stops them—Then I'm alone beneath the river—my heavy clothes pulling me under, I don't want to live—

Those night-words formed in air. But in the graveyard I didn't repeat them, didn't want the girl to know of her mother's despair. She'd started bringing me things—hunks of bread, chocolate, oranges, a pen, but I left them on the stone untouched.

One time she left a note: *Why won't you come out?*

Meanwhile I kept reading:

"I . . . Robinson Crusoe, being shipwrecked during a dreadful storm in the offing, came on shore on this dismal unfortunate island, which I called the Island of Despair . . . I had neither food, house, clothes, weapon, nor place to fly to . . .

"Yet how wonderfully we are delivered when we know nothing of it: how, when we are in a quandary, as we call it . . . a secret hint shall direct us . . . I made it a certain rule with me, that whenever I found those secret hints or pressings of my mind . . . I never failed to obey the secret dictate . . ."

~ ~ ~

"Soundness of understanding is inconsistent with prejudice.

"Soundness of understanding is connected with freedom of enquiry.

"Soundness of understanding is connected with simplicity of manners."

~ ~ ~

"Let us cast our eyes over the history of man, and we shall scarcely find a page that is not tarnished by some foul deed, or bloody transaction. Let us examine the catalogue of the vices of men in a savage state, and contrast them with those of men civilized; we shall find that a barbarian, considered as a moral being, is an angel compared with the refined villain of artificial life. Let us investigate the causes which have produced this degeneracy, and we shall discover that they are those unjust plans of government, which have been formed by peculiar circumstances in every part of the globe."

~ ~ ~

"David's Deer live on the eastern coastal plains of China. Although they are very beautiful, many of their parts resemble the parts of other animals: their tails are similar to that of the horse, their hooves to those of the cow, their antlers to the deer's, their body to the donkey. Hence, they are also called 'non-descript animals.' Their normal life-span is twenty years."

~ ~ ~

"This want of tools made every work I did go on heavily, and it was near a whole year before I had entirely finished my little pale or surrounded habitation . . . Having made me a table and chair, and all as handsome about me as I could, I began to keep my journal . . ."

Claire,

The more he included Robinson Crusoe among his reading, the more I spent nights picturing a world more desolate and unsalvageable than Crusoe's. There was something about Crusoe that bothered me—his faith, his belief that things could be "for the best," though I admired how he forged tools, built a table, explored the island, gathered grapes to dry and store as raisins. Part of me wanted to be like him but part of me didn't. I'd say to myself, "It's the year 2094. The plague has spread through the entire world. There are riches but what's the use of riches? Crusoe could hope to be rescued, but there's no hope of rescue here. And after a while Crusoe had Friday, though he called him a 'creature,' not a man. And yet he loved him. But here there's only the empty buildings and the ruins . . ." Yet you were sleeping nearby, and our father, your mother, Fanny and others nearby. But in the bushes, he was all alone. If he were the product of such solitude, such unrelieved withholding and recoil, what would that do to him, what violence might that carve in him, what would he become? Sometimes I wondered if I hit him with my fists would that forge a connection between us stronger than the one we had which felt like the most tenuous thread, as if at any moment, without warning, his voice could disappear forever—

William, I'm underneath the water and don't want to come back up. Plunder. Vengeance. Atrocities. All this talk of "political liberty" while we build walls and more walls—Walls to enclose, walls to pummel, tear down, build back up again—And even though they've had their revolution the Americans still trade in slaves, thousands each day. What stubborn ignorance cuts the name of hope with cruelty?—Thomas Paine returns to America distraught and sickly. You don't know me yet—I have a child by Imlay. I lay her on the shore then wet my shoes and dress to help me sink more quickly. I'm wrong to do this, I know—But everything's in ruins—Somehow a boatman finds me unconscious washed up by Putney bridge. Brings me to Fulham for help and I start breathing, decide right then I'll write more Vindications—Man preys on man. Such misery demands more than tears—

Those days in the graveyard I traveled across many pages which frequently ended in mid-sentence—the books I found were mostly torn—so my travels were wayward, random, disrupted, though maybe the mind mostly travels in this way. Sometimes a page's beginning was missing, or part of a paragraph remained while another part was gone:

"The first use of zero as a fully formed number seems to have appeared around the time of Brahmagupta in the seventh century, when this great Indian mathematician tried, but failed, to explain how zero could be divided by itself. The Maya"

The Maya what? I couldn't know—

Or:

"hdad a city that would have rivaled Rome at its height. But the truth is that no one will ever know for sure the splendor that was Baghdad, for it was utterly destroyed, almost to the last brick, first during a period of civil war among the later Abbasids, and then in 1258 by an invading"

Or:

"The southern part of the city of Aosta
deserted, and seems never to have been greatly
ulated. One sees ploughed fields there, and mea
bordered on one side by the ancient ramparts ere
by the Romans to serve as the city's enceinte, a
the other side by the walls of a few gardens.
Solitary site may, however, be of interest to tr"

Mostly I tried to read from books that were at least intact for long stretches:

"In a little time I began to speak to him, and teach him to speak to me. And first, I made him know his name should be Friday, which was the day I saved his life. I called him so for the memory of the time. I likewise taught him to say Master, and then let him know that was to be my name. I likewise taught him to say Yes and No, and to know the meaning of them. I gave him some milk in an earthen pot, and let him see me drink it before him, and sop my bread in it. And I gave him a cake of bread to do the like, which he quickly complied with, and made signs that it was very good for him."

And of course I read the paragraphs in air, Mary's mother's words, that came like wounded soldiers, determined, emphatic, unafraid:

William, it was cold under the water but I didn't care—Cold the way the deepest convictions of mind are cold, the deepest contradictions—Rights aren't favors—Why should the poor, should women, be expected to act grateful? I'm accused of inflaming their minds. But my voice is almost nothing—I can't tell if I have a body anymore, can't see you—Justice mourns in sullen silence. The river a struggle of mind. Accountings of privilege aren't history. Where is my writing desk, my—Torn pages of light—Out of ideals of liberty and equality— terror, bloodshed—Nothing makes sense. And still one needs to try—This has been such a period of barbarity and misery I shouldn't complain of having my share. Such pictures in my mind: the King's head buried under mounds of lime. Marat dug up, re-buried in the Pantheon—At least Robespierre's finally gone but what of the 7,000 market women who rose up with such hope, what do they have now? Burke called them "the vilest of women." Yet they wanted justice, wanted a world that made sense—I don't know if I have a body anymore—My baby's hungry I must go into the air—

Claire,

Over time I brought him things, biscuits, chocolate, some bread. Sometimes I imagined we were friends. But often he felt more like a kind of infection to me than anything else—something awful that I'd caught—that burned me yet I didn't want it to stop. And even though I didn't fear him, I came to believe I sensed beneath that steady reading voice something I began to tell myself was hatred. Was it hatred of me? Years later when I got smallpox it was as if that hatred was finally writing on my face. Scrawling all over it. That it had been waiting all those years—brewing, taking root, increasing. That he'd planted it somehow, those hours in the graveyard. My ugly, ruined face. I remember walking through the streets glad, finally, to be damaged in that way. The harm visible, overt. The disgusted looks of strangers. Lowered or averted eyes. The giddy justice of it then. Did he hate my fresh-scrubbed skin, the fact that I had a bed to return to every night? Yet he read to me such wondrous things, so why did I even think of hatred? Why did I dream of guillotines, of shredded, mud-stained dresses? Corpses. Atrocities. Bodies floating face-down in the river. Guns. Sabers. Severed limbs—

Week after week of rustling pages. Hush of the river. Clicking of pebble against pebble in her hand. In my mouth the threatened shelter of each word, outlaws, vagabonds, chained yet wildly tender, weirdly free. My voice for hours on end from the bushes, she listening from the other side:

"Curse on all laws but those which love has made."

~ ~ ~

"Ideas are to the mind nearly what atoms are to the body. The whole mass is in perpetual flux; nothing is stable or permanent."

~ ~ ~

"An infinite number of thoughts passed through my mind in the last five minutes. How many of them am I now able to recollect? How many shall I recollect tomorrow? Some may with great effort and attention be revived; others obtrude themselves uncalled for; still others are perhaps out of reach of any power of thought to reproduce, having never left their traces behind them for a moment. If the succession of thoughts be so inexpressibly rapid, may they not pass with so delicate a touch as to elude forever?"

~ ~ ~

(I'd lost my Crusoe, which was, in any case, missing its last fifty pages. I could no longer read of making tools, planting corn, and finding Friday, couldn't know how they'd fared.)

~ ~ ~

"Kue-lin-fu contains three very handsome bridges, each one more than a hundred paces in length and eight paces in width. The women there are also very handsome. The people live in a state of luxurious ease, as the city possesses much raw silk and exports large quantities of ginger and galangal. The city is well-known for a species of domestic featherless fowl clothed in black hair resembling the fur of cats. Its eggs are of a pale violet tint, and are said to taste of rose-petals mixed with fresh rain."

~ ~ ~

"When thou cam'st first
Thou strok'st me, and made much of me; wouldst give me
Water with berries in it; and teach me how
To name the bigger light, and how the less,
That burn by day and night: and then I lov'd thee,
And showed thee all the qualities of the isle . . ."

Claire,

If Crusoe could give bread and milk to Friday, why would he who read to me take nothing? As if, through his refusal, he meant to starve us both—not of food but of something else I couldn't name. Each time the bread or chocolate went untouched, a feeling surged in me that said he could vanish any time, even in mid-sentence, leaving me suddenly alone. No trace of him anywhere. With one ear I listened to his words and with the other to their threatened absence. I trusted nothing. Could absence and silence themselves be forms of hatred? I was a knife sharpening myself against that question. And then I came to wonder (though I wondered this in different words, since I was 9) is there something in the mind that needs to starve and wants to, that craves only famine and extinction?

And still I picked up each scrap or note he sometimes dropped, secret pages, maybe, he'd meant to keep only to himself. Slept with them under my pillow, then locked them in my secret box—:

"What was I? When I looked around I saw none like me. Was I, then, a monster? I cannot describe to you the agony I felt at these reflections. I tried to dispel them but sorrow only increased with knowledge."

"Of what strange nature is knowledge! Once it seizes the mind it clings to it like lichen on a rock."

"Under your friend's careful tending, you slowly recovered. 'You'll be well soon, Victor,' he whispered, his hand on your forehead as you woke. But who would say such things to me?"

"I cleaned and bandaged the wound I had received."

All this in that large, awkward hand, as if written with a mud-tipped stick—

But William, does progress exist? We use the word but naming doesn't make it exist—There are so many deformities inside each seeming freedom—I keep thinking of your description of prison, the straw mat for sleeping, the 'detestable uniformity' of the hours. What it was like to have no books, no pen, no paper— Underneath the water I thought I would feel the end of perplexity and disorder, but I was wrong. I felt them to the very end. And after they fished me out I felt them too but with less anger. I understood they stay the way rocks and grass and planets stay—Our human selves the things that leave—Our smallness. Why should mystery and disorder bend beneath our narrow will?—I've wanted to believe the human mind can be freed—but what would that mean? You worry over the ambiguities in my unfinished novel, think I would have resolved them if I'd lived—But I think they'd be there even so. In my mind, in anyone's, so many barriers and faults of understanding—My hands so cold—Everything unfinished always—White X on a door—Faces at the barricades—The storming—

Claire,

All those words but I felt I was starving. Nights I dreamed of cattle so thin their ribs were butchers' blades, their knees brittle twigs. Voices cut from their throats. They were stumbling through mounds of snow. Yet there were handsome bridges in Kue-lin-fu. Love made laws. Count Waldstein read Caroline's letters and Crusoe offered bread and milk to Friday. In Kinsay one could find the most fragrant white-fleshed pears. Each day so many stories, so many words . . . so wasn't I a hunger being filled? The only time I'd ever glimpsed him he looked so big and ample. Yet more and more I pictured withered limbs, sallow skin, his back hunched and fragile, eyes dully fading while his reading-voice grew plump—as if that voice were feeding off his sight, draining it as flames use air. I believed there was something starved inside his mind (but what could I know of his mind?)—Wasn't he starving himself as well as me, willfully and cruelly? And yet could tenderness still dwell within a cruelty? Of course I couldn't know his mind . . . my own more blindfold than anything, a knot tightening as I slept. I'd think, if he would just take my bread or chocolate, if he would come out again, just once . . . But then the cattle would come back and I knew he wouldn't. I went to the graveyard every day, waited for his voice. The air between us burning—

Then one day I came upon her mother's book, *Maria.*

(the deepest convictions of mind are cold, the deepest contradictions)

Wiped off the grime, opened it just like the others, pried apart the stuck pages.

All the while the girl waiting on the other side of the bushes.

(I don't want to think about this now. Why must I think about it now?)

Looking down at her mother's pages, my eyes, by chance, landed on these words:

"Treated like a creature of another species, I began to envy and at length to hate."

I read them only to myself. Read further:

"the very air I breathed tainted with scorn."

Then:

"I had not even the chance of being considered as a fellow-creature. I had no one to love me. I was an egg dropped on the sand. I belonged to nobody, despised since my birth."

And:

"To be cut off from human converse was to wander a ghost among the living."

I felt she knew me, but how could she know me? I was reading the words of a dead woman

(My hands so cold—the barricades—the storming—)

but suddenly I had no tongue to speak them. The air turned hot and swelled and filled with waves. My skin breaking into curving, beating waves.

(William, there are so many deformities . . . and walls to tear down and where is my writing desk, my . . .)

The girl still waiting. The plain intactness of her face. Her eyes. Slow pull of the river. The graves.

I knew she expected me to read, but how could I read? I had no voice, could think only of her mother's book and the detested creature. The more I tried not to think the more I thought. Of your horror of me, how it feels to be hated. That night I dreamed I was in an old, abandoned garden. A vine-covered trellis stood about three feet away. I could see her on the other side, a large white bandage over her mouth, her eyes bandaged also. I started to read but when I opened my mouth a stream of blood came out. Then I was walking in an ice-field. There was no sign of anything alive. Why can't I at least see a mirage, I wondered, would that be so hard? I felt your eyes on me though I couldn't see you. I tried to give you the bloody handkerchief I'd used for my mouth, but when I reached into my pocket it was gone.

She came and waited the next day, and a few days after that. But I read nothing, or rather, read silently and only to myself, words distant planets on the page.

Can thoughts build and stab themselves at once? My mind frightened me—thoughts of you, of how I'd lived and what I was.

And she—she was still waiting—ignorant, protected.

My throat an ugly flower poisonous to the touch. I couldn't heal its torn stem, its clenched, red blossom.

William I can't see you anymore—Am I at home have I just had a daughter?—My limbs are heavy, it's dark, I'm walking through a London street I'm stealing whatever I can—bread, books, jewelry, money. I feel such hatred and I don't know why. I hide in an alley with my books near the hospital where the doctors are experimenting on the poor—You'll finish my sentences, you'll—Something monstrous in me. I crouch in rags—In the poorhouse the women are mocked for the smell of their dirty linen—My body no longer female nor male my limbs large somehow, awkward—No law governs what I am—I'm nameless you can't find me. I watch your walls from outside, always from outside, snow falls on me, a girl drowns herself in a well, a dog overturns a garbage can, I'm stealing whatever I can—My skin a covenant of what?—But I have no body, and skin is alien, opaque, un-meaning. A form of misunderstanding only—Why do we need to despise? What is it in us that has no country?

Claire,

Of course one day his voice stopped as I'd feared. Suddenly, without explanation. After a while I didn't wait for him. I'd sit in my room, pick up a book, read from it out loud, imagining I was him: "Meng Tian is credited with the introduction of the Chinese brush pen, which is made of sable, fox, or rabbit hairs, set in a bamboo holder. He died in 209 B.C. and is worshipped on his birthday by pen-makers." Or: "If rubbed on the lips and tongue Chinese ink is considered a good remedy for fits and convulsions." But all the while something in me hardened. As if each word contained a harsher, stricter word— braver, unforgiving, more alert. Keener, cold. Each word isolate at its core like him, mysterious, unknown like him, making chains all over me like him. I sat at my desk writing lists: cleft, strike, copper, kindness, carry. Heard the sounds strike themselves, strike air. (And yet when I'd glimpsed him I'd wanted to touch him, he'd seemed a hurt presence, ashamed.) All I had left were scraps of paper. Sometimes I imagined him at my window, just standing there watching—wanting what? But I knew I was ignorant, mistrusted everything I thought—

William, Do you think you can see me?—You read my words, annotate the text of my unfinished novel, write your book about our years together and the years of my life before you knew me—I can't feel my arms, don't know if I even have a body—One daughter will take laudanum in a rented room. No one will know who she is or even claim the body—I called her the barrier-child—You call me "incomparable," write that I was "affectionate and compliant to the last, not tormented by useless contradiction." But isn't everything contradiction in one way or another? Facts are merciless—My ignorance as real to me as anything— The barrier-skin of the body, charged pathways of the brain in which we are hidden even from ourselves. I can't tell you why the word "destroy" keeps rising in my mind, or what was in my silence when you asked what I wanted for our child—I scrawl a white X on my shoulder, stand in the poorhouse smelling of urine and old food, I lie in the hospital where the doctors are experimenting on the poor, they come near me, it's my turn—A mind can't look at itself, not really—Words in the wind. Rebellion. Trespass. Consequence. Disorder.

I touched my fingers to my lips to wipe away the blood, that taste of iron and salt, but each time my hand showed nothing.

One day she was no longer there.

Bandages in the air around me. Voice on the edge of Vanished. Reason's shore.

Rough husks of lungs and yet they flowered. Monstrous. Harmed.

I didn't know if I lay there for weeks or was it longer? I kept touching my mouth, my bloody mouth, but each time no sign of blood.

Where was she? What was she thinking?

And then one day a voice again, not mine—sharp needle through the fever carrying its single thread:

> *William, A storm of pages—I'm revising as fast as I can—Words spill in the margins some upside down some sideways no top or bottom anymore, the words all wrong anyway—I should keep the strike-outs but not the words—signs of annihilation—signs of needing to try again yet again—Everything's taken away and this tracelessness in me, this not-quite-rightness—Something in me too quiet too apart—Something that hates though it doesn't know why, feels alone though it doesn't know why—Something harming and harmed—Once we lay so close I could taste your breath, the smell of you all over me but we are taken away even from ourselves, especially from ourselves—Inchoate—Cold—These fractured instances of what I was—*

That voice. But not the child, Mary's, voice.

My skin as if belonging to another. Wavery. Hot. The air by turns yellow, sallow green, a bluish-red. Steely, impersonal, cold, moving in and out of the lungs. Something very patient and cold inside me also.

Fever-tree, I thought, then *fever-grass, fever-trap, fever-fire, fever-cooling, fever-dream.*

I remembered what Aristotle said, that a chain of words would lead to the word you're trying to remember: *milk* to *white, white* to *mist, mist* to *moist* and finally *moist* will lead to *fall,* season of mists and light rain you were trying to arrive at.

But nothing in me moved in a chain. There were bandages and x's, pebbles, barricades, *must go into the air.* There was "despised," bread, your name, walls, stealing, slaves, the poor.

Aristotle used the word *soul.* When affection "is implanted in the soul memory exists." I knew I couldn't use that word, couldn't find a chain of words to get there.

Recollection, he said, is a form of investigation.

The air turned yellow again, then white, then the sour orange color of my skin. All the while that salt taste on my lips. No voice in me. Taste of broken words, of wrongness.

Claire,

Who could I tell? Each day his voicelessness grew louder, built in me a coarse, deserted city. After a while I wanted only to flee—not to some far, exotic sea but to a place so drearily inland no one would go there. Some flat heath with spiky grass and rock. Once, in the middle of the night, I imagined he sent me a letter: "My dear Child, I betrayed you by not keeping my distance, and so in ways you can't understand, though maybe even now you sense them, I harmed you with my proximity, the monstrousness of what I am. I took something from you, twisted and scarred something in you. I never should have let you hear my voice. You'll never hear it again. Not once. Not ever. This I can promise. I ask neither for your pity nor forgiveness, and understand you may come to abhor me. Maybe you've abhorred me all along. I intend that no one will ever catch sight of me or hear from me again. In sorrow and with the plain, cold will of one who knows what must be done, and maybe also with remorse, I leave you."

Why couldn't I read even to myself?

The words from her mother's book still reeled inside me: *"hide my head,"* *"shall not,"* *"detested creature."* *"Shut out from humanity,"* *"the severity of my fate,"* *"branded with shame,"* *"how could I be such a monster?"*

Every now and then her bandaged mouth and eyes. Sky full of clouds, of voicelessness.

No chains of meaning in me.

Sometimes numbers marched, rigid soldiers, through my brain: 1, 2, 3, 4, 5, 6, 7, 8, 9, then I'd start the same sequence again.

Leafy branches all around me but I saw a desolate shore.

Aristotle said remembering the future isn't possible. I didn't know.

Once a hand resembling hers but older seemed to leave a trail of ink across a page.

Aristotle said no one could say he's remembering the present since at that moment it's complete within him. But was this so?

Bandages. Salt. Voicelessness. Precipices. Seas.

The fever wasn't florid or flowery, not gaudy or dramatic as I might have supposed. Instead, it was austere, almost modest in its ardor, stripped.

Claire,

Then we moved, remember? Father found the house on the corner of Skinner Street, on Snow Hill. You liked it there. But all I could think of was how far it was from the graveyard, and even though I'd stopped going I never stopped wondering if one day he might change his mind, read to me again, maybe even show his face, not shun me. I'd go over the letter he sent (the one I made up in the night) thinking about proximity, monstrousness, harm, forgiveness, all those words knotted up inside me, a knot I couldn't undo. Why did it have to be that way? My mother had written "misery wanders in hideous forms over the earth," yet her portrait on the wall looked mostly gentle, benevolent, undisturbed—and I'd sensed a gentleness in him even as parts of me recoiled. Even as, sometimes, I thought of hurting him, making him suffer for reasons I didn't understand. Sometimes I wondered if I wanted to hurt him <u>because</u> he was alone, that I was tempted to try my hand against a lonely, breathing being no one loved. But I knew no single explanation would ever be quite right. It was like standing out in a storm and the storm is everything at once—bright and dark, violent and calm, fractured and intact. Our new neighborhood was filled with butchers' shops, booksellers, prisons—the oddest combinations. (Remember the huge crowds gathering for the public hangings?) Flies in the cattle market, the fetid stench in summer. And still his apology echoed in my head, if it was an apology, or was it a way to be rid of me, vanish from my life forever, and in vanishing make me always remember. More and more my memory felt like a kind of operating theater, or the butchers' shops I passed each day, their deliberate, wet dissections. Blood on the butchers' blades. Shining knobs of leg-joints, gristle, bone.

I walk around for hours, try not to think of her.

I pass: ALLEN'S ALLEY VIDEO (WE RENT AND SELL), TOWER RECORDS, J&R MUSIC WORLD, FANELLI ANTIQUE TIMEPIECES, TRUE VALUE HARDWARE, MERCHANTS BAG & PAPER, DEGAMBA PAINT REMOVAL, AMERICAN SELF STORAGE, UBS BANK, ICON PARKING, EXPERT DATA RECOVERY, CAMERA LAND, DUANE READE.

A man stands unmoving on the corner even when the light shifts, *Everything Will Be Taken Away* stenciled in henna on his forehead.

If my fever had stripped itself to the core, then found words for what it was, would those have been its words?

William, I lived among watchmakers, engravers, the crippled man pushing his cart of wheat cakes through the grimy streets—Tall elms and banishments and findings—poorhouses, gardens, public squares—I was broken over and over yet intact. When I think of the portrait Opie did of me, I want to take a cloth and smear it—Leave smudges, marks—No clarity of skin, no—Then you wouldn't know whose it was, that face. Everything's taken away, nothing's ever really kept—I would do this to your portrait too. Gray smudge of forehead, eyes—Gray sweep over everything I wanted, fought for, ever was—

The fever kept building, but how could it go on like that? Why was it still building?

The air increasingly colder, sharp, the trees duller, bare.

Sometimes her hand coming as from nowhere, writing of Skinner Street, cattle markets, butcher shops—things I hadn't seen. And always the feeling that if I parted my lips and tried to speak I'd hemorrhage from the mouth.

Memory is investigation, Aristotle said. But each time I remembered her, part of me went blank. As if I were meant to answer a list of questions written in invisible ink. So how could I investigate? And what was I seeking?

One may conduct investigations into absences, causation (my books had said this). One can do careful and minute research.

And still I thought: *fever-tree, fever-nests, "fever-like I feed."*

One can examine systematically, in detail. "This learning . . . cleare, playne and open that does search or will investigate."

The bees were "light horsemen investigating where they maie passe."

If she returned would I read to her of bees, "light horsemen"?

Meanwhile the air continued growing splinters, scars—crevices hidden in plain sight.

Claire,

Increasingly I came to understand the mind doesn't live in just one place. Skinner Street, Snow Hill, its butcher shops, the horrid public executions—I moved among them but in my thoughts I was often in the graveyard, that place emptied of his voice, emptied, even, of his breathing, faint rush behind the bushes. The sound of nothing there, like the sound of my mother, that's what I heard. I craved his voice, those hunger-pangs I felt as I'd listened, even those pangs of maybe I hate him and I want to hurt him but I don't know why. Craved the way his voice had sought me out, but had it ever really sought me? Or had it simply been indifferent all along? Maybe I had to accept that I was of no consequence, meant nothing. Meanwhile I kept thinking of that desolate place I might run off to where no one could find me. I would carry a letter from him, "My Dear Child, I should fear that if I let you regard me with less abhorrence . . ." I didn't know what would come next. Maybe, ". . . the peace and security of your pure mind destroyed . . ." Something like that. I'd read it in my solitary cottage. I would be the sole depository of my own secret. I'd become as quiet and extreme as he, as voiceless. Hidden. Merciless. Proud—

Then one day the fever stopped. No blood taste in my mouth, no mix of salt and iron (though off and on for years it would come back). Touching my lips, I felt no wetness. I opened my mouth.

All around me branches were honed to extreme versions of themselves, clearer than I'd ever seen. All the edges of things gleaming. And those edges felt *helpful*—I didn't know how else to put it and still don't—they seemed just wholly themselves, far from human feeling. As if sight could cleanse itself, though I knew this would be a temporary feeling.

Still, at that moment I thought *branch, dirt, river-sound, books*—

The air untouched by the mind's complications, moving in and out of the lungs. Not ghosted or complicitous or wanting. Not treasonous or fraught or haunted.

Claire,

Dr. Cline came, and Dr. Lawrence. Our father had sent for them. My skin burned, was covered with red scales and itched. My right hand hurt, my right arm felt always weak, sometimes I kept it in a sling. They said "failure to thrive" and "troubled" and "would be good to send her away for a while." Said, "tensions in the family." They couldn't know the graveyard lived in me, or that the far place where desolation would be my only comfort kept looming in my mind. I was the torturer and the tortured, the one who taunted and the one who crumbled, the one who maybe even murdered (Was he alive? Had he left me or had I left him? Had my wish to hurt him landed like a poisoned needle in his brain? Had he stopped breathing?). Once after Aaron Burr visited our father, he came upstairs to our playroom and pretended to have tea, then came back later with presents of elegant stockings which he was too shy to give us—he carried them home in his pocket still secretly folded. I felt like that—like someone who kept something tight inside her pocket—I couldn't bring myself to stretch out my hand. My skin red, hot, but I had no fever. His letters in my mind, "My dear Child, I have betrayed you . . ." "My dear Child, we must separate forever."

If I'd kept reading . . . If I hadn't recoiled . . . If the words hadn't harmed me (but *how* had they harmed me?) . . . If I could have stepped from the bushes . . . faced her waiting eyes . . . then what might have become of her and me, how might things have been different?

Claire,

My skin was burning, every thought seared red and burning. Skinner Street, the butchers' shops, the grave, the air, his voice. Scales on my arms, parched and burning. Why did I feel such pride as I burned? (Ugly nerves, electrified, raw, flailed much too close to the air). Monarch of my own destruction. Was I showing him that no silence or withdrawal—nothing he could inflict—could rival what I inflicted on myself? That I could outdo him? Or was it he who was writing on my skin until I was all fiery scaliness and itch? Or was it all of those and more? His absence an invisible hand, willful, cruel. I lay in the burning sea of my body. Admired in secret my own fortitude. Turned my face to the wall. Spoke to no one. Scratched until I bled, then watched how the skin, temporarily and with patience, mysteriously reknit. Its smooth rebuke of me. Its desolate faithfulness, but to what?

I could read again, but not out loud.

Sometimes her mother's hand came in air, sometimes hers. Each of them writing.

I held my books close, moved my lips as I read. The smooth or jagged letters rising in my throat, stopping short of open air. Secretive, withheld inside me.

Though my mind netted words and hauled them in, I knew even the smallest was more powerful than I:

"There are many names for rice in its different stages and qualities, e.g., *Ku,* the ripe grain or husk; *Su,* paddy; *No Mi,* glutinous; *Mi,* hulled; *Fan,* cooked; etc. Rice straw is employed to make paper, matting, sandals, rope, thatch, fertilizer and cattle fodder."

~ ~ ~

"Nature is an infinite sphere whose center is everywhere and whose circumference is nowhere."

~ ~ ~

"But if our own Biography, study and recapitulate it as we may, remains in so many points unintelligible to us, how much more so must these millions of lives which are the essence of History, and which we know not and cannot know!"

As I read, I listened for her breathing, the click of pebbles, faint scraping on the gravestone as she left a piece of bread, though I knew I would hear nothing. I hadn't forgotten her mother's words: *"shut out from humanity,"* *"How could I be such a monster?"* *"branded with shame,"* but thought maybe I could live with them, carry them not as enemies but as companions speaking of the life I was given to live. I turned this possibility over in my mind, wasn't sure what I thought.

I waited for her hand, often young but sometimes older, balancing, unbalancing in air. Leaving edges, marks. And I waited for her mother's hand. But never for yours, though I carried your laboratory notes still folded in my pocket all those years—

William, Our daughter will learn to read from the letters on my gravestone—
Will find the words of me but not my body—Those letters arranged, rearranged,
to form a world: stone, ray, one, all, far, tower, craft. And "mar" as in to harm,
as in: hamper, hinder, impair, damage—But "mar" also means the sea: Mar
Roja, Mar del Norte—That far uncrossable of me—I'll be the mar that is to
trouble and perplex, to grieve—And mare: swift horse, its terrors in the night—
It's said a "mare-stone" keeps away all fright, so maybe I'll be that as well.
I'll be the "mare" which is a snarled thread. How will she ever untangle me—
lost and wild in her mind I must leave her this snarl that is my self—knotted—
impossible—The flat basaltic planes of the moon are "mares," once they were
considered distant seas—Nights when she looks up, fierce eyes with their per-
plexities and angers, she'll see those planes of moon as me, desiccated, lifeless—
Monstrous of me to leave her in this way—And yet . . . and yet . . . I feel oddly
happy, but how can I be happy?—All the towers in me crumbling, only the word
"one" echoing where her cry breaks into such dust—I can't hear her anymore—
(how can I be happy?)—Can't see the prisons either, the barricades, guillotines,
dirty outstretched hands, the mind preying on the body, the washer-girl too poor
to buy shoes—

Claire,

This was before "Buy mourning and work in the evening." Before my "Journal of Sorrow," and Shelley's heart snatched from flames on the shore. Before "&I but a shadow," and "for eight years ~~my soul~~ communicated with unlimited freedom . . . conversed with him, rectified my errors . . . obtained new lights and my mind was satisfied." Before "My dearest Hogg my baby is dead—will you come to me as soon as you can—I wish to see you—you are so calm a creature, and Shelley is afraid—." Before, "They are all gone and I live." Before "I am perfectly detached from the world, I cannot be part of it." This was before France, before Switzerland and Italy. Why did I feel so proud? I burned, plotted, thought of him and I was proud. Proud to be burning in that way, to possess a monstrous and consuming passion. To have hurt or been hurt beyond anything I'd dreamed. Faithful listener. Martyr. Scorned. Aldini was traveling across Europe, reanimating corpses with jolts of electricity. Decapitated oxen heads shuddered and opened their eyes. If my skin burned as it burned and I could stand it I knew I could stand anything—the sight of those oxen heads, a murderer's corpse lifting, suddenly, one rigid greenish hand. His silence had made me a soldier, but of what? Still sometimes I felt the slightest breeze could bend me—

I could read again, so why couldn't I say the words out loud?—I was alone, there was nothing to stop me. Something inside me sharpened itself, then recoiled, damaging and damaged, an *afterwards* I didn't understand. The air against my lips a raw and too-thin skin. Sometimes in my mind, bandaged eyes, her mouth covered with white cloth. I wondered where she was, what she was thinking.

Her hand sometimes old, sometimes young. I could never predict when it would visit. I noticed her strings of misspellings:

> untill, agreable, occured, confering, meaness, receeded, hopless,
> lonly . . . Seprate, extatic, sacrifise, desart

saw she had trouble with words that involved doubling. Were there two *l*'s in *until*? Two *r*'s in *conferring*? She gave *until* one letter too many, *conferring* one too few. As if it was too hard to balance the relation of one thing to another, assess what might be companionable, what must stand alone.

Often she wrote *Teusday* for *Tuesday*.

She wrote on small slips of paper, then pasted them over other pages. Wrote a name then crossed it out or changed it:

Welford

became

Lovel,

then

Herbert,

then

Woodville.

Next to this a date:

1819.

Some dates were much earlier: On a scrap of paper:

~~the whole sea of me burning~~.

Next to this:

1811.

Sometimes her hand stopped in mid-sentence:

"the intricacy and perplexity of"   "unspeakable xxxx doctrines."

Other times whole lines or paragraphs were scored out:

~~tell your story that weighs heavily upon you~~

Time meant nothing to me. Past, present, future, all wrapped up as one.
I waited to see what she'd keep, what she'd cross out:

~~Claire if I could confide in you but I can't~~

~~xx I hear the slaughtering of animals in the night~~

~~Father says Mr. Burr is so poor he had to sell his watch to buy coals~~

After a while the quieter I grew the louder and more *visible* the outside world became. I couldn't explain it. Wasn't I part of the outer world as well? And yet I grew more quiet and more hidden.

Robertus Mut and Alanus le Mute couldn't speak. My books don't say why. The black-necked swan's born mute. A Languedoc wine stopped in the process of fermentation is said to be mute. (But I was born with a voice then lost it, if one could say that I was *born*.)

Coleridge wondered how humankind would seem if mute. And Sir Philip Sidney said there's a "dubble Speech; the one in the mynde . . . the other the sounding image thereof."

If I could hear my voice move outside my mind . . . but even now this voicelessness, and all these years later. It had harmed her and myself, but how had it harmed us? Those words I read not even mine. There was just the hook of my voice lifting them off the page.

"The flesh of the visible," one wrote. I think of the flesh of the audible, what's that? My voice a skin that troubles and frightens me. Didn't I touch her with that skin as I read? Borderland, strung syllables, breath. Site of harm, layer upon layer of what?

Once the sky over the graveyard filled with eyes. I lay mute and watchful in my fever as if I were one of their kind, but distorted, earthbound, odd. Then the rain came with its broken sounds and the wind, and my mind made sounds also, but they were guarded, watchful, raw.

Claire,

I kept thinking I would go away to that desolate place I imagined—would
leave no tracks, everyone giving up on me, believing me dead. I'd walk on bare
land, shun all humankind, trust no voices but the birds'. Not even my own.
Especially not my own. If he could see my burning skin what would he think?
Would he see how he'd harmed me, that absence and quietness also are a form
of violence? I lay in the burning sea of my body thinking: red that pools in
butchers' sinks and spews from volcanoes, red fibers of revolutions, red threads
sewn into banners of resistance. Red alert, red attempt, red stain on a napkin,
red dress. The whole sea of me burning. The visible can't rest within itself,
keeps trying to break violently out or plunge more deeply in. But can do
neither. The visible trapped as he and I are trapped. But in my desolate place
I'd spend my days reading books, re-reading his letters, though I couldn't
decide what those letters should say. Would they be pathetic attempts to
explain why he'd left me, crass manipulations, hooks to still maim me, or the
words of a being I'd harmed or even murdered? I listened to your footsteps and
Fanny's in the hall, your complaints and laughter. But everything had changed.
I lived in a world of punishment and pride and damage. Red stain embedded
in each naked molecule of air—

William, *The woman I was is sitting at her writing table filling notebook upon notebook, a child sometimes beside her, sometimes not—I tell her books are skins and nervous systems, not lessons, don't turn them into lessons—But her hand's moving fast she doesn't see or hear me, barely feels the dissonance humming through every layer of her skin—She's rushing to make points—Single-minded. Urgent. Fierce—But this confusion of surfaces, this—You think I'm in those books and I am, but there's so much of me that isn't—Vigilance fails, the visible fails—I'm ambiguous, indecipherable, lost—No name for me, no . . . I wanted vindication, I don't think I was wrong to, for myself, for others, but a nervous system doesn't explain doesn't argue—Our daughter will feel how being tries to rise through words, how the mind mutinies against itself, violates each seeming certainty until each single thing is several things at once, decentered, precarious, unsolved—I stood in the visible world, a tree with tough roots and sturdy trunk, wind whipping around me—But I was also the shadow of that tree and the empty space beside it—Ferns that thrive only in the forest's filtered light, dirt, slugs, earthworms, fallow seeds.*

And so I came to understand I would always be silent. The skin of my voice never touching another.

Out of nowhere—out of air—her hand continued to come, moving back and forth in time, though I could never go to her.

My eyes sharpened themselves on the world's abundant angles, its likenesses and differences, my ears always listening, and my mind. Each morning I opened my books, read to myself all day. Tried not to think of her, of you, of anyone:

"They say there is no straight line in nature. This is a lie: every line exists in nature. But I will tell what there is not; there is no even tint in nature. Nature's shadows are ever-varying, and a ruled sky that is quite even never can produce a natural sky. The same with every object in a picture, its spots are its beauties."

~ ~ ~

"Dictating his recollections to his friend Rustichello, Marco was intent on the description of things in his memory, and talked as if looking back from the outside. He was not interested in the autobiographical and injected himself into his account very little."

I kept my eyes to the pages, as if, were I to raise them, I'd feel the air rip against my skin.

One day, without warning, another hand appeared. Whose handwriting was this? It moved close to hers.

I'd been trying to figure out what she meant by,

"We agreed perfectly and yet there was a great dissimilitude in our characters,"

when the other's hand—its handwriting quicker, wilder, more free—wrote beside hers:

"yet there was a harmony in that very dissimilitude."

I saw it cancel her words with wavy lines, insert its own. Often it made suggestions:

"I think the journey ought to be Victor's proposal. That he ought to go for the purpose of collecting knowledge, for the formation of a female."

Mostly it lived in the margins.

Over time it came often with hers, but never when her hand was small as in the graveyard. At those times her words remained uncommented upon, uncorrected:

> Father's writing an essay on the importance of gravestones. They want to send me away, say it's for my own good but I feel I'm being punished

> I'll go away to some desolate place. ~~I'm not~~ I'm not gentle like Fanny. ~~Why after all those weeks did he . . . this silence that angers and frightens me~~

I lay in the world's profuse brokenness where, among the many names, I heard a namelessness, private and denied, unspoken.

Claire,

Then one day as I daydreamed of walking in my desolate place, I suddenly felt I could know him without really knowing him. No one knows anyone, the silence between us just more visible, overtly cruel. And all meanings stricken, traumatized, suffering at the core, clawing toward some imagined center. It was as if he was standing there, waiting for me to stroke or hit him, either one. I could make of him anything I wanted. My mind the cage of him, the laboratory, the shackles. I would construct of him what I needed. He my prisoner, my experiment, after all. Part of me pulled back, shuddered at my faithlessness, arrogance, sensed that other being who I knew I couldn't know (yet I'd felt I'd grasped him in some way) and who had left me. I turned him over and over, a secret rock lifted from the soil, seeing what grew on the damp underneath when no one was looking. I'd find that rock, hold it a few minutes, lose it. Find it again. Turn it over and over. Never really see it. Lose it. Knew I wouldn't let it go. Slowly my skin grew smoother, milkier, and often people commented on how beautiful my complexion was, though they said I seemed distant, rather cold.

Industrial zones, financial centers, meatpacking districts, train yards, dirt roads. Everywhere I went I waited for that hand, sometimes older, sometimes young. Slender letters slanted rightward, lithe but not delicate, *t*'s crossed with long, determined slashes.

She corrected misspellings:

> not a leaf ~~stired~~ stirred   each ~~proceded~~ proceeded ~~imolation~~ immolation,

or crossed out a word, replaced it with another: *better* became *mild*, *unhappy* became *sorrowful*. She wrote *depressed in my mind* then underlined *mind*, jotted next to it—what?—I had trouble deciphering the word: it looked, maybe, like *remorse*.

I followed each mark as if it could hold me to the world (but how could it hold me?). It was baffling reading whole strings of words without context:

> was made a prisoner   and would not disturb   You cannot be so wicked as to murder a child

> Tell me you haven't injured the child   ~~through the dark what has kept you~~

There came:

> *do not understand and ask for my*

Then she signed herself:

> *Yours Entirely, Mary*

I wondered about that "*Entirely.*" There was no date. If she'd come to truly trust another, how had that happened, who was she writing to, and when? (I thought of the hand that had moved so close to hers.)

Then came:

but cannot compose my thoughts it is all so strange   You do not write and I
despair of ever hearing from you again

Eventually this long, broken string arrived, forming much more slowly than the others:

I am silent and serious . . . a wrecked seaman's plank . . . the air bitterly cold and this sharp wind . . . I have nothing else except my nothingless self . . . I have heard from no one. I see no one . . . the annihilation of study and pleasure . . . then the stream of thought which has struggled against its [illegible word] through the busy day makes a prison, and sorrow and memory

After that her hand was gone for weeks.

worldonline   bibliomania   wikipedia   answers.com

If I could find her . . .

Light fading now between the buildings, reddish glow spreading over the East River.

No hand alights in air. No words take flight before my eyes.

www.bartleby.com/65/sh/ShelleyM.html
                                        www.findagrave.com/pictures/1617.html
www.answers.com/topic/Mary-Shelley
            www.readprint.com./author-71/Mary-Wollestonecraft-Shelley
www.literarytraveler.com/authors/Shelley_Mary_Wollestonecraft.aspx

Yet long ago it came to me, that hand, came often.

    I have heard from no one. I see no one.   I am ashamed that I
    and what am I then in this world?

    and these thoughts stain this paper

Claire,

This was before "Shelley's boat is a beautiful creature." Before "the <u>reality</u> of my lost life," and "grief makes my mind active." Before "Yours Entirely." Before "Then he told us the haze of the storm hid them from him & he saw them no more . . . when the storm cleared he looked again—but there was no boat on the sea." Before "(so bitterly)." Before "I often see both he and Dear Edward in dreams." Before "I see no one. No one at all." Even then I grieved. Thought maybe I could go to America, its land harsh and unsettled enough to match the brutality of my thoughts. They enslaved people there, "brought their cargo of muscles and sinew from the old world to cultivate the new." Their soil was "defiled by slavery's miseries and crimes." As I had defiled my own mind. Defiled my memories of him, had with my own mind laid waste to myself, my own kindness . . . burned my own skin . . . Each night I imagined constructing him—he, helpless, strapped down on a table before me. His voice not under his control. I held off giving him a mouth or throat. Until I didn't hear the silence of the graveyard anymore but the brutality of my own imaginings, my need not to have been left. Even as I thought this, part of me still felt he had done nothing wrong, that there was something I could never know—that I was wrong, ignorant, to have turned from him and from myself, though I watched my skin grow smoother, whiter, all the while thinking Chains and ropes, experiments, scalpels.

William, A mind must become both unsparing and kind or it is nothing—I tried to see clearly but proximity confuses, distance confuses. It's just how it is— The mind chained to itself either way— Sometimes our talks unchained me, long evenings by the fire, the words moving back and forth between us as if changed—My eyes less vicious then, less harsh—I wanted to understand the words as you meant them, the angles (surprising) (not mine) from which you saw—I expected, with my breathing shallow and my pulse slowing, I'd turn increasingly inward, everything fading, falling away. But the opposite has happened. Everything outside me more present than myself, though my skin no longer feels it—Skin has little to do with it after all, I wouldn't have guessed this—Have I already left you? Will our daughter know that feeling of another's mind close to hers, a hand moving along a page to the rhythm of her hand?— When I was still pregnant . . . Those days feel far away—Do we grow harsh because most of what we know is inaccessible to us even as we know it? There must be tenderness somehow or there is nothing—I hear her name in mine, branching, intertwined—

Claire,

This was before "mad with introspecting joy," before "the children bear the journey exceedingly well," before "my milk comes more easily now." Before "Dear Love I will meet you at three," and "Dearest Shelley you are solitary and uncomfortable yet I know how much you love me." This was before Casa Magni, Allegra, walls, Clara in fever. The burning was gone but my skin had become laboratory glass. I was a vial horribly smooth yet easily shattered, a slide on which samples had been smeared. No nerves dwelled in that skin, no veins or lines or pores—its taut presiding smoothness holding back a world. I could feel nothing. So if he'd come to me then, or if I'd gone back to the graveyard and he'd stepped from the bushes and started to speak, what would I have felt? What would he have thought of my glass skin, newly hardened as it was against him? Or would my skin have suddenly softened upon his return? Or might it have gone on glittering the way loss and hurt and hatred glitter? Meanwhile I became the laboratory, the cage, the instruments of dissection. My days spent imagining his parts. I'd look through the microscope, see the mute cells, skin cells and brain cells like wriggling protozoa. But what did magnification give me in the end? Those cells still impenetrable though I spied on them with my powerful glass eye. Nevertheless, each day I watched them as long as I wanted: my glass eye held them captive, those worlds within worlds of him, the way the early Romans kept fleas under glass until they burned.

~~Carignan~~ was the son of a merchant   and never completely happy when Clerval was absent

but in ~~Clairval~~ Clerval I saw the image of my former self; he was inquisitive & anxious to gain experience & instruction

Why was she writing of Clerval? And why was she changing his name around like that?

(I remembered those scraps of paper I'd dropped in the graveyard.)

Then:

~~in a most painful degree~~MWS.

Where had the *S* come from? Why was that part of her name? I couldn't know then how that *S* would change her.

And:

I am having my character, Walton, write to his sister Margaret—I've given her my own initials: MWS

Her hand signed many different ways:

*Your Affectionate Companion Mary—W.G.—; Runaway Dormouse; Your own Mary who loves you so tenderly; Adieu Yours MaryS.; Mary W. Shelley; Ever Affl*ᵞ *Y*ˢ *MWS.; I am dear Sir Yours truly MaryShelley; Ever Yours MWS.; Your attached friend Mary W. Shelley; Yrs my dearest friend ever Mary Shelley; I am &c &c MaryShelley; Vostra Aff*ᵐᵃ *Amica—Mary Shelley.; Your own Mary; I am dear Sir Yours Obliged MaryShelley*

Sometimes she didn't sign her name at all—

You must forgive [   ] as I am only convalescing [   ]—and still very weak

I tried to piece together what I could. The lost Atlantis of her. Substance and error. Visibility's brief promise. Far-off shore—

Claire,

How long could I remain so brittle? Though I imagined him my creation, sometimes even my slave, wasn't I equally controlled by his silence and withdrawal, my response to him largely making me into what I'd become? And in that way wasn't I enslaved by him as well? I missed the world. Missed dailiness. Whatever freedoms I might find there. Even so, when I thought of my glass skin, I admired its genius as one admires an ice-field or the cooled gleaming surface of spilled lava. That vial-skin so fierce and without compromise—alien, unforgiving. Father's friend John Newton had published his book The Return to Nature, remember? But what did that really mean? What was truly natural? And even if the skin were to be left in its natural state, uncovered, and all of us were to go around naked, what of the mind? Nature seemed to me less penetrable all the time—brutal, full of violations, and when I considered my own thoughts I wondered if the human mind is built to turn on itself and others, if this is natural, the ways it complicates, withdraws, turns against, and circles. Even if the Newtons were choosing to go around without clothes, and feeling close to nature in this way, they still lived on their income from slave plantations in the West Indies. So what was I to make of that? Meanwhile, Father worried about money and debtor's prison. Fanny stayed to herself. You and I passed in the hall like strangers. When finally they sent me away to Scotland, to the Baxters, Father wrote to them of my "excessive reserve." The sea voyage took 6 days and on board I somehow lost all my money—arrived with nothing. Maybe my skin will feel different in this new place, I thought, maybe I won't recognize myself and will be free, though I could feel his silence travel with me, his withdrawal as strong and mysterious as ever, and what I came to think of as his "frightening detachment"—this traveled with me also, though I knew I had no idea of what he truly felt.

William, a chalk-white film sifts onto your skin—I'm trying to wipe it away, scrutinize your features, know you—Always I felt a certain barrier inside myself vivid as pain or the smell of kerosene—I turned to the muteness of books, gave myself to them wholly, fearlessly, and often when reading I felt neither female nor male—But with you, with anyone living, it was different—I held myself back—In Paris when they marched the king to his death I was the stranger, alone, watching from outside their language, their history. Even the particularities of their silences differed from my own—That distance was a fact of nature— My distance from you felt more secretive, illicit—I think we are ever-changing meanings to each other—If we could have been facts—Clarities—not immolations of meaning, edges, shadings, risks of meaning, not hiddenness, or—If humans could be actual facts to one another—My child's body's clear to me but not her mind—How will you know her, this child? Will she come to understand what an other is—To what extent does a mind construct what it knows, what it touches— What will she construct of me? I listen to your voice your hands turning pages but you were never a narrative as I was not a narrative but clusters of increasing and decreasing perceptions—Uneven. Contradictory—The mind's never sufficient to its needs.

London, Pisa, Genoa, Naples, Lerici, Putney, Dover, Lyons. It was hard to piece her story together. What was fiction, what fact? Was there always a difference? Was it possible that what at first seemed fiction was more factual than not, and what seemed fact was less truthful in some way?

Letters, journals, notebooks, shadow-shapes of pages: lime green embossed with a delicate fan, cream-colored with the watermark *JL*. Then white and lined but with no watermark. Sewing holes in some. One page was stamped with a kneeling figure offering flowers within a circle topped by a crown.

Often I read without understanding:

for

    The shapes which drew in thick lightnings

read

    The shapes which drew it, in thick lightenings

for

    seem,

read

    seems

for

    shrine,

read

    shine

for

    wait,

read

    wail.

Then

    —I feel a cold northern breeze upon my cheeks which braces my nerves and fills me with delight. Do you understand this feeling? This breeze, which has traveled from the regions towards which I am advancing, gives me a foretaste of those icy climes. You will rejoice to hear that no disaster has accompanied this beginning of my journey

And:

    —A Storm has come across me—I thought I heard My Shelley call me— ~~the~~ My Shelley—my companion in my Daily tasks—I was reading—I heard a voice say "Mary"   We go out on the rocks and Shelley and I read part of Mary, a fiction

    Monday 13th S. and H. & C. go to town—stay at ~~ho~~ home net & think of my little dead baby—this is foolish I suppose yet whenever I am left alone to my own thoughts & do not read to divert them they always come back to the same point—that I was a mother & am no longer—Fanny comes wett through—she dines and stays the evening—talk about many things—she goes at ½ 9—cut my new gown—

One day—almost nightfall—this came:

    as if I had already entered my grave

I kept what words I could. Tried to know her. Those shards and darks of who she was.

www.maryshelley.org   **Error: Can't find website**   www.maryshelley
.com   **Error: Can't find website**

www.marywshelley.com   **Error 500** www.marywshelley.com
Unknown Host

These walls so quiet. Across the street, the PARK sign red and blinking.

Infrared security eyes, high-definition face recognition, gesture-tracking
video cameras, infrasound, ultrasound, passwords, PINs, lasers, parabolic
microphones, X-rays . . .

Everywhere a sense of watchfulness, suspension.

But once the whale calves looked with mild eyes into the whalers' eyes
then past them. If I could have looked into her eyes, what might I have
seen?

Claire,

The Baxters were Glassites, that's what the sect they belonged to was called.
They held to the doctrine of "bare faith" (wasn't my vial-skin stark like bare
faith?), believed that faith is the "bare belief of the bare truth"—that truth
presides through its starkness, isn't arrived at through merit or striving but
simple assent. I wondered, could assent be simple? They ate nothing bloodied,
touched no meat from strangled animals. Their faith pure, severe, unbending. I
was trying to break free of my glass skin, make it soft again, yet the feeling of
glass had followed me even there. As if I lived in a glass dwelling among
others made of glass. I imagined his skin, also, was glass, his heart black glass,
so dark it reflected shapes but no clear features. So if I looked into it I might
see the shape of my head, but not the eyes to know him with or the mouth with
which to speak. And isn't that how slaves feel?—faceless within the owner's
eyes, annihilated though breathing. I remained there for almost two years,
climbed the tall hill called Law Hill, watched the whaling ships entering and
leaving the bay, scratched my initials into a back room window. Thought
about him. Wondered where he was, how he was doing, was he even alive. All
the while I continued to build my laboratory, adding new instruments and
devices as he lay on my table, helpless, still partial, wholly mute.

I liked it best when her hand came small and alone as it had been in the graveyard. Then I could think of her as the girl near the bushes, solitary, missing her mother. What would I read to her next? More selections from Marco Polo? Augustine's *Confessions*? Boethius's *Consolation of Philosophy*? The *Letters of Abelard and Heloise*? Or:

"Wednesday (27th June)—A very rainy day. I made a shoe. Wm and John went to fish in Langdale. In the evening I went above the house, and gathered flowers, which I planted, foxgloves, etc."

Would she wonder how one makes a shoe? Was it the left one, or the right? Was another made to match it? When, and out of what?

Her hand still leaving fragments from a life I could barely understand:

those heavy hours but I have nothing

Dear Sir I am in great want of a book which describes minutely the Environs of Constantinople

and shut out as I am

I am impatient for the papers I mentioned. I wish particularly also for my two journal books—(one a green covered book & the other a little one bound with red leather). I shall not be easy until

Walk out—work—S comes down on friday evening

3
4 10
1–19
5
3–15
2–19–9
1–11–~~116~~
3
2 6
75
5 5

I

—

10

Unable ^{to endure} the aspect of the creature I had ^{being} created

He <u>then took</u> me into his ~~workroom~~ ^{laboratory} and ~~showed~~ explained to me his various machines

Teusday 26th—Walk—read Pamela—Shelley reads Gibbon—in the evening
S goes out to take a little walk and loses—himself—

Clary in an ill humour—Shelley sits up & talks her into reason

I felt great relief in studying with my friend Clerval, and found not only instruction but consolation in the works of the orientalists. Their melancholy is soothing, and their joy elevating to a degree I never experienced in studying the authors of any other country.

So the days passed. My reading the words she left so briefly in the air before me.

William, There's a dream I meant to tell you—I was in Lisbon, Fanny Blood and her baby had just died. The walls were covered with her botanical drawings, plants from England—She'd wanted to draw the plants of Lisbon but Mr. Curtis wouldn't let her—I lay in a white bed next to hers and after a while a nurse came in, handed me my baby. Such a small soft bundle. From the moment I held her I knew she was glass, and that glass had shattered—There were cracks like fault lines all over and through her but the outer form still held—I got up to get help but when I stood I was glass, a broken vase but moving—No one was around it was so quiet I went back to bed, picked her up, held her, looked into her newborn eyes—This is what I want to tell you—There were no cracks no fault lines in the eyes —Whatever it is that's word-blank in me, word-blind and word-deaf and leaving, I want to say I saw her newborn eyes and nothing stopped them—Nothing hurt or labeled or restrained them—They looked out with such great calm and pleasure—How does the mind move when it no longer moves in word-time?—What was she thinking, she who had no words?

I could see she kept track of everything she read:

1814

Mary. Those marked ✗—S. has read also

✗ Letters to Norway
✗ Mary, a Fiction
✗ Wordsworth's Excursion
✗ Madoc. By Southey. 2 vol
✗ Curse of Kehama
✗ Sorcerer. A novel.
✗ Political Justice
✗ The Monk—by Lewis—
✗ Thaliba
✗ The Empire of the Nairs
✗ Queen Mab
✗ St. Godwin

The list broke off, then continued:

1816

Mary

✗ Park's Journal of a Journey in Africa
Peregrine Proteus
4 Vols. Of Clarendon's History
✗ Modern Philosophers
The Opinions of Different Authors upon the Punishment of Death,
    selected by Montagu
Erskines speeches
✗ Caleb Williams

Had she kept lists of what I'd read? Or had she hated all along those rough sounds that broke from my throat?

Claire,

It was wearying controlling him, constructing him but giving him no mouth, no means of speaking, yet I couldn't stop. I'd feel my own lips harden as I spoke, tendons rigid, constricting in my throat. This was when Robert Owen was pursuing his "experiment in perfectibility"—he believed in fundamental human goodness, but I knew I could never perfect what I was making. He persisted in so many ways mysterious, unyielding. So a slave's a mystery too, I thought, a slave's an other *unconquered after all. No one owns anyone. I sailed back home on a ship called the Wishart. Thought about that word with all its innocence and bitterness. The allies were entering Paris, claiming liberation. Bonaparte dethroned. One rigid power replacing another. There would be a monarchy again, the restoration of the Bourbons. That same corrupt monarchy my dead mother had despised. How could I dethrone myself without replacing myself with another unjust power? Something merciless in me, unkind, unforgiving, monarchy or not. And he, impoverished, uncompleted, without rights, still strapped on the table. Each night as I built him I made sure to keep him unfinished. As much as I built his flesh how could I even begin to build his thoughts, the private currents of his brain? Those parts of him that knew but wouldn't speak. England felt strange when I returned, I'd been so long away. Like him, I belonged nowhere, wondered where I might go. Knew I'd take him with me.*

The more the other's handwriting came with hers—he finishing her let-ters, his words in her margins, she signing a letter

your own Mary who loves you,

—the more I felt like a ghost. Why had I wondered if she missed my books, the graveyard? How could I have been so foolish?

"A truth wastes away when it becomes integrated into other ones," I'd read. Had I merely been of use to her until she'd met him? Each mind, the book said, "preserves and suppresses, realizes and destroys."

Meanwhile I watched their hands moving closely together. Their words intertwined and overlapped. Each following and guiding. The quiet shore of them. Wing-beats. Turnings. Consent.

Often they wrote of a monster, a creature, a feared being. It pained me, but I wasn't surprised.

Where she wrote,

I sprung on him ~~that I might destroy so hateful a monster,~~

the other wrote above those words then continued in the left-hand margin:

~~and~~ impelled by all the feelings which can arm one being against the existence of another

Where she wrote,

A creature whom I myself had created and endued with life,

he crossed out

creature

wrote in:

being.

She wrote,

> I lived in daily fear lest the monster whom I had created should perpetuate
> some new wickedness. I had an obscure feeling that all was not over

and he added,

> there was always fear so long as anything I loved remained alive.

His hand so often in the margins:

> distrusting the very solace

and

> lulled

and then,

> my disorder owed its origin to some uncommon & terrible event

When she wrote fast she left out letters:

> remeber for remember

—his hand inserted the

> m.

The more I watched, the more I felt alone. Still, I didn't want them to
stop. Feared one day her hand would leave forever.

William, I see you and the children eating breakfast—Or they're outside in the evening fighting and playing—Sometimes I see my hand writing, "the unswervable principles of justice and humanity," something like that, or "send me some ink," or "I'm glad there's no perhaps"—I see Goethe's book we were reading. Words I underlined but can't remember why: mortal, selfishness, traffic, impulse, flies, great, little. Why underline those above others?—I hear your voice say "it's cloudy"—Then you're telling Dr. Clarke you won't attend my funeral—I see moths, candles, a horse running away from you (though that's something I never really saw), Fanny Blood in fever, my father hitting my mother on the stair—I hear the black doors of the Thames, their hinges—My hand writes, "must learn to brave censure," "I'm not fond of vindications," "Fanny sends her love to Henry"—I watch all these words brightening, fading— I can't tell if I have skin or has it vanished? How vivid everything is now that it's leaving—The trees' soft pulsings, Joseph Johnson's kindness to me, Fanny Blood's botanical drawings—

Not once did she change because I thought of her or watched her. What would I have changed? Her love of him, her blindness toward me and toward herself, our days in the graveyard, her rage at what she thought I was?

When flowers open they're said to "watch." My watching had little openness in it.

I was "vigil-strange," "vigil-wasted," "vigil-patient," "vigil-keeping," "vigil-blind."

www.google.com

search for: mary shelley   mary shelley monster   mary w shelley
mary wollstonecraft shelley   mary shelley creature   mary wollstonecraft
godwin   mwgodwin shelley   maryfannyclaireallegra

[refine search]   [key words]

[Push the refresh button. Redirected to]:

My Hideous Progeny: Mary Shelley–Home Page

ON THIS SITE YOU WILL FIND EVERYTHING YOU HAVE EVER WANTED TO
KNOW ABOUT MARY SHELLEY. THERE ARE PAGES DEALING WITH HER LIFE,
HER FAMILY, HER FRIENDS AND HER NOVELS.

But I was not confined to my own identity—

she'd written that in air. So how could I have found her? How could I find her even now?

Claire,

Why couldn't I forget him? Not even after those beginning secret hours with Shelley, our love for each other, our thoughts of running away. When Shelley gave me Queen Mab, I pretended I was reading to a girl on the other side of the bushes in a graveyard. Or I'd sit in my room wondering what he'd think of the tiny printed hands in the margins of Shelley's notes. Those notes reminded me of how he wandered through so many texts, surprising me—I never knew what would come next. I felt a sudden softening in myself as I thought this, the laboratory far from my mind, the idea of him strapped to the table much too far from my mind. So I pulled back, strapped him to the table once again, took away his mouth, his tongue, sometimes took away a hand, a leg, made sure he was powerless, unfinished. In Queen Mab Shelley celebrated liberty, equality, critiqued the monarchy, commerce, religion. Yet the copy he gave me had been printed with his name deleted—he feared reprisals—so what liberty did he really have? What walls did he stare into? What hiddenness even in him? Even more than the poem I loved the notes best—: "beyond our atmosphere the sun would appear a rayless orb of fire in the midst of a black concave." "In one year light travels 5,422,400,000,000 miles, which is a distance 5,707,600 times greater than that of the sun from the earth." "The plurality of worlds,—the indefinite immensity of the universe, is a most awful subject of contemplation. He who rightly feels its mystery and grandeur is in no danger of seduction from the falsehoods of religious systems, or of deifying the principle of the universe." He cited Nicholson's British Encyclopedia, our father's Enquirer and Political Justice, the Bible, Homer, Lucretius, Gibbon's Decline and Fall, Sale's Preliminary Discourse to the Koran, Rousseau . . . Worlds within worlds unfolding on the page before me. Seventeen notes in all. He wrote of how "we see a variety of bodies possessing a variety of powers" but we are in "a state of ignorance with respect to their essences and causes." Wasn't I in a state of ignorance? Though I'd strapped the one from the graveyard onto the table to control him, I was ignorant all the same of who he was, the truths of him, of what he thought and how he'd come to grow so silent. Hume, Locke, Newton, Plutarch, Lambe's Reports on Cancer, Thomas Cadell's Return to Nature or a Defense of Vegetable Regimen—I read on and on through those notes as if in challenging my mind they could tame me, maybe even make me burn or dismantle the table where I held him. Instead, I polished that table even more, tightened the straps, sharpened my instruments. Collected, hoarded, rearranged—

A few times his hand came alone. I felt like a ghost as I watched, but grew to feel a certain tenderness as well, wondered who he was.

His hand wrote feverishly, leaving cross outs and drawings. There were ink blots, water stains, burns, some on pages so small they'd fit into a pocket.

Once he filled up a whole sheet of paper with just this: Na na , na na ná na. Why would he do that?

He'd write something, suddenly stop, then weeks later write the same words in other notebooks, though not one of them was filled. Often he wrote in several at one sitting. Great swirls of words. Yet he was the one who was patient with Mary, pausing to hear her, soothe, consider.

He came in fragments just like her:

in a sea and my sail has been torn   the tender and impartial love
overcoming all insults and crimes

      thus the life of a man of virtue and talent who should die in his thirtieth year, is, with regard to his own feelings, longer than the life of a miserable Priest-ridden slave

        the laws of nature   have undergone violation

Over the faint penciled words:

Yellow & black & pale & hectic red,

one day he wrote in blurred dark ink a draft of something else,

Una Favola,

which began

"l' ~~imagine di questa angelica donna ci sedava,~~

When he wrote too fast, or wrote in streaming rain (the letters blurring, misshapen), or spilled ink on his pages, I imagined making of myself for him some sort of shelter. Still, I wished him gone, remembered her hand and those pebbles, days she left chocolate, hunks of bread.

Claire,

I finally managed to shed my glass skin (to this day I'm not sure how this happened), but part of me was always in the graveyard waiting for him to come back. We live in the present and not. Days passed and years—so many visible events and changes, those outward manifestations so often mistakenly equated with a life. Our running away to France, you and Shelley walking together for hours, the village of St. Aubin among the trees, then those first days in Italy, so much that I wrote in my notebooks: "Dream my little baby came to life again—that it had only been cold & that we rubbed it by the fire and it lived—I al awake & find no baby—think about it all day—Fanny comes a little before 9." When my babies lived for a while I felt their cries, always went to them quickly. Nothing more real to me than them. Watched how they turned their infant hands in front of their eyes, a wild wonder at the thing before them. I think they didn't realize those first months the hand was attached to their body, not something mysteriously visiting that at any time could suddenly be gone. Everything vivid: Shelley's hands, his kindness, the way we shared a notebook, finished or began each other's letters. All the while wasn't part of me expecting him to come back, to finally explain, to make the cruelty or mystery or inevitability or whatever it was of his silence more overtly explicit? Maybe I could release him from the table then, imagine him at large in the world with a life of his own. But of course he never explained. My waiting had a cruelty in it, this I knew—a shard of something sharp or weapon-like wrapped inside a longing, a jewel hidden in layers of gauze. He didn't come and so I kept him strapped down, though sometimes I also felt I sheltered him in some way—that my waiting did this—if a shelter can be partly cruel, ambivalent, ruthless. Sometimes I believed my waiting kept him warm—

Nothing mattered but her hand in air:

I long for some circumstance that may ^assure me^ that I am not utterly disjointed from my species

Why would she write that? She who had Shelley. Her skin looked older,
dull.

most women I believe wish that they had been men—but I don't wish to
change my sex & do not think my talents would be greater if I had been
born male   these hours that have destroyed my happiness   ~~but all my~~
~~many pages future wastepaper surely I am a fool~~   yet cannot forgo the
hope of loving & being loved   I am a fool—poverty-stricken—deformed
squinting lame   I will bury myself alive among flowers

That page was torn off and another appeared:

Winter passed, and summer.

Her hand looked young again, the skin brighter, smooth:

Henry^clerval^~~Carnigan~~ was the sons of a merchant ~~an~~ of Geneva ~~and~~ an
intimate friend of my father's when he was only nine years old he wrote a
fairy tale which was the delight and amazement of all his companions

it was with these feelings ^that^ I began the creation of a human being. As the
^minuteness^~~smallness~~ of the parts ^formed^~~were~~ a great hindrance to my speed I
resolved, contrary to my first intention, to make ~~him of~~ a gigantic stature

Here S's hand crossed out

"him"

wrote

"the being"

instead. The rest of the page was in her hand:

But how How can I describe my emotion at this catastrophe; or how delineate the wretch whom with such infinite pains and care I had endeavoured to form. His limbs were in proportion and I had selected his features ~~h~~ as ^{beautiful}~~handsome.~~ ^{Beautiful}~~Handsome~~; Great God! His yellow ~~dun~~ skin scarcely covered the work of muscles and arteries beneath; his hair was ^{of a} ^{lustrous black &}flowing

I came to believe she was constructing some skewed version of me. A version she needed to believe. Yet she used the words *handsome* and *beautiful*—what was I to make of that? All the while I imagined the two of them curled in their bed. My eyes a hushed river as I watched.

Why had she written, *I am a fool—poverty-stricken—deformed squinting lame?* Why had she feared herself *utterly disjointed from my species?* And how odd that she'd describe me as *handsome,* even *beautiful.* I who was the one cast out, disjointed, deformed. What had happened to make her so despairing?

William, I'm thinking of margins—How what's written in them isn't governed by the monarch text, that central ruler—How there are margins of rivers, woods, systems, habits of thought—In his Optics Brewster wrote, "the central parts of the lens refract the rays too little"—But margins are active, wild, refractive, not obedient to the laws of the center—I want to dwell among the smallest things, the cast-aside, banished, dismissed, discounted—There are hands at the barricades making visible the margins in air, can you see them? Such margins where the poor fail, thrive, suffer, go on—I would live on the margin of doubt—Lilies are marginals—Any plant flourishing at pond's edge—I would breathe from those edges—We married, should we have married?—All those books I wrote, their texts are disappearing in front of my eyes I see this right now, but the margins remain someone's writing all over them I walk into them alone, my feet stepping among so many questions, calculations—No monarch of my mind, no town square, no penal code, no prisons—

Wasn't she trying to create a story that would move into the silence and confusion we'd become? She needed to take hold of me, explain me. I saw there was a violence in her need.

Her hand moved back and forth in time:

I have been an altered being since your silence
I tried to keep you, feeling the while that I had lost you
Do not think that I am not fully aware of the defects on my part that might
call forth your reprehension
How hateful I must have appeared to you   thought presses & stings me
I have known no peace since that summer—
I never expect to know it again—
Were I to say forget me, would you reply?   I cannot forget you
I can only be an object of distaste to you—
so isn't it best then that I be forgotten—

Could those words be addressed to me? Yet I was sure they weren't. Then:

by the magic of words   between the most barren clefts   into the
    regions of frost

the destroyer   the murderer   the creature

I have also finished the 4 Chap. of Frankenstein which is a very long one & I
think you would like it.

I believe William Gifford advised John Murray against publishing my
Frankenstein. Murray rejected it on June 18.

When I can get out and about again   The blue eyes of your sweet boy are
staring at me as I write this.

Sir, I am anxious to prevent your continuing in the mistake of supposing that
Mr. Shelley is the author of this juvenile attempt of mine and from which I
abstained from putting my name. I have kept my authorship of Frankenstein
concealed out of respect to those persons from whom I bear my name.

and loathed his deformity   and had created a fiend whose unparalleled
barbarity   the death of my little Clara   soon William fell ill and
we were frightened   i

*you see how blind we mortals are—We came to Italy thinking to do Shelley's
health good—but the Climate is not warm enough to be of benefit to him & yet
it has destroyed my two children—*

to ~~loose~~ *lose two only & lovely children in one year—*   *Shelley says
that he will finish this letter—*

Claire,

*If I could experience him as an unhealed injury I carried within me, keep him
alive in me like that, would that be less wearying, more practical, maybe even
more effective and efficient, than keeping him strapped down without a throat
or mouth? I considered giving him a voice—not his voice exactly, but the voice
of the wound in me speaking. Something like that. I wasn't sure. I didn't
want anything so rampant as what had happened with my skin—imagined
instead a coin-shaped wound near the heart, but festering, signaling its redness
to my brain. That summer of 1816 at Villa Diodati and then traveling
through the Alps, through all those huge storms, looming peaks outside
Chamonix, rumors of a gigantic glacier edging ever closer, that summer of those
discussions of the slave-trade, the Treaty of Paris securing for France slave-
trading rights for another five years—through that whole summer of your secret
pregnancy, remember?—I tried to hear his voice as the voice of a wound that,
if I could both feel and contain it, might make me less vicious, less cruel.
Wouldn't a wound be something I'd want to tend? Might I even feel toward
it an odd tenderness, protectiveness, knowing it couldn't heal itself? His voice
not chains all over me this time but fleshy, raw, unable to close over, form a
scar. And still I felt a cruelty in myself, the need to hurt him, make him pay.
The words* monstrous *and* murderer *festering in my brain. But what had he
murdered?—the deluded place in me that thought there could be answers, clear
meanings in the world? Or the place that believed abandonment, fear, and
shame could be eluded? Or the place that hoped I might one day hear my
mother's voice? Of course when anyone asked how and when he'd come to me
(after my book they asked often) I gave contradictory accounts—"In a waking
dream," I'd say, or, "Everyone was making up stories and I couldn't think of
one, and then . . ." Or, "We'd been reading Mrs. Utterson's translation of
German fantasy tales, Tales of the Dead, and in one of them a gigantic spectre
was doomed to kill all the heirs of his house with a kiss." Such distance
between any breathing thing and another. Is seeing always partly a travesty of
seeing, touch partly a travesty of touch?—though of course I never touched him.
The brain a desperate, entrapping thing.*

I stand upon a precipice and cannot
                              The vale is like a vast Metropo[lis]
<u>*I have been reading Calderon without you*</u>.

This from his hand, not hers. Then:

Italy. I only feel the want of those who can feel, and understand me.
Whether from proximity and the continuity of domestic intercourse, Mary
does not.

I felt I'd glimpsed something hideous. Those two whose hands moved
side by side finishing each other's letters, helping with each other's books,
who slept entwined in the night—even between them a loneliness, a
wrongness. (I thought of her sad skin, the redness spreading.)

His hand continued:

Concealing and containing   And ~~the atoms of chaos~~   And the <u>waves</u>
of ~~its~~ chaos are

                    Making captivity a barren coffin

I sold my watch, chain, & etc which brought 2 napoleons 5 francs

I was not before so clearly aware how much the colouring of our own
feelings throws upon the delineations of other minds

We arrived at Paris. Mary showed me the papers in her box, promised I
could read and study them. I intend to claim this promise.

His hand returned a few more times through the next weeks. Then
abruptly, not at all.

Meanwhile I kept reading. Pictured them reading also to each other. Their words in air made clear they often did this:

Teusday 21st

(she was misspelling *Tuesday* again)

Shelley reads Livy and then reads Gibbon with me till dinner; Monday 8th—
buy Shelley a pencil case—talk with him for hours—read Ovid together—
S. finishes the 17th canto of Orlando Furioso; Wednesday 23rd—Mary not
well. Visited Minerva Library. Brought home Adolphus's Lives to reads with
her in the evening.

My books as close and real to me as flesh. Often they seemed almost to breathe:

"Noble deer.
But man lives in huts, wrapped in the garments of his shame . . ."

~ ~ ~

"What does it mean to speak of Hölderlin's madness? The official record tells us he loses his mind toward the end of 1806. Released from a clinic after a year's unsuccessful treatment, he will spend his remaining days in a small tower overlooking the river Neckar, passing his time playing the flute, reading, going for long walks, and every now and then, under the mysterious heteronym of Scardanelli, composing a few small, rhymed poems."

~ ~ ~

"The *Cha no yu,* or tea-making ceremony, is an elaborate ritual invented, so it is said, in the sixteenth century by the great Hideyoshi, to turn the thoughts of his men away from war. Perpetual peace was to be kept by means of pursuing artistic grace. Although this policy failed, it gave rise to a flowering of the ceramic arts."

~ ~ ~

"Nothing sets us upon a change of state, or upon any new action, but some uneasiness. Uneasiness is the great motive that works on the mind."

Now there are no hands to wait for. I look out at the stone face across the way, the PARK sign, read MTA posters as I ride:

IF YOU SEE SOMETHING, SAY SOMETHING. THERE ARE 16 MILLION EYES IN THE CITY. WE'RE COUNTING ON ALL OF THEM. BE SUSPICIOUS OF ANYTHING. PLEASE TAKE YOUR THINGS. OR WE WILL.

Call the anti-terrorism hotline: 888-NYC-SAFE · Be alert to unattended packages or luggage · Be wary of suspicious behavior · Take notice of people in inappropriate or bulky clothing especially in warm weather · Keep an eye out for exposed wiring or other irregularities · Report anyone tampering with surveillance cameras or entering unauthorized areas · Be wary of someone nervously checking belongings or clothing · And remember, if you see something, say something.

REMEMBER. YOU ARE THE EYES AND EARS OF THE SYSTEM.

Didn't your world fill with suspicion because it had me in it? From the moment I opened my eyes, you couldn't trust who you were, what you had made or done, what I was or might become. Yet mostly you said nothing, until maybe those last hours of your dying. In that way weren't we alike?—we kept our secrets, fed the isolate silence of our eyes.

William, Do you remember when Dr. Singleton told us some day they'll invent a cream that's a barrier between skin and toxic chemicals—You just rub it in, it leaves an invisible glove on your hand—But what if the workers' materials, the air, weren't toxic?—Even the barriers in our cells, will they try to make them more vigilant, less supple?—When the water went into my lungs I thought maybe I could be the water, but they fished me out, they—And hands are barriers, and eyes. Sometimes when my pen moved across the page there was no barrier between my thoughts and the words—Between the things I felt and the people I wrote to, the person I thought myself to be—But that happened rarely— Why did it have to happen just rarely?—Our new daughter, what barriers will she find in the world she'll grow up in without me?— What barriers will rise up in centuries to come?

Why was her hand absent for long stretches? His was always hurrying. I knew from her pages his body often pained him.

One day he wrote that animals were slaves:

> They are called into existence by human artifice that they may drag out a short and miserable existence of slavery and disease, that their bodies be mutilated, their social feelings outraged. It were much better that a sentient being should never have existed, than that it should have existed only to endure unmitigated misery.

This was in his

"A Vindication of Natural Diet."

Though I'd eaten only leaves and berries, never tasted flesh, I hadn't thought of animals as slaves until he wrote that, realized he was right. If he could recognize that animals had "social feelings" might he recognize such traits in me?

He was the one, kind, protective, who held Mary as she slept, calmed Claire, looked for a house for them in Hampstead; who sold his watch to buy them food and passage. The one who wrote,

> I went the other day to see Allegra at her convent, & stayed with her about three hours . . . at first she was very shy, but after a little caressing . . . led me all over the garden & all over the convent, running . . . and showed me her little bed and the chair where she sits at dinner . . .

One day, his hand left this:

The conclusion wonderfully

I pondered that a long time. Though I envied him his life, I imagined his voice not faltering in his throat. Wondered how she felt each time she heard it.

Claire,

Even as I wrote my book part of me believed he'd try to find me, that one day he'd come back—that in the end he couldn't forget me. But the longer his silence continued the more I remembered the hatred I once sensed in his voice, though I never could be sure that it was hatred. Maybe it was loneliness or fear or . . . Meanwhile each morning I pursued the construction of my creature: "with yellow, watery, but speculative eyes," I wrote. (If he ever read it, if he ever sought me out, wouldn't he be particularly pleased by 'speculative'?—that gesture toward the nature of his being.) Wrote: "Shall I respect man when he condemns me? Let him live with me in the interchange of kindness, and, instead of injury, I would bestow every benefit upon him with tears of gratitude at his acceptance." But the fact of his not coming ate away at me. If it was true he'd been cold and cruel all along, if he'd planned all along to vanish and so pain and haunt me, then what was I to make of all the words he'd read me? Had they been weapons? Traps? Subtle instruments of coercion? If he had never felt what he read, then all along I was the one strapped down and he the scientist experimenting, controlling. It was I who was his creature. But how could I know? How could I interpret silence? Often in the afternoons Shelley's hand moved next to mine as I went over my work, assessing how I'd built my creature, built cruelty into him, and longing, betrayal. I wrote in gray ink, not brown, different from my letters, the gray of her gravestone or the pebbles I held in my hand as I listened.

Last night I dreamed of Claire. She was standing at the window in Moscow in the cold, wearing Shelley's shawl. Then she turned to me and said,

"I'm not in Moscow like you think. Don't you know where I am? I'm on the island of Gloskar. The cattle are starving, walking on snowdrifts high as roofs. Everyone's sick here. I'm sick too, don't you see I can't close my eyes? And my hands don't work right, I'm always dropping things. We're all starving, there's not enough food. You think about the kindling in your brain, you quote Shelley's lines, but what about the kindling on this island?—it's all gone. Why don't you think of me anymore? When will you ever open your eyes? What did I mean to you? What did your watching mean after all?"

Then she was gone. My hands cold when I woke.

He was writing over a household list she'd made:

gowns—	hope as2 is the	sick despair of good
sheets—	certain4ty of ill	
shirts—	11	
towels~~such~~ doubt	5	
tablecloths~~powerless~~	a2nd the spirit with all her brood	
napkins—	4	

I watched him fold the paper, address it *alla Signora Shelley, Casa Galetti, Lung' Arno,* so knew they must be apart. Beyond that I knew nothing.

I glimpsed her hand (somewhere far from him, but where?) leaving a few words—

appears tranquil   yet who knows what wind

Where was the monster they'd been writing? Or, rather, *her* monster?— the monster, the creature, the being, the despised, the mistake, the beautiful, the handsome, the ill-led, the aberration? The monster he'd been commenting on, fine-tuning, critiquing? I missed those echoes of the time we'd spent together (but could I say we had ever really been together?). Echoes that, however ugly and distorted, were more comforting than silence. In truth I found them partly tender.

His syllables lengthened into words:

I fear you are solitary and sad at Villa Magni. I plan to sail back tomorrow with the first good wind—

Poor Clare has borne her loss with great fortitude after the initial shock   My boat has arrived and Williams and I are delighted with her. She serves me at once as a study & a carriage.

Then came a swarm much harder to discern:

~~sustaining~~ hands   and many were hurt

The <u>fevered</u> motes of a ~~sick~~ ^ eye   Suffering makes suffering—ill must
follow ill

~~Hard~~ Harsh words beget ~~ill~~ hard thoughts

Stray pen marks, smears, drawings of a face, a bridge, a tree . . .

As   sunlight   ~~on~~   a   prison   which   And   h ate____
and   terror   ; and   the poisoned   rain

Hadn't I come to think of them as some sort of makeshift family, the only one I'd ever have? Even as I feared she'd leave me. Even as her monster burned and plotted—threatened, murdered, harmed.

Claire,

Sometimes I'd stop building my creature in my copybook, start a letter to him instead. It had been so long since I'd seen him. But what was I after? If I were to blame him didn't I first need some sense of what had happened? Some version I could live with? Once I started, "You don't even have a name, yet I want to speak plainly to you. I think often of the word 'plain,' that it means frank, clear, unequivocal. It can also mean complete. You read to me so many things. I believe you must like to think about words as much as I do. But I know I should presume nothing, not even that. I want a plain sense of what happened between us. I dream of mountains, huge peaks, crevices, dangerous steep slopes, but Wesley wrote, 'I recovered some strength, was able to walk again on plain ground.' And a calm wind is said to be plain. I think you must dislike elaboration as much as I do—you live with the harsh fact of who you are, how you were made, your awkwardness, your hiding. Remember when you read to me from Robinson Crusoe? Defoe wrote, 'a tradesman's letters should be plain, concise, and to the purpose.' I would like mine to be like that. And Anderson asked, 'Tell me in plain words, do you or do you not have a soul?' But the problem is I don't know exactly what I want to ask you. I want to be straightforward like Jacquard's loom that took the most complicated patterns and wove them with the same ease as the plain. I guess I want to ask you why you stopped speaking, why you went away. But then I need to wonder why you started speaking in the first place, why you read to me like that. We speak of the 'plain truth.' I wonder what you think of this expression? What if ambiguity is part of that plain truth? Even if you were to answer, how could I trust what you say is truthful? In my mind I strapped you down, held you prisoner. But in the end my instruments were too blunt, your ambiguities escaped me. Is there a plain truth of you, can I know it? Why should I assume you even knew why you read to me. Maybe it just happened. Why should I assume you understand your silence, or that you'd even tell me. Yet you must understand it better than I do. I remember the graveyard I believe you know my name it's Mary."

William, I'm remembering Blake's etchings, the ones he did for my book of stories—The people look troubled, unhappy—Hatched, wavery lines everywhere over their limbs, spidery, entrapping— He etched such scars on them, the limits and distortions of their thinking. I hadn't thought I'd written of unhappiness, believed I was writing of improvement, instruction, peace of mind, but I see now—I didn't know—He knew but I didn't—I was writing of constriction and imprisonment—I was young, William. All those faces in Blake's etchings aren't looking at each other or anything nearby— Nothing real to them but their thoughts so what will they ever see when they're not really looking?—What if I had written of a pebble, just that? Looked a long time at a pebble—I still think of reaching hands, barricades, the storming—But think of a drop of water, William—Think of a pebble, a branch, a hunk of clay, this wooden desk, a seed, a spider—

Her fingers traced words he'd left behind, touched, sometimes, pages they'd worked on together.

His voice in her margins. Where she'd written

disturb,

he'd crossed it out, replaced it with

destroy.

Where she'd put

diminish

he'd written

extinguish.

For

wretched

he substituted

excluded.

For

cause

he wrote

author. Surprised

became

astonished. Ideas

became

experiences & feelings.

Consider the being.

He stressed this often.

Had she considered that her names for me—the wretch, the creature, the fiend, the monster, the enemy, the daemon, the hideous, the miserable—were softened by him, made by him more subtle, layered? *Being* so much closer to what I was, and she the one who should have known this.

His words so solid on the page, and yet she couldn't touch him—

He'd crossed her *t*'s when she'd forgotten, though often he forgot his own. He'd inserted missing letters, his hand overlaying her hand. He'd written in periods, dashes, commas. His ink stain spread where Carignan's name was first changed to Clerval.

Reality is of little worth,

he'd written, and in a margin otherwise blank, the single word:

solitude.

On another page:

gradually saw plainly.

She turned to the passage where her monster considers a family:

Yet why were these gentle beings unhappy? They possessed a delightful house for such ^it was ^in to my eyes and every luxury. they had a fire to warm them when chill and delicious viands when hungry—they were dressed ~~in clothes that kept t~~ in excellent clothes and still more they enjoyed one anothers company ^& speech—and ~~saw~~ interchanged each day looks of affection & kindness—What did their tears mean? Did they really express pain? I was at first unable to solve these questions

Beneath that he'd written, using her pet name:

o you pretty Pecksie!

Maybe her tenderness had moved him; in that passage her monster was a lonely, striving being.

She came to his:

that I may not be

and

driven from joy for no misdeed

Her hand stopped, touched nothing. It seemed to stay that way for hours, unable to find a right place to come back to—there was no right place—all surfaces alien, comfortless, infected.

Claire,

I was often ill, and like you I wondered was it my body that was weak, too vulnerable, and so suffered, or was it the sufferings of my mind speaking through my body? I wondered this each day I built him. One morning I woke from a dream of prison. I'd been surrounded by turnkeys, bolts, all the miserable apparatus of a dungeon. When I looked up I'd seen barred windows. My bed was a slab of gray stone, the guards had confiscated my copybook and pen. Lying there, Shelley still sleeping, I thought of the prison I'd built in my mind, the ways I'd locked myself in. Considered the harsh words I'd put into my book: my enemy (I used that word often), hatred, anger, revenge, devilish terror, everlasting war. The list went on and on: eternal hatred, everlasting hatred, adversary, rage, maddening rage, fiendish, agony, vengeance, deadly revenge. If I could feel his wound more, trust in it more like I'd wanted to before but couldn't, maybe I would suffer less. But if he were not just evil, then what was he? I would let him read books, allow his reading voice not to be just a trick of hatred or revenge. But I could go only so far. I still kept him "hideously deformed and loathsome" (since truly I couldn't trust who he had been). But I let him find in the woods a leather satchel, and inside it some books. So he could read to himself, think about the things that Shelley and I also read and talked of: the rise and decline of empires, the nature of power, sympathy, friendship, the art and poetry of the Greeks and Romans. I even let him feel affection for a family he watched from a distance (though it made me nervous to do this). All those years I never told Shelley what I'd seen. He believed I made it all up, often wondered at my harshness, said there was something cold in me he didn't understand. Something unforgiving, preoccupied, mistrustful. I couldn't bring myself to tell, I don't know why. After he died I'd lie there in the mornings imagining him next to me, thinking I'd finally tell him. And still I couldn't. Did I believe that the one who once read to me might yet, after all those years, come back, and something be released in me? Or that maybe he'd been watching all along? If he had been watching, would he see that my secret never strayed from my lips (even if I disguised it in a book)? That I hadn't once in all those years betrayed him—

Time moved forward, back, always in no particular order.

It was clear he'd died:

> the watery surface was blank   at the age of seven & twenty I find myself
> alone.

(His hand never grew old.)

Two—or was it three?—of her children had died:

> the death of my little Clara   has destroyed my children.

Her monster read, though only to himself. She gave him Volney's *Ruins
of Empire*, Milton's *Paradise Lost.* He was trying to teach himself about
humans and the world:

> . . . these books . . . produced in me an infinity of new images and feelings,
> that sometimes raised me to ecstasy, but more frequently sunk me into the
> lowest dejection

(Is this what she thought had happened to me?).

> I was similar yet at the same time strangely unlike the beings of whom I
> read . . . I sympathized with them and partly understood them, yet I was
> unformed in mind; I was dependent on none and related to none . . . there
> was none to lament my annihilation. My person was hideous and my
> stature gigantic. What did this mean? Who was I? What was I? Whence
> did I come? What was my destination? I was unable to solve these
> questions . . .

Shelley had written in the margin:

> Whence did I come? What was my destination?

This she had inserted later.

Often his copybooks were back in her hands:

I wish no living thing to suffer pain.
~~he bends his head as in pain~~

And thou,   & thy self torturing solitude

Grief for awhile is blind

I imagined him coming from the shadows, pressing her hand to his face. But of course he never came.

I sensed a deepening quiet in her hands. Only few words came, white space around them an ice-field or a windless shore:

so destitute of every hope of consolation

the offspring of solitude

my life as it passed . . .

Again her hand left only a few words. She wrote them slowly:

having nothing, I can lose nothing   from this solitary and wind
stricken hill

The desk has arrived—with several letters in it from me to mine own S.
from when he'd gone, briefly, to Marlow all those years ago—they are full of
William—Clara & Allegra—I was in another world while I read them—for I
am still alive and they are not. My diamond cross was also in the drawer—
the pledge of his safety who is no longer safe.

(I have nothing. I've become nothing—)

I feel a strong need to close the shutters. To sit where no one sees me.

Can quietness be visible? It seemed I saw it spreading.

Claire,

Geneva, Chamonix, Portsmouth, Bath. Charles dead, newborn Clara dead, Fanny dead. London, Marlow. I gave birth to Clara Everina. Meanwhile the one in the graveyard still rampaged through my mind, plotted, murdered, taking his revenge. I'd given him a mind that could investigate and wonder. I'd allowed him to read, feel loneliness and hurt (even though I'd never had an explanation). Wasn't that enough? Now I was a mother of dead children and young children. Had seen them suffer. So how could I keep strapping him down, how could I keep stabbing him? (and still I often stabbed him, strapped him down). Why couldn't I be like Shelley's copybooks where the words of the despised and dispossessed would have a voice? Why couldn't I be kinder? I looked down at Shelley's pages: "In mine own ^{heart}soul I saw as in a glass/The hearts of others" and "thine atmosphere which penetrates mine." Saw how he changed "clothes" to "fills," "buried" to "happy," "green" to "brown," "day" to "[truth?"]—How he considered alternatives: "[?swift / dwell], [?truths], [?Indian], "[wide, caverned]," "overspread," "unremembered." Nothing locked in, nothing rigid, cold as my instruments, my table. If he could write upside down and every which way, why couldn't I turn my thoughts upside down? (I'd seen my own children die, hadn't that disarranged my mind, set aflame the cold table in my mind?) Maybe I could send him North, as far away as I could manage. Maybe then my thoughts wouldn't stab him. On the other hand, if I killed him maybe that would be best, I'd be rid of him completely, his voice and inexplicable silence finally dying. Or would he live on inside my mind? Might I even in some odd way miss him? In his notebooks Shelley drew firecracker trees, suns, mountains, huge X's over the contents of entire pages. I thought of Shelley's phrase, "the human love that lulls." Wondered if that was something I could offer my creature—

William, North can be a verb I hadn't known this—So one can say "gently nor-
thing" or "I northed until he couldn't see me"—Or "northing and flaming, trav-
eling far from where I meant to get to"—I said I wasn't cold but I'm cold—
I remember my trip to Norway, Sweden, Denmark. I sent letters back to Imlay,
then turned them into a travel book for Joseph Johnson—It seemed I never knew
what my life was without turning it into a book—In those frigid villages the
women spinning, the men weaving, anything to keep out the cold—The same
cruelty there as here. They had no slaves, but still the man in charge was
allowed to beat the others—I northed, William, I flamed—"Cold as charity"
Lamb wrote. Isn't there a cold that drives itself almost out of itself, the way steel
crystals bend and disarrange under pressure? That steel changes itself,
William—All those days in Sweden a slow fever. In Denmark I looked out on
stretches of cold land, imagined in a million or two years all of it covered with
people—What will humans do when the earth is used up by our breathing, our
construction, and can no longer feed us—In that time of my fever I saw a body
burning in the snow—This really happened—There had been an execution.
Women and children in pretty dresses walking slowly back, grown tired of
watching—Where is my baby is she hungry?—I said I wasn't cold but I'm cold—
This north in me watches I'm northing away, trees flame in my brain, red leaves
and yellow, their trunks and branches white ice.

Claire,

I would send him North. As far away as possible. And in that way I would protect him from myself and my unkindness (always I thought of my dead children). I'd try to set him free. But even as I thought this—those vast irregular plains of ice, bright masses drifting—it occurred to me the ice resembled my glass skin. So I wasn't really sending him away after all, but exiling him to the site and memory of my own affliction—that vial-trap I'd felt, brittle bitterness and ruthless gleaming. I wanted him to know how it feels to live inside glass skin, have no access to the world but through glass skin. Ice/glass—that feeling of not knowing where one ends and ice begins—he would know how I suffered. But wouldn't he have known this on his own? Wasn't that a crucial aspect of his affliction (and at least, unlike him, I had a name), being forced to live always apart, never touching or being touched by (so I thought) another breathing thing? I'd hoped I'd softened . . . wanted to soften . . . but I was wrong. Nights as Shelley and I held each other, I'd feel that glass climbing back inside me, small branches, brittle twisted vines. Everything unsafe, on the edge of being atomized maybe. Yet Shelley's hand on my shoulder was the simplest, most trustworthy thing. It's not that I was waiting for anything particular, my hours were busy with writing, reading, and then, while they lived, caring for my children. Shelley's hand on my shoulder—if I could place such a hand on the shoulder of the one who'd read and then left me . . . But all I had was North, the idea of sending him away, out of reach of my barbed thoughts, and even that, I saw, was flawed. Still, every now and then I'd try again to write him a letter:

> Each time after one of my children dies I hear my voice as if originating from outside my body. It comes from an automaton who looks like me, opens and closes her eyes like me. When I open my mouth I hear metallic words come out: "cloudy today," or "are you in the mood for potatoes or bread?" or "I'm so sad I don't know what to do." Whatever I say the voice is tinny, strange, lives in a world I feel no part of. I wonder if this happens to you . . . if it happened to you in the graveyard. Sometimes when you read I felt you hated me, that your voice could feel only a programmed hatred for those who touched each other, had families, changed. Yet in my book I put these words into my creature's mouth: "My heart was fashioned to be susceptible of love and sympathy." I believe this must be true of you. So why did I come to suspect you hated me? Why did I send my creature into ice so vast it was vivid distrust? After you left I grew glass skin. Do you know how it feels to walk around inside glass skin? Everything hurts, is brittle, and at the same time numb. But maybe you know this, maybe that's why you walked with that lumbering

gait, even though your limbs seemed beautifully made. Maybe it was your own skin you hated and that pained you, not mine, your own mind you hated . . . because it wouldn't free you, not even after all those books, that reading. Do we both have a North inside our minds? Cold winds that strip the raw voice from the throat, make it shatter—

Once I came across a copy of Godwin's *Memoirs of the Author of a Vindication of the Rights of Woman,* its margins filled with the handwritten daily diary of someone else's life. Only the margins around the account of Mary Wollstonecraft's suicide attempt were kept blank. Why would a stranger write his life into the margins of another's?

Wasn't I lingering at the edges of another's life, mixing in my thoughts and longings with hers?

(Your notes I kept folded. Your notes I didn't want to get near.)

Sometimes I considered writing her a letter. Maybe I could do it if I promised myself I wouldn't send it. Anyway, I wouldn't have known where it should go; time and place continually shifting. London, Pisa, Naples, Lerici, Rome, children dead, living, then dead.

~~You may wonder why I stopped reading~~

Right away I crossed this out, knew it was a terrible beginning. There was no way I could explain.

I tried again:

> *You've made your monster capable of vicious, hideous acts. Don't think I hold this against you. Yet I who partly recognize myself in your pages hobble my voice, keep always to myself. If I could read to you of Theoclea, I'd tell you how she climbed a ladder in air. Her eyes were closed, but she was seeing. "Where are you?" Pythagoras asked. "I'm climbing . . . I continue climbing." Then she loosed her black hair and fire was streaming through it but the flames couldn't harm her. She was listening to him read, she climbed higher, she continued climbing.—For many years I've been a silent being, the silent e in* hide, *the silent i in* pain *and* recoil. *The silent g in* sign. *I've watched your hand, watched S's, watched your two hands moving together. Was it wrong of me to do this? If I could move my hand without fear . . . I live in a glass voicelessness, a silence.*

That night I thought of your laboratory notes, wondered why I kept them. Waited for her hand, but never yours.

Claire,

We were in Rome. Two of our children had died, both buried in unmarked graves. How could I have left them like that, and in places we were only passing through? (If I hadn't been able to sit near my mother's grave, hadn't known where she was . . .) Cattle grazed among ruined columns, marble torsos, scattered, broken heads. Shelley pried a sliver from the wooden door of Tasso's prison cell, slipped it in his pocket. We traveled over desolate land where just a few years before Lamartine had passed burned carriages and corpses. All the while Shelley was writing mournful poems he never showed me (I found them after his death). Yet we loved each other ~~how is it that~~ ~~our babies had died, something silent and terrible came into me something not glass or ice at all~~ *I wasn't sure I understood Shelley's words to Peacock about vacancy and oblivion, only that they felt desolate like my feelings for the one who'd read and then stopped. By thinking constantly of the graveyard, by keeping his presence in me alive, I had peopled my mind with what <u>felt</u> like vacancy and oblivion, or, rather, had kept open in myself areas of vacancy and oblivion active as atoms or the hidden, violent collisions we call thinking. (Claire, I'm telling you this as if you weren't traveling with us but of course you were there too . . . there was such a far-awayness in me then that I think of you as elsewhere though you weren't. I was often angry with you, wished you simply gone.) In Pisa there were chain gangs working in the streets. How could they do such heavy work with chains around their arms and legs? I thought of my two creatures—the one in the graveyard and the one in my book—how each was hobbled in his own particular way, my mind hobbled also, chained to them both. I had wanted to free him, free myself, yet the more I wrote the more the ice built up around me, the more the chains thickened, multiplied, complicating the shadows on every wall I saw. Sometimes I think history <u>is</u> slavery, or at least the record of slavery in its numerous guises—the ways the human mind chains itself and others intricately, cruelly. Piazza dei Miracoli, the river Serchio, Casa Bertini, Bagni di Lucca, Este, the Villa I Cappuccini. My baby Clara's body somewhere under the sand on a stretch of beach along the Lido. And under it all, the fact of his silence—hole in the world, oblivion, relentlessness, chaos, confusion—*

Our lives are the embodying of quiet—

Her hand was back (so quiet). I couldn't tell where she was, saw only those words, not even a window, a desk, part of a wall. Her skin was reddened, worn.

they say I look fragile but could still pass for a girl. Robinson says I seem sickly. I still hear waves against rock

my cruelty that last winter, I—
                          my face so often turned away

Hunt says I'm a "torrent of fire under a Hecla of snow" but he knows nothing of me

               grief is quiet loss is quiet

        a living corpse such as I ✗✗✗

If I am to receive even the smallest allowance from Sir Timothy I must agree never to bring S's name into the public eye and can sign none of my own writings "Shelley"

(So in a way she was like me, left without a name, and hidden.)

~~Dear Claire~~   *another landing on this staircase I am climbing   his dead body stained blue by the lime*

                    I hate the sound of the sea

then they knew it was him from the book of Keats's poems in the pocket

She was transcribing his unpublished writings.

(I have become a cowardly . . . I agreed not to publish them, but what choice did I have . . . I can't)

I could tell she found the handwriting hard to decipher. She turned the notebooks sideways, upside down:

the plague of ^{xxx} gold and blood   as one whom years deform

     of that cold light whose airs too soon deform

Her hand paused for several minutes. Did she feel that cold light he wrote of, the ways in which she also felt deformed? I'd seen her write:

that winter of my alienation . . . my babies had died . . . but I believe his heart would have warmed to me again.

Her hand continued its transcription:

I have suffered what I wrote . . . and so my words have seeds of misery

    To [?spare] [me] from words

                 To save ^{me} from more words

    Must sail ~~alone~~

~~Must~~ ~~sail~~ ~~alone~~   [?toward] [?~~question~~] [?]

After the notebook closed, those words still lingered. *To spare me from words . . . to save me from more words.* I waited till they faded. Wondered if I wanted to be saved from words. Tried to think what I would be without them.

Must sail alone toward question   our lives are the embodying of quiet

Those words remain inside me.

    sail alone toward question

Isn't that what I do when I wonder who I am and why you made me?

That wondering so quiet (*our lives are the embodying of quiet*). I remember her eyes through the bushes, her small hands.

Claire,

North, ice, snow, ashes, immolation—I'd tried to send him away, kill him off or forget him. I promised myself I'd think of something else, banish him from my mind no matter what. This was after Shelley drowned. I was writing a new story. In it Valerius had been dead for hundreds of years, woke to find himself in Rome. Everything strange to him (not unlike how I felt upon my return to England, but of course more extreme). He hated what he saw. Only the Mediterranean (beautiful, blue) seemed unchanged, everything else bore "the marks of servitude and degradation." What he saw disturbed him so deeply he fell mute: "I became agitated with a thousand emotions. I refused to speak to anybody . . . I saw the shattered columns and ruined temples of the Campo Vaccino . . . the Roman Forum degraded and debased . . . ideas floated in my mind like broken columns . . . The moon shone through the broken arches and around the fallen walls . . . and I stayed mute, I uttered not a single word." After a while a young woman approached him, "You're unhappy," she said, "cast upon our modern world without friends or connections. Consider me your daughter, come with me to our house; you'll be cherished and honored there." But he couldn't bring himself to go. He dreamt of shattered walls and towers. Why can't human language express human thought? Then one day he met a man who, not unlike the young woman, also wanted to help him. They read together—Valerius knew nothing of Virgil, Horace, Ovid or Lucan, Livy, Tacitus or Seneca. All had been born years after his first death. So the man and he read those authors, discussed at length what they read. Yet his companion still felt he couldn't reach him: "there was a sadness . . . he wasn't a being of this earth . . . his semblance was of life yet he belonged to the dead." What did this man, then, feel toward Valerius? "I did not feel fear or terror" (remember what I told you of the graveyard, Claire, and what I felt there?), "I loved and revered him, yet mixed with these sensations was another feeling—I cannot call it dread, yet it possessed something allied to that repulsive feeling—a sentiment for which I can find no name." Claire, I abandoned the story, but these were its last words: "the earthly barrier placed between us." So you see, I wasn't writing of the one who read to me, and yet I was. North, ice, ash, snow, it didn't matter. Why couldn't I leave him behind? When I was writing I thought I was focusing solely on Valerius, picturing only Valerius, and Rome, broken columns. Not the muteness of the one who'd read and then suddenly stopped. Not those books we shared. Not the pebbles in my sweaty hands, or the mystery of who he was, the sadness I wondered if he felt. Not the not-quite dread (but what was it?) that I couldn't name, or the barrier—was it within or outside me or both?—for which I had no name—the shattered, the debased, the mute, the ruined . . . the barrier itself a kind of ruin, partly crumbled partly weakened but still there.

Theoclea climbed a ladder in air as she listened to Pythagoras reading, until there was no barrier between his voice and her mind anymore, no North in her at all, no place he couldn't reach—

"Where are you now?"

"I'm climbing . . . I continue climbing . . ."

Behind her eyes she saw the horrors of the Cambyses, pillaged cities, sacred books thrown into flames,

slaves walking in chains, charred and gutted animals . . . heard invisible colors speaking . . .

And still she kept climbing—

"Where are you now?"

"Fire's coursing through my hair but the flames can't hurt me and I'm climbing. A white shape's gliding by the Fountain of Castalia but I'm far above it now I barely see it. I'm climbing the rungs of your voice and there is no sanctuary there are wars and terrors I can't name and still I'm climbing there are no gods but I'm climbing . . ."

Pythagoras turned the pages of his book as he read to her long into the night and through the next day and the next . . . for weeks he did this . . .

as world upon world formed in Theoclea's eyes . . .

Claire,

All these years since Shelley drowned, and often I still take out our copybooks, though by now many have been lost, just look at his handwriting and mine. I randomly turn pages, stop for a minute here and there: "I will not attempt to ɇ console you"—this from my Frankenstein, the first draft of volume 1. As though, if I could only stare hard enough, Shelley's hand will appear in the margins, write: "but I will console you"—or, "explain consolation" or just leave a stray ink spot. I look for where his words mix with mine: "could not extinguish my grief." I remember when he wrote that.

He changed my "sometimes amused" to "sometimes lulled." Such a little thing, yet I go back to it, looking for some clue. My choice more lively, his more dreamy. But he was rarely lulled. Remember his nightmares, his sleep walking, the way he cried out in the night?

I linger over his "housekeeping marks"—those small, tedious corrections that strengthened my text: commas, periods, the crossing out of "each," replacing it with "every." Some changes seemed larger—he changed my "little animals" to "little winged animals," so one could see the forest more clearly through the monster's eyes. He had the monster notice cheese at the cottagers' windows, say that it "allured" him. Often I felt he could sense the monster nearly as vividly as I—his need for warmth, his loneliness, his longing. He let him speak of "sensations of a peculiar & overpowering" love for the cottagers—a mixture "of pain and pleasure such ɇs as I had never experienced either from t̶h̶e̶ hunger or cold, o̶r̶ ̶f̶r̶o̶m̶ or warmth or food . . . I was unable to bear these emotions." All that still in my copybook, in his hand. Still I couldn't speak to him of my confusion, or ask him what it was in me that needed to condemn the one who'd read then left me—

As I watched her turning light-blue pages, I saw some were torn, others loosed from the notebooks' careful stitching. Some were soiled, though I couldn't say from what. Sometimes the ink bled from one page to another—I thought of his vanished hand, its shadow. Quarter-pages were inserted over whole ones. Unexplained lists of numbers showed up oddly in margins. Had Shelley done their accounts at the edges of her story?

Claire, if I could show you this page I've just come to—he wrote: "renew the spirit." And here: "whom the spoiler has not seized." And here: "the work of my own hands," "affirm." But Claire I've got to close this notebook now, I don't even remember where we bought it, do you? Probably Geneva. I remember sitting all one long afternoon, penciling in the margin lines, counting the five sewing holes before I even began. The blankness of the pages didn't scare me. As if by foraging through that blankness I might find him—

Years later, when she was no longer alive, I came across this passage in a book I found beneath a bench: "We possess nothing in the world—mere chance can strip us of everything—except the power to say 'I.' There is absolutely no other free act which it is given us to accomplish—only the destruction of the 'I.'"

It went on: "Nothing is worse than extreme affliction which destroys the 'I' from outside . . . So long as we ourselves have begun the process of destroying the 'I,' we can prevent any affliction from causing harm. For the 'I' is not destroyed by external pressure without a violent revolt."

At first I felt very confused. Why would it be a good thing to destroy the 'I'? But the more I thought about it the more I thought back to the graveyard. Wondered if what troubled her in part was that I had, in a sense, by the ugliness of my birth, been destroyed from the outside from the start, and she sensed but couldn't say this. I'd been born not out of love but coldness, calculation—maybe, even, out of hatred. So how could I go back to an untainted beginning from which I could, of my own will, destroy and thus possess myself? Was that why despite all of Shelley's efforts, she couldn't bear to call me "being"? Always I was the creature, the fiend, the evil one, the miserable, the monster. In truth I often shared this revulsion. Was she revealing what she *sensed* of my beginnings, though she couldn't quite pin down what they had been (yet she had those notes I'd dropped in the graveyard).

Given who I was and how you made me, why had I even tried to give her comfort? What good could my voice have ever brought to her, and how?

Claire,

Each time I thought my glass skin was finally gone it came back. As if it had
been hiding, dormant all along, only to surge forward at the oddest times. So
I'd be rolling a ball with William, or tending little Clara, or in the years after
their deaths, sitting at my desk trying to make a living writing those short
biographies of "eminent men" for Lardner's Cabinet Cyclopaedia, and
suddenly I'd feel it—that rigidity, that fierce, glittering refusal—but of what? I
hardly expected him to come, so how could I be steeling myself against him?
Why did I need to be so armored and hardened, horribly smooth? The armor,
in any case, was fragile—glass being so easily shattered. I'd be sitting at my
desk, trying to decipher Shelley's writing, or sometimes just touching the words
in his copybooks, or I'd be out tending my garden, or once, having returned to
Italy, I was just standing in my rented room looking at a washstand like the
ones we'd had when we first traveled, and suddenly I'd start thinking about
Charles VI of France, how he believed he was made of glass. At first, when he
was young, the people called him Charles the Well Beloved; later he was
known as Charles the Mad. (What would people call me if they knew I had
glass skin like his? Of course I kept this to myself.) Once he chained himself to
his men, made them dance with him in a wild frenzied dance, until one, still
chained, was flung too near the torches and caught fire. He burned in his
chains while they kept dancing. I'd think of the king and his glass skin and
my skin would grow harder, more glittery, reflective, smooth, though it never
would have done that in the graveyard when I felt the words come into me like
light into water, or the sound of footsteps or the barest wind.

Late in her life she wrote of a girl who exchanged her body with the body of a fiend. Though she shivered like *"broken glass"* each time she heard his voice, and recoiled from his *"unnatural ugliness,"* she felt *"a certain fascination,"* so agreed to an exchange of bodies for three days.

Now I lived in that hideous body. I began to walk towards Genoa, growing somewhat accustomed to my distorted limbs

If someone saw me wouldn't they stone me to death, taking me for a monster?

it became necessary that I should study to conceal myself; and yet I longed to address someone, and to hear another speak

(but I will not blacken these pages with   must not blacken)

None knows that once   and now I abhor myself in recollection

As she wrote that, was she thinking of me? How she and I were intertwined, and all the silence that came after? I watched her hand slow; it seemed, almost, to soften. I sensed she'd decided to give the girl back her body, would offer her this kindness.

Even so it was long before I recovered. I have never, indeed, wholly recovered my strength. My cheek paler, my spine a little bent

my tongue can't speak of what befell me
                I keep silent to this day and turn my face from the sun—

Such silence in my head as I think of her. Even the jackhammering and sirens outside seem wrapped in gauze and distant, less real than my flawed memory of one single human hand.

I sit at the computer, reading headlines:

- **Russians have "Derailed" Reforms, Bush says.**
- **Hillary Clinton Opens Up About Faith, Bill's Infidelity**
- **Transplant Team Crashes, Six Feared Dead**
- **Two Grocery Chains Recall Ground Beef**
- **Judge Awards Woman $184 Million in Divorce**

Then:

May 01: Ten bodies found
tortured, shot in Baquba

May 01: One killed by roadside
bomb, al-Bunouk, north
Baghdad

May 01: Head of
kidnapped police officer
found near Beiji

May 01: One shot dead in
Doura, Baghdad

May 01: Three by mortar
rounds, Khalouf, Bani Sa'ad.

April 30: One by roadside
bomb, Talbiya, northeast
Baghdad

April 30: Four by car bomb,
Bayaa, southwest
Baghdad

April 30: 32 by suicide
bomber at funeral in
Khalis

April 30: Five shot dead at
fake checkpoint in Latifiya

April 30: 11 in minibus shot
dead in Iskandariya

April 30: Laborer shot
dead in al-Musayyab

April 30: 27 bodies found
tortured and shot in
Baghdad

Hide not thine ear at my breathing, at my cry

(I remember her copying that down in her notebook). Then:

but so much is strange and bitter

given so much horror how does one not travel only into bitterness?

ashes   bewilderment   chaos   the hauntings of the mind

Claire,

I'd gone to Paris but when I got there I could hardly stand. My legs ached and my skin burned. The Douglases lived on the Rue Neuve de Berry; they took me in, took care of me. I didn't know what was happening. Didn't know, even, really where I was. (Did I think I was that girl with skin that burned but would grow soft again and white then turn to glass and she'd be sent away to Scotland?) Six days of fever, headaches, then the spots began— they didn't want me to look into a mirror but I looked—got up in the middle of the night when they were sleeping. Stared into my ruined face. My mouth hurt, the raw inside of my mouth. Weeks, and it had spread all over me, the smallpox—face, chest, hands, legs, everywhere. How had I caught it? If even just breathing wasn't safe . . . if ordinary breathing could bring this to me and into me . . . Or had I touched some contaminated bedding or clothing, but whose could I have touched? My eyelids swelled, I couldn't see. Then I heard him near me, "Maybe now you understand why I fell silent. You feel those sores inside your mouth, how it hurts even to speak." Even in fever, part of me suspected I was the one making up those words, making him speak, that what he said was my conjecture, my stubborn wish for a clear answer. I lay there thinking <u>I'm like him</u>. Always he felt nearer to me than the anxious, efficient ones busying themselves around my bed. Hadn't I become, like him, a creature, a deformed and monstrous being? A being from whom everyone would flinch? He and I the only ones who understood. Or could it be I <u>was</u> him, and yet I heard him speaking from outside me. Was this how I'd brought him back to me, brought him close again after all? I'd sent him North but he'd come back. Not even my glass skin could sustain itself, keep hard enough and cold, keep him away. In my book he'd set dwellings and trees on fire, torched in malice and longing—now had he somehow set fire to my skin? If he had, should I fear him, should I try to run away? Sometimes I felt frightened, at other times comforted. Would feel him at my bedside, just the two of us in the room with its white curtains billowing in and out of the open window as if the air were innocent. But why should I even expect a benign world, think it possible? Why should I think he should be benign, or the air innocent, untainted? Everyone said my lesions were pustules, but in fact they were filled with the debris of my own tissue, so I was carrying on the surface of my face my hidden taint made manifest. They said I would get better and I did, though my hair never shone like before, and my skin remained more clay-like, tinged a faint, dull gray. Sometimes the inside of my mouth felt raw and burned for no reason though they said I was completely healed.

She lay in her bed with the smallpox covering her face, felt me beside her. I know this—her hand left the evidence, the traces.

Always he felt nearer to me . . . hadn't I become like him, a deformed and monstrous creature?

What would she have felt if I died? Who would have watched over her, kept vigil in his mind as she lay in the shadows or looked in the mirror at what she thought of as her ruined face, her young husband long dead, her children in their unmarked graves? Who would have remembered her small hands, how smooth they'd been and waiting, as she lay in that far room fiercely burning?

In her book she hadn't killed me. Was there some way she wanted to release me? For every stab she gave, she also had a wound. I knew this. I'd left her in a silence she couldn't understand. I thought of her hurt skin, and her mouth, that place of speech, so blistered and raw no words could come out. Weren't words what she lived by, words what held her to the earth and made her who she was? No words, not a single one, could come out.

Her hand among messy piles of papers, writing:

it was his frequent habit to read aloud to me   lived in utter
solitude

was pursued by hatred and calumny   was treated with revolting
cruelty   denounced as vicious

cast forth as a criminal   never expressed the anguish he felt

built up a world of his own   wandered among the ruins

thought himself defective   sheltered himself against memory and
reflection in books   made various notes

my life a desert since he left

Was she writing of me?

Then I saw she was writing about Shelley, drafting her Preface and Notes
to his *Complete Poetical Works,* 1839. Many years had passed since he'd
died.

She dated the bottom corner: Putney, November 6, 1839, and another
page: Putney, May 1, 1839. Were those his manuscripts strewn all around
her? Her hand shook like blown rain, or a branch against a window.

She called her task *inexpressibly painful,* and wrote of how difficult it was
to extract his lost poems from *so confused a mass, interlined and broken into
fragments* (But wasn't I trying to do that very thing with her?).

These Notes are not what I intended them to be . . . my strength has failed under the task . . . my health has been shaken . . .

She wrote of having found things

which he hid from fear of wounding me . . . I never saw them till I had the misery of looking over his writings after the hand that traced them was dust.

She wrote that he'd suffered:

constant pain wound up his nerves . . . he died and the world showed no outward sign.

I could tell this cruelly pained her. (Thought about how so much of wounding happens in severe and private silence.)

he knew every plant by its name   his days were spent chiefly on the water

he possessed a quality of mind which experience has shown me to be of the rarest occurrence among human beings: this was his UNWORLDLINESS

he loved democracy and his fellow-creatures   looked on political freedom as the direct agent to effect the happiness of mankind

disappointments tortured but could not tame him

Wasn't she trying to draw him near, deny the futility of her wish? I think she sensed the desolate nature of her act, her hand trembling, frailer by the hour.

William, What if gravity didn't exist? What if everything were angles, glimpses, endlessly unfolding questions—No central place to look out from, no one irrefutable law—These rips in me, these—I thought becoming untethered in this way would feel noisy, tumultuous, hard, but I'm not chasing after one thing or another, not worrying about one right place to come back to or another—Everything is so light—My body, your hand where it touches your watch-face, even my memory of my pregnancy, the king walking to his death, even the word subjection—Once I wrote, "and here I throw down my gauntlet, for man and woman truth must be the same, the principles they live by the same."—But if there's no gravity I can't throw anything down can I though I still believe what I said of men, women, truth, and those angles come at me the questions come at me—If there's no gravity what's a storm, what's wind what's thunder—Marie Antoinette floats free of her aggrandizement, her ridiculous and trivial indulgences, and the king floats free of his gluttony, brutality—There are so many hands in the air—impoverished, dirtied hands—turning this way and that, trying the angles, floating out past the ceiling—Curious—Expectant—Not free—

Claire,

Where does one being end and another begin? Why did I think this could be clear? When Trelawny wanted my help with his book about Shelley—wanted facts about our life together—I refused: "It would destroy me to be brought forward." My hair was straw, chopped short after the smallpox, my skin sallow, almost gray. I thought of the one in the graveyard, wondered if there was some way he also felt this—that it would destroy him to be brought forward. Large as he was, might he somehow still feel endangered, unprotected in some way? Maybe he'd <u>needed</u> to hide behind those bushes, read from where I couldn't see him. When he fell silent, was there some way in which that feeling of endangerment had increased? When I had smallpox I walked the streets of Paris bravely. Showed my ruined face. It was a novelty to be so ugly, I'd never in my life been ugly. And as I walked he burned through me— unquiet, fierce, accompanying me everywhere, demanding I take him. So I never felt alone. Who I was had partly turned to ash, what was left was traces of myself mixed in with traces of him. I was walking through the world as both of us, or, rather, as some strange hybrid, though I still couldn't read his mind, wondered what he wanted. Did he want anything from me at all? If he wanted nothing then was everything I felt only from the needs of my own mind? (Godwin was writing Lives of the Necromancers—his book about famous alchemists, remember?—I thought about all the alchemy inside each one of us, the combinations, burnings, transformations.) If I could walk bravely with my ruined face, walk with my scars and pustules, my straw hair (my legs stiff and hurting from the sores) was there a way I was aiding him by taking him with me, helping him somehow to be brave? Was I speaking to his need? Maybe I was just walking alone. Maybe he never thought of me at all. Or as I've said many times, maybe he'd even meant to hurt me. Still, as I walked I felt I was bringing him into the world—the rue Saint-Honoré with its hats and prints and arcades, and the cafés, parks, bakeries, bookstores. Sometimes when I woke I couldn't tell who I was. Was I myself or the one from the graveyard, was I Shelley? Then I'd recognize my hand against the sheet, see I was myself, though what that meant became increasingly murky, or, if not murky exactly, then more layered, less evident, more complex. So that when I needed money and was finally forced to sell Shelley's traveling library, as I signed the papers I wasn't sure if it was Shelley's hand that signed, or even the hand of the one from the graveyard, or mine—we'd all lived so long together by then—though to all appearances we'd each been only alone for many years and far apart.

Though often desolate, her hand still sometimes came:

In the deepest solitude of thought I

~~in the fiercest solitude~~   ~~For one tone of your voice~~   what I would
give for that one moment of your voice

   how painful all change becomes when the <u>internal</u> life is completely
   different from the outward and apparent one

         I have no friend now   myself a faint continuation of
         his being

his vanished voice his   in the mind's most desolate solitude

         One meaning of bond is "a force that enslaves the mind"

   why does ~~the~~ this pen so lag   and expression fail when I would

         pollas d' odous elthonta phrontidos planois

lake & craggy height & olive wood & cypress
                              & try in vain to bring him back—

At times I'd forget I was myself, would sit there missing my drowned husband, Shelley, or I'd be walking down the street in Paris thinking of my ruined face, or lying in my bed feeling my glass skin. Once I thought, *I must create a second life within the outward one* (the outward being blighted from the start) then remembered those words were from her journal—they weren't mine at all.

I felt the quiet absence of her hand. Even though she shifted back and forth in time, or, rather, my sightings of her shifted, a quietness seemed to seep ever deeper through her skin, like the knowledge of my leaving, or the grayness of her mother's grave.

and I think now this grief would destroy me   broken up

                                borne away on the tide of

             I loved Italy best but Italy is a murderer

     I write but double sorrow comes ~~th~~ when I feel that Shelley no longer
reads what I write—

and the   ~~shadow~~ of   and ~~cond~~emned to   the power and
presence of his voice—

Her hand returned to the pages she'd worked on with Shelley, tired fingers lightly tracing.

   would restore my tranquility

Here he'd penned an ✗ beside her words.

   Which Lord Chancellor Bacon^the discoverer of gunpowder

Beside that he'd written in her margin—this in the draft of Chapter 11

   —no sweet Pecksie-'twas <u>friar</u> Bacon the discoverer of gunpowder

She found this in his hand:

   the bitterness of recollection.

Paused a long time at those words.

Then lingering in her margin (did she remember when he wrote it?):

   imagination   supposed the safety of

This in Chapter 10.

As she stumbled on those words, I thought I saw her hand grow grayer—
whatever she'd once let herself imagine, none of it had kept him safe.

I wonder what she'd think of this Golden Lion *Frankenstein* edition (Lion Book No. 146, New York, 1953; the price on the cover 25¢) I found in the trash the other day.

THE GREATEST HORROR STORY OF THEM ALL it says above the title, and beneath, a man with huge bloodied hands stands at the bedside of a murdered young woman. BETTER BOOKS FOR EVERYBODY along the bottom of the title page, and then: "And so was born the monster Frankenstein, the freak who murdered and pillaged, who thrust naked terror into the lives of half the people in the world." Those words she never wrote. Instead, she'd given her creature/monster/being books to wander in and learn from, had let him think about the things she and Shelley talked of—slavery, oppression, loneliness, friendship, faithfulness, freedom.

On the back there's an ad for another Lion book:

ROOMING HOUSE

by Berton Roueché

> "It was a house of sin, and the people in it were a neurotic girl and her mousy husband . . . a refugee and his mistress . . . and a flighty little man who only wanted to mind his own business. And they were all prey to the grotesque whims of the bulgy-eyed landlady who surrounded herself with potted plants and pornography and lavished mournful affection on the memory of a husband she never had . . ."

> **"A FREUDIAN SHOCKER . . ."**
> —*The New York Times*

Would she laugh out loud at that? (All those times in the graveyard I never heard her laugh.)

Claire,

I felt some relief writing my essays on Eminent Men of Italy for Dionysius Lardner's Cabinet Cyclopaedia. *Petrarch, Boccaccio, Machiavelli—those lives so far from mine, from Lerici, glass skin and burning skin, the graveyard, and* "the boat was flawed in its design and never should have sailed." *Far from* "his voice, a peculiar one, engraved in my memory," *and* "joy would destroy me." *My task was to make a life become a kind of story, not to dwell in its intricate unsolvable mysteries. To build a life like an equation but not quite—even with those far-off lives I knew there could be no definitive summary or angle. I pared away so much, ignored so many shadows (had little access to those shadows). I was an outsider, there was much I couldn't know, wouldn't even know I didn't know, didn't sense (unlike the way I'd sensed in the one from the graveyard things for which I had no words). I knew I was writing a kind of lie, that to sum up a life at all is always in some sense a lie. But I liked the straightforward, practical feel of it, the steady* task. *Godwin said I did it well—had a gift—could do it better than he. And of course it brought in money. So I could write the most straightforward facts, and take pleasure in those facts:* "When Petrarch was eight years of age, his parents moved to Pisa." *Or* "At the age of fifteen Petrarch was sent to study at the university of Montpellier." *I could write,* "Niccolo Machiavelli was born in Florence on the 3d of May, 1469" *and not worry I was wrong. Those spare facts comforted me, stood like massive walls but even more so, stronger and more stable than anything I'd known. When I quoted from Machiavelli's letter recounting how the duke, no longer needing his cruel underling Ramiro* "caused him one morning to be placed on a scaffold in the marketplace of Cesena, his body divided in two, with a wooden block and bloody knife at his side," *I barely felt the horror. It seemed distant, unreal, though I knew it was more* fact *than much of what went on in my own mind. I could write,* "The great doubt that clouds Machiavelli's character regards the spirit in which he wrote the 'Prince'—whether he sincerely recommended the detestable principles of government for which he appears to advocate, or used the weapons of irony and sarcasm to denounce a system of tyranny which then oppressed his native country." *But I didn't have to worry much about it, didn't have to hear the stirrings and nuances of his voice, whatever tinge of pleasure, dread or hatred might have been there, or a mixture of all three. I didn't have to know. And absences didn't haunt me. I quoted a letter from Machiavelli's son written after his father's sudden death (some wondered if he died by suicide, a deliberate overdose of pills, but I don't think so):* "Our father has left us in the greatest poverty, as you know. When you return here, I will tell you many things by word of mouth." *Whatever was said* "by word of mouth" *had long been lost, no more than air in air. I found that freeing. There was so much I didn't need* to know with Petrarch too. His copy of Virgil for instance: on parchment hidden and glued beneath the cover a note by him was discovered with writing so faded it was nearly effaced. It held dates recording the loss then recovery of the book, the death dates of various friends mingled with expressions of regret and sorrow, his feelings of increasing isolation. But if that leaf hadn't begun to peel (in 1795, in the Ambrosian Library in Milan) no one would have thought to look or found the ghost-note underneath. I didn't feel responsible for such mysteries, such chance discoveries, the absences and presences, we call a life, call <u>knowledge</u>. I could write, "This is a brief and imperfect sketch of Petrarch's Life," and not worry. Could write, "This letter of Machiavelli's is lost; and we are thus deprived of a most interesting link in the correspondence, and an insight into Machiavelli's feelings." And I'd still sleep well that night. I accepted my distance from those "eminent Italian men." Didn't harden myself against them or feel their voices mingling and stirring on my skin or how they were like nets to those who knew them.

William, I say "my voice"—I'm used to thinking "my voice" as if it were a thing I owned, my great possession—I've gotten used to the sound of it, this sound I think of as my being, my knowing, my property—But I realize now there are other ways to see it—If there were parts of me that were utterly separate and alone, never spoken into air, that stayed always unknowing and unknown, maybe that's not so important after all—Can't not-saying be a voice, just different and more mute from what we'd thought?—Eyes a voice, even hands, unmoving, a voice—Hesitation, swerve, pulling back, refusing, a voice—I used to think the withheld parts of myself were a wound, but now I don't think so— that's just one piece of who I was, no more or less important than the others—not something that needed to be healed—Your hand nearby, opaque and full of questions, soundless spot on which my eye alights for a moment then moves on—

but I am not confined to my own identity   yet I am still here, still
thinking, still existing

When she didn't come I read to calm myself:

"An author, therefore, is a human being whose thoughts do not satisfy his mind."

~ ~ ~

"So far as is known, Epictetus left no philosophical writings. The *Discourses* (or *Diatribes*) is a transcription of some of his lectures made by his pupil, Arrian. In one, he addresses the slave owner: 'Will you not bear with your own brother? Will you not remember who you are, and whom you rule, that they are kinsmen from the same seeds, brethren by nature, that they also are the offspring of Zeus? To be just you must use the right words. Does a man bathe quickly? Do not say he bathes badly, but that he bathes quickly. The right name puts the right thing in the right light. Use the right word for your relation to your brother and your treatment of him. Right names disclose true relations.'"

~ ~ ~

"If one is doubting, one exists."

~ ~ ~

"Diderot believed there are no true and meaningful divisions within the animal kingdom: 'Imagine the fingers of a hand bound together and the material of the nails increased to envelop the whole: in place of a man's hand you would have a horse's hoof.' "

(I stopped to think how Shelley would have liked this.)

~ ~ ~

"The English word 'utopia' is derived from the Greek term for 'nowhere.' It suggests nonexistence. The English inventor of this term, Thomas More, applied it to a mythical community, using his account as a means of criticizing certain social and political practices."

(That sense of *nowhere* was so palpable every time I glimpsed her hand, though it didn't seem like *nonexistence,* but a pane of glass retaining every shadow that passed through it.)

yet cannot forgo the hope of loving & being loved

    these hauntings of the mind   this bewilderment this chaos

      I long for some circumstance that may assure me that I am not
      utterly disjointed from my species

I feel a strong need to close the shutters

Your Affectionate Companion   Vostra Affina Amica
           Yours tenderly   Your own attached friend, Mary Shelley

Claire,

If I could accept that Machiavelli's approach was "enigmatic," that one could never fully discern whether he was satirizing the Prince's harshness or genuinely recommending those harsh ways (the text provided evidence for both)—then why couldn't I accept this lack of clarity with the one in the graveyard, hold the various possibilities in my mind, realize doubt is as much a part of our natural lives as anything? Isn't ambiguity in itself a kind of truth? Unknowing a kind of truth? Confusion and ambivalence, both truths? My laboratory was gone, and that hard table I'd strapped him to (though sometimes I felt it hovering just as fierce and cold as before) . . . I was the mother of dead children and one living child. We'd moved to Harrow for his schooling. Shelley had lived on the water but now I almost never went near water. The mind wants justice, mistakes knowledge for justice. Thinks they're the same thing. Thinks certainty, balance, calm are justice. But they're not. Even with us, we remain in darkness to each other, don't talk anymore, and still I write to you as though this weren't the case. The two of us the only ones left. All those years I never told you . . . We're such strange, contradictory creatures. Look at Godwin—he starts out an anarchist and ends up a government employee. Is solitude desolation? I've been writing to Mr. Murray, hoping he'll decide to let me author books for his Family Library. I need to make money. I've proposed a life of Mahomet, and a life of Madame de Stael. Also the conquest of Peru and Mexico, and a volume on the history of the Earth before written history begins—such speculations excite me. So far he's said no to everything. Something's rigid in me. maybe the greatest wisdom is in suppression, maybe and this bitterness and the world designed by a blind watchmaker. Sometimes I wonder if we could see into our cells would we see them changed by what we think and feel, by what and who we've known? Would my cells look like his now, even if years ago in the graveyard he hated me for my warm bed, my family, my smooth skin? Why do I keep thinking I was hated? . . . Sometimes when I'm writing I look down and think it's Shelley's hand that's moving or even the other one's . . . "What am I then in this world" . . . it writes, or, "No one can console me," or "I plan to sail back tomorrow with the first good wind." All these living faces around me, and still the laboratory in my mind, that hard table in my mind. I said it was gone but it's not. My scalpel, my surgeon's mask over my mouth, always that white mask over my mouth. My hands building, dissecting. How does a mind find its freedoms?

~~But all my many pages future wastepaper surely I am a fool~~   I will bury myself alive among flowers

    ~~outlives our feelings~~

in the evening S goes out to take a walk and loses—himself—

    I am dear Sir Yours truly   ~~*in a most painful degree*~~

We see an immense hawk ~~rid~~ sailing in the air for prey—

    ~~imagine di questa angelica donna ci sedvava,~~

the laws of nature   my life as it passed

William, When I was learning the alphabet the world became more precise, but more obscure at the same time. More focused, less hidden, but in another way more hidden and less free—So I'd lie awake at night wondering whether to let it in—Why did I think I had a choice?—Now I see an index, but of what?—My name's entered under Prostitution—Why would they put my name there, whoever they are, why would they do such a thing what could they be thinking—I see . . . Brown, Browning, Brunel, Bulwer-Lytton, I see this list of names, this index but from what? See: Geneva, Genoa, Germany, Girondists . . . attempted drowning, and melancholy, influence on Godwin—French Revolution, reputation and influence, Williams, Winckelmann, Windsor, Winter's Wreath—I had motives, scars, cruel and barren places, intricate and fearful places—Places northing away from you, places smoldering, burning—When I lay awake those nights wondering if I should let the letters in I didn't know if they would comfort or hurt me—Remember how we used to read to each other at night—You're turning pages even now when I can't see you and yet I somehow see you—They're blank and burning— You still turn them and I'm listening— What does their burning sound like, what are they saying now that they've been stripped of words—

Online for hours, I come across *Contagious Magazine,* "We identify ideas, trends and innovations behind the world's most revolutionary marketing strategies."

"The media landscape has fragmented. Across all product categories, the way in which people's purchasing decisions are influenced has changed beyond all recognition."

"From design to marketing to retail, *Contagious* analyzes the strategies behind the brands that work."

My dear Sir, I received your letter of November 17, explaining that the sale, in every instance, of Mr. Shelley's work has been very confined. Will you have the kindness to deliver to me any copies of the works as you still retain: 4 Hellas (sewed), 18 Proposal for Reform (stitched), 41 Adonais (quires), 15 Revolt of Islam. I hope that Mrs. Ollier and yourself are in good health. Your obedient servant Mary W. Shelley

They will print only 500 copies of my Frankenstein. It is a small amount, the offer is not handsome.

My dear Sir, You brought me two propositions from Mr. Colburn concerning my book—I am no woman of business. I would not know how to divide the profits as you suggest and so accept your second offer of £150. With many excuses for the trouble I give you—I am Yours Obliged MaryShelley

Sir, A poem entitled Queen Mab was written by me at the age of eighteen, I daresay in a sufficiently intemperate spirit. I doubt not that it is perfectly worthless in point of literary composition . . . I fear it is better fitted to injure than to serve the sacred cause of freedom. I have directed my solicitor to apply to Chancery for an injunction to restrain its sale . . . I am your obliged and obedient servant, Percy B. Shelley.

Claire,

*My head aches, I'm tired all the time and clumsy. My right hand's not
working right, I drop things for no reason. I've been wanting to write my book
about Shelley and my one on Godwin, but each time I try I feel ill. I don't
know what this is . . . ~~and fearless quiet and a storm across the~~ . . . ~~xxx~~ . . . ~~in
my mind this odd mixture of . . . and Lerici . . .~~ the doctor says I'm just worn
down, need rest . . . But I feel it's something else . . . I don't even feel I'm
writing to you anymore . . . If my cells have come to resemble his, if I could
look into my body and see inside myself <u>his</u> cells, if the cells in my right hand
and brain are closer now to his than anyone's, chained or carried forward (into
what?) like his . . . marred, dirtied, silenced, corrupted, or purified like
his . . . but I don't know why I say this. If he and I are strapped down on our
tables . . . and it seems there should be more freedom overall but as it is there's
little freedom . . . Memory is a form of investigation, Aristotle said, but I feel
torn by it, feel pieces of ripped things in me, detritus, scraps. ~~and cast down
from the precipice~~ I want to travel, go back to Paris (nothing seemed to
frighten me there, my smallpox-badge shining), and to Germany, Switzerland,
Italy . . . then move back to London, maybe to Park Street or Half Moon
Street—I always liked that name. I want to say my faults injure each other,
but I'm not sure what that means. I sit here and Shelley's hand sometimes
visits: "the shattered masses of precipitous ruins," or "despair itself is mild," or
"Tasso's handwriting starts out large and free but then his letters constrict into
a smaller compass toward the ending of each word as if admonished to pull
back by the chill waters of oblivion." Sometimes I'm in Lerici, the sea loud in
my ears, I'm reading Hunt's letter: "Shelley mio, Pray let us know how you got
home the other day with Williams, for I hear you must have been out in the
bad weather, & we are anxious—." Or I take out Amelia Curran's portrait,
the one everyone likes so much, but I think it looks more like anybody else in
the world than Shelley. The mouth's all wrong, for one thing. Sometimes his
hand's so feverish I feel I should calm it but then I think it doesn't even know
I'm here it's so lost in itself so busy crossing things out: "~~[build?] homes, warm
homes, I feared that they exist & being free~~ a slave whose ~~garnered~~ cells,
~~the waxen hive. words words.~~" Does there exist an unalterable gentleness
even so? If I could restore my health . . . but something's erased in me,
something's . . . inside each word a mutilation . . . I don't know if I believe
that. The light's so bright it's hurting my eyes, and the*

In handwriting jerkier, much larger, more clumsy than before, she was writing on stray scraps of paper; her *t*'s no longer crossed with that strong, steady line I'd grown used to. The curves of her *m*'s seemed to crumble.

~~then taken from~~   xxx   all   burning   mute

~~De~~

~~Dear Claire,~~

but I don't feel like I'm writing to you anymore. Can't feel you anymore, or that idea of you I held in my mind. Am I writing to anyone? To him? I keep thinking of how Aristotle said recollection is investigation but I don't know. My whole body's a question, everything I am a ~~questionxxxAnd the que~~ *And the question's inelegant, rough, barely reachable with words* xxxx ~~my eye~~ *My right eye hurts, I don't know why. I gave him that large ungainly body, attached to him the words "filthy," "deformity." I wonder if that hurt him. But how could he even have known? Didn't I also make him beautiful in a way— as a troubled sea or a breaking iceberg's beautiful? I let him speak of delighting in the sight of flowers, let him find, under the trees, a huge cloak to warm himself, let him listen, wonder, read . . . Still, it was cruel of me, it was*xxx *and what was Machiavelli's tone really when he wrote of the Prince, "let everyone see what you seem, but let no one know you."* ~~he knew~~ *He saw the uses of cruelty but thought cruelty should stay hidden, don't let them know that's what you are or they'll try to hurt you, bring you down. Seem to your subjects benevolent, loving. Then hurt who you need to . . . but in secret . . .* xxxx *But I laid him out on a table and my instruments were too blunt, unworthy. And this pain in my head as if something I didn't even know was protected is now unprotected, something I didn't think about at all . . .* xxx *I still want to go to Italy, to Germany, still*xxxx *want* xxx

I felt my muteness seeping even deeper and more dark.

The taste of blood back in my mouth, my throat once again an ugly blossom. I couldn't touch her hand or help her.

my box with the papers being gone

              and all being broken

my best love I haven't heard from you today we have had bad weather

   ~~pe~~ Petrarch had many ~~fr~~ dear friends, but the plague ~~ea~~ appeared and
their silent graves were soon all that remained to him of them

           I must study—the rest is all nothing

would you buy for me also a gown of a close pink stripe

         I do not think that you will ✗✗✗ find me what I was

he fixed to the binding of his copy of Virgil a record of her death

Claire,

Or, no—I'm not really thinking of you am I? Then who am I speaking to, why do I need to speak to anyone at all? The headaches ~~have . . . the headaches~~ come more frequently, are stronger. I'm in Italy. Pine forests. Chestnut groves. The fertile valley of Chiavenna. And now Cadenabbia. Mornings I watch the girls walk to their jobs at the silk mill. I watch them and wonder, Do they know they're being watched? ~~Such distances in me such~~ And always now the light too strong for my eyes ~~and I but a shadow~~ There's a man here who believes when people pass him on the street they scatter a poisonous powder over him. He grew so frightened he didn't eat for 10 days. I tried to bring him some tea but he refused me. This morning he finally reached into the deepest corner of a basket of pears, selected one and ate it. ~~such mistrust in us such deformed, peculiar mourning~~ I watched his bony hand, my eyes scattering their poisons, he would have hated it if he knew I watched. Often my hand shakes badly and I don't know why. Just yesterday I suddenly remembered (after how many years?) that Cervantes lost his hand in battle. Strange to think about that now. My own hand tense, odd, as if burdened by a hidden contempt, but of what? Or as if it's been in battle also. I try not to think of it, I try . . . xxxx There's a sect here that wears woolen clothing even at the height of summer. They've done this since the plague when their ancestors pledged that if their village was spared they'd wear only this burdensome dress. The cloth's a heavy dark-blue with a red stripe around the bottom. Such faithfulness and yet it's like chains, isn't it—they were spared but they wear these woolen chains . . . The mind lets go of so little. I don't know how to . . . and . . . I watch my hand shake and think, what does a hand leave in the end? His hand left me this: "And [softer] constellations [?hover]." Left: "Where Ruin broods over a world" and: "I should not infect my own Mary with dejection." Left: "leaves no trace of" and "piu fresca che la Maia quando." All those hours I spent with his copybooks studying, transcribing. Recently I learned the term "silent corrections," meaning changes a publisher makes to small, assumedly accidental deviations within a text, corrected "silently" for accuracy, without comment: "cunning, intriguing" for "cunning intriguing" or "Mestre" for "Mestri." "I don't know why" for "I don't why." If there are silent corrections in me, the smallest shiftings, rearrangings, I can barely feel them yet I think they're there. Everything's hazy, it's hard to concentrate, to read, so maybe my mind isn't correcting itself silently at all but building into itself new errors, deviations . . . and I just want to look at the girls walking back and forth from the silk mill, go to the Opera, visit the olive-wood near Menaggio, not think about this. But then I feel the table against my back— is it _my_ back or _his?_—I feel the cold instrument, not deft enough as it makes its incision or attaches one horrid part to another . . . I wonder whose hand it's in now, the instrument, now that my own hand's so shaky. Each thought an ignorant wave breaking over me—

She'd grown weaker, had returned to London. As I watched her hand sicken (I was surprised it still came) I felt my muteness spreading even further, past my ugly throat, past anything to do with words.

The Dr. says it's a "functional derangement in the nerves." But what's that? Even he seems puzzled

Now he says it's a "neuralgia of the heart."   nobody knows what's wrong with me

they say they can operate to relieve pressure on the spine. But I feel there's something in my brain, Ixxx . . . and nothing's like it was . . . sometimes the whole right side of me goes numb

last night in my dream there were silent corrections but they were correcting the things that were right and not touching the wrong ones. everything is mixed up

"Cosi al vento nelle foglie lievi/ Si perdea la sentenza di Sibilla."   six years now since I've kept my journal

to investigate: to search or inquire into, to examine systematically . . . to trace out . . . to track . . .

my first Chapter wasn't good enough. I wish I could re-write it . . . those letters from Walton to his sister

I need to cross out "situation," replace it with "solitude," need to cross out "wonderful" put in "strange"—and my creature, is he cold beneath those trees? I should have kept him warmer

but I also hated him

Need to cross out "Carnigan" and put in "Dearest Clerval" . . . need to . . . but that's Shelley's hand writing in the margin

"Maie's not well. Mary continues to feel unwell" "Wander no more from kindling brain to brain"

I'm not gentle like Fanny. ~~Why after all these weeks did he~~ it was his
frequent habit to read aloud to me

I have also finished the 4 Chap. of Frankenstein which is a very long one &
I think you would like it.

Last Wednesday I saw Dr. Bright at Guy's Hospital. He said to me, "I am
very fond of seeing," and observed me for some time. He's diagnosed me
with a tumor of the brain.

I loved Italy best but Italy is a murderer   I shrank from the monster—he
held out his hand but I couldn't touch it

so quiet now, where is he?   I abhor myself in recollection   these
pebbles in my hand these . . .

why won't he take the bread I leave?   Why does he have to shrink back
behind the bushes? Is he there or has he vanished?

never to reveal to human ears—

I sit in this cold building and remember, but don't want to remember. I should pick up a book to distract myself, do something, anything. But what would I be without her hand that visited even as it sickened, and those days in the graveyard, the ways she tried to build me, send me north, how she thought for a while that might protect me. Nameless as I am, wouldn't I be even more so without those few moments she glimpsed me, and how she didn't run away, even if, over time, a feeling much like hatred—(*call him being not creature*)—a feeling she didn't understand—blended with my face, my voice, my silence, until she burned then turned to glass.

    Dr. Bright says I have a tumor of the brain   I am very fond of seeing,
       he said.

    Your friend in truest truth Mary Shelley   Yours in Exile, Mary W.
       Shelley   Believe me your affectionate friend
    MWS

             Votre Amie tres sincere MS   Your very true friend MaryW
    Shelley   Your Runaway Dormouse
    MS

    Believe me ever Y^s—MWS.—

    (Maie's not well . . . Maie continues to feel unwell)

If, as Giordano Bruno wrote, we can know the world only through its traces (he was burned at the stake for what he thought) then I know it partly from the trace of her hand that came and went without warning, and when young left chocolate, hunks of bread.

There was so much I couldn't touch, so many ways I couldn't bear to touch.

"Matter has the capacity to be other than in actuality it is," Giordano Bruno wrote. Yet I sit here in this horrid body. And I watched her shaking, often-paralyzed hand as she sickened, that hand I couldn't force into wellness or to be other than it was. There seemed no hidden capacities of the kind Bruno wrote about within us. Still, if appearance is only part of what we are, if *seeming* is, in the end, a small part of who we are, if there are aspects of our being that have capacities I can't even imagine, then how might I think of her even now?

If I could have helped her when she sickened, or if she hadn't sickened like that, or if I'd not been so other, and her sickness not spreading . . .

Matter is that which "enfolds out of itself, and contains within itself all forms it is capable of taking on," Bruno said. Even if those forms aren't visible. So what does that make of her, and of me?

What forms were within her even as she sickened? What forms are within me even now?

In Bruno's dialogues Theophilus says "all forms of natural objects are souls."

All forms. If this is so, and you'd believed this, would it have been so easy for you to hate, mistrust, and pull back from my body?

He said the world presents to us a "bewildering number of aspects and angles" from which we must view it.

Maybe this is partly what troubled you, you made something you could never understand.

Yet Bruno believed that, however varying, the world's unified at its core and imbued with goodness, whether or not we see or feel it.

I remember when she read about his burning, her hand still young then, steady. He'd moved from place to place—France, England, Germany, Switzerland—provoking criticism wherever he went. In Italy he became a victim of the Inquisition, was imprisoned in Rome (the city she most loved—*I loved Italy best but Italy is a murderer*) and burned there at the stake in 1600. All this I learned as her hand jotted notes, turned pages.

~~Claire, no, Shelley, no, the one from the graveyard, no,~~ then who am I writing to—to anyone? My hand hardly moves anymore—Do I write on the page or in my mind? (Do I have a voice anymore or has it vanished like his?) I keep thinking of Dr. Bright in Guy's Hospital saying, "I am very fond of seeing." In the graveyard I tried to see I wanted to see. His voice like two dilating eyes. Two eyes that held me, took me in. And then I didn't know how to go on, didn't know how to live without those eyes. Everything dark. I tried to see him but my mind got in the way. Burning skin, glass skin. I didn't know that burn can mean a stream, a river, a fountain, a spring. My whole body on fire, but what if I'd known that burn could be water, something nourishing, cooling. Even now that I know it I can't feel the water. I feel fire, glass skin, the straps on the table. And burn also comes from "burden." Didn't I burden him, make him pained and rigid like me? Creature, monster, fiend, dreaded, daemon, wretch, abhorred, miserable . . . I hobbled him I tried to . . . I can't move anymore, my right eye hurts but how can it hurt when I feel numb? The Glassites held themselves apart, refrained from eating the flesh of animals, ceremoniously cleansed their feet . . . And glass is made lustrous from such modest materials: a fusion of sand and silica or potash. (Shelley liked to learn about such things, he liked to . . .) His sail going under, and the water dark. I never did kill the one from the graveyard, couldn't bring myself to do it, though I know I was cruel—. Just left him to be borne away by waves, lost in darkness and distance. Who knows what happened after that? And Shelley under the waves and never coming back. Once when Fanny and I were young and in the garden, she said the worm we found was a glow-worm but I said its other name was glass-worm. She didn't believe me but I was right. My skin hadn't burned yet, I hadn't longed for it to turn to glass, anything to save me from that burning (though that burning made me proud— I could suffer like him, inflict pain, be relentless like him). And I can't move anymore is this what he felt in the graveyard?—that he wanted to speak but couldn't? I strapped him down, wanted to know who he was, but my mind got in the way, it still gets in the way. Dr. Bright said I am very fond of seeing, but it's hard to really see. Does he know his patient's glass, that I've turned again to glass, can he see this? So I'm brittle after all, but when he read to me I wasn't brittle . . . and the waves at Lerici and the . . . and that hand that moved next to mine, that hand in the margins . . . Is this what slaves feel, is this how his silence felt . . . Is he even alive anymore and where is he if he is? But what if he can't die? All those parts he was made from, what if they just go on forever and won't die? How could I have sent him north like that, alone as he is, if he can't even die? I watched the girls coming back from the silk mill in Cadenabbia, laughing and talking, watched the frightened man pick out his pear. He would have hated it if he knew I watched him. But if the one who read to me can't die, what then? Will anyone watch him, will he hate being watched or is that something he needs . . . Who'll think of him as I do? . . . I must study the rest is all nothing . . . would you buy for me also a gown with a close pink stripe . . . Petrarch had many dear friends but the plague appeared . . . my box with the papers being gone, and all the rest broken—

We're in the graveyard. It's afternoon, in summer. The River Fleet moving sluggishly nearby. Faint wind in the bushes. Brittle clicking of pebbles in her hand.

I'm reading and she's listening:

"Secluded-Streamlet Pavilion is one of a number of 'protecting-stone pavilions.' Erected around a stone known for its beautiful shape and clear yellow grain, it is also known as Wind and Rain Pavilion. This name is in commemoration of a young woman fighter who, disguised as a boy, sheltered there one stormy night after battle, never to be seen again."

~ ~ ~

"A plum tree holds the moon; a secluded path is added to fresh wind."

~ ~ ~

"The biographical tradition, full of contradictions, says of Sappho: that she married a merchant of Andros, named Cercolas, and had a daughter Cleis; or, contrariwise, that Cercolas is a fictitious name, and that Cleis was not her daughter."

~ ~ ~

"But it must be stressed that metaphor is not a completely successful or controllable means of communication. We employ inadequate language always."

~ ~ ~

"With only coarse bread to eat, water to drink, and my bended arm for a pillow, I feel joy."

~ ~ ~

"Can perplexity be stabilized? There is no simple solution. We must find a way to live with it. Since there can be no escape from perplexity, it must be seen as a starting point and a necessary condition."

As I read I listen for her breathing. Is that the sound of the river or her breath? Are they mixing with each other? If I could hear her listening, but what does listening sound like? And if she could hear me listening for her breath, listening for the way she hears me . . . And then I'm not turning pages anymore, though I still hear pages turning. Is she turning them from where I can't see her? Is she reading to me?

Who's the reader? Who's the listener?

(And I who will never belong in the world. And she who is dead.)

The graveyard's deep in snow, but we're still reading. Our skin's on fire and then it's glass but we're still reading.

The pages turn. Her hand's not old, it moves the way it used to. I don't know who turns the pages but they turn—

SOURCES

THIS WORK IS A FICTION. Although it roughly follows the events and trajectories of Claire Clairmont's and Mary Shelley's lives, my intent was not to construct historically accurate portraits. In the Ice Diary and Metropolis/The Ruins at Luna sections, I have nevertheless incorporated phrases, word clusters, and sometimes whole sentences or lists from Claire Clairmont's and Mary Shelley's letters and journals, and in Mary's case, from her fictions and manuscripts as well. In the Metropolis/The Ruins at Luna section, I also used some of Percy Shelley's writings from his letters, poems, and the facsimile editions of his notebooks and some from Mary Wollstonecraft's letters, and other writings. Of course all the letters here, except for one of Claire's noted below, and a few short ones from Mary and Percy about the publication of their work, are fictional creations. In the Metropolis/The Ruins at Luna section, the facsimile edition of Mary Shelley's *Frankenstein,* edited by Charles E. Robinson, was an invaluable resource.

Throughout the book, I have taken liberties small and large with many of the sources I have used, including the writings of Mary Shelley, Claire Clairmont, and Mary Wollstonecraft. Claire's note to Leigh Hunt after Shelley's drowning, for example, uses nearly her exact words, but I have greatly shortened the letter and slightly rearranged it. In another case, Claire's thoughts about the German word for *ghost* in the Ice Diary section were actually expressed by her brother, Charles Clairmont, in a letter of February 26, 1820, from Vienna, to Claire and Mary in Pisa. And when in these pages Claire writes, "Fanny, I'm not well. My mind always keeps my body in a fever," this is in fact a sentence from one of Fanny Imlay's few surviving letters to Mary (written in 1816): "I am not well my mind always keeps my body in a fever. But never mind me—." Fanny Imlay's obituary is reproduced here word for word as it appeared in *The Cambrian* on October 12, 1816.

In the Dream of the Red Chamber section, Clerval's friend in Aosta is based on a man who is said to have lived there in the eighteenth century. A brief account of his life can be found in *The Italian Valleys of the Pennine Alps* (1858) by Reverend S. W. King. This man subsequently became a character in Xavier de Maistre's *The Leper of the City of Aosta* (1811). Henry Clerval, in the Dream of the Red Chamber section, figures in Mary Shelley's *Frankenstein* as Victor Frankenstein's dear and devoted friend, who is killed by the monster. Of Clerval's love for things Eastern, and his desire to go East, Mary Shelley wrote, "He came to the university with the design of making himself complete master of Oriental languages . . . he turned his eyes towards the East as affording scope for his spirit of enterprise. The Persian, Arabic, and Sanskrit languages engaged his attention." In *A Monster's Notes*, Clerval is not murdered after all; I have sent him East as he wanted, but to China, not Persia, where he translates the Chinese classic *Dream of the Red Chamber*.

Red Inkstone, the commentator on the *Dream of the Red Chamber* manuscript, is in fact thought to have existed, though there is much speculation as to who he might actually have been. The majority of his marginal comments in this book, as well as all of Cao Xueqin's notes, are my invention. The excerpts from the novel, *Dream of the Red Chamber*, are actual quotes I've often slightly adapted. I used Yang Xianyi's and Gladys Yang's excellent four-volume unabridged translation, published by Foreign Languages Press in Beijing under the title *A Dream of Red Mansions*. Although technically Clerval would have used the Wade-Giles system of transliteration in his work as a translator, for the sake of clarity and consistency I have used pinyin, which is now considered standard. It is this form of transliteration that is used in newspapers and in most current literary translation, such as David Hawkes's relatively recent translation of *Dream of the Red Chamber* (*Story of the Stone*).

Below is a list of main sources consulted for each section and sources for specific quotations the reader might be curious about. I have often used inexact or foreshortened quotations, adapting them as necessary. As the monster is a note-taker, not a scholar, I gave him quite a bit of leeway.

10   **"Q. 'What exactly do people do' "**: The interview with Dr. Anne Foerst, adapted and rewritten by me, is from Claudia Dreifus, "Do Androids Dream? M.I.T. Is Working on It," *The New York Times*, November 7, 2000.

ICE DIARY

Main sources for this section include: *The Clairmont Correspondence*, edited by Marion Kingston Stocking (Baltimore: Johns Hopkins Univ. Press, 1995) and *The Journals of Claire Clairmont 1814–1827*, edited by Marion Kingston (Cambridge: Harvard Univ. Press, 1968). Other main sources I used for details of Claire Clairmont's life include: R. Glynn Griylls, *Claire Clairmont* (London: John Murray, 1939) and Robert Gittings and Jo Manton, *Claire Clairmont and the Shelleys* (New York: Oxford Univ. Press, 1995).

Throughout this section, information on the Northern explorers is from *Arctic Explorations and Discoveries*, edited by Samuel M. Smucker (New York: Orton & Co., 1857); Pierre Berton, *The Arctic Grail* (New York: Viking Penguin, 1988); J. Douglas Hoare, *Arctic Exploration* (New York: Reaktion Books, 2005); *Tragedy and Triumph: The Journals of Captain R. F. Scott's Last Polar Expedition* (New York: Konecky Publishers, 1993); *The North Pole: A Narrative History*, edited by Anthony Brandt (Washington: National Geographic Classics, 2005); Valerian Albanov, *In the Land of the White Death*, edited by David Roberts, Introduction by Jon Krakauer (New York: Modern Library 2001). Details and quotes from all of these books are often adapted and altered by me. I have also invented some of the quotes attributed to Albanov and others. For information on Percy Shelley's writings, see the Metropolis/The Ruins at Luna section.

21   **"Hear how it glows":** St. Augustine, *Confessions.*

28   **Shen Kuo information:** http://en.wikipedia.org/wiki/Shen_Kuo.

29   **"Waves of light drive violently":** Payer's description of northern lights is from Julius von Payer, *The Austro-Hungarian North Pole Expedition of 1869 to 1874* (Vienna, 1876), rewritten by me.

34   **On this map I've found:** This map is from Fridtjof Nansen, *Farthest North,* 2 vols. (New York: Harper and Brothers, 1897).

37   **I wonder who left this copy:** Index from Nansen, *Farthest North.*

44   **"What we call monsters are not so":** Montaigne, *Essays.*

45   **If, as Plato said:** Plato, *Laws,* trans. Benjamin Jowett, Books 7–12.

46   **I would call a Difference Engine:** The "Difference Engine" was actually invented by Ada Lovelace, Lord Byron's daughter.

48   **A melancholy discovery was made:** Fanny Imlay's obituary, Oct. 12, 1816. This can be found in Miranda Seymour's *Mary Shelley* (New York: Grove Press, 2000).

57   **"Cold burns the eyes":** Olaus Magnus (1490–1557), as quoted by Peter Davidson in *The Idea of North* (Chicago: Univ. of Chicago Press, 2005).

72   **"Extreme disturbance possesses our whole mind":** John Locke, *Essay Concerning Human Understanding,* 1690.

77   **"I've finally reached home":** These are Nansen's dreams as rewritten by me.

79   **"It was fear first in the world made gods":** This is an inexact quote from Ben Jonson's *Sejanus: His Fall,* 1603.

79   **"O Monster! Mixed of insolence & fear":** From Alexander Pope's translation of the *Iliad.*

85   **"a weariness of heart":** This and other northern quotations here were altered by me, from Samuel Smucker and A. M. Miller, *Arctic Explorations and Discoveries* (New York: Orton, 1857).

92   **"From half past nine till half past two":** William Parry, from his *Journal of a Voyage to Discover the Northwest Passage,* 1821, adapted by me.

95   **"I brought with me Spurr's *Geology*"** and other quotations in this list: From *Arctic Explorations and Discoveries,* 1857, altered by me.

95   **"Loveliest of what I leave behind":** Fragment 1, Praxilla of Sicyon (c. 450 B.C.), translated by Richmond Lattimore, *Greek Lyrics* (Chicago: Univ. of Chicago Press, 1949).

95 **"I am a flood"**: From "Song of Amergin" (ancient Celtic poem), translated by Robert Graves, in Robert Graves, *The White Goddess* (New York: Farrar, Straus and Giroux, 1966).

96 **"To speak is pain but silence too is pain"**: From *Prometheus Bound* by Aeschylus as translated by Edith Hamilton, *Three Greek Plays* (New York: W. W. Norton, 1958).

100 **"A disorder of the nerves"**: Information on Albanov's nervous disorder is from David Roberts's Epilogue to Albanov's *In the Land of White Death* (New York: Modern Library, 2001). The other Albanov quotes on this page were altered or invented by me.

107 **"From this comes our Ghost"**: Comments on the German word for *ghost* are adapted from a letter by Charles Clairmont in Marion Kingston Stocking, ed., *The Clairmont Correspondence* (Baltimore: Johns Hopkins Univ. Press, 1995).

111 **Yuan Mei wrote of the "impenetrable north"**: Yuan Mei was a Qing Dynasty poet and scholar (1716–1797).

115 **When the Goddess of Consolation came to Boethius:** The description of her robe is from Boethius, *Consolation of Philosophy*, translated, with an introduction and notes, by Joel C. Relihan, (Indianapolis: Hackett Publishing Co., 2001).

115 Ibid., adapted by me.

122 **"Lips covered with foam"**: The Archilochos fragments here are from Guy Davenport's *Seven Greeks* (New York: New Directions, 1995).

146 **On Parry's second Artic voyage:** The information is from Parry's journal, published in 1821.

154 **"I walk each day"**: The journal entries found in a metal box have been adapted from Richard E. Byrd, *Alone* (New York: G. P. Putnam's Sons, 1938).

164 **"I decided I needed strategies"**: The quotes are adapted from *In the Ghost Country*, a memoir by Peter Hillary with John Elder (New York: Simon and Schuster, 2007).

173 **Socrates, that "self-stinging stingray":** This notion of Socrates is from Gareth B. Matthews, *Socratic Perplexity and the Nature of Philosophy* (Oxford: Oxford Univ. Press, 2004).

176 **Dr. Joseph Vacanti directs:** Information on Dr. Vacanti can be found at http://www.hsci.harvard.edu/pri-fac-profile/285, and on Dr. Langer at http://en.wikipedia.org/wiki/Robert_Langer.

179 **In 1298, in a prison in Genoa:** Much of the information on Marco Polo is from John Larner, *Marco Polo and the Discovery of the World* (New Haven: Yale Univ. Press, 1999), and from *The Travels of Marco Polo*, introduction by F. W. Mote (New York: Dell, 1961).

184 **At Lille the leper carried:** Information on leprosy is from Peter Richards, *The Medieval Leper and His Northern Heirs* (London: D. S. Brewer, Rowman, and Littlefield, 1977); Saul Nathaniel Brody, *The Disease of the Soul: Leprosy in Medieval Literature* (Ithaca: Cornell Univ. Press, 2001); Tony Gould, *Don't*

Fence Me In: Leprosy in Modern Times (London: Bloomsbury, 2005); and from Internet sources.

Dream of the Red Chamber

The primary translation I used of Cao Xueqin and Gao E's *Dream of the Red Chamber* was Yang Xianyi and Gladys Yang's translation for the Foreign Languages Press (Beijing, 1986), published under the title *A Dream of Red Mansions* (4 vols.). Other translations referred to are David Hawkes, editor and translator, *The Story of the Stone or the Dream of the Red Chamber,* vols. 1–3 (New York: Penguin, 1974–1981), with subsequent vols. 4–5 (1982–1986) translated and edited by John Minford. Their textual notes also inform Clerval's and Cao Xueqin's notes in this text. A valuable source for passages on Red Inkstone was Shih-ch'ang Wu's *On the Red Chamber Dream* (London: Clarendon Press, 1961). Other works consulted include: "Excerpts from the *Red Inkstone Commentary*" at www.geocities.com/littlebuddhatw/commentaryenglish.html; *The Dream of the Red Chamber,* abstract and translation by Henry Giles, in *Chinese Literature* (London: Appleton, 1909), edited and with footnotes by Richard Hooker, 1996, at www.wsu.edu/~dee/CHINESEDREAM.HTM; and David L. Steelman, "Introduction to Editions of the Red Chamber," *The Scholar* (June 1981), at http://etext.virginia.edu/chinese/HLM/hlmitre2.htm.

Information on nineteenth-century China is mostly from Constance Gordon-Cumming's *Wanderings in China* (London: Chatto & Windus, 1886). Medical details (adapted by me) on leprosy were taken primarily from R. G. Cochrane's *Practical Textbook of Leprosy* (London: Oxford Medical Publications, 1947). Other leprosy details are from Peter Richards, *The Medieval Leper and His Northern Heirs* (London: D. S. Brewer, Rowman, and Littlefield, 1977); Gerald Lee, *Leper Hospitals in Medieval Ireland* (Dublin: Four Court Press, 1996); and Rotha Mary Clay, *The Medieval Hospitals in England* (London: Methuen, 1909). Much of the information on Aosta is derived from S. W. King's *The Italian Valleys of the Pennine Alps* (London: John Murray, 1858).

192 **Ever since that strange man, Morrison:** Information on Robert Morrison (1782–1834) can be found at www.babelstone.co.uk/Morrison.Biography.html.

192 **Lady Su Hui's *Xuan Ji Tu Shi*:** Information on Lady Su Hui came from www.metmuseum.org; Poems in Pictures, www.cityu.edu.hk/ccs/Newsletter/newsletter5/Poems.htm; and David Hinton (conversation).

203 **There's something called the "Mass of Separation":** The text of the Mass of Separation can be found in Peter Richards's *The Medieval Leper and His Northern Heirs.*

218 **"Confuse the musical scales":** The Zhuangzi quote is from Herbert Giles, *Chuang Tsu,* 1889, 2nd edition, 1923. Other sources consulted for Zhuangzi elsewhere in this section are: Burton Watson, translator, *Basic Writings* (New York: Columbia Univ. Press, 1996) and Arthur Waley, *Three Ways of Thought in Ancient China* (Stanford: Stanford Univ. Press, 1982).

221 **"eyelids pierced and sewn with iron wires":** Dante Alighieri, *Purgatorio,* translated by John Ciardi (New York: Penguin, 1961).

241 **the frescoes at Issogne:** Reproductions can be found in Sandra Barberi, *Il Castello di Issogne in Valle d'Aosta* (Turin: Umberto Allemandi & Co., 1999).

251 **It's a simple piece of Attic pottery:** This description of lekythoi is indebted to Maia Sian Peck's "Dining with Death: An Analysis of Attic White-Ground Lekythoi and Athenian Notions of the Afterlife in Classical Greece," *Brown Classical Journal,* vol. 19, 2007.

259 **your question about the Confucian temples:** Information on Chinese architecture, temples, gardens, etc., are from the following sources: Zhu Junzhen, *The Art of Chinese Pavilions* (Beijing: Foreign Languages Press, 2002); Ronald G. Knapp, *The Chinese House* (Hong Kong: Oxford Univ. Press, 1990); Joseph Cho Wang *The Chinese Garden* (Hong Kong: Oxford Univ. Press, 1998); Young-Tsu Wong, *A Paradise Lost: The Imperial Garden Yuanming Tuan* (Honolulu: Univ. of Hawaii Press, 2001); Edwin T. Morris, *The Gardens of China* (New York: Scribners, 1983).

287 **the Athenians tattooing:** Some of the thoughts on skin are informed by Steve Connor in *The Book of Skin* (Ithaca: Cornell Univ. Press, 2004), including the detail of the Samian prisoners and the manacles being thrown into the water; Nina G. Jablonski, *Skin: A Natural History* (Berkeley: Univ. of California Press, 2006); Maurice Merleau-Ponty, *Signs* (Evanston: Northwestern Univ. Press, 1964), and Maurice Merleau-Ponty, *Sense and Non-Sense* (Evanston: Northwestern Univ. Press, 1964).

289 Some of the thoughts about blinking are indebted to Samuel Beckett.

331 **From the early 1960s until her death:** The information in these notes is mostly from the 2005 Drawing Center catalogue on Martin's work, *3 x Abstraction: New Methods of Drawing by Emma Kunz, Hilma af Klint, and Agnes Martin* and from *Agnes Martin: Writings,* edited by Dieter Schwartz (Berlin: Hatje Cantz, 2005). Her quotes are at times adapted by me.

334 **He believed there's no such thing as silence:** John Cage, *Silence* (Hanover, N.H.: Wesleyan Univ. Press, 1973). I have slightly altered some of Cage's quotes.

337 **The Nuremberg code states:** The code can be found online at www.csu.edu.au/learning/ncgr/gpi/odyssey/privacy/NurCode.html. Information on John Moore vs. Regents of the University of California can be found at www.richmond.edu/~wolf.moore.htm.

341 **His body was his exhibition space:** Information on Stelarc can be found on his Web site. His words have been adapted by me.

344 **From 1964 until her death:** The information in these notes is mainly from Elisabeth Sussman and Fred Wasserman, *Eva Hesse: Sculpture* (New Haven: Yale Univ. Press; New York: The Jewish Museum, 2006) and Catherine de Zegher, ed., *Eva Hesse Drawing* (New York: The Drawing Center; New Haven: Yale Univ. Press, 2006).

347 **"Do there exist many worlds"**: Much of the information on Albertus Magnus is from Wikipedia and other Internet sources.

METROPOLIS/THE RUINS AT LUNA

Main sources for this section include: Percy Bysshe Shelley, *The Mask of Anarchy Draft Notebook*, edited by Mary A. Quinn, vol. IV, a Facsimile of Huntington Ms. HM 2177 (New York and London: Garland Publishers, 1990); Percy Bysshe Shelley, *Shelley's 1819–1891 Huntington Notebook*, edited by Mary A. Quinn, vol. VI, a Facsimile of Huntington Ms. HM 2176 (New York and London: Garland Publishers, 1994); Percy Bysshe Shelley, *Shelley's 1821–1822 Huntington Notebook*, edited by Mary A. Quinn, vol. VII, a Facsimile of Huntington Ms. HM 2111 (New York and London: Garland Publishers, 1996); Percy Bysshe Shelley, *The Prometheus Unbound Notebooks*, edited by Neil Fraistat, vol. IX, a Facsimile of Bodleian Mss. Shelley E.1, E.2, E.3 (New York and London: Garland Publishers, 1991); Percy Bysshe Shelley, *The Hellas Notebook: Bodleian Ms. Shelley adds. E.7*, edited by Donald H. Reiman and Michael J. Neth, vol. XVI (New York and London: Garland Publishers, 1994); Percy Bysshe Shelley, *The Homeric Hymns and Prometheus Drafts Notebook: Bodleian Ms. Shelley adds. E.12*, edited by Nancy Moore Goslee, vol. XVIII (New York and London: Garland Publishers, 1996).

The Letters of Mary Shelley, vols. 1–3, edited by Betty T. Bennett (Baltimore: Johns Hopkins Univ. Press, 1980); Miranda Seymour, *Mary Shelley* (New York: Grove Press, 2000); Muriel Spark, *Mary Shelley* (New York: Sphere Books, Penguin Group, 1987); *The Mary Shelley Reader*, edited by Betty T. Bennett and Charles E. Robinson (New York: Oxford Univ. Press, 1990); Mary Shelley and others, *Lives of Eminent Literary and Scientific Men of Italy*, vols. 1 and 2 (Philadelphia: Lea and Blanchard, 1841). Mary Wollstonecraft Shelley, *The Frankenstein Notebooks*, edited by Charles E. Robinson, Facsimile Edition of Mary Shelley's Manuscript Novel, 1816–17 (with alterations in the hand of Percy Bysshe Shelley), Parts One and Two (New York and London: Garland 1996). I have used various editions of Mary Shelley's *Frankenstein*, including *Frankenstein; Or, The Modern Prometheus* (London: Lackington, Hughes, Harding, Mavor & Jones, 1818) annotated by Mary Shelley; *Frankenstein*, with an introduction by Diane Johnson (New York: Bantam, 2003); *Frankenstein Or, The Modern Prometheus*, foreword by Walter James Miller (New York: Penguin, 2000). Also, Frankenstein File, compiled by David S. Miall, University of Alberta, www.ualberta.ca/~dmiall/Shelleys/FRANKDOC.HTM. *Letters of Percy Bysshe Shelley*, vols. 1 and 2, edited by Frederick L. Jones (Oxford: Clarendon Press, 1964). *The Journals of Mary Shelley*, edited by Paul Feldman and Diana Scott-Kilvert (Baltimore: Johns Hopkins Univ. Press, 1987).

Mary Wollstonecraft, *A Vindication of the Rights of Woman and the Wrongs of Woman, or Maria*, edited by Anne Mellor and Noelle Chao (New York: Pearson Longman, 2007); *Collected Letters of Mary Wollstonecraft*, edited by Ralph M.

Wardle (Ithaca: Cornell Univ. Press, 1979); Lyndall Gordon, *Vindication: A Life of Mary Wollstonecraft* (New York: HarperCollins, 2005); Janet Todd, *Mary Wollstonecraft: A Revolutionary Life* (London: Weidenfeld and Nicholson, 2000).

Victor Erice's film, *The Spirit of the Beehive*, 1973, was an inspiration.

353 **"the tornadoed Atlantic of my being":** Herman Melville, *Moby-Dick*.

356 **two limestone eyes can't close:** Details of stone faces in New York City are based on photographs by John Yang, *Over the Door* (New York: Princeton Architectural Press, 1995).

357 **"like the last column":** Herman Melville, "Bartleby the Scrivener."

362 **I only ever wanted to be a continual experiment:** The notion of Mary Wollstonecraft's wanting to "be an experiment" is based on Virginia Woolf's comment on Wollstonecraft's life in *The Common Reader* (London: Hogarth Press, 1932).

365 **"In France they have a dreadful jail":** This is adapted from Mary Wollstonecraft, *Original Stories* (Chapter 3, "The Treatment of Animals").

365 **"Loveliest of what I leave behind":** Fragment 1, Praxilla of Sicyon (ca. 450 B.C.), translated by Richmond Lattimore, *Greek Lyrics* (Chicago: Univ. of Chicago Press, 1960).

365 **"We are not as hardy, free":** Diogenes (ca. 5 B.C.), translated by Guy Davenport, *Seven Greeks* (New York: New Directions, 1995).

365 **"I have just completed a forty-two-day voyage":** From Xavier deMaistre, *Voyage Around My Room* (London: Hesperus Press, 2004).

372 **"The Emperor Ling Ti":** This quotation and the one following are from C. A. S. Williams, *Outlines of Chinese Symbolism & Art Motives* (New York: Dover, 1976).

372 **"Why is our fancy to be appalled":** Political pamphlet, Mary Wollstonecraft, *A Vindication of the Rights of Men* in a Letter to the Right Honourable Edmund Burke; Occasioned by His Reflections on the Revolution in France, 1790.

372 **"although I hear people say 'Moses meant this' ":** From St. Augustine's *Confessions*.

374 **"Man has been changed into an artificial monster":** Mary Wollstonecraft, *A Vindication of the Rights of Woman*, adapted by me.

374 **"There are authors whose object":** Montaigne, *Essays*.

374 **"A Robin Red breast in a Cage":** William Blake, "Auguries of Innocence."

375 **"Ivy grows best when wild":** Montaigne, *Essays*.

375 **"Be very careful, in painting, to observe":** Leonardo da Vinci.

375 **"Now I will tell you about the city of Kinsay":** Marco Polo, adapted by me.

379 **"Isabelle de Montolieu"**: Mary Wollstonecraft is known to have read works by this author.

379 **"Personal size and mental sorrow"**: Jane Austen, *Persuasion.*

379 **"Caroline wrote the letter"**: From Isabelle de Montolieu's *Caroline de Lichtfield,* translated by Thomas Holcroft (London: Robinson, 1786). The quote has been altered by me.

379 **"I was born in the year 1632"**: Daniel Defoe, *Robinson Crusoe.*

380 **"I . . . Robinson Crusoe"**: Defoe, *Robinson Crusoe.*

380 **"Soundness of understanding"**: William Godwin, *An Enquiry Concerning Political Justice and Its Influence on General Virtue and Happiness* (Dublin: printed for Luke White, 1793).

381 **"Let us cast our eyes over the history"**: Godwin, *An Enquiry Concerning Political Justice.*

381 **"David's Deer"**: Zhang Cizu, *Rare Wild Animals.*

381 **"This want of tools"**: Defoe, *Robinson Crusoe.*

384 **"The first use of zero"**: This passage and the one following are partial quotes from David Ewing Duncan's *Calendar* (New York: Avon, 1998).

387 **"Curse on all laws but those which love has made"**: Alexander Pope, *Eloisa to Abelard* (1668–1744).

387 **"Ideas are to the mind"**: Godwin, *Enquiry Concerning Political Justice.*

387 **"An infinite number of thoughts"**: Godwin, *An Enquiry Concerning Political Justice,* slightly altered by me.

387 **"Kue-lin-fu contains three very handsome bridges"**: Marco Polo, *The Travels of Marco Polo,* altered by me.

387 **"When thou cam'st first"**: This is spoken by Caliban in Shakespeare's *The Tempest* Act 1, Sc. 2.

398 **Recollection, he said, is a form of investigation**: Aristotle, *On Memory and Reminiscence.*

402 **Everything Will Be Taken Away**: Adrian Piper, performance art, New York City, 2007.

403 **"This learning . . . cleare, . . . playne and open"**: This quote and the following are from the OED entry for "fever."

409 **"There are many names for rice"**: Various online sources.

409 **"Nature is an infinite sphere"**: Blaise Pascal, *Pensées.*

409 **"But if our own Biography"**: Thomas Carlyle, *Essay on History,* 1830, adapted by me.

417 **"They say there is no straight line"**: Leonardo da Vinci.

417 **"Dictating his recollections"**: This information is based on John Larner, *Marco Polo and the Discovery of the World* (New Haven: Yale Univ. Press, 1999).

438 **"A truth wastes away"**: Maurice Merleau-Ponty, *Signs.*

441 **My Hideous Progeny**: Web site http://home-1.worldonline.nl/~hamberg/.

453 **"Noble deer"**: Friedrich Hölderlin, *Hymns and Fragments,* translated by Richard Sieburth (Princeton: Princeton Univ. Press, 1984).

453 **"What does it mean to speak"**: This is from Richard Sieburth's Introduction to Hölderlin, *Hymns and Fragments,* adapted by me.

453 **"The *Cha no yu*"**: Bayard Taylor, ed., *Japan Illustrated* (New York: Scribners, 1893).

453 **"Nothing sets us upon a change of state"**: John Locke as quoted by Godwin in *An Enquiry Concerning Political Justice* and amended by me.

454 **"If you see something, say something"**: MTA posters and official MTA Web site, 2007.

471 **I flamed**: Shakespeare, *The Tempest,* Act 1, Sc. 2.

483 **"We possess nothing in the world"**: Simone Weil, *Gravity and Grace* (London: Routledge, 2002).

486 **"May 01: Ten bodies found"**: From Antiwar.com.

503 **"An author, therefore, is a human being"**: Mary Shelley on Alfieri, in *Lives of Eminent Literary and Scientific Men of Italy, Spain and Portugal* (1835–1837).

503 **"So far as is known, Epictetus"**: Frank N. Magill, ed., *Masterpieces of World Philosophy in Summary Form* (New York: Harper, 1961), adapted by me. The reference to More's use of *Utopia* is adapted from the same source.

503 **"If one is doubting, one exists"**: Descartes.

503 **"Diderot believed"**: Magill, *Masterpieces of World Philosophy.*

508 **"We identify ideas, trends, and innovations"**: Adapted from the online site for *Contagious Magazine.*

516 **If, as Giordano Bruno wrote**: Giordano Bruno, *Dialogues Concerning Cause, Principle, and One* (1584).

519 **"Secluded-Streamlet Pavilion"**: Zhu Junzhen, *The Art of Chinese Pavilions* (Beijing: Foreign Languages Press, 2002), adapted and added to by me.

519 **"The biographical tradition, full of contradictions"**: Mary Barnard, "A Footnote to the Translations," in *Sappho* (Berkeley: Univ. of California Press, 1958).

519 **"But it must be stressed that metaphor"**: Maimonides, *Guide for the Perplexed.*

519 **"With only coarse bread to eat"**: Confucius.

519 **"Can perplexity be stabilized?"**: Maimonides from Magill, *Masterpieces of World Philosophy,* adapted by me.

Acknowledgments

IT WAS my great good fortune to have an uninterrupted year of writing as a Fellow at the Cullman Center for Scholars and Writers at the New York Public Library. My boundless and most heartfelt thanks to its director, Jean Strouse. To Drew Gilpin Faust, former dean of the Radcliffe Institute for Advanced Study at Harvard, and Judy Vichniac, its director, I also extend my warmest thanks for a fellowship year during which time this project began to take shape.

My gratitude, too, to Pamela Leo, Betsy Bradley, and Adrianna Nova of the Cullman Center; also to the Cullman fellows, especially Sharon Cameron, Clive Fisher, Jim Shapiro, and Will Eno.

Thanks also to Charles Carter, Laura O'Keefe, and David Smith of the New York Public Library, and to Daniel Dibbern Doucet, David Fischer, and Donald Reiman at the Carl H. Pforzheimer Collection of Shelley and His Circle.

Christine Nelson, Inge Dupont, and John Bidwell at the Morgan Library arranged for me to read and study for one magical afternoon Mary Shelley's annotated copy of the 1818 edition of *Frankenstein*.

Phyllis and Burtin Sheck, Jim Peck, Maia Peck, and Dr. David L. Mayer gave abidingly to this project in ways both practical and immeasurable.

Deborah Garrison, my editor at Knopf, has taken this work on the journey from manuscript to book with great grace, ingenuity, and care. To her and to her assistant, Caroline Zancan; to Maggie Hinders, who gave the monster's unusual manuscript an especially beautiful design; to Victoria Pearson, production editor; and to everyone else who worked on this book at Knopf, I offer my most heartfelt thanks.

Short excerpts from the book appeared, sometimes in slightly different forms, in the following publications, to whose editors I also offer thanks: *A Public Space*, *Bomb*, *Ploughshares*, *The Paris Review*, and *TriQuarterly*.

A NOTE ON THE AUTHOR

Laurie Sheck is the author of five books of poetry, including *The Willow Grove*, which was a finalist for the Pulitzer Prize, and *Captivity*. Her work appears widely in such journals as *The New Yorker*, *The Paris Review*, and *Boston Review*. The recipient of fellowships from the Guggenheim Foundation, the National Endowment for the Arts, and the Ingram Merrill Foundation, Sheck has also been a Fellow at the Radcliffe Institute for Advanced Study and the Cullman Center for Scholars and Writers at the New York Public Library. She is on the faculty of the MFA Writing Program at the New School and lives in New York City.

A NOTE ON THE TYPE

This book was set in a version of Garamond, a type named for the famous Parisian type cutter Claude Garamond (ca. 1480–1561). Garamond, a pupil of Geoffroy Tory, based his letter on the types of the Aldine Press in Venice, but he introduced a number of important differences, and it is to him that we owe the letter now known as "old style."

COMPOSED BY NORTH MARKET STREET GRAPHICS
PRINTED AND BOUND BY BERRYVILLE GRAPHICS, BERRYVILLE, VIRGINIA
DESIGNED BY MAGGIE HINDERS